More praise for

The Last Summer of the Camperdowns

Washington Post Notable Book of the Year
Cosmopolitan Best Book of the Year for Women, by Women
Indie Next Pick
Amazon Best Book of the Month
Barnes & Noble Best Book of the Month

"A wonderful novel is like an orchid: smooth, creamy, full of unexpected crevasses. The more you look at it, the more surprising it is. *The Last Summer of the Camperdowns* . . . is like that, giving us characters you've never seen before, worlds we never knew, crimes we never thought of. Of course, some of us raise horses for the fun of it and run for Congress and may be bona fide movie stars, but not too many, and as purely escapist literature, *The Last Summer* works beautifully. . . . Really terrific fiction."
—Carolyn See, *Washington Post*

"These vibrant personalities jump off the page individually, and the collective dynamic is as lifelike and scintillating as beautifully cast actors in an artfully directed play. . . . The scenes and dialogue unravel organically, and razor-sharp witticisms tumble out so effortlessly."
—Hannah Hickok, *Redbook*

"A witty, suspenseful tale of murder, marital conflict and agonizing secrets. . . . [T]he exuberant story is transporting and delicious, a worthy summer read."
—Robin Micheli, *People*

"The novel acquires a crackling tension that doesn't ease until you've turned the final page. A pure pleasure read, *The Last Summer of the Camperdowns* will remind you of sweating glasses of ice tea, fireflies in the backyard, and lost innocence."

—Julie Buntin, *Cosmopolitan*

"Twelve-year-old Riddle James Camperdown witnesses a crime that will change her life and lives of those around her. A story about the family ties, the quest for status, and the secrets that kill."

—Gabrielle Too-A-Foo,
Good Housekeeping's Best Summer Beach Reads

"Dripping with Gatsby-esque tragedy, this story of a wealthy family's [summer in] Cape Cod mixes malcontents and murder in a raucous cocktail." —*Barnes & Noble Review*

"Riveting. . . . Riddle perfectly narrates the events of one crazy, harrowing summer against the tumultuous backdrop of the 1970s. Written with cutting wit and intensity; it doesn't get any better than this." —Donna Bettencourt, *Library Journal*, starred review

"Have you ever had a 'wow' moment in a book? It's that page or scene where a good book suddenly turns into a great book, a book you can't put down, a book that deprives you of sleep and compels you to sneak pages beneath your desk at work. *The Last Summer of the Camperdowns* has one of these incredible moments. . . . I can't give away more without depriving you, dear reader, of the experience of reading this fascinating novel . . . but I will whet your interest by saying there's a twist at the end you won't see coming." —Jennifer Hufford, editor-in-chief, *Mystery Guild*

"Elizabeth Kelly . . . takes readers to the Cape of the early 1970s. The narrator, a 12-year-old Wellfleet girl with eccentric 'Me Decade' parents—her mother a retired movie star and her father a candidate for Congress—is plunged beneath the surface of the idyllic summer setting when she discovers dark family secrets and witnesses a sinister crime she won't soon forget."—*Boston Magazine*

"The unfolding story burrows into new and long-buried secrets, both inside and outside of Riddle's seemingly charmed family circle. . . . Well worth reading for its exploration of a sensitive child's interior life, the novel probes deeply into the far-reaching consequences of not telling when we know we should."

—Ellen Boyers Kwatnoski,
Washington Independent Review of Books

"*The Last Summer of the Camperdowns* is both spooky and smart, with a fun-house-mirror cast of Cape Cod Irish aristocrats like no other. It's as if the Kennedys had catapulted themselves into a tale by Edgar Allan Poe—with rollicking, harrowing, and above all highly entertaining results." —Holly LeCraw, author of
The Swimming Pool

"There was no putting down this book. Elizabeth Kelly's riveting *The Last Summer of the Camperdowns* left me breathless."
—Marcy Dermansky, author of *Bad Marie*

"Elizabeth Kelly's second novel (after the critically acclaimed *Apologize, Apologize!*) continues to explore—in her characteristically tight, witty prose—the dysfunctional American family. . . . *The Last Summer of the Camperdowns*, with its vivid and notable Cape Cod setting, is a unique beach read, the kind that might keep you glancing over your shoulder to make sure no one is sneaking up behind your beach chair." —Book Reporter

"Kelly's raucous, deliciously creepy novel about the dysfunction of the über wealthy begins in 1972 as the hoity-toity Camperdown clan prepare for another summer of horseback riding, fox hunting, and hors d'oeuvres in their cushy Cape Cod enclave. . . . When the truth finally emerges amid a whirlwind of flying accusations and shattered lives . . . no one, not even the creepy killer, escapes unscathed. And everyone, at least in part, is to blame."

—*Publishers Weekly*

"The best-selling author of *Apologize! Apologize!* (2009) returns with another witty take on a dysfunctional family. . . . Kelly is a very entertaining writer with a digressive style and a way with metaphor. . . . Readers will find much to like in this colorful story peopled with larger-than-life personalities."

—Joanne Wilkinson, *Booklist*

"Kelly's new novel is just as scathingly witty as her best-selling debut but better plotted and even more emotionally harrowing. . . . Kelly skillfully builds almost unbearable tension, slipping in plenty of dark laughs en route to a wrenching climax that leaves in its wake some painfully unresolved questions—just like life. More fine work from a writer with a rare gift for blending wit and rue."

—*Kirkus Reviews*

"Kelly brings each character to life with such vivid language, it is almost possible to hear the tones of their voices and see the subtle shades of their hair. . . . At its core, *The Last Summer of the Camperdowns* is a novel of self-discovery, honesty and forgiveness. However, the path Elizabeth Kelly takes to the final reveal is fantastically developed and well written, combining bits of Gothic fiction with more modern American wit."

—*RVA News*

The Last Summer of the Camperdowns

Also by **Elizabeth Kelly**

Apologize, Apologize!

The Last Summer of the Camperdowns

Elizabeth Kelly

LIVERIGHT PUBLISHING CORPORATION

A DIVISION OF W. W. NORTON & COMPANY

NEW YORK | LONDON

For information about permission to reproduce selections from this book,
write to Permissions, Liveright Publishing Corporation, a division of
W. W. Norton & Company, Inc., 500 Fifth Avenue, New York, NY 10110

For information about special discounts for bulk purchases, please contact
W. W. Norton Special Sales at specialsales@wwnorton.com or 800-233-4830

Manufacturing by Courier Westford
Book design by Fearn Cutler de Vicq
Production manager: Julia Druskin

Library of Congress Cataloging-in-Publication Data

Kelly, Elizabeth, 1952–
   The last summer of the Camperdowns / Elizabeth Kelly. —First edition.
      pages cm
   ISBN 978-0-87140-340-7 (hardcover)
   1. Girls—Fiction. 2. Parents—Fiction. 3. Eccentrics and eccentricities—Fiction. 4.
Cape Cod (Mass.)—Fiction. 5. Family secrets—Fiction. 6. Domestic fiction gsafd
I. Title.
   PR9199.4.K448L37 2013
   813'.6—dc23
                                    2013003876

ISBN 978-0-87140-745-0 pbk.

Liveright Publishing Corporation
500 Fifth Avenue, New York, N.Y. 10110
www.wwnorton.com

W. W. Norton & Company Ltd.
Castle House, 75/76 Wells Street, London W1T 3QT

1 2 3 4 5 6 7 8 9 0

for Team Dean

The Last Summer of the Camperdowns

"I do not wish to live like a baptized person.

I wish to live like a dog of the wood."

—OLD ROMANY SAYING

Chapter One

———

I RAN INTO HARRY LAST NIGHT.

It was inevitable. I knew it would happen someday—in the same way that I have this nagging hunch I'm going to die. Eventually. For me, eventually arrived yesterday in Nonquitt, Massachusetts, at a Democratic fundraiser held at the hundred-acre estate of a New England philanthropist by the name of Edgar Rutherford.

Still, it was a shock.

He'd been living abroad. Hong Kong. Rome. Dublin. Lhasa. I've kept track. Just back from a trip to the Darien Gap jungle, he made a documentary film about his trek across the remote Atrapo Swamp, a place so inhospitable you'd need a chain saw to tame the spiny undergrowth, and rabid dogs proliferate like perverse tour guides. I heard that he got married to some shiny object he picked up along the way. Her father was the French ambassador to the United States. Harry always did have a taste for thoroughbreds.

You know the type. Refined neck and long legs, glistening mane, traceable lineage and exotic temperament. The only thing missing was an appetite for hay. Someone who knew her told me that Élodie Héroux suffered from the classic racehorse afflictions of low fertility and small heart. An unkind remark—it reminded me of something my mother would say—even if it did taste good going down, though not for long.

I've never married. It's all right. I'm young and anyway, I have my dogs. I have my horses. I've done okay, even enjoyed some success as a competitive rider. To think that Harry used to kid me about making a good match, as if marrying well in my case was preordained, an unavoidable rite of passage.

Harry was always teasing me about something.

BEFORE I SAW HIM, I heard him. That voice! My only experience of synesthesia. He sounded the way a graham cracker tastes. We were at opposite ends of the massive living room, an old and fading beauty, a bit desperate, one of those cosmetically enhanced spaces that make a vocation of overdecoration to the point of malpractice.

He came around the corner, pausing for a moment to take in the view. If Harry was surveying the forest, then I was focused on the tree. Warm and robust, he crackled like a campfire, flickering with all the colors of autumn—russet hair with gold and amber highlights, fair skin rosy and burnt by the sun and the wind. Slim but strong and athletic, sporty as a lacrosse stick. But for the subversive kindle of intelligence and humor in those balmy blue eyes, he might have escaped from a Ralph Lauren print ad.

My heart did a quickstep. I felt sick to my stomach. An enormous mixed bouquet of gardenias and white Madonna lilies sat on the table next to where he stood, their musky fragrance and his unblemished confidence filling up the room. Gripping the armchair beside me, I took a deep breath, inhaling that wonderful combination, certainty and the scent of flowers, and I was instantly transported back to the moment I met him.

It was 1972. I was thirteen years old. My father, Godfrey Camperdown, was running for the House of Representatives. He was an unlikely candidate, a labor historian and activist, a celebrated biographer and an aspiring musical composer whose stage productions had appeared off Broadway. ("So far off," as my mother delighted in reminding everyone, "you could smell the lilacs from the Brooklyn Botanical Gardens.") We were attending yet another fundraiser, the ballroom stacked with a handpicked crowd that alternated between two extremes, the charmless rich and the rancorously blue-collar.

I was standing next to Mirabel Whiffet, notorious busybody dowager and scandal archivist, when he walked in the door, his arrival causing a shimmer of excitement from the packed crowd.

"Ooooh!" Mirabel made a whooshing, satiny sound at first sight of him. She tweaked me with her elbow.

"That boy could attract bees," she trilled. My mother, the actress Greer Foley, star of stage and screen, initially feigned indifference—the only grand entrance that interested her was her own—but then even she came around, nodding in grudging concession to his appeal.

I watched him furtively and from a chaste distance, flattening my bangs over my eyes in a pathetic attempt to veil my curiosity. Sipping his drink and chatting, he surveyed the room, nineteen years old, genial and easy; he stopped talking to listen to my father, my father's voice ringing out like Sunday morning. How Camp loved any opportunity to sing! Egged on by staffers and friends, he launched into his signature number—"The Daring Young Man on the Flying Trapeze"—the eccentric linchpin of an unchanging repertoire he'd performed in camphorated living rooms from Los Angeles to Boston to New York City, his unvarnished tenor soaring.

Plainly mortified, pretending more enthusiasm for my father's performance than I felt—with parents such as mine, embarrassment and humiliation clung to me like remoras—I looked up, nervous and gawky, taking in the genteel scenery of Harry. To my amazement, he joined in with the crowd as they sang along, my gaze shifting back and forth like a swing, looping between my father and Harry, from one to the other.

A tall man in a dark blue suit caught my eye as he made his way through the crowd. He attracted Harry's attention, too, which was evident in the way his expression changed, the corners of his mouth lifting. I watched the man approach my father; the two began to speak and then all hell broke loose. I can see it and hear it and smell it—the disarray. My father red-faced and brawling, the man in the blue suit reeling backward, my mother running across the ballroom in her skyscraping heels, women screaming, men shouting, flashbulbs popping, tables overturning and glasses shattering, hitting the wooden floor, one after another, exploding like machine-gun fire. Boom. Boom. Boom.

Now SEEING HARRY AGAIN, I ached with loss; it blew through me like a cold wind across an empty field. He stood among a large appreciative group, the women in black cocktail dresses and rosy-white pearls, the men in soft bespoke suits and summer-white shirts, sophisticated human scaffolding erected around the charismatic centerpiece of Harry Devlin.

It was June and the garden doors were open, white flowers lightly infusing the house with the lacy odor of late spring. He was laughing, and his laughter traveled from one end of the room to the other, carried along on the jaunty breeze.

I struggled to breathe. "Are you all right?" the woman next to me asked. Nodding, smiling, I pretended interest in the origins of the oil painting on the wall. A beach scene. Waves crashing. Tall grasses waving. Seagulls tucked together on the sandy dunes.

A smartly dressed couple across the room pretended not to

look at me. Others stared openly, pointing and rude, as if the usual rules governing intrusiveness didn't apply in my case. My face burned the way it does after a day on the beach. I was calm on the outside, but the winds inside me were picking up. Reaching for the nearest chair to steady myself against their swirling effects, my past roared into present view.

I grew up alongside the Atlantic Ocean, alert and attentive to the battering of the breakers and the separate wilderness of the wind, the air soaked in brine. Each day I awoke to the feel of my bare feet sinking with a salty gush into the cool morning sand, tide receding, the beachfront littered with the damp dead and the dying. Until that last summer, I imagined that it was the one season with nothing to hide. Now I wake up knowing that the sea conceals more than it ever reveals about the true terrors of summer.

"Oh, my God, isn't that Harry Devlin?" The same solicitous woman reached for my forearm. I didn't know her but it seemed that she knew me. "Look, if you'd like to leave . . ."

I put my drink down on the closest table and considered my answer just as the great, carved, mahogany double doors leading from the dining room into the living room blew open and Edgar Rutherford appeared, loud and vulgar, surrounded by a human tsunami, an overflow of people pouring into the room.

"Jesus, Dev! Is that really you? Where the hell have you been all my life? It's about bloody time you came home!" He was shouting, infecting the room with his studied exuberance—Rutherford held the patent on formulaic outlandishness—and Harry acknowledged him with an extravagant wave, everyone laughing and clapping, ripples of excitement seen and heard and felt, formally attired staff struggling to make their black-and-white way, tripped up at every turn, gleaming silver trays over their heads, as they winnowed, unsmiling and solemn, through the creamy crush of the crowd.

Edgar grabbed a bottle of champagne from a passing tray and lobbed it like a football in Harry's direction. Harry leapt forward, lunged for it and missed, the bottle exploding on the hardwood, champagne surging like a geyser, spraying him top to bottom with bubbles and fizz. Everyone gasped, the circle of glamorous disciples that surrounded him cleaving neatly down the middle.

Harry hooted noisily as if he'd just been tossed into an unheated pool, wiped the champagne from his eyes and started to laugh. "You son of a bitch," he said as he headed for the nearest window, and much to everyone's combined amusement and dismay, used the faded antique curtains to dry his face and hair.

I was afraid he might see me. I was afraid he might not see me. Over the fireplace mantel there was a large and ornate mirror, vaguely oriental. Spotting his reflection, I relaxed into the intimate safety of watching him remotely, light from wall sconces and candelabra a golden blur. Harry, slightly bent at the waist, rubbed his hair on the pale imported silk. Then he glanced up at the mirror.

His reflected gaze met mine. It was the first time I had seen Harry Devlin in two decades. His eyes registered brief surprise, then something more. There was a whole lifetime in that look. He hesitated and then he started to walk across the room, talking to this one and that one, casually making his way through the crowd. I didn't turn around, but watched him in the mirror, walking in a straight line, heading right for me.

Someone whispered, someone else murmured, someone tittered, someone groaned, the room got quieter and shifted edgily from one foot to the other foot as people began to understand what was happening. They knew our history, after all.

"Shit," Edgar said, loud enough for everyone to hear.

I held my breath as he drew closer, so near that I could smell the champagne. For a moment I thought he was going to stop. For a moment I thought . . . well, it doesn't matter what I thought.

Harry walked right past me and through the open doorway, into the hallway and out the front door.

The crowd dispersed as the orchestra leader tapped on the dais with his baton and the band began to play something pretty. The music filled me up and the few people that remained behind, more curious than courteous, gradually withdrew until I was left alone with the same question that I had asked myself every day and every night for more than twenty years.

Why, oh why, didn't I tell?

Chapter Two

———

I CAN STILL SMELL THE AIR THAT MORNING. SMELLS LIKE JUNE. Smells the way the hermit thrush sings. If I listen hard enough, I can hear the metallic ripple of the old gray fan swiveling back and forth, wobbling on the uneven dresser top, my basset hound, Dorothy, softly snoring at the foot of the bed. It was an old-fashioned room in an old-fashioned house, florid wallpaper pattern of cabbage roses covering the plaster walls, a room out of step with its cranky, opinionated occupant. I was twelve—almost thirteen, as I reminded everyone incessantly—and desperate for modernity with my melodramatic shrine to the late Brian Jones, with its pop colors and angular graphics, its collage of newsprint pictures torn from the pages of *Fab* magazine, an embarrassingly earnest art installation at aesthetic odds with the chenille bedspread, the handmade quilt and the botanical prints.

My bedroom was my private refuge and lucky for me—and for my parents—it took up the entire third story, affording me the luxury of a separate wing all to myself.

The ancient dollhouse next to the window seat made it plain that it was a girl's room, though in decor it was matronly rather than feminine and featured good traditional pieces. Darkly veneered four-poster bed, tallboy, a mirrored vanity with velvet chair—my sanctuary was filled with the kind of furniture that gets passed down through generations, which meant that I spent most of my childhood feeling as if I was channeling the musty spirit of my maiden aunt Kate, the one whose breath I still vividly recall as having the power to curdle my will to live.

We lived in the town of Wellfleet, on Cape Cod, in a weathered cedar-shake house with robin's-egg blue shutters and a salmon door. My father, then forty-six years old, had grown up in that house, one of two heritage properties located at the end of a long private road. Our place sat on top of a soaring sand dune overlooking the Atlantic Ocean, part of a large parcel of land that ran along the Outer Cape shoreline.

The walls were painted in the rich saturated hues that my mother loved, blue and coral, orange and yellow, red. From top to bottom, you could feel her refined sensibilities at work in every inch of our old house, with its miles of buffed herringbone floors. My father had no interest in decor—he would have been more inclined to get a perm than comment on a fabric choice. Because my mother relished discord, nothing matched. She detested conspicuous decorative effects, preferring the conspiracy of random elements to create a seemingly accidental chic.

Outside, white-capped waves rolled in with sublime efficiency.

That dear old house. If there is a heaven, I will spend eternity on the back porch, sipping iced tea and eating radish and mayonnaise sandwiches, listening to the birds chirp, watching the mulberries ripen, hearing the waves roll in, reading Sun Tzu when my father is looking, Trixie Belden when he isn't.

It felt so alive where we were, everything seeming to happen all at once: sun, sea, sand, wind, blowing grasses, tangled woods and secretive wildlife. Even the roof was covered in thick layers of actively growing green moss. We were bound by a conservation area on one side, with its circuitous trails and cluttered enclaves of trees, their trunks congested with matted vines, and on the other side was a small stable with a paddock where my mother and I kept my horse, Eugene Debs, and her horse, Joe Hill. Across the road, deeply forested tracts of land, along with open fields of pasture and wildflowers and kettle ponds both small and large, offered a spectacularly different vision of the natural world. My father used to say that the only thing we were missing was a view of the Matterhorn—in which case, according to him, we weren't missing much.

It was the start of summer holidays, and I felt so light and liberated I practically had to anchor myself to the ground to keep from floating away. I hated school. St. Patrick's Academy was my own private Leavenworth, criminally earnest, a school that promised to develop physical, spiritual and intellectual greatness in students whose parents were inclined to interpret life's disappointments in terms of a mediocre wine list. Despite my worst efforts, I was a good student and had just graduated from grade eight.

A loner by choice, I viewed the summer months as my time— to ride my horse, play with my dogs, read my books, run on the beach, gaze out over the ocean and daydream. My father was running for Congress, unfortunately for me, since it meant there was always the implicit threat that with school out I was available to attend endless fundraisers and help out with the campaign.

Politics was an inherited affliction in our family, passed on like a weak chin from one generation to the next. My grandfather, a fervent Democrat, had been an early labor activist and union leader who scandalized his blue-collar disciples by marrying the boss's daughter, a concert pianist.

"I believe the term 'limousine liberal' was coined with your paternal grandfather in mind," my mother used to scoff at every opportunity.

Any time there was a major strike or a serious bout of labor unrest my father talked about running for office, a constituency of powerful union supporters and left-leaning pedigree pals urging him on, but it was Vietnam and the release of the Pentagon Papers, his growing disillusionment with the ethical failures of leadership, that pushed him to finally make good on his word.

IT WAS JUNE 4, 1972. The day started out peacefully enough, a creamy soft Sunday afternoon, a sweet do-nothing day. My mother called them tea-finger-sandwich days. A day with the crust removed. My parents and I were in the dining room eating lunch. The garden doors were open. The late spring sun poured in, conferring a brilliant sheen to the ocean air, the exuberant complementary colors of the fabric on the chairs, orange and blue, fading against the natural light.

The election was five months away, and we were enjoying a rare quiet moment as a family. Camp had promised to take the day off and unplug the phone, but not before receiving the news that one of his biggest supporters had died unexpectedly the night before.

"Terrible about Franklin." My mother unfolded her napkin and positioned it in her lap.

"There's a goddamn bullet for everyone," my father said, not for the first time, from his position at the head of the long table as we sat together in the cherry-paneled room. Four courses. Soup. Salad. Entree. Dessert.

"I'd settle for a goddamn hot dog," I said, grousing, unconvinced that a stranger's death was worth my attention, pulling a paperback novel from my back pocket. *Diary of a Nobody*. Lifted from my mother's nightstand. At that stage of my life, I was persuaded that curmudgeonly complaint lent me a certain gravitas that belied my age, which is not to say that whining didn't come naturally to me.

"Riddle, you sound like a hockey player," my mother said as Louise, called Lou, our durable staff of one, emerged from the kitchen with a pot of coffee, steam pouring from the spout. "How many times must you be told not to read at the table?"

"Better a hockey player than a debutante," my father said, patting my hand, indicating his ongoing support for my minor acts of rebellion. Grateful and a little bit smug, I smiled back at him.

"Shall I pour?" Lou asked no one in particular, the coffeepot poised in midair over my mother's empty cup.

"Yes, thank you," my mother said.

"No," my father interrupted. "We are quite capable of pouring our own coffee. Just leave the pot. Thanks anyway, Lou."

Lou smiled nervously as my mother sighed in annoyance.

Everything about Lou was short: her stubby legs, her thick waist, her spiky hair, a kind of electrified crew cut. The only thing long about Lou was the extent of her suffering—she had taken care of my mother as a child and continued to perform the same penance now that she was an adult. She cooked and cleaned and ran the household, subject to occasional cursory inspection by my mother, who made it clear to everyone that when it came to what she found interesting, housework and children ranked just above medieval fairs and slightly below collecting bottle caps. I generally felt the welcome mat yanked from beneath my feet after ten minutes of undiluted exposure. Her impatience with my father hovered at the five-minute mark, at which point her fingers would begin their deadly tabletop drumming.

She was tapping up a storm that day in the dining room. "It's when the drumming stops you start to worry," my father said, inexplicably in thrall to her sleek furies.

When it came to my father and what he had to say, the bar was always open. He served up endless rounds of proclamation and intimidation, each garnished with a spritz of soda and a wedge of lime. He liked fizz. Try to imagine *North Korea: The Musical* and you might begin to understand the ruthless carbonated foundation on which Godfrey Camperdown was built.

"Your father makes Fidel Castro sound like Gilligan," my mother said with practiced indifference. "I'm going to buy him a lectern for his birthday."

She reached for four strips of bacon and, bending down, fed them to the dogs, her beloved basset hounds, Dorothy, Madge, Hilary and Hilary's three-month-old puppy, Vera.

Dunhill cigarette in hand, her sixth finger, she straightened up and exhaled in my direction, a plume of silky smoke winding through her yellow hair like a gray ribbon. I breathed in deeply of her sophistication, imprinting forever that angular and archly feminine aesthetic native to her but elusive to me. I still find the malignant trinity of cashmere sweater set, French manicure and cigarette smoke irresistible.

I'm a good listener. Maybe it comes from being an only child living in a large house with high ceilings and wide baseboards, wandering through rooms as elegant in their quietude as the first hours of morning. Growing up in the exclusive company of my parents, I was attuned to all the things that tend to go unsaid between adults in a relationship of long standing. My mother and father were great talkers, their conversation part of the electrical circuitry of the house, lighting up rooms, propelling forward the machinery of our daily lives.

Nodding enthusiastically, in thrall to the idea that my father could diminish Castro to the status of little buddy, I scooped up a grape and popped it into my mouth with relish, juice trickling down the back of my tongue. Like my mother, I deplored all that bored me—unlike her, though, I absolved myself of any obligation to be entertaining. I might as well have been born with a pistol in my hand, firing furiously at the floor, ordering life to dance.

There were four members of the private club that made up my immediate family: my father, my mother, me and World War Two, which I had come to think of as an unfunny uncle with a penchant for fighting and moodiness. My dad had volunteered in 1943 when he was only seventeen years old, lying about his age, and served in Europe in the infantry. For him, the war was a present-tense event against which all other experiences languished in pallid comparison.

He was hell-bent on making a man out of me. I was his special project, one of several missions he'd undertaken both on and off the field of battle, where his role as a frontline combatant had permanently blurred the lines of distinction between war and peace. Preoccupied with my personal safety, troubled by my inability to defend against the world's evils, he taught me to conceal a rock in my fist whenever I left the house. You never know when you might need to shatter an unshaven cheekbone or crack open a resistant skull.

"Castro? Since when do you take your mother's side against me?" Camp said, glancing in my direction as I grinned over at him. He picked up one of Lou's freshly baked biscuits and lobbed it at me, hitting me in the cheek.

"Oh, Lord," my mother said as he followed up by reaching over and pinching my forearm.

"Ouch!" I yelped.

"Don't tell me you're going to just sit back and take it," he said, playful and challenging as I reached for an olive, pinging him in the forehead.

"Finally! Now, we're talking." He stood up, gesturing with both hands, daring me to launch a full-scale reprisal. "Punch me in the stomach. Come on. Hit me as hard as you can. Don't hold back."

"For God's sake, Camp, she's twelve years old . . ." my mother said.

"Almost thirteen," I interrupted.

"This is Cape Cod, not the Russian front," my mother protested.

"What should I teach her? How to iron?" My father reluctantly sat back down in his chair, unable to conceal his contempt for the so-called feminine arts. He was a true anomaly, an alpha male with suffragette sympathies. I sometimes suspected that his militant feminism had its roots in his desire to rid both sexes of all traces of effeminacy.

My mother's attempt to speak devolved into a low grumble deep in her throat. Greer was a master sigher. Then she brightened. She had decided on a different tactic.

"So, it's interesting timing for Michael Devlin's return from Italy, what with the election, I mean." She glanced downward at the antique Aubusson rug on the floor, as if something remarkable might spring up from beneath its faded tapestry.

"Hmm." Camp seemed as remote as my mother seemed engaged. His hands opened in front of him, he extended his fingers and then tightened them together into a fist, gathering up the loose ends of a waning Sunday morning and tying them into a knot. My mother intuitively responded to the sudden tension by loosening the ribbon that held back her hair, which fell onto her shoulders in a single sleek, swooping motion.

"I hear they've done so much work at the house in Truro in anticipation of the great homecoming. Apparently, he's bringing some of the horses up from Virginia. Can't wait to see them. Brooklyn is expected to take the Derby. I'm not surprised. Even as a boy, Michael always was the first to cross the finish line."

I glanced at her sideways. Italics became her. "Who is Michael Devlin?" I asked.

"Well, good luck to Michael Devlin, Esquire, and his fantastic horses," Camp said. In Camperdown-speak, "esquire" was a pejorative.

I repeated the question. "Who is Michael Devlin?"

My parents continued to ignore me. Camp turned back to his newspaper, the reading of which was a form of ornate daily ceremony that would have impressed the Aztecs. My father took current events personally. Every day brought some new confrontation with a foreign leader with his head up his ass. I watched, flinching in anticipation as his demeanor abruptly changed, his eyebrows meeting at a bitter point of consternation. Uh-oh. I braced for point of impact. Looked as if another CEO son of a bitch had backhanded the proletariat.

"Goddamn it," he said.

"What is it now?" my mother asked warily, glancing over at me, trying to recruit my silent commiseration.

"Looks like we have our answer for why Michael is back."

"Would someone please tell me who Michael Devlin is?" I asked.

"Oh, for heaven's sake, Riddle," my mother said. "You've heard me mention him in the past. You've read about him, I'm sure. Everyone's heard of Michael."

"I probably blocked him from my mind after hearing you talk about him so much." I spoke flippantly enough, though even as I said it, it occurred to me there was some truth to the allegation.

Camp folded the newspaper in half and handed it to me, vigorously pointing to an article, the tips of his fingers sparring with the newsprint.

"Here, Riddle, read this."

I grimaced—in those days, my range of expression was limited to eye-rolling and sneering—my deepening curiosity about Michael Devlin wrestling with my contrived ennui. Why should I read it? What did I care? I looked into my father's eyes and saw simmering lakes of lava just looking for a reason to overflow. Choosing the prudent course for once, I kept my thoughts to myself and did as I was told. "International playboy and renowned horseman Michael Devlin, heir to . . ."

My mother interrupted. "Well, don't read the whole thing verbatim. This isn't a home for senior citizens. I loathe listening to people read aloud, especially when it's poorly executed. Such a bore! Next thing you'll be telling me what you dreamt about last night."

"I dreamt that I murdered my parents," I mumbled to an unappreciative audience.

"Condense it, for heaven's sake!" She was still carrying on.

"All right. All right. Hold on," I said, scanning quickly. "It says that he's finishing up a book about his war experiences . . ."

"Jesus Christ!" Camp's anger rattled the chandelier overhead. I could practically hear him ticking.

"The book promises to be controversial . . ."

"Ha!" Camp snorted.

"Rumor has it that it contains explosive content . . ."

"Let's hope it blows up in his face," Camp said.

"Should I keep going?" I said.

"Well, of course, keep going," my mother said.

"Um, it says here that he got a big advance from Simon and Schuster. Oh, and that he's going to donate the money to some charity for the preservation of wild horses."

"Good for him," my mother said. "He has been a marvelous force for good in the racing world, Riddle."

"Alert the world press! Contact the Vatican. We have a saint that needs crowning. St. Michael of Bullshit." My father spoke directly to me. "Riddle, do not listen to your mother about Michael Devlin. She has a splinter in her eye the size of a two-by-four when it comes to that man."

"Riddle, look at me," my mother ordered, going so far as to physically turn my head in her direction, my chin cupped in her hand. "Your father has been jealous of Michael since we were children. It's embarrassing."

"You listen here, Jimmy," my father countered, invoking my pet name, his hand on my wrist. "That is a goddamn lie. This book, as your mother well knows, is a deliberate act of sabotage."

My mother leaned back in her chair. "It's not the end of the world, Camp."

"This is a direct threat against me and my election bid. Devlin's out to get me. Well, he's not going to get away with it." My father jumped up from the table, spilling a mug of hot coffee in the process. "Jesus Christ!" he said, grabbing a napkin and wiping the top of his pant leg.

"Calm down, Camp, for heaven's sake," my mother said, patting the seat of his chair. She looked over at me. "Please, tell him to take a deep breath before picking up that phone."

"Are you serious?" I was fuming. "Tell him yourself. Talk to each other. Leave me out of it. I'm not the referee."

"Someone is a little touchy today," my mother said before turning to speak to my father directly. "Camp, relax, have lunch, cool down and then deal with it."

Acceding reluctantly, Camp sat back down in his chair as my mother poured him another cup of coffee. "Here," she offered. "Have a piece of chocolate cake. It might cheer you up."

"He's picked the wrong man to tangle with," Camp said. "I haven't worked this hard, come this far, to have it all undone by some effete occasional expat with a gift for revisionism."

"Why do you hate Michael Devlin so much?" I asked as I bent down to disentangle little Vera from my shoelaces. My father's dislikes were interesting to me. My mother, on the other hand, loathed everyone, which had the effect of curtailing my curiosity.

"I don't hate him," he said, a tad unconvincingly.

"How do you know him, Camp?"

"His family lived on the estate across the road, before they sold the place to the Whiffets. We played together as kids, went to the same schools, the usual nonsense."

"Oh," I snapped my fingers. "That Michael Devlin."

My mother couldn't resist chiming in. "The Devlins are enormously rich . . ."

"For Christ's sake, Greer, rein in your fetish. I won't have you talking to Riddle about money."

"Relax, will you?" I could stand no more. "Why are you two so obsessed with him?"

"We are not obsessed," my mother said. "He and your father were best friends. They even served together overseas." She paused, considering. "I've known him for years. He's an interesting man. Good-looking, too. You should have seen him when he was young."

My father laughed in some disbelief and stared at her, a pattern of response that tended to act as precursor to the sudden appearance of a mushroom cloud.

"Ha! Inherited wealth is all that stands between him and a sink full of dirty dishes in some greasy spoon in Dorchester."

"Ignore that man behind the newspaper," my mother directed me. "Gin says the Devlins are the richest family on the eastern seaboard." Gin was my mother's combination best friend and worst enemy. He lived across the road and made a point of knowing everyone's business. Gin was also the official president of her fan club and was frequently called on to deal with avid admirers who showed up on our doorstep, pleading for her to fulfill her regular threats to stage a comeback.

Greer was eighteen when she starred in *The Heir and the Spare* in 1946, her first big role. She won a supporting Oscar for *Brazen* in 1957 and except for the occasional stage appearance retired from performing when I was born two years later, claiming that she couldn't be bothered any longer. No one believed her and there was ongoing speculation about why she had abandoned acting at the peak of her power and popularity, all that speculation only contributing to her mystique.

The truth is, she really couldn't be bothered.

MY MOTHER CALLED FOR Lou and then, exhausted by the thirty-second wait, impatiently poured herself a glass of ginger ale.

"Did your good friend Gin also say how they acquired all that money?" my father said finally, intruding on her money-induced reverie. "Devlin-owned factories were a disgrace, violating every tenet of decency in the history of labor relations in this country. Riddle, did you ever hear of the Thanksgiving strike in 1923?"

"Uh, I think so," I said, pretending knowledge, a hobby of mine that has persisted into adulthood.

"Michael's grandfather presided over one of the most violent strikes in the country, all designed to break the union. Four strikers were killed by company security men when they brought in a group of scabs to cross the picket line. And the old bastard laughed about it as he carved the turkey."

"Pardon me if I don't lose sleep worrying about people who buy their wine in gallon jugs," my mother said. "Anyway, that's just one more example of your father's infuriating union propaganda. It's positively un-American, Camp."

"Oh, is it? You had better take up your concerns with your capitalist hero. He's the one who told me and quite cheerfully, too. Recited it as if it was a recipe. He's a pirate at heart, just like his old man. Just like his old man's old man."

"Michael was telling you what you wanted to hear. A common affliction among those close to you, I might add. Anything to stave off the effects of another spirit-grinding sermon."

My mother twisted the end of her cigarette into an ashtray

and reached for her omnipresent antique cigarette case, expertly extracting a fresh recruit. "Riddle, Michael has been a very successful businessman. A diplomat, too."

My father, who had resumed his lunch with some relish, stopped eating and dropped his knife and fork. They landed with a dull thump on the tablecloth.

"Unbearable. Just intolerable. The truth is he inherited the family business, sold it for a fortune, made a phony show of abandoning his father's politics, reinvented himself as a liberal democrat and got a sweetheart diplomatic appointment as a result of enormous campaign donations. Now he fancies himself a historian and an author, a Jesuit, too, if I'm not wrong, and a fashioner of public opinion." Steam from his coffee curved round his lips, creating the illusion of smoke, as if he was setting fire to each word. "Despite his highly vaunted sense of self-importance and his desire to be seen as a serious man, the truth is that he's playing tennis, for Christ's sake. His life is one, long, achingly dull tennis match among lesser players. End of story."

"Well," my mother said, running her fingernail around the rim of a coffee cup, "at least he's in the game."

Grinning like a big cat poised to strike, my father said, "Just once, Greer, I would like to see you defend me with the same enthusiasm as you do the great Michael Devlin."

"Why do you court disaster by being so abrasive? Michael has his weaknesses and you could use them to your advantage. He never could resist flattery. Strike a conciliatory note. Appeal to his sense of himself as the good and compassionate king. Approach on bended knee. I'm telling you, a little humility on your part and a couple of moonlit dinners with your wife will do the trick." She smiled as I looked at her in disbelief. "I know just the outfit, too. Think how advantageous it would be if he were to endorse you for the House or throw his weight behind the campaign financially."

"I don't need any favors from Michael Devlin and I'll be damned if I will abase myself to get them," my father said. "The kind of people in the party that support me have long memories and would be appalled to see me crawling before Devlin. Anyway, you've lost your mind if you think Michael intends to do me any favors when it comes to getting elected. In case it escaped your notice, his support and his friendship have been conspicuously absent for many years. He's made it quite plain where he stands concerning my candidacy."

A look passed between them. Its intensity was bewildering—and compelling.

"What do you mean? Doesn't he like you?" I said, unable to resist all that was going unspoken between them. Their silence frustrated me. "Camp, why do you have to run anyway?"

"I'm running for office because the like-minded bastards have taken over and . . ."

"And it's time for a different set of like-minded bastards to assume power," my mother finished the sentence. "Michael doesn't like your father because . . ."

"Because I know where the bodies are buried, which is a powerful position to be in and a vulnerable position. Makes a person both predator and prey at the same time."

"Interesting interpretation," my mother said, savoring some secret amusement clearly designed to be provocative.

"Son of a bitch!"

I jumped as my father slammed his fist down on the table, sending the dogs scurrying beneath it. The puppy, Vera, sought refuge at my mother's feet.

"I don't understand," I said, feeling confused and even a little unsettled.

"You're not meant to," she answered.

"Always the loyal wife. Greer, you amaze me. Your pragmatism is astounding. Which is why I leave the cultivating of others to you." He turned to address me. "Your mother could make corn grow on Leonid Brezhnev. But then she is a performer, after all. There is a reason she was picked to play all those treacherous dames in the movies."

"Is it treachery to want the best for your children?" Now she was mad. "For yourself?" Hissing, she recoiled deep into her chair. Yikes. I nibbled on a piece of toast as, face flushed red, skin so fair you could see the blood boil, she sprang forward, striking out. "I didn't sign up for a lifetime of cotton-knit sweaters, coupon clipping and date squares."

My father for once chose to ignore the sweeping theatricality of her declaration, continuing to talk to me instead of her. He had a preacher's instinct for the teaching moment. "You listen to me, Riddle. Money does not equal success. Criminals have money."

"It would seem we're the only ones that don't have any money. But thank God, your father's integrity is intact," my mother interjected, calmer now, basking, her natural chilliness restored, the reptilian coolness of her denunciation a familiar poison.

There it was, making its daily cameo. The M word. Our secret shame. No money. We didn't have any money. What we did have was debt. Of course, it's clear to me now as an adult that a bigger problem than not having any money was behaving as if we did. You might as well have told my mother to join a bowling league as suggest that she live within her means.

Money was the thing we never talked about publicly but never stopped discussing privately. Money was the crazy aunt we kept locked in the attic, our lives measured in food trays and inelegant deceptions. "Aunt Loretta? Oh, she's decided to stay on in Palm Beach. Sometimes we wonder if she will ever make her way back here." In a way, it was part of the shared delusion of our household, this idea that we were broke. We didn't have the kind of money needed to maintain a position of tribal significance, which was an ongoing source of frustration, especially to my mother. She had a generous annuity and could still have commanded a big salary if she decided to perform again.

Camp wasn't interested in money, maybe because he'd grown up with it and took its advantages for granted, or maybe because he viewed money and its pursuit with a combination of artist's disdain and Teamster's suspicion. He was a cultural schizophrenic who responded to any number of competing voices in his head. He wrote a prizewinning biography of James Riddle Hoffa— yes, that's how I got my name, Riddle James, and my nickname, Jimmy—along with several respected volumes about industrial relations, trade union formation, strikes and the working class, but his true love was songwriting and composing. A failed songwriter and composer, as my mother never tired of reminding him. A warrior with a melody in his heart and a hole in his pocket, she mocked.

No one spoke.

"Oh, look at Vera," I said in a vain attempt at distraction as the puppy clamped her teeth onto Dorothy's ear and tried to drag her across the floor. Anything to disperse the unaccustomed silence.

My father stood up, chair tumbling to the floor, mercury rising, totally eclipsing me as he confronted my mother. Hopelessly intimidated, I receded back into my chair.

"Greer Foley," he thundered, "whose side are you on anyway?"

Caught up in the whirlwind of his anger, I looked on simultaneously riveted and detached, as if I were watching a tornado touch down, caught up in his swirling colors as they engulfed me, so much like the natural world, sea-green eyes, chestnut hair, ruddy skin. I was being swept away by forces over which I had no control.

The Last Summer of the Camperdowns

. . .

I'M THIRTY-THREE YEARS OLD and the memory of that long-ago summer remains as alive to me as something I can reach out and touch, a secular rosary upon which I frequently meditate. I run the tips of my fingers over their firm smooth surfaces, feeling each individual sphere, cool and detached, fiddling with ideas and scenarios and endless possibilities in the hope that things could somehow have been different. If only. If only I could somehow poke a hole through time and space and reach into that old house and shake that girl, slap her silly, tell her to shout out from the rooftops what she knew.

There was time. I had the time. It only takes a moment to do the right thing. But maybe that was part of the problem. I took my time. All those hours devoted to thinking about what to do were just a prelude to letting myself off the hook.

Something I've learned: once you postpone doing what's right, you become a big part of what's wrong.

Chapter **Three**

———

WHISTLING FOR THE DOGS, I DARTED OUT THE FRONT DOOR, the crashing of the waves and the wind obliterating the last remnants of staccato bickering emanating from the dining room. I rubbed the back of my neck, joints sore from swiveling from one point of view to the other. To spend time with Greer and Camp was to experience firsthand the effects of a ping-pong marathon between two warring countries.

Breathing deeply of the ocean air, my sighs of blessed release mingling with the sweet music of songbirds, I chased Vera to the far reaches of the garden, to the grassy tree-lined area near the little barn, the horses watching from the paddock. I threw a ball for her, the only one of the bunch young enough to still see the value in fetching.

"Riddle!" My father appeared from around the corner of the house and called out to me from several yards away, clearly annoyed. "Do you have any idea what's happened to my navy blue socks? Dozens of socks and I can't find a matching pair."

I shook my head and waited for what I knew was coming next.

"Did you notice the cobwebs in the living room? It's like we live in some neglected Romanian castle. Why in the hell I'm spending valuable time looking for socks and knocking down cobwebs . . ." He turned around, cheeks flushed, and headed back toward the house. He was more upset than I suspected. Whenever Camp started looking for socks or complaining about cobwebs, it was time to seek refuge in the nearest underground shelter.

I flopped down in the long grass, the basset hounds panting and jolly and curled up around me, cocooning me with their warmth. Sometimes, alone with my dogs and my horse, I felt as if I was the only person in the world. It wasn't an unhappy feeling. The puppy licked my face and thumped down on my chest as I thanked God for being wise enough to withhold from dogs the gift of speech.

An hour later, the dogs passed out and snoring in the shady grass, I was hanging above them, upside down in a hammock, squinting up at my toes, floating and inaccessible, in that prepubescent realm harrowingly located somewhere between heaven and earth and Kraft dinner.

Way up in the tree canopy, perilously high off the ground, sun shimmering through the leaves, hair in my eyes and red paint on my toenails, rosy and glowing, a ripening peach in a cotton-string pouch anchored between two ancient chestnut trees, I watched an endless parade of navy blue cars arrive one after another as the house filled with campaign staffers, my father laughing and greeting them loudly. So much for our family day.

The door snapped open. A flock of grackles blew up around me in an indigo swirl of noise and panic. My mother appeared on the side verandah. Cheeks pink, hand at her brow, she called out, "Riddle, would you come in here please and smile for these idiots? If I have to perform like a trained seal, then so do you."

"What do you want me to do?" I groused. "Bounce a ball on my nose or devise campaign strategy?"

"Don't be a wisenheimer. Just get in here and be pleasant and polite and serve some cookies. What are you doing up there anyway?"

I shinnied down and was almost at the bottom of the tree when a solitary crow landed in the branch beside me, a baby bird in its beak, still alive, tiny chest rising and falling, otherwise motionless. That captive terror! That expression! The very thought of it all these years later is still enough to catapult me into the open arms of the nearest exclamation point.

It was my first personal experience of certainty. Horrified, I lost my grip and then I lost my balance. I let out a single yelp. That's when my foot began its long irreversible slide. The sharp edge of a broken branch scraped my flesh, making a shallow surgical incision that started at my ankle and came to searing conclusion along my inner thigh. It hurt like hell. I hit the ground standing but with a mordant thump.

"Shit!" I hollered, blinking back tears.

"Riddle! Honestly. I've had enough of your feral word choices," my mother said, her smoky shadow unsympathetically blocking out the sun.

Yeah, well, I've had enough of your bullshit. Why can't you talk like a normal human being for once? I let the thought go unexpressed, savoring for a change the rebel joy of keeping something secret. I swallowed a whimper. No bawling in the Camperdown house.

"Once a person starts crying, they never stop," Camp liked to say.

It wasn't until we reached the door to the house that we realized the puppy was missing.

"Honestly, Riddle, one thing I asked of you. All you had to do was watch the puppy. Where could she be?" My mother couldn't conceal her annoyance with me as we searched for Vera, conducting a thorough sweep of the inside and the outside of the house, guests be damned. From the foyer my father started to speak before stopping himself. He knew better than to interfere with my mother's relationship with her dogs, watching in silence as we headed back outside.

From where I crawled among the dense undergrowth in the wet wilderness outcropping at the outer limits of our property, I could see my mother standing at the top of the dune overlooking the ocean. She had her hand to her forehead, an awning for her eyes as she surveyed the empty beach below for any sign of the missing Vera.

I stood up, my palm gripping a fallen log for support. "Shit!" I said, as the top of my head skimmed along the surface of an encroaching bush and I realized that my hair was congested with nettles. I was officially at the end of my ability to absorb setbacks. That's when I walked into a sticky web roughly the size of Tanzania. In its center, a monstrous black and yellow spider indicated its intention to bind, torture and kill me.

"Vera, where are you?" Darting into the relative safety of a tiny clearing, I tried to banish my growing suspicion that I was a complete and utter fraud, a hopeless girly-girl in combatant's gear. I searched my immediate surroundings in a mindless effort to somehow prove my manhood. Pissing seemed out of the question—I lacked the equipment. In desperation, I spit on the ground. A grasshopper sprang from the long grass and landed on my shoulder. I sprinted toward my mother, who was already walking in my direction.

"This is terrible," she lamented. "Awful! Where is she? Could she have wandered across the road and over to Gin's?"

"I don't know. Maybe." Gin Whiffet owned the former Devlin estate, vast lush acres of woodland trail, open pasture, wet marshland and dense forest. The Devlins had bred some of the finest thoroughbred horses in the country on that land. Part of what was now Gin's property extended to the point at the end of the road where the beachfront met "civilian" ground. He operated a private riding stable for elite equestrian students who came from around the world for advanced instruction in eventing, dressage, jumping and steeplechase.

Gin and my mother had been friends since childhood. She treated his land as if it was her own, and for his part, he seemed to enjoy her abuse and her trespass as well as her cultish celebrity. Gin taught me early the true meaning of reflected glory.

When I was growing up, people said that along with being one of the country's great celluloid beauties, my mother was the finest horsewoman in New England. It was a clear case of form triumphing over function—an aesthetic victory for Greer, who longed to be taken seriously as an equestrian without doing any of the work. She never competed in a show ring but created the impression that she did. Her real achievement lay in her talent for looking good on a horse, glamorous for sure, and sophisticated. Remote, detached, stylish—she made Audrey Hepburn seem like Minnie Pearl. How she detested naïveté! If Cole Porter's music could be taught to ride a horse, it would capture some of what my mother evinced in the saddle.

We walked back to the house together, not talking, sand filling up my running shoes, the specter of Vera's disappearance becoming a sadder reality as I tried unsuccessfully to banish thoughts of whatever hideous fate she might have met as a result of my negligence.

"Camp!" my mother called to my father through the screen door at the front of the house. "Riddle and I are going to Gin's to see if Vera found her way across the road."

"If you're not home in an hour I'll alert the Coast Guard," my father said, aides at his side where he stood in the doorway.

"Honestly, that's not the least bit amusing. Can't you see how worried I am?"

"Greer, worry is a way of life for you. I'd be worried if you weren't worried."

"Don't be absurd. You make me sound like one of those women in a housedress with nothing better to do than wonder if everyone has had a proper breakfast."

I heard a round of nervous laughter from campaign staffers inside the kitchen. Greer, rippling with exasperation, was midway down the flagstone walkway before I'd stepped off the verandah. I was busy pouring sand from my shoes onto the ground.

"Riddle!" she called back. "Keep pace!"

"Release the hounds!" My father playfully unlatched the door.

The screen door banged open then shut as the three basset hounds spun past me and set out in braying pursuit of my mother. Reluctantly I followed them down the walkway as she waited for me farther down the path.

"Oh, Jimmy . . ." Camp called out in a singsong voice.

I paused and turned to face him.

"Look out for Gula!" he teased.

If he was looking for a dramatic response, he got it. Without thinking, purely reacting, I stopped altogether, my feet riveted in place.

"Camp, stop behaving like such an ass," my mother ordered. "You, too!" She pointed, calling me out, turned around and kept right on walking as I dashed after her, Camp shaking his head in the doorway. I marched along in silence, my father's taunt reverberating in my head.

"It's your own fault. I told you not to tell him," she said. "But you won't listen to a word I say."

A few weeks earlier, I had made the mistake of confiding in Camp that Gula gave me the creeps. Why did I say anything? Knowing my parents, I would soon be reading about it in the *Saturday Evening Post*. I still had the scorch marks from Greer's interview in *Ladies' Home Journal* when she talked about buying me my first bra.

"He's a bloody janitor. Your fear of him is an embarrassment," Greer said by way of ongoing rebuke. Gula Nightjar was Gin's caretaker and stable manager. A European immigrant, he had only been in the States for a few months when he came to work for Gin the previous fall. He knew a lot about horses and running a stable, as Gin never stopped reminding everyone. Soft-spoken, well-spoken, gentle in his demeanor, Gula was considered charming by some people who admired his composure, his self-containment.

I didn't like Gula. There was something unsettling about his watchfulness. He made the earth beneath my feet rumble, as if he was spreading underground. Quiet as nightfall, his unctuous attributes of mannerliness and humility were better suited to the saloon than the drawing room, seeming less like social graces and more like weapons that he used to disarm others. He had this way of speaking to me—as if I were an adult, as if there were no distinctions between us. Of course, I thought that's what I wanted until the moment I got it.

My parents and Gin dismissed my uneasiness, seemed entertained by it, attributing it, in the jaded way of adults, to the affliction of adolescence.

A loud yodeling sound went up as Dorothy picked up a fresh scent, running in frantic circles, trailed by Hilary and Madge, before deciding on a course of action, booting away from the beaten path and heading out across the field.

"Dorothy!" Greer shouted after her, to no avail. The hunt was on. I watched as my mother, not hesitating for a second, took out after her rogue posse, dashing purposefully across the open pasture to corral the runaways, who finally, tails wagging in good-natured apology, reconciled themselves to her will and trotted along obediently, forming an honor guard around her.

My mother had made a halfhearted attempt to breed basset hounds—her kennel was called Jolie Laide—in an era when breeding dogs was still considered a genteel aristocratic pastime, a sort of cultural imprimatur, like wearing a strand of pearls or a pillbox hat. That morning, surrounded by her horizontal hounds, striding across the fields as if she were anointing the ground with every confident step, she was eminently vertical, sheathed in riding breeches and herringbone jacket, black boots eschewing vulgar shine, blonde hair trailing like a keffiyeh in the dry wind, an icon of privilege so recognizable she was almost self-parodying.

I trundled along like one of the pack. Basset hounds and I have lots of things in common. Short legs for one. Friendliness. Nosiness. A distinctive bray. Spots. Red hair. Big ears. An obsession with gravy. The desire to please, despite evidence to the contrary. We also have our differences. Basset hounds have a good sense of humor. They're easygoing. Earnest would be a charitable description of me.

Greer ordered the dogs back home as we crossed the rarely trafficked road that divided our two properties, me struggling to keep up with her as she briskly negotiated the uneven ground, easily outstripping me as we started the arduous upward climb. Gin's big pink house sat on the other side of a steep hill. I hesitated. So much work for so little reward.

Huffing and puffing from resentment and physical effort, I felt thin lines of sweat run down my cheeks. My mother, on the other hand, looked crisp as a white blouse fresh from the clothesline as I stood next to her at the top of the hill and looked down at the house, abloom in lavender wisteria and nostalgia, its faded rosy exterior aglow in the soft sunlight.

"Gin's house is so old-fashioned-looking. The same color as pink lemonade," I said.

"More like Pepto-Bismol," my mother replied, starting down

the incline. I lingered before descending, watching her make her surefooted way down the path. My lunchtime session with Camp and Greer had been exhausting. I'm sure people have gone to the gallows feeling more lighthearted than I did at the prospect of now spending social time with my mother and Gin.

A long, wide driveway cut a meandering swathe through the property, dividing the land into forest and marshes on one side and open field and fenced pasture on the other side. The hill conquered, it was a healthy walk to reach the house, which was positioned in a fertile clearing surrounded by informal gardens and a splendid range of enormous weeping willows.

Built in 1700 in New York, the original house had been moved to Wellfleet in the early 1900s by Michael Devlin's father. With its exposed beams, coffered ceilings, antique furnishings and imported cherrywood floors, the pink house shone with the slightly tarnished patina of days gone by.

A corridor of dead trees lined the last part of the route to Gin's house. All the bark was gone, every tree stripped bare by the cormorants, hundreds of them, winged undertakers, perched in the twisted branches of all those looming gray ghosts. Among them, there was a distinctive giant tree, thick and contorted, its living identity erased long ago. I could see it rising up in front of me, poised way above my mother's head as it stretched its long surrendering limbs across the sky, dozens of cormorants positioned on its branches like hooded points of time on a Gothic clock face. Unnerved, I broke into a run, and propelled by the power of my short legs, I raced ahead of my mother and directly into the heart of the Cormorant Clock Farm.

Chapter Four

———

GIN, AS USUAL, MET US AT THE GATE, DUTIFUL AND DUPLICI-tous as a seventeenth-century eunuch lining up for his daily beating from the empress. He never had to wait long.

"Oh, my, Greer, I'll keep my eyes open. We'll find her. Don't you worry. Poor little thing. Lost in the woods. It's not safe in these woods, you know. She could drown in the kettle pond. What about the predators? Coyotes, owls and don't even think about the fishers. Oh, the fishers! People say there aren't any in the area but I've heard them crying out in the night. Horrible. Why did God make fishers, do you think? For that matter, why create mosquitoes? Well, that's why I'm an atheist. Mosquitoes propelled me into agnosticism. Fleas were the last straw."

"Oh, heavens, Gin, I stopped believing the first time I saw pleather."

Gin shrugged and nodded, pushing his dark hair away from his forehead. Slim and narrow, looking like something Evelyn Waugh might have doodled on a napkin during a lull at a dinner party, he wore his traditional daily uniform of classic black riding breeches and Dehner field boots in aesthetic lockstep with my mother, a tasteful pair of matching lamps. Ha! How my mother would detest that description! "There is nothing tasteful about matching lamps, Riddle," she would protest. "Good taste occurs in odd numbers."

I cleared my throat and coughed. Gin's house was immaculate—he had staff to make it so—but it always felt as if there were particles in the air, soot or sand, as if it was forever Ash Wednesday in that big old house, with its dead rooms filled with uncirculated air and no pulse beating. His collection of Victorian taxidermy, on display throughout the house like an overdose of rouge, inflamed the intimation that you had somehow stumbled into the perverse past as it played out on a slightly off-kilter planet. Gin had spent the last two decades putting his indelicate fingerprint on the pink house, and the result, in especially florid evidence in the living room where we stood, an ungainly trio, my mother humming in agitation, waiting for him to get going, was roughly akin to what the bastard offspring of a forced union between a bordello and a funeral home might look like.

I stood in the middle of the room and looked up as I had done a million times before, one of the rituals of my childhood. An Empire-style antique chandelier hung from the ceiling, a gilt bronze and cut-crystal centerpiece with beaded chains and crystal drops dangling. If you positioned yourself directly beneath it, you could see a large emerald and ruby star glowing on the bottom.

Gin and Greer continued to bicker back and forth, the moist pettiness of their mutual complaints beading on my skin like an oily drizzle. So it went. Around and around. Small circles. Big circles. The circuitous chatter of the damned, my father called it. He nicknamed my mother and Gin the Sisters.

I left them to navigate the fog and the mist generated by their conversation—between them, Gin and Greer produced all kinds of weather—as I tiptoed across a threadbare Persian carpet and over to a large antique display case positioned in front of a vast casement window. Kneeling down to examine its familiar contents, I saw dozens of exotic stuffed birds posed in static impersonation of the natural world. Beautiful in its own way, but grotesque. Maybe becoming an ornament was the animal equivalent of being consigned to hell. Everywhere I looked there was another example of living death—a zebra's head mounted on a plaque, a feisty border terrier encased in glass confronting a hissing, scratching calico cat, and, on the mantel over the fireplace, a baby rabbit in Edwardian costume playing an oboe.

"Zombie memorabilia," my mother called it. Sinking down into a plush purple velvet chair, I reached for a diorama crammed with butterflies and birds, every one as recognizable to me as my own face. I had been analyzing each captive still life since I was a little girl, and it never failed to induce in me a sense of brooding nihilism.

"Honestly, Gin, you should mothball this stuff," Greer said, surveying the immediate vicinity, her scorn picking its way through the room. "It's disturbing. I swear you'll have your mother stuffed and under glass, tarted up like Queen Victoria, before you're through."

"How many times must I tell you, Greer? It's an art form. An authentic slice of Victoriana. I find it transporting. Then, I'm different from most people—I have no fear of mortality. My only real dread is a world devoid of the creative arts and culture. I would happily donate my body in the service of art."

"If only you could be disposed of that easily. I'm trying to imagine the kind of artist interested in working with you in life or death," my mother said, calling after Gin as he disappeared into the kitchen. "Someone who enjoys the idea of dogs playing poker, no doubt."

Gin emerged carrying a tray with a ceramic pitcher filled with some kind of sparkling fruit punch and three tall glasses. He offered my mother a drink. She reached for it, then hesitated. "I trust this isn't formaldehyde," she said as I hastily gulped down my juice.

"Let's get going," I urged, frustrated by their relentless sparring. "What about Vera?"

I spent the next hour calling for little Vera as Gin and my mother searched together. They combed the area at the back of the property, bordering a large tract of forested land navigable by a man-made trail that wound through the woods from one end to the other. It was covered over by cedar chips. Alone, and grateful for the reprieve, I wandered through the early summer gardens, diminished tulips and narcissus, brilliantly colored poppies and fragrant orange and pink honeysuckle robustly clinging to ancient wood.

"Puppy! Puppy! Vera!" I called out as, in the background, Gin and my mother did the same.

"Maybe she's shown up at home," I said wanly as the three of us met in the pasture, surrounded by curious horses, my distress growing in direct proportion to the level of guilt I was feeling over having lost Vera.

"Oh, I hope so," my mother said. "I can't stand to think of that little thing being on her own. When you think of the awful things that could happen to her." It wasn't unusual for my mother to become emotional about one of the dogs, though she rarely extended the same feeling to the people in her life. Gin read my mind. "Too bad we walk on two legs instead of four, isn't it, Jimmy?" he said in rueful aside.

She smiled defiantly and lit a cigarette as Gin recoiled and fumed. He had a stable owner's instinctive dread of fire. "Greer, you are wicked with those stinking things. I swear you do it just to be, well . . ." He looked around, searching the summer faces of a separate clump of horses as they stood next to one another beneath a trio of apple trees, his arms waving so wildly that a bay filly shied sideways and kicked the air with her rear hooves. "Jimmy, what word am I looking for?"

"Inflammatory," I supplied. "Incendiary."

"Exactly." Gin snapped his fingers and laughed. "Someone's been hitting the books. Inflammatory. Incendiary. She sure has your number, Greer."

My mother, irritability levels percolating to the point of steamy overflow, brought the flattened palm of her hand down on the show jumper Delano's rump, the loud plain slap scattering the small herd that had settled around us. "Gin, it's a cigarette. It's not nitroglycerine. Not another word, please." She reigned over the compliant silence until she decided we had been sufficiently subdued. "Anyway, on to more interesting matters. Where's the poor woman's Heathcliff?" Specializing in getting to the wicked point of it all, she grinned and glancing downward, used the toe of her boot to dig a hole in the clay.

"You tell me where he is," Gin said, staring at the delinquent cigarette. "I haven't seen him for the last couple of days. Gula is a regular phantom. Here one moment, gone the next."

"I'm confused. I understood that he was working for you, not the other way around."

"He is my employee, Greer, not my slave. He asked for a few days off. He never takes a holiday. I could hardly say no under the circumstances."

"Getting any closer to revealing the glorious secret?" My mother had such an arch delivery that someone once asked her at a funeral if she was being sarcastic when she expressed her condolences to the family. When she intended sarcasm, she peeled the bark off trees.

"Never you mind."

I couldn't quite decide whether Gin spoke with a Southern accent or a British accent. In the end I decided it was a defeatist hybrid.

"Ha!" My mother laughed. Her laugh sounded like mockery in any language.

"What glorious secret?" I asked, unable to resist such a tantalizing tease despite my worry about the puppy and my exasperation with current company.

"Gin's not talking. He and Gula are in cahoots on some special project. I suspect it has something to do with a horse."

"You'll see," Gin said.

She rumbled with impatience. "Oh, for heaven's sake, Gin, what are you hiding? You act as if you're planning to invade Turkey. You've been downright surreptitious since Gula arrived on the scene. There is something about this man that you aren't telling me. Out with it—or perhaps you're embarrassed. From what I've heard, he's nothing more than a low-rent gigolo."

"Greer, that is a terrible way to talk about a man with such an unhappy past," Gin said, looking instantly regretful for responding to her bait. If Gin had fins, he would have been one of those hapless fish that gets instantly hooked again the moment he's thrown back into the water.

My mother pounced. "What's this? What unhappy past? Since when do you keep a confidence?" She looked over at me as if she suddenly remembered my presence. "It's when your uncle Gin stops talking that he has something worthwhile to say," she added confidentially. "Maybe Riddle's instincts about Gula are right after all. She's terrified of him."

I looked up sharply. "I am not," I protested. Surely, Gin would recognize a compliment directed at me as the ultimate manipulation.

"He's got the thousand-yard stare, all right. Why wouldn't he, with all he's seen? The horror of war and all that sort of thing. Man at his worst et cetera, et cetera," Gin said. "But look, Jimmy, the man is harmless. I would go so far as to say he has a gentle soul. He's interesting, too, in his way. He takes a little knowing, that's all. I wouldn't have him around otherwise. My God, but he is an absolute magician with horses. I think he is quite brilliant, really I do."

"Enough!" My mother was impatient of any conversation that did not feature her at its epicenter. "Where did he come from? You've evaded and obfuscated forever. Time to tell, finally."

Gula's professional and personal background was mysterious and malleable, highly changeable. I heard so many stories: that he had gone from being a stable boy at a number of European race-tracks after the war to supervising the breeding program at a racing stable in Saudi Arabia for a member of the royal family.

"He trained polo ponies for one of the Rothschilds!" Gin said. He was especially enamored of the Rothschild connection.

"A Rothschild! Oh, my, you don't say. Did he wear sunglasses to protect his eyes from the glare?" Greer's contempt for others was not dependent on class or race. The whole world was her killing field. "I don't care if he shoed horses for the Holy Ghost, however has he become such a fixture around here? He's like some sort of Rasputin knockoff."

"First, Heathcliff, now Rasputin. Greer, you are positively melodramatic in your judgments about people. God knows how you describe me."

"Topo Gigio," I said. "She calls you Topo Gigio."

"It's a term of endearment," my mother said, vibrating with annoyance, giving me a quick pinch, unmoved by Gin's sharp, shocked exhalation of breath and my exclamation of pain.

"Anyway, don't change the subject. I swear you're frightened by the man, though I can't imagine why." She glanced over at Gin, eyeing him peripherally.

Gin was sputtering. "Now that is the most spectacular lie!

Afraid! The idea! There's no great mystery. Why must you make theater where there is none? The poor man grew up during the war in France, or was it Belgium? Some godforsaken place. He's practically a refugee. His family suffered terribly, and yet he pulled himself up from all that depressing reality, got an education, and used his talent with horses to work among the world's great stables." He paused. "I'd like to think my little enterprise here has made its own mark in that regard."

"I'd like to think that Riddle's hair color is just a bad dream, but then garish reality intrudes. Really, Gin, if you truly believe what you're saying, you're an even bigger fool than your advance publicity suggests."

I could almost see my mother sharpening her blades. Gin was a butter knife, no match for her serrated edges. "The truth is the man is a two-bit Porfirio Rubirosa wannabe whose riding skills aren't confined to the stable. Marion Bingham swears she witnessed him climbing out of Myrna Stevenson's bedroom window, shoes in one hand, riding crop in the other. Rumor has it he taught Holly Laidlaw dressage by day and the Kama Sutra by night and then extorted huge sums from her to keep quiet about it."

She glanced over at me. "Slack jaw isn't a good look for you, Riddle."

"I've heard all the stories, Greer," Gin said. "Typical tiresome chat. I don't pay attention to gossip."

My mother laughed in astonishment. "Who are you trying to kid, Louella? Obviously, it's all true. You are so transparent." Greer was enormously impressed with herself and the skill with which she extracted information from Gin. There was something else, too. My mother would never admit to her fears, but her curiosity about Gula, so uncharacteristic, was unsettling. I wondered at its meaning.

"I prefer to judge people based on my own experience of their behavior." Gin defaulted to loftiness. "All I know is that Gula's conduct has been beyond reproach during his time here. I don't care what you say. I don't care what anyone says. Thanks to him, I shall finally realize a great dream!" Gin's voice lurched several octaves as he struggled to find his emotional equilibrium.

"Now I get it. You plan to have yourself stuffed and Gula has offered to do the honors."

Gin was still wrestling with my mother's accusation. "Honestly, Greer, scared of Gula? Whatever in the world is there to be frightened by? Sometimes you make me cross."

I looked at him sideways. Gin's indignation wasn't entirely convincing.

"Gin Whiffet, you are notoriously yellow. I have no patience for a cowardly man. Say what you will about Camp, but he has guts." My mother tossed her head and stamped her foot, attracting the notice of Gin's warmblood stallion, the notoriously temperamental Mercurio, who snorted noisily from behind the fence, sensing a kindred spirit. "I'm not afraid of anyone, let alone someone who makes it their business to be intimidating."

"Do you think that Gula is intimidating?" I asked, surprised at her unexpected admission.

"Hardly," she snapped. "Trying and succeeding are two different things."

"The only person I know who makes it their business to be intimidating is you, Greer." Gin cleared his throat, unaware that he had just conferred on her a great compliment. "So, I guess we've avoided the topic long enough. How do you feel about Michael coming home? How did Camp take the news?"

My mother tossed her lit cigarette to the ground, grinding out the burning embers with a precise stomp of her heel. She nodded in my direction, then looked back at Gin by way of exasperated explanation.

"Jimmy, why don't you run along and check out the stable?" Gin said, winking over at my mother, persuaded that he had a talent for making orders seem like playful suggestions. "There's a new foal that was born over the weekend and who knows? You might come across the puppy. We didn't think to look there earlier."

The Sisters had a limited tolerance for the companionship of children. It worked both ways. I was thrilled for the opportunity to escape their oppressive prattle. Besides, I wanted to keep looking for Vera. On the other hand, I was intrigued by discussion concerning Michael Devlin. My mother was obviously trying to get rid of me. Things so rarely went unsaid in the Camperdown household that when they did it usually meant I had stumbled across a mystery worth exploring.

As I was walking away Greer called out to me, "Find that puppy! Don't you dare come home without her. If anything happens to Vera you have only yourself to blame."

She turned her back on me and took up with Gin in her brittle way—the uninflected chilliness, the precision of her evisceration, her aloof sociability. She was a late frost and I could feel my toes curling.

I walked away, her heedlessness a listless wind against my back. I broke into a jog, then a run. Sprinting toward the barn, shouting for Vera all the way, I shivered to think my mother might be right.

Chapter Five

———

I RACED ALL THE WAY TO THE STABLE, PRAYING FOR MY LOST puppy as I ran. "Please, please, let Vera be safe at home with Camp," I said, coming to a stop, eyes shut, hands forming a steeple, fingers touching my lips.

Gin had two barns. I sprinted past the big white stable, heading toward the yellow barn, which was smaller and less grand, a kind of poor relation. Off the beaten path, remote and largely unused, it housed a handful of mares and their foals. The first three stalls were empty, their residents turned out to pasture. I surprised a mouse in the feed room that popped out of a bag of oats and then just as quickly vanished into a worn section of barn board. Shoulders slack and feet dragging, I continued down the broad aisle of the stable.

A dapple gray mare whinnied at my approach, head extended over the door of her stall. Her tottering charcoal-black foal peeked out at me from behind her. "Come here, I won't hurt you," I crooned, extending my arm over the top of the stall door. Unlatching it, I slid inside; the mare greeted me with interest, pushing against me with her head, looking for a treat. I reached into my pocket and gave her a carrot. The baby horse cautiously approached my outstretched fingers, standing just outside my reach, bobtail flicking back and forth as his mother munched on my gift.

Sun streamed into the stall, thick yellow bedding of clean straw warm and glowing, breeze blowing soft and mellow through the stable. I felt more truly myself when I was with my dogs and my horse than I ever did with most people. Grabbing the mare's mane, I hoisted myself onto her bare back, the foal looking on. Her back was hot from the sun's rays; tail flicking lazily, she nuzzled through the hay, snacking. I lay down on her back, a human blanket, arms and legs extended downward, limp and defeated, my face pressed against her withers, soaking up her body heat even as she absorbed mine. For the next few minutes, I breathed in the dusky rich scent of horse, my adolescent girl's version of an intoxicant, and I felt comforted even through my anguished thoughts of Vera.

I heard a muffled voice coming from somewhere both near and far. My first thought was that it was my mother and Gin. My second thought was that it wasn't them at all. Hastily I dried my eyes, vaguely uneasy. My instinct was to get away from there, though I couldn't say why exactly. I sat up to go but uneasiness, like a hand against my chest, held me in place.

Slithering back down to the floor, embarrassed and confused by my fear, I receded into the far corner of the big stall, wedging myself behind a stack of straw, the foal peering at me as I pulled my knees into my chest. The door to the tack room at the far end of the aisle opened and thudded shut, startling me. The foal's head jerked up. I pressed myself against the wall, instantly alert, radar twitching. Someone was running down the long stable corridor and past the stalls, heading toward the door. It had a frantic quality, part shuffle, part awful scurry.

Panting, whoever it was ran first one way, then back, mindless and without direction, in terrible desperation—that panting! The tack room door opened again with a whoomph. More of the same fugitive flight sounds, like wings flapping against a windowpane. I felt as if a bird was trapped inside of me, flailing against my rib cage. It was hard to breathe; the air around me, only moments before so sweet and comforting, now felt thick and debauched, musky and wild, as if someone was pumping squalor through the vents. Suddenly something wicked oozed from every pore of that barn.

A horse whinnied in alarm.

There was a frenzied scuffle. It grew louder and louder and it came closer and closer, rhythmic and churning, my terror increasing incrementally in jolts of electricity. Dizzy and disoriented, a violent bang brought me round as someone or something landed against the stall door where I hid. My head snapped back. I buried my face in my knees and clamped shut my eyes and tried not to scream. I heard a ragged scrambling, a helpless floundering, and down the corridor the discomposing tread of dragging.

There was something else, something rasping, halting and breathless. Scared. It sounded like a word. "Why?"

The door to the tack room thumped shut and there was silence.

ALL I WANTED WAS to get out of there, but where to go? How to get there? Shaking with fear, I was incapable of sustaining a logical sequence of thoughts. I sat with my eyes shut for a long time. When I dared to unlock my eyes for a quick peek, the top corner of the stable door was visible from where I sat hunched against the wall behind the straw. That door represented freedom and home. Home! However was I to find my way back home? Even thinking about escape was proving too harrowing an exercise—any idea that I might be exposed made me lightheaded. Curling up into myself, I listened and waited. It was so quiet that even the slapping of the horses' tails as they whisked away flies, the occasional muffled stamp of a hoof on straw, resounded like a thunderclap and I covered my ears, afraid of what I had heard, terrified of the erratic pulse of my own breathing.

I remained in that twilight state for what seemed like forever, a prisoner of shock and impending stasis. Too terrified to make the slightest movement, I sat rigidly in place for so long that when I finally tried to stand and walk it was like taking a mallet to limestone, parts of me crumbling with every stiff and painful step. The door to the tack room remained shut. I had no idea who or what was inside that room, or if they were still inside. Had they left? The tack room had its own separate entrance. My temples pounded. Should I stay or should I go?

I imagined the heart of the barn itself beating in unison with my own as I made my way slowly and mechanically upward until I was standing, holding my breath so successfully that by the time I reached the stall door I felt faint. Outside the stall, tiptoeing toward the stable door, barely resisting the urge to bolt, I counted each step as I quietly focused my whole being on that door. I was almost there when I heard a faint cry.

My knees buckling, I strained to hear, the insistent buzzing of flying insects and the crunch of straw now the only sounds. Then I heard it. Whining. How I wanted to find Vera, but why now? I looked cravenly beyond the door and into the fields.

Whimpering. It was coming from behind me. Behind me was the tack room. Behind me meant going away from the stable door, which had become the central focus of my life. Jostling currents of fear, anger, self-interest and my love for little Vera swept over me. I took two steps forward and then, mustering what little courage I had, I spun around and hastened back down the long center aisle of the stable, passing two more mares with foals and then a series of empty stalls. At the end of the aisle was a large box stall filled floor to ceiling with hay. Next to it was the tack room. The gray mother horse neighed in the background as I reflexively breathed in the familiar smells of horse and saddle, burnished leather, bridle and hay, humid straw, moist and woody exposed beams.

"Vera?" I whispered, frantic and with more hope than conviction as I neared the closed tack room door. My voice slowly drained of volume until it was little more than the silent formation of letters and rush of adrenaline that pulsated in my throat, thumping along with the sound of scraping nails against the opposite side of the door. Wanting to go back but compelled to go forward, the scratching growing louder with every step, I crept up to the large, heavy wooden door.

Momentarily faltering, I took three steps back. I couldn't do it. I could not open that door. I was at the outer limits of my courage. This was a job for Camp, not me. The door opened a crack just as I was about to flee. Gasping, I dropped to my knees.

Vera! Her little tricolor face was there in front of me, ears dragging. She was smiling, her low-slung body wriggling with the joy of being found. She bounded toward me, wagging her tail and licking my face, clamping down on the red fringe covering my forehead. "Ouch!" I muttered, trying to extricate my hair from the unforgiving trap of puppy teeth.

"Thank you! Thank you!" I spoke silently to myself and to any god that would listen. Vera finally released my hair and, ignoring my hushed entreaties to stay, wheeled around, her long thick tail accelerating like a windshield wiper, circulating the otherwise dead air, whirring flecks of straw and hay and dust made visible by the sudden incursion of sunlight.

"Come here!" I hissed and darted after her. She stopped abruptly and I tripped over her hind end; lurching forward, I fell with arms outstretched, landing in an undignified splat.

"Dammit!" I lay there stunned, profanities springing up inside of me like internal bruises. I caught sight of something on the floor next to me. A clump of hair, russet hair and amber, the color of tree resin; the tips were wet, as if they had been dipped in crimson dye.

Panicked, I rolled over onto my side, the dull jab of something hard and intrusive poking and resistant against my abdomen. The toe of a riding boot. Scuffed and scratched, well worn—I stared at it long enough, focused on the leather's matte finish. It took what felt like years for me to generate the courage to look up.

Deep-set black eyes stared down at me where I lay. I realized then that there is a third option to the primitive responses of fight-or-flight—spontaneous brain death. My first sputtering cognitive thought was a decidedly adolescent one: his pants were too short, hovering just above his ankles.

He held his hands out in front of his chest, rubbing them together as if he was warming them over an open fire. Tall and thin, unshaven, neither young nor old, with longish dark hair that curled round his shirt collar, he seemed to be growing, soaring smoothly upward to the rafters, reaching greater heights with each passing moment. Extending his arm, he took me by the hand and pulled me to my feet. His palm felt damp and limp, flaccid—something else I've learned, a weak handshake isn't an accurate forecaster of strength of purpose.

I could have pulled free, but I was being held in place by a force greater than anything imposed by his grip.

"Well, now," Gula said finally. "What are you doing here?" He sounded indiscriminately European, a mishmash of accented inflections, with a subtle British top layer. His gift for dry understatement conferred on him an unsentimental refinement.

Too frightened to speak—a unique experience for me—I looked around for Vera in the hope that she might somehow answer for both of us.

"You need to take better care," Gula said, as he let me go and leaned his back into one of the tall stacks of hay. "I found her running up and down the aisle in here." He spoke calmly, though I could detect a note of stern inquiry in his voice. "How long have you been here?"

My mouth was so dry I would have had more success building a sandcastle than formulating a response.

"Not long?"

I shook my head.

"I see." He reached out and touched my hair. It was warm in the barn, but I began to shiver.

"You have straw in your hair," Gula said, removing a long yellow stalk and rolling it between his forefinger and his middle finger before casually putting it between his lips, teeth holding it in place as he began to chew. I looked down at the ground.

Vera came around the corner carrying something in her mouth. A shoe.

"Where did you get that? You bad puppy." Gula reached down and grabbed Vera by the scruff of her neck, causing her to cringe. He took the shoe from her, started to stand back up and then in one fast swooping motion reached back down and slapped her across the muzzle, sending her rolling across the aisle of the stable. "That's what happens to bad pups," he said.

She yelped, and for a moment the blinds went down and I could not see.

"It looks like something Gin would wear, don't you think?" Gula held up the shoe, a topsider, brown leather, expensive but frayed, and he laughed without laughing as he turned it over in his hands and then set it down on a window ledge.

His reptilian languor, the torpid absence of any overt aggressiveness, was more disturbing than if he had dragged me off by the hair. Gula and I had entered into a kind of listless war, and his lack of specific animation was disconcerting. I had an idea of how villains should behave, and he wasn't playing along with my expectations. It's terrifying to find yourself dealing with someone who hasn't read the handbook.

He took up a spot in front of the tack room. Leaning his head back against the closed door—which, in my mind, had assumed the malignant proportions of the Berlin Wall—he closed his eyes as I struggled to remain upright, the force of his secret thoughts threatening to knock me down.

"So," he said, using his foot to open the door a crack wider. "Do you want to come in? See my secret project? I'm working on something special. Are you interested?" Speaking in that quiet unperturbed way of his, he might have been folding laundry. The low haunting register of his voice had a kind of depraved elegance.

"I have to go home," I said, finally finding my voice, each word scraping against the cloistered air.

"Where is your spirit of adventure? Home is highly overrated."

"I guess." Shuffling backward, I made a stumbling movement toward the door when I felt his hands on my shoulders, his fingernails digging into my flesh with an intensity that went right to bone. I caught my breath—I knew what it meant to be a rabbit snatched from the long grass by a raptor. Jerked skyward, my feet left the ground and as he lifted me higher I felt certain that he was going to throw me into the tack room where I would shatter into a million tiny pieces.

"Are you sure?" he teased, lowering me back down to the ground. "Aren't you the least bit curious about what's behind the door?"

I had never been less curious about anything in my life. I turned my back to him and started walking.

"Wait!"

I willed myself to turn around.

"Aren't you forgetting something?" Gula had Vera tucked into the crook of his elbow. His gaze locked on mine, he shoved the puppy rudely into my arms, her long ears flattening against the velvet dome of her skull in sweet submission. She licked his fingers in misguided appeal, the tip of her tail fluttering.

Holding Vera tight against my chest, I turned around and walked slowly toward the stable door. I was remembering something I once read and kept repeating it as if it were a prayer: I want to live for another thousand years. I don't know if it's true that there are no atheists in foxholes, but there were no twelve-year-old unbelievers in the stable that day.

The barn door was within reach, my hand was on the handle, when I heard glass shatter, reverberating like a minor explosion coming from inside the tack room. It was followed by a long low moan, lonely and disconnected, with only a tenuous claim on consciousness, and all I could think of at that moment was, Thank heaven that's not me. Urine streamed down my legs as Gula sprang toward the open tack room door; I felt a cold rush of air as he pounced, the door shutting behind him in a heartless thud.

I ran. Ran from whatever was going on behind that door. I ran from the yellow barn, Vera in my arms, straw blowing in the wind. I ran through the grazing pasture, the horses lifting their heads in unison, ears slowly twitching, idle antennae signaling their indifference. Gin's old Shetland pony, Judy, chased Vera and me from the field, sent us clambering over the old wooden fence and into the forest, propelled along a path that represented the long way to our house.

I ran toward home. I ran and I ran. I kept running. I ran for another thousand years.

Chapter Six

———

CARS LINED THE DRIVEWAY, FOUR OR FIVE OF THEM IN VARIOUS shades of dark blue, parked on the diagonal next to one another. I sprinted past them and up onto the verandah. The screen door banged shut behind me as, shaking from exertion, throat burning, I leaned for support against the staircase in the hallway.

"Riddle?" My mother called out to me from the living room. I could hear voices, men and women, exuberant voices I didn't recognize, Camp's voice, everyone excited and happy. "Is that you? Did you find Vera?"

She wandered out into the hallway carrying a glass of wine. "What happened?"

Vera hopped from my arms. My mother dropped to her knees, smothering the joyful puppy in kisses. "Thank God. Where did you find her?"

"Gin's," I said. "I found her in the woods." I was lying and though I didn't fully understand why, I knew enough. I knew that something had happened in that barn, something bad. I just wanted it to be over, to be done. I wanted to make the events of the afternoon vanish, as if nothing at all had happened. I didn't tell my mother. I didn't tell my father. At that point I didn't even tell myself, but I can never say that I didn't know.

So I lied. The tiny voice in my head that urged me to tell was no match for the thunderous knocking of my knees. It didn't stand a chance against the living memory of Gula's hands on my shoulders, in my hair. In those days, I was all about the soft landing, especially when I was the one plummeting through the atmosphere, the earth rising up to greet me. Something wasn't right with what had happened in the yellow stable, but I was determined never to know what was wrong about it.

"When are they going home?" I couldn't catch my breath.

"When the booze stops flowing. As usual, your father reneged on his promise. You can't believe a word that man says. Oh, Vera, you dear little thing! Whatever would we have done without you?"

Camp came around the corner. "Whoa," he said, mildly taken aback when he saw me. "Jimmy! Are you all right?"

I glanced at myself in the hall mirror. My knee was cut. My lip was bleeding. My skin was so white I looked as if I had been systematically stripped of pigmentation. My hair, on the other hand, was so alarmingly red it was standing in the middle of a crowded theater screaming "Fire!"

"I'm fine, just . . . Judy chased me across the field," I said. "I scraped myself on the fence when I was trying to get away from her."

"That pony is a menace," my mother said. "She came after me last week, too. Gin won't hear a word against her. He insists that she's 'complicated.' Crazy. Heavens, Riddle." She got back to her favorite pastime, assessing my dishevelment. "You look as if you've been in a bar fight." She inhaled and grimaced. "Good God. Is that urine I smell? Riddle! Look at you. You've wet yourself. What's happened here?"

"Nothing!" Embarrassed and at a total loss, I stamped my foot in a gesture of pure emotion. "I ran as fast as I could. I didn't make it home in time. All right? Are you happy now?"

"Leave her alone." Camp patted me on the back and looked admiringly at my bruises. "She fought the underbrush and Gin's psychotic pony to bring home your lost dog."

"The dog she lost," Greer interrupted.

"Regardless." Camp's frequent use of the word "regardless," his favorite arch dismissive, inevitably sounded like the precursor to a physical threat. "Riddle's got more on her mind than how she looks." He lobbed that grenade in my mother's direction. My father despised personal vanity. He fought so many wars on so many fronts; among his softer targets were the great fashion houses of Europe. What did I expect? After all, this was a man who once watched a tank carrying one of his best friends blow up: "All that was left of him was a smoking black scorch of ash on the ground."

A warrior in her own right, Greer bit back a retort; apparently she had decided to regroup. She dismissed us with an elegant but crushing wave of her wrist, the sun shining on her golden hair as if it had nothing better to do, her profile more devastating than all the bombs dropped on Dresden. I wondered if my father understood the battle was already lost.

"Come on. Clean yourself up. There is someone that I want you to meet," Camp said. I stared at him, searching his face for signs, for confirmation that I was the same girl I had been when I left the house a few short hours before. Had the whole world changed? Was it just me?

"Riddle?" My mother touched my hand. "Did you hear your father?"

I nodded as both of my parents looked at me expectantly, slightly perplexed. I stared into their faces. I knew they were there, the problem was me. I wasn't there. I was back in the yellow stable with Gula, his hands permanently affixed to my shoulders.

"I don't want to meet anyone," I said unreasonably, tears falling. "Why can't you just leave me alone?"

"Baffling," my father said, watching me torpedo up the stairs. "What's that all about? Crying never solved anything," he called after me as I stopped on the second-floor landing, just out of sight, where I collapsed in a humid heap on the stairs.

"Well, that's helpful advice, Camp. Honestly. What you don't know about young girls would fill an encyclopedia. I'll go talk to her," my mother said, her voice following me up the stairs to where I sat, my head in my hands, her hand on the top rail of the staircase, her foot on the first step. She started up the stairs after me but Camp stopped her.

"She'll be fine. Let her be. Expiation through conversation is a cliché, Greer. Anyway, you're not exactly the picture of the sympathetic mother. You'll do more harm than good. There's a reason you and Donna Reed were never up for the same parts."

I lurched to my feet and ran up to the third floor. Slamming the bedroom door behind me, I threw myself onto the bed and pulled the covers up over me, trying to obliterate the noise in my head. That obscene scrambling, that helpless scurrying—the furtiveness settled somewhere in the deepest, most primitive part of me. It was as if I had found a secret staircase that led to a hidden room, previously undiscovered and buried inside me. Gula's damp detachment, those fingers in my hair. Repulsed, I threw off the covers and darted into the bathroom. I ran the water in the bath and slid down onto the floor.

Where had I gone? The brave girl I had only imagined myself to be.

Scrubbing myself with a bath sponge, steaming hot water skimming the edge of the old claw-foot tub, its porcelain flaking and chipped, I rubbed my skin until it was raw and red, but there wasn't enough bubble bath in the world to sanitize the effects of that afternoon.

To this day I wonder how different things might have been had my mother simply yielded to her first impulse and followed me up those stairs.

IT WAS LATE. EVERYONE had gone. The house was silent except for the occasional muffled exchange between my parents. Crawling on top of the covers, my old bed creaking in aged response, I worked on revising my understanding of what had taken place in the barn.

Gula talked about a secret project. Maybe he was referring to the glorious secret that Gin was talking about. Maybe it was Vera running back and forth. The more I thought about it, the more convinced I became that it had to have been Vera. As for the shoe, well, who knew? The shoe was no big deal. Gin had so many riding students, most of them from privileged backgrounds. Bare feet and topsiders—classic private-school boy insignia, the sheen of wealth encapsulating them like a glistening force field. The kind of boys I publicly ridiculed but privately yearned after.

The clump of hair probably belonged to a little creature attacked by a predator. It was a woodsy color, a color more wild than domestic. Poor dead rabbit.

The sound I'd heard. Thought I heard. Was it human? Unlikely. Or maybe it was me. Maybe I had cried out. Maybe I no longer recognized the sound of my own voice.

What else could I have done? Squeezing my eyes shut, all I could see was the inglorious sight of myself running away, fear elevating me several feet off the ground, the soles of my running shoes caked in straw and horseshit. It wouldn't be my last experience with misguided supplication. I had a talent for asking myself the wrong questions.

"Riddle?" The doorknob twisted. I scrambled under the covers.

"Come in," I said as my father entered the room, stopping at the doorway.

"How are you doing? We missed you at supper."

"I'm fine."

He hesitated, shifting awkwardly in place before approaching my bed and sitting down next to me. "Listen. I know this is a tough time for you, for all of us, your mother especially—as she reminds me on a regular basis. Running for office is sometimes more diffi-cult for the family than for the candidate. After all, you didn't sign on for this. In the end, you are sacrificing a lot in support of my goals and ambitions. I realize that and I sympathize . . ."

"It's all right, Camp," I said, interrupting.

". . . to a point," he said, completing his thought in a way that suggested his empathy levels were more reminiscent of a fast-drying creek bed than an overflowing reservoir. "So there have been some challenges in the past year. Big deal. It's a pain in the ass but we're in the home stretch. The election's in November. We just need to keep our cool and remember that there are things greater than ourselves. It's important to have a sense of humility. We're at war. People are dying, Riddle, suffering, and not just Americans. Do you see that? Do you think about it?"

I nodded.

"Good. Because you should. You have a moral obligation to think about others, especially now with social upheaval every-where. The country is undergoing fundamental changes; the world is changing. Democracy can't function effectively when its leaders speak with one voice. I want my dissenting voice to be heard. Do you understand?"

"Yes," I said.

Camp looked at me intently. "Do I sound as if I'm giving a speech?"

"A little bit." We both laughed.

"You know, Jimmy, God never promised us a rose garden."

He took my hand and held it in his, the clasp of his hand filling me with such warmth. I snuggled down into my bed feeling safe and secure. A calmness came over me, settling round me like a gentle mist. My father smiled. I smiled back. I would tell Camp everything.

"Camp . . ."

Bang! A broken branch, buffeted by a sudden loud and swirling gust of wind, hit the window, rattling the glass. I jumped. My father looked startled. A long, low, howling whistle signaled a sudden shift in the weather. Sitting up straight, startled and disoriented as if crudely ejected from a dream in which I felt loved and protected, I covered my heart with my hand.

"What were you going to say?" Camp asked.

"It doesn't matter."

Camp patted my hand, kissed me on the cheek and said good night. As the door clicked quietly shut behind him, I got up and walked over to the window. On my knees, I looked out onto the deserted road, randomly illuminated by stars and distant lights. The quiet deepened but for the intermittent rumble of thunder and the pulsating roar of the waves as they crashed against the shoreline. I heard the casual swish of my horse's tail where he stood beneath the tree in the paddock. The flick of Eugene's tail, the stamp of his hoof—I've imprinted both. I'm habituated to them. Like cues in a stage play, they announce the next entrance.

The shadows parted like theater curtains, and there he was, visible in the golden lamplight, a smoky puff of gloom and silence, soundless as suffocation, smoothly gliding like a snake across the surface of my fear. Tall and lean. His mouth hung open. Loose.

A ramp with a broken hinge. Gula leaned slightly forward as he walked. He walked slowly. He had his mongrel dog with him, brown and sable, ears flattened against its skull, its tail hanging down, ribs visible, matted fur, tufts of hair missing, on a short taut leash. In the same hand he carried a large stick that rested rigid against the dog's flank, a fixed reminder. They walked together, taking synchronized steps, moving in slow unison as if they were conjoined, cruelty's ultimate cruelty.

The dog! Oh, Hanzi! They stopped at my mother's perennial garden. Flashes of lightning overhead illuminated him in the blackness. I could see him clearly one moment and the next moment I couldn't see him at all. He dropped the leash. The dog slid down onto the ground in a single slinking motion. The leaves on the trees rippled. I watched as he pulled an army knife from his coat pocket and began cutting wild roses in the rain. A sudden surge of wind and the whole world seemed to shift, then bend backward at the waist. Unhurried, he went from bush to bush, collecting orange, yellow, red, white and pink blossoms, oblivious of all that was blowing around him, unmindful of me.

I let the curtain slide slowly back into place as he and his dog vanished into the blackness. Gula was picking roses in a storm in the dead of night and I couldn't have been more afraid than if I'd witnessed him digging his own shallow grave beneath the moonlight.

Back in bed, I tried in vain to sleep. After a while, it started to rain lightly, then hard. Rain sprayed through the open window and made tiny pools on the pine floor. I jumped to my feet and closed the window, the wind banging against the glass to get in. Raindrops from the giant oak tree clinked downward against the gutter, a cascade of individual coppery notes clanging like unlucky pennies.

You could see the ocean from my bathroom, a kind of simmering, limitless horizon of hope or doom, depending on the day. We were on top of a cliff, the highest point of a series of graduated dunes—the lowest point towered one hundred feet above the Great Beach, which was accessible only by a narrow wooden staircase built into the sand on a sheer vertical angle. The obliterating view of the ocean and the sky from the edge of the bluff was nothing short of astounding, made all the more so for its utter lack of announcement—you couldn't see anything at all until you were right at the edge and then you could see nothing else—and left the uninitiated wordless.

"Edmund Burke would say that what you're experiencing is true astonishment," my father used to tell gaping first-time visitors. "The terror and beauty of the sublime."

"As a bonus, along with the view, comes instructions on how to stuff a wild bikini," my mother would add, flicking cigarette ash onto the sand. No one knew how to rob a moment of its majesty better than Greer.

On rare occasions, including that night, rogue winds and wild weather patterns would join forces with the tide and the ocean would surge to the top of the dune, making you feel as if you were perched on the dark edge of infinity, as if the whole world was a giant witch's cauldron, gurgling black abyss, sky overhead filled with steam, ruination everywhere. Even now, the thought of it fills me with desolation.

I caught sight of myself in the old iron mirror that hung over the sink. My tomboy cap of tropical red hair, hair the color of a geranium, rude hair that openly defied gravity by growing up rather than down, shrieked back at me.

There was an enormous clap of thunder followed by a ghostly quiet. From across the road came the sound of a loud boom, then the high-pitched whinnying of horses. I called for my father. He was already midway down the stairs, my mother following. He reached the last stair and sprinted toward the living room. My mother froze on the landing. I rushed passed her and ran after him.

She shouted out my name. "Riddle!" She called for my father. "Camp!"

Boom! There was a stupendous crashing sound. Through the living room windows I could see the contorted silhouette of the big cormorant clock tree and far behind it the silvery outline of the yellow stable as the sky blew up, turned red and gold, black and gray, ash and cinder and flames soaring beyond the trees. The ocean behind us was roaring in the background, rising waters like claws scraping away at the containing range of cliffs.

"Jesus Christ!" my father said. "Gin's yellow barn is on fire." He reached for the phone.

"My God!" My mother's arms dropped to her sides.

I was standing at the window when I heard the explosion. The roof blew off the stable and the walls burst away from their foundation, windows detonating like small-arms fire, horses screaming, the line of oak trees melting, my father running from the house, across the fields, racing toward the fire that had become the whole world.

Chapter Seven

I T WAS THE FIRST TIME I HAD EVER SEEN A MAN CRY. NOT JUST cry. Sob. Wail. Wring his hands, tear out his hair and foam at the mouth. Gurgling and roiling—you could have gone white-water rafting on all that hysteria—Gin was bent over at the waist, clutching his abdomen as if he were trying to keep himself from ripping apart at the seams. A thin string of drool ran from his lips to the kitchen floor. One of the dogs hurried over to lick the slick little pool of spit off the wood plank.

Reaching down—Gin was always conducting a cursory self-inspection regardless of his personal drama—he brushed away a nettle loosely clinging to the hem of his shorts. He was crisply turned out, sharply pleated, meticulously pressed—ludicrously outfitted as if for a Patagonian safari—although his most dangerous meeting that day was with my mother. Which just goes to show that some people are never too upset to pay attention to how they look.

"All that's missing is the pith helmet and veil," my father had said as he watched Gin walk down the driveway to the house a few minutes earlier, hysteria preceding him.

"Calm down," Camp said, his hand at the base of Gin's neck,

one part comfort, one part strangulation. His tone was flat but I could tell that he was making some attempt to control his disdain. My mother was sitting at the kitchen table, a remote outcropping of frozen tundra, the temperature in her immediate vicinity several degrees lower than the air around her. My parents looked at each other and exchanged deadly sighs that only I could hear, my eyes and ears sharpened by years of exposure to their marital Morse code. I stood in the doorway, receding, one foot in the kitchen, one foot in the hallway.

"Three mares, three foals! Incinerated! The barn gone. It was the wretched cigarettes. I told you, Greer. How many times did I tell you about smoking? Oh, my God. Oh, Jesus." Extending his arm in front of him as if he were trying to feel his way through a thick fog, Gin stumbled into the nearest chair where he collapsed, burying his head in his hands.

"It was a lightning strike. It was not a cigarette," my father said, emotionless and matter-of-fact, countering Gin's allegation with the intractable firmness that characterized most of his views.

"It was a cigarette! I'm telling you. If you don't believe me then speak to the fire department. They found a charred package of Dunhill cigarettes at the barn. That's your brand, Greer!" Gin pointed to an offending red package with gold lettering on the kitchen table.

"I was nowhere near that barn! I was with you the whole time. Speak to a fireman?" Stimulated by digression, my mother had a habit of interrupting her own train of thought. "Are you serious? Have you ever spoken to a fireman—or to a policeman either, for that matter? Why not ask the refrigerator for an opinion? Dorothy has better instincts." She gestured at the tricolor hound whose head was buried in a wastepaper basket. Hearing her name, she lifted her head and wagged her tail, an empty toilet roll in her mouth.

Gin was weakening under the onslaught. "Maybe you stopped in to look for Riddle on your way home. Maybe you were distracted. She went to the barn to see the new foal, do you remember? She went to look for the puppy. All those babies, burned alive. How could you be so reckless?"

"You go too far, Gin," my father said, his eyes narrowing.

"How dare you?" My mother burst from her chair like a lit firecracker, sparks flying. Greer only ever operated at the two extremes of hot and cold. "You accuse me even after I've told you I was nowhere near there. I don't care what they found, where they found it or why they found it. Have you ever known me to be careless about anything? You're upset about what happened? Well, so are we all."

Leave it to Greer to make it about her. I thought about the little foal and her mother. I rubbed my eyes, country dirt under my bitten nails. There weren't enough sandbags in the world to prevent the flood of tears.

She bumped back down onto the seat of the chair. "One more thing, you little toad. If I were to set fire to your barn, you'd never know about it. What do you take me for? I certainly wouldn't be stupid enough to leave behind evidence. To what end? The fire was an act of God. Who knows? Maybe God smokes Dunhill."

My father looked at her, admiration evident in the flexible curve of his open mouth, ardor glistening like a polished trophy. He never could abide conciliation.

The best defense is a good offense.

It was silent except for the sound of the dogs panting and Gin's loud sniffling. The furrow between his eyebrows deepened into a crevasse. His jaw clenched and twitched; he flinched. He was thinking about something and it hurt. His shoulders slumped and slid slowly downward in a defeated sag. The logic of what my mother said rang indisputably true—the fact is, she wouldn't do anything that dumb, neither accidentally nor intentionally. Self-incrimination eluded her.

Finally, Gin spoke up in a voice more plaintive than belligerent. "Well, all right, if it wasn't you, then who was it?"

My heart started pounding with so much force I thought for sure everyone in the room could hear it. My sense of complicity was so great at that point that I had convinced myself it was me.

"Who left the cigarettes at the barn? I mean, now I've let you off the hook, Greer, then you must be willing to at least entertain the idea that it was a cigarette that caused the fire."

"Well, how should I know? Have you ever thought it might have been the Gypsy King?"

I sucked in a loud breath.

"Don't be ridiculous," Gin said. "You might as well accuse me. Anyway, Gula doesn't smoke. He loves those horses. He risked his life trying to save them."

"Oh, what difference does it make?" Greer snapped. "What's done is done. The stable is gone. The horses are gone. It's sad, of course, it's dreadful." She watched Vera chase the other dogs around the base of the table. "You are insured, after all."

My father raised his eyebrows and cleared his throat. I wondered where that came from.

"If this was a deliberate act or even if it was carelessness, shouldn't I know?" Gin was begging for answers.

"Well, that's up to you to pursue or not, but I don't see the point. You'll just be wasting energy better spent on rebuilding. Onward and upward and all that sort of thing."

"But what about consequences, Greer? Surely, there should be consequences for someone. Why should I be the one to pay?"

"You mean now that your little plan to blame me has gone kaput? Why should you be exempt from the vicissitudes of daily existence?" How my mother loved to invoke humility as a status to which others should aspire. "That's life, isn't it? As far as that goes, you've done all right." Her victory was complete.

My father, entertained but increasingly impatient, put a mug of coffee in front of Gin, who, shuddering, wrapped both palms around its steamy porcelain sides. He watched as Gin took a lingering sip and then he remembered the small matter of me. I had been at Gin's, too.

"Riddle." He swiveled round to face me in the doorway. "When you were at the barn, did you see anything suspicious?"

My mother and Gin looked over at me, but it was my father's gaze that held my attention. His manner was casual, his tone friendly and interested—his relaxed demeanor a temperate oasis amidst the scorching intensity emanating from the other two. He glanced away and reached for a lone surviving scone in a basket on the counter. Breaking off a piece and popping it into his mouth, he waited for my response, comfortable that he could count on me to answer honestly.

Our eyes locked. Lie to my father? I had never lied to my father in my life. He trusted me.

"Riddle?" He looked amused. "Where are you?"

I shook my head until I thought it would fall off. "I didn't see anything. I wasn't there for more than a few minutes." I took a deep breath and felt my spine stiffen—it was an unpleasant sensation. I was proving to be an astoundingly resilient liar. My fear of discovery was so great it had the ironic effect of making me heroically duplicitous. Shoulders back, chin forward, it was official, I had become the ferocious guardian of a terrible secret, a sudden sharp jolt of self-knowledge shredding all that I had believed about myself and the kind of person I was. Of course I was confused and upset by what had happened in the barn, but at that point I was more troubled by my cowardice. Now I had lied to my father.

Gin stared dully back at me. Then his eyes popped like the flash on a camera. "Riddle, you weren't smoking, were you? Experimenting maybe? Did you take your mother's cigarettes? Tell me, please. I won't be mad."

"Oh, for Christ's sake," my father said.

"Well, she wouldn't be the first kid to sneak a cigarette," Gin said.

"No. No," I said, my face reddening. I felt as if someone was blowing up a balloon inside of me. With each pump the pressure intensified until I exploded. "It wasn't me!" I was shouting. I was aware of the proviso about excessive protest and its relationship to guilt, but I couldn't seem to help it.

"No one is accusing you of anything, Jimmy," my father said.

"Why are you crying?" Gin asked. He assumed that the right to weep was his alone.

"I'm not crying," I wailed. "Don't say I'm crying when I'm not."

My mother was watching me. I could feel her piercing scrutiny from across the room. Her eyes widened and then elongated. She leaned back in her chair. Then she leaned forward and with two twists she crushed her cigarette into an ashtray, grinding it into ash.

"This is bullshit," I said, taking two steps back. "I didn't do anything. I didn't see anything."

"Yes, this is bullshit," my mother said. "Run along, Riddle. This has nothing to do with you."

Heavy footsteps on the front porch started a deafening round of braying and barking among the dogs. "For heaven's sake, who is this?" my mother said, furious at yet another intrusion.

It's the infamous Mr. Nightjar," my father said as the dogs flowed out onto the verandah to greet our visitor.

"Gula! What now?" Gin said.

Gula. I couldn't feel anything at all.

My father opened the door. I looked at him in disbelief. He opened the door! Let him in? Had everyone gone mad?

"Don't let him in!" I said. Covered in sweat, my clothes felt wet—I was saturated in terror, practically marinating in guilt. I kept expecting the police to show up at any moment—or worse, God Himself.

My mother and Gin looked over at me. My father hesitated and frowned. "Why not?" he asked, even as he gestured for Gula to come inside.

"Because . . ." I said. "Because he . . ." I stole a glance at Gula. His eyes met mine with the force of a lunge, his quiet violence quelling my voice like fingers wrapped around my neck.

"Because he what?" my father persisted impatiently.

"What have I done now?" Gula said, half in, half out of the kitchen. "Whatever it is, I plead guilty to all charges." He looked over at me and smiled, a silent, wet snarl.

"Riddle?" Camp said.

"Because . . . He'll see that I'm crying," I said finally.

Gula stood on the opposite side of the screen door, his long black shadow casting about, searching and filling every corner, a vandal on the prowl, his smile acting as camouflage. Instinctively, I pressed my back up against the wall, flattening myself against the rippled palm plaster, hiding in plain view.

Gin was needed back at the house, he said, hesitating for a moment, seeming to want to come in even as he was backing away, head slightly bowed in arrogant impersonation of deference.

"I should go." Gin stood up with a grimace, the backs of his thighs sticking to the seat of the wooden chair. "Ouch."

"Serves you right," my mother said. "Those shorts are an abomination."

Gula's eyes shifted sideways, contempt flickering briefly then just as quickly dissipating. I averted my glance, but not fast enough.

The trace of a smile lingering on his face as he caught me staring at him, he nodded in my direction as he held open the door for Gin. I watched him as he walked down the lane, his car parked behind Gin's, and drove away. I wanted to make sure he was gone.

My mother, whirling with fury, picked up Gin's coffee mug, walked to the kitchen garbage receptacle, stepped on the foot lever and dropped the cup into the trash. "Who does he think he is, coming into our house and accusing me of such a thing? Why not just connect me to the Manson murders while he's at it?"

"Greer, relax," Camp said as he stood at the kitchen door and observed Gin clamber behind the wheel of his station wagon. "Why would you take anything that a narcissist like Gin Whiffet has to say seriously?"

She grabbed a wet dishcloth and began to wipe down the counter furiously. Any attempt at housework on her part was a sign of incipient madness. "I'm sorry if I'm a human being and feel the need to defend myself against false accusations, regardless of their origins. Camp, you know as well as I do that he'll tell everyone who will listen that I set fire to that stable and killed those horses."

"It doesn't matter. No one pays any attention to anything he says. He's been making a fool of himself since he was a kid. His universal status as a flibbertigibbet is firmly established. What I don't understand is why you continue to have anything to do with such a duplicitous man."

She tossed the dishcloth into the sink and turned on me, still sniffling in the corner. "What I don't understand is what has gotten into you? What in God's name is wrong with you, Riddle? Why are you crying?"

"I don't know."

"Leave her alone," my father said, encouraging me to sit down at the table. "All those horses. It's a hell of a thing that's happened."

"Is that what this is about?" my mother asked, staring at me, incredulous as I pulled up a chair and sat down, head bowed, shoulders slumped. "So is this your idea of a proper response to a challenging situation? Emotional collapse every time you break a nail?"

Her scorn was lacerating. I straightened up and wiped my eyes.

"It's no accident that Greer rhymes with sneer," my father said, offering up mild humor as comfort as my mother vanished into a puff of cigarette smoke, rematerializing seconds later in the living room. We watched her from the safety of the kitchen, poking around the magazine rack, looking for something to shred. He patted me on the shoulder. "I've got a few appearances to put in today." He paused, mindful all of a sudden of what lay ahead. "Jesus, if I have to watch one more overweight Rotarian eat with his mouth open and spray minced chicken on my tie, I'll pray to go blind. Goddamn campaigning. I swear, I look at these assembled herds and it's like a convergence of ketchup bottles. I'll be glad when the election's over."

Me, too. Camp was always traveling. When he was home he was on the phone or planning to be. I tried to think of the last time I had heard him singing around the house. He kissed the top of my head and headed for the stairs—I could hear his familiar two-step bound.

I sat alone in the kitchen just long enough to pull myself together. Wandering into the living room, I curled into an armchair and watched as my mother, appearing thoughtful, stood at the window in profile, looking out over the dunes and the ocean.

"So what was that little performance of yours really all about?" she asked me. "Did something happen that you're not telling me about?"

"No."

She turned to face me. "Are you sure about that?"

"Yes," I said, chewing on my thumb.

"Stop mangling your fingernails. You look like a farmhand." She paused. "Listen, Riddle, if Gula is bothering you . . ."

I stopped gnawing. "What do you mean?"

"Do I need to spell it out for you?" She clapped her hands as if she were trying to jolt me out of a deep sleep. "Time to grow up. You know perfectly well what I'm asking you."

"No! Oh, my God . . ."

"Calm down. Fine. That's good. I just don't want you to be one of those neurotic little ninnies that goes along with God-knows-what in silence, too silly to come forward. If any man so much as . . ." She was looking around the room as if she were searching for a weapon. "You scream bloody murder, do you hear me?"

"Yes, I hear you," I said, my anxiety giving way to annoyance.

She crossed her arms and tilted her head provocatively, staring me down. It took all of five seconds for me to avert my gaze. She lifted her chin and relaxed her stance a little. "Let me tell you something, Riddle. When I was your age my parents threw a huge garden party. I got bored and sought refuge in the library. There was a man alone in there. A business associate of my father's. I began to leave. He started to chat me up. Offered me a sip of his drink, if you can imagine anything so patently ridiculous. Well, I'm sure you're able to guess where this is going. He tried to kiss me. He put his hand on my breast."

I flinched but remained rapt. "Jesus."

"Oh, don't you worry. I picked up the nearest vase and smashed it over his head and then I brought the house down with my screaming. I can still see the water and the blood running down his forehead. He was covered in long stems of freesia."

She was rapturous remembering.

"What did he do?"

"What could he do? It was a silent movie. No one needed to say a word; the visuals were powerful enough to convict him. My only regret is that I didn't murder him when I had the chance." She sat down on the sofa and clicked her cigarette lighter with so much ferocity, I thought for a moment that she would ignite.

"Weren't you upset? Wasn't it . . . ?" I searched for the right word. "Traumatic?"

She looked at me, disbelief degenerating into pity. "Traumatic? That," she said, spitting out the word as if it were a tooth knocked out in a street fight, "will be the day."

"Not everyone is like you," I said weakly. The more I thought about it, the more I realized there was no one like Greer Foley. Her only living counterparts wore stripes, ate a side of raw beef for breakfast and worked for Ringling Brothers.

"You think I was born this way?" she said.

"Yes, I do." Greer was an act of God, of that I was certain. What else could explain this woman?

"You're wrong. Give me some credit, will you? I decided when I was very young that I didn't want to be a mouse in a world of cats. You'd be surprised what you can accomplish when you make up your mind. I'll tell you a little secret." She leaned forward. "I enjoyed it. Splitting his head open with that vase. I loved every moment of it." She took a long drag on her cigarette. "There's something to be said for violence. To tell you the truth, I think I've been looking for an excuse to smack someone else ever since."

Her eyes were so blue that the sky and the ocean seemed pigeon-gray by comparison.

"I hate to break it to you," I said, "but that isn't a secret to anyone."

Chapter Eight

———

AROUND EIGHT O'CLOCK THE SAME EVENING THE PHONE RANG. A Molotov cocktail tossed through an open window into the living room where we sat could not have generated a more outraged response from my mother, who viewed the most banal domestic intrusion as an act of hostility.

"What now?" She tossed her arms into the air and looked heavenward. Greer was in the daily habit of demanding answers from God, treating Him as if He were a henpecked husband. Lurching theatrically from the sofa, she stalked into the library and picked up the receiver. The sound of her voice radiated into the living room. Camp looked over at me and groaned when he realized it was Gin. I got up and headed after her into the library where I found her listening intently—the rarity of her silence enough to make me wonder what was going on.

"Oh, honestly Gin, how would I know? No, I'm quite sure Riddle doesn't know him." She tapped her foot as she listened. "Well, of course, if something's happened, it's awful but I think you're being a bit premature." Taut with consternation, she held up her hand to enforce my silence, shushing me as Dorothy and Madge came careening around the corner, mad to see me, panting, whining, nails clicking on the hardwood. Kneeling down to meet them, I glanced up and saw Vera bringing up the rear. I covered my eyes with her long velvet ears.

A cheer rang out from the living room. Camp was watching the televised replay of an earlier boxing match between Muhammad Ali and George Chuvalo. He leapt to his feet, pumping his fists, shouting and exultant when Chuvalo landed a right cross. The dogs wagged their tails in bewildered acknowledgment, Hilary rushing over to take his empty spot in the armchair.

"Camp, please, I can't hear." My mother's voice stamped the ground in a fit of impatience. "Say that again, Gin."

He ignored her. "Riddle, come here. You have got to see this."

I stood up and headed back, dogs trailing behind me. He turned up the volume on the TV and then, deferring to Hilary, sat down on the sofa, the roar of the crowd filling the room, an incongruous accompaniment.

"Camp!" my mother called out.

"Did you see that, Jimmy? Fantastic. Unbelievable. What a fight! Jesus!"

"Oh, dear. Oh, no, well, let's hope not." My mother said the same things over and over, a baleful chant, its effect so unsettling I slid down onto the sofa, the world around me tilting in ominous new directions.

"Camp! It's about Michael Devlin. Something has happened."

But the TV was too loud, his preoccupation was too great, his willful indifference to my mother's dramatics too ritualistically enforced. The crowds were cheering and my father was now sitting on the edge of the coffee table, leaning forward, and elbows on his knees, engrossed.

"Bam!" He was up on his feet. Jumping side to side. Boxer's stance. Throwing fists. One. Two. "Jab. Jab. Right cross. Uppercut." He was simulating each move. "Bam! Look at that guy Chuvalo.

Boom! Boom! Boom! He just plants himself and takes it and then he gives it back. Slug. Slug. Slug. None of this sweet science nonsense."

He was standing in front of the floor-to-ceiling window. I could see the sun dropping in the charcoal-blue sky; orange and red, it hovered just beneath the top of the tree line as Camp continued to battle his invisible foe.

"You're awfully quiet," my father said, glancing sideways, breathing heavily, still absorbed in the fight.

"Mom is talking to Gin about Michael Devlin. I think something's wrong."

"Camp!"

He looked over his shoulder, expressionless, and then he turned his attention back to the TV screen.

"Give me a minute," he said so quietly she couldn't possibly have heard him.

A few moments later, my mother joined us in the living room, lacquered in composure, shimmering with the kind of bleak wintry poise that strikes fear in every living heart.

"Anything interesting on TV?" she asked, sitting down in the armchair across from where I lay on the sofa.

"Just the fight," I said, searching her face for information, for explanation. Her seeming indifference was bewildering, though a familiar tactic. There was obviously something wrong. Why did she always feel the need to be strategic?

"I said, 'interesting,'" she editorialized as she got up to change the channel. She stopped to watch a special news story that flashed across the screen, attracting her attention.

"What was all that with Gin?" my father asked, resigned to playing his part in the protracted unveiling of what she knew.

She paused, pretending distraction and staring at the TV screen, visibly working to put emotional distance between herself and the phone conversation. "Oh, earlier this evening, Gin's mother Mirabel called, wanting to know if he knew anything about where Michael Devlin's younger son Charlie was. She thought maybe one of his riding pupils might have said something. You know how Mirabel loves to feel important by insinuating herself into these things."

"Is he missing?" Camp asked.

"I assume. Gin was a little vague, short on facts as usual. He asked me if we had heard anything about him. Why would I know anything about the whereabouts of a teenage boy? The assumption is that he's holed up somewhere with friends and Michael is trying to track him down. Gin was speculating that he's run away. Can you imagine? Who in their right mind would run away from all that? He was just back home for the summer from Georgetown Prep. He disappeared last weekend, apparently," my mother said offhandedly, as if she and Gin had been discussing the rising cost of grain. The screen filled with the stark, static shot of a little girl running naked down a bleak road in Vietnam surrounded by fleeing villagers.

"Charming world we live in." She nodded toward the image on the TV screen as my father urged her to be quiet. Camp always would choose the universal over the personal. Greer could have announced that I had vanished in a puff of smoke and he would have waited until Walter Cronkite signed off before reacting.

"How old is his youngest? Fourteen, maybe fifteen?" My mother was talking to herself.

"Jesus, turn that up," my father said as the screen boiled over with still photos of smoke and ash and burning flesh, a village on fire.

"His eldest boy, Harry, what would he be now? Eighteen? Nineteen? He's at Yale, or so Gin says. I saw Harry in Provincetown at the horse show not long ago, the image of his father at the same age. Not a bad rider."

Now I was intrigued. Not bad was as good as it gets from Greer. Harry Devlin must have been a centaur.

"Goddamn it," my father said, shaking his head, concentrating on what was happening on TV.

My mother sighed and rolled her eyes. "Oh, Camp, how many wars do you intend to fight? What has it to do with you?" She walked over to the sofa. I reluctantly made a spot for her next to me.

"Wonder who the younger boy looks like?" she asked. "Let's hope for his sake it's not his mother."

Camp finally looked away from the news story and frowned over at her.

"For Christ's sake, Greer, the poor woman has been dead for a decade."

"Well, of course, I'm sorry."

My father hooted as my mother pursued the point she was born to make.

"But what does that have to do with her face? Believe me, Riddle, in Polly Devlin's case, decomposition would be an improvement." Her remark produced a weird round of enthusiasm from the dogs, their tails banging on the wood floor.

"What a fiasco," my father said, turning his focus back to the TV.

"Poor Michael," my mother said, surprising me with her sympathy. "He must be worried, thinking about all the possibilities. I can't imagine."

"You can imagine," my father snapped, finger thrust forcibly forward. My mother and I were jolted from our private thoughts by the violence of his response. "You can imagine anything. Anyone is capable of anything. Do you hear me? And by the way, how about a little perspective? Starving children being burnt alive and we're supposed to wring our hands over some spoiled rich kid like the Devlin brat just because he can't be bothered to call home?"

I nodded, too timid to speak, feeling pulverized by the rogue elephant of male rage. For once my mother had nothing smart to say. My father churned from the room, glass ornaments trembling in his wake. His feet were loud on the stairs. I jumped when the door to his bedroom slammed shut. Moments later I heard the bludgeoning sound of him on the phone, talking about the incident in Trang Bang. Animated speech, angry, pounding out each point as if he were trying to break something into pieces, killing it with the blunt force of his point of view.

MY FATHER WAS PASSIONATE about being right. To him, being right was a thing of violence and covered vast territory: moral, factual, ethical, social, philosophical. His certitude ran bloodred; his belief in himself was starkly anatomical. You could smell the rawness of it. His confidence was an athlete. Lift the lid, look inside his head, and you'd see goalposts and a megaphone.

I worshipped my father. So, why was I listening to him and thinking about Gula, so soft-spoken, so watchful and self-editing? I could feel myself shrinking under the enormity of their separate angers even as I hated myself for indulging such a hideous comparison. I blinked and swallowed, the events of Sunday acquiring new life in the wake of my father's rampage.

Anyone is capable of anything.

Camp might as well have been talking about me.

LATER THAT NIGHT, THE house in darkness, I was in bed unable to sleep when I heard a sharp noise coming from the kitchen. Glass shattering. Sitting up, rigid, I struggled to understand what I was hearing. The old pipes rattled in the walls. Water ran from the faucet.

Slowly, I crept from my bed, navigating past my parents' room where my father slept on, seemingly oblivious, then through the library, and into the dining room where I watched from my concealed position behind the half-closed door as my mother bent down to pick up something—a wine glass—that lay broken on the floor.

She was washing the crystal, head bowed at the sink—goblets, glasses, bowls, candlestick holders, the stuff of inheritance and commemoration—everything spread across the counter, each piece simultaneously special and banal. Whenever she was really upset, my mother washed the crystal. Holding a wine glass up to the light, contemplative but purposeful, she inspected it, then shone it with a white cloth, vision turned inward, as if she were polishing a dim memory.

What could be so awful that it would drive my mother to plunge her arms up to her elbows in dirty dishwater?

The windows rattled, tree branches banging against the glass. Storms always catch me by surprise. I grew up next to the Atlantic Ocean and yet I'm no good at charting the weather. It seems I never correctly anticipate what's incoming.

The washing and drying done, the crystal put away in the cabinet, its luster restored, my mother stared out at the night from the window over the sink. After a few moments she straightened her hair, rearranged her nightgown, tied her cashmere robe at the waist and clicked off the light. She walked through the kitchen door and out into the hallway.

"Hello, Dorothy," she said reaching down to pet her favorite. It was with a shocked sense of self-recognition that I watched my mother behave as if everything was fine. Apparently, she and I had more in common than I knew.

Outside an animal cried out, a deer, maybe, or a rabbit, something dying, something ending, saying goodbye, a piercing shriek. The cormorants flew off in a single startled motion—the cormorant clock, shuddering in the wind, tolling in its tomblike way, hollow flap of wings marking the hour.

Chapter **Nine**

———

A FEW DAYS LATER, I AWOKE TO THE HOSTILE RAT-A-TAT-TAT of my parents fighting in the bedroom below. I pulled a blanket up around my head to block their increasingly shrill back-and-forth even as I strained to hear what was being said. They were arguing about money and about my father's decision to fly to Saigon. Knowing him as I did, I thought he might have signed up for a tour of duty, but in fact he was helping to organize, along with a number of prominent Democrats, including senators and members of Congress, an independent fact-finding mission concerning what happened in Trang Bang. My mother said we couldn't afford to finance the cost of his unnecessary involvement.

"What about the election?" she demanded. "Do you really expect me to campaign in your absence? I've seen one supermarket. I don't intend to see another." Her voice registered disbelief and anger in even proportions.

"Thanks for your unstinting support. I can always count on you to put yourself ahead of any and every other consideration. Anyway, there are more important things to consider here than shaking hands. I can miss a few chicken dinners, and if my candidacy can't survive my temporary absence," he fired back, "to hell with it."

Drawing the cover away from my face and blinking in the streaming sunshine, my respect for my father propped me up like a pillow.

"Oh, I know, you have whole worlds to save. What would posterity do without you? What about your family?" my mother said, going for the low blow. "What about Riddle and me? We have every cent tied up in this stupid campaign. I don't want to even think about the debt . . ."

"So like you to put a price tag on my role as father and husband," my father retaliated, almost shouting.

"Won't you reconsider, Camp?" She retreated slightly, knowing that she had taken the wrong tack, bringing up money. "I don't know . . ." She paused, uncharacteristically subdued. "This thing with the Devlin boy still missing is a little unsettling. No one knows where he is or what's happened to him. For all we know there could be some lunatic on the loose."

"You can't be serious! You expect me to put everything on hold because fifteen-year-old Charlie Devlin is off raising hell somewhere? If this was any kid other than Michael's it wouldn't even be a blip on the radar. Frankly, I couldn't be less interested in anything that has to do with Michael Devlin, though obviously the same can't be said for you. In any event, I feel quite confident leaving you alone. In a contest between you and a lunatic, God help the lunatic."

I was sitting on the edge of the bed, bare feet dangling, relieved that the conversation had veered away from the always explosive topic of money, when Greer decided to venture into even more fraught territory. "Why can't you be more moderate? You've already made up your mind about Michael's boy though you haven't a single fact to support your conclusions. God knows, you've made your views on the war abundantly clear. By now, Ho Chi Minh must be ready to surrender rather than listen to another word on the subject from you. How far do you intend to go? Isn't it enough that you wave the union label at every opportunity? You live and breathe controversy. It's like a shtick. Why must you be so adversarial? Sometimes I feel as if we're chained to Krakatoa, waiting for the inevitable explosion."

"That's a hot one coming from you, Miss Congeniality. Is that your idea of a joke? Don't be so goddamn melodramatic. Why the hell would I run for office if I didn't have something to say?"

My mother laughed. Idealism amused her, or so she pretended. "Save it for those gullible legions of factory workers. Do everyone a favor and quit deluding yourself about the purity of your motives. No saint ever survived the election process." Her words sounded dirty, as if she'd swept them from the floor.

"Oh, I don't know about that." Camp was shouting at her now. "Only a saint could put up with you."

Their bedroom door opened and banged once, twice, as he stormed into the hallway, a permanent dent in the plaster where the door handle met the wall. Sometimes I wondered if my father realized that doors didn't need to be banged open or slammed shut to work correctly.

"Camp!" my mother shouted at him from the top of the stairs. "Will this fucking war of yours never end?"

I had never heard my mother use the word "fuck" before. Wham! Camp slammed the front door with so much force that it shook the foundation of the house.

I guess she got her answer.

Sinking back down in my bed, flopping onto my stomach, I buried my face in my pillow. Soon I had forgotten whose side I was on.

AFTER THAT MONUMENTAL BATTLE, an equally epic silence crept into the house and lingered for weeks, my parents barely speaking to each other. The absence of conversation was so unusual and disarming, it felt as if it must be a sign of the impending apocalypse.

Riding was my only distraction and I spent the first part of every day training for the fall shows. I wanted to be an eventer and I needed the practice. Sitting at the vanity in my bedroom, I pulled on my riding pants and my boots, ran my fingers through my hair—a brush only made matters worse—and headed downstairs intending to go for an early ride cross-country.

Greer glanced up from where she sat at the table as I walked into the kitchen. She was on the telephone, its lax cord wound loosely round the two fingers that she held up to shush me. Blooming like an extravagant lavender border, she wore a deep blue cotton dress with black polka dots, the perfumed effects of its wide shoulder straps, sweetheart neckline and fitted bodice creating the impression that she was her own garden party.

Lou smiled over at me from where she stood at the stove and whispered her willingness to make me breakfast. Did I want French toast? I nodded, slightly distracted as Vera jumped up and tried to yank my riding gloves from my hands. Lou and I, resigned to our rampant status as itch grass alongside the exotic cultivar of Greer, shared a brief commiserating glance as I tossed a tennis ball into the hallway, Vera in clumsy pursuit. Then I pulled up a chair and sat down at the table as Lou poured me a glass of orange juice.

"So the police definitely think he ran away. What does Michael think?" My mother wasn't usually so attentive when speaking to Gin. That was before Charlie Devlin disappeared. She and Gin talked about it compulsively, to the point that it was hard not to conclude that the worst thing to happen to Michael Devlin was also the best thing to happen to them. Several moments passed without any interruption from her, her cigarette burning away neglected, the embers collecting in the bottom of the ashtray.

"I don't know this boy, of course," she interrupted finally, "but it's been three weeks, wouldn't you think he would have relented and called home by now? The fact that none of his friends know where he is—or claim not to know anyway—seems significant to me. Maybe there's been an accident of some sort, or God forbid, a kidnapping. Oh, but then, wouldn't you expect a ransom demand, given Michael's wealth? Honestly, the more I think about it, he's probably holed up in some dive in Haight Ashbury reeking of incense and fey girls. Anyway, very sad. Poor Michael. I feel terrible for him. I would be frantic if it were Riddle."

Surprised to hear her say such a thing, I looked at her in some disbelief and felt mildly relieved, my comfort levels restored, when she rolled her eyes in annoyance at my silent profession of skepticism. I took a bite of my toast, Lou and I sneaking amused glances—now there was the mother I knew! My faith restored, I took a moment to survey my immediate area. Spread across the table were the daily newspapers, all of them featuring stories about the missing boy. When a rich and famous man's son vanishes it doesn't go unnoticed.

I glanced down at the headline: "Where is Charlie Devlin? Private Schoolboy's Disappearance Remains a Mystery." The more I consumed about the case, the less real it seemed, as if the flesh and blood of Charlie Devlin had been supplanted by a boy in a fixed number of infinitely repeating poses, a boy constructed of ink and newsprint and projected emotions, his shallow biography bolstered by predictable personal anecdotes and photos in black and white.

Charlie loved sports, played baseball, played tennis, was a promising rider, a gifted writer and a talented musician, an accomplished pianist. Charlie was funny. Charlie was smart. Charlie was popular. A good student, he was high-spirited and got into a few scrapes at school, was always playing pranks, was a regular in the headmaster's office.

Reading about my mother and father in the press over the years had produced the same anesthetizing effects. Stripped of their humanity, they were editorial caricatures, lifeless as Gin's taxidermy collectibles, with no connection to me, to themselves or to the living world.

A FEW HOURS LATER, HOT, scraped, scratched and dirty, back from my ride, I found Greer in the library. She glanced round, greeting me offhandedly.

"What's that doing on the desk?" I asked her, pointing to a favorite watercolor of hers. My mother had an avid interest in art and collected what she could. She had inherited several fine pieces from her mother.

"I'm selling it." She stood over the painting, running her fingers along the carved detailing of the rosewood frame. "Someone has to pay for your father's excesses," she said, a trace of bitterness evident.

"Are we that broke?" The familiar jangle of our chronic money worries clanked inside me like loose change.

"Well, of course we are," she snapped. "I'm not the Shah of Iran. I don't have a bottomless trust, although Camp seems to think I do."

"Camp puts other things ahead of money. He has principles and he's angry about what happened in Vietnam."

Bristling on cue, in keeping with my self-righteous view of myself as an incipient idealist and aspiring pundit, I was reluctant to acknowledge that when it came to politics it was simply easier and more comfortable to take up arms alongside Camp. Inwardly, I flushed to hear myself talking about upholding principle, making the moral choice.

"Don't we all have principles?" she barked back. "Look, Riddle, time for a little perspective. No one cares if your father and his smug little committee go to Vietnam cherry-picking evidence to support their biases and prejudices. What a crock! I can write the report now and spare them the phony exercise of a trip. Anyway, what's it got to do with him? He's not the center of the universe, you know. Why must he always put himself there?" She looked down at her painting. "And so the Trang Bang atrocity becomes the Camperdown Comedy."

"How can you compare the loss of your painting to what happened in that village?" I was shocked and dismayed. My mother could be astoundingly solipsistic.

"You're right," she conceded, much to my surprise. I looked at her with suspicion; concession wasn't exactly her long suit. "There is absolutely no comparison in value between a magnificent piece of art and a human being. People are a dime a dozen. That's what makes the forced sale of this painting so tragic."

At one time I might have argued with her or even been entertained by the sheer cultivated awfulness of her remarks, but now I began to see my mother's glamorous misanthropy as proof of my own dubious origins.

My father came in from outside and walked up behind me. He avoided looking at my mother, who flapped from the room on the noisy wings of a loud sigh.

"I'm heading into Harwich. I've got a few things to take care of before I leave the country. You want to join me?"

"Sure," I said.

I SAT IN THE PASSENGER seat of our old sedan—according to Camp, owning new cars was something to which bankers aspired—filled with stale smoke from my mother's cigarettes. Rolling down the window, I searched in vain for an unobstructed breath, but there was no respite anywhere. The air outside was still on fire, seared by what had happened weeks earlier, the sky gray as granite, smoke damage permeating everywhere I lived, inside and outside, deep within, seeping like heavy fog into my lungs, acrid smell rolling across the dunes and dispersing over the Atlantic.

"Will that smell ever go away?" I asked my father as he slid in behind the steering wheel.

"It stinks all right," Camp said as we drove down the lane to the road.

"What's that supposed to mean?" It was obvious that Camp wasn't referring to the lingering odor of smoke in the air.

"There is something very fishy about what happened. Methinks it's a classic case of friction. You know . . . the mortgage rubbing up against the insurance policy."

I was stunned. "You mean, you think . . . ?"

"I think Gin burned down the barn to collect the insurance money. The convenient placement of the Dunhill package was a dead giveaway, as far as I'm concerned, though Gin's notable lack of character is all the evidence I really need."

"But Gin loves those horses," I said. "He would never . . ."

"Never what? Put his interests ahead of theirs? If it comes right down to it, most people would choose money over just about anything or anyone. Gin is dependent on handouts from his mother to survive and she is notoriously punishing. Sure he loves his horses. He loves your mother, too. Gin loves his horses the way he loves your mother. Capisce?"

He looked at me sideways, his eyebrows forming two matching arcs in his forehead. Our eyes briefly met, me hoping that my expression conveyed the kind of world-weary acquiescence that I contrived to parrot rather than the shock and horror that I felt.

"What does Mom think?"

"I haven't a clue."

Inching forward in my seat, I held my head out the window, the wind flattening my hair and streamlining my features, compressing my view of things as it blew through me like a funnel, emptying my brain of all its troubling thoughts. For a little while at least, I was a voluntary captive of the sun and the wind and the carefree road.

HARWICH WAS A POWERLESS prisoner of the summer tourist season as cars jockeyed for position on the main drag. Parking spots were at a premium. "The nightmare continues," Camp growled as someone in a jeep cut him off.

We parked in front of Pilgrim Congregational Church. I loved that little white church, plain and simple and resonant with clarity, its tall steeple frank and reassuring. We walked side by side down Pilgrim Road, crowds jostling and competing for sidewalk space, as I listened to Camp describe in detail his reasons for going to Vietnam. He was in the middle of explaining the difference between what had happened at My Lai as opposed to what had happened at Trang Bang.

"My Lai was murder, pure and simple and premeditated. Those soldiers are war criminals. The napalm assault on civilians in Trang Bang appears to have been unintentional, although . . ."

He was just getting wound up when we ran into the first of many friends, acquaintances, motivated strangers, potential supporters, the curious and the committed. In every case, Camp dropped anchor and talked and laughed and cajoled and expounded, riveted, and treating every conversation as if it was his both his first and his last.

"Jesus, is that the one and only Patrick Flannery? The world's greatest defense attorney? I ran into James Connor last week. He told me about your courtroom victory against the mighty Andrew Peters. Congratulations on being the one who finally took that bastard down."

Flannery beamed, the two men laughing as Camp praised and teased and challenged and gossiped. How he loved to talk, to listen, to kibitz, to dismantle, to fight! Mowing the lawn or mowing down the enemy, my father approached the mundane and the profound with equal intensity. Oh, I did my share of sighing and blushing, but I never tired of listening to Camp talk. So many people are limited in scope and opinion to what they're doing for dinner—not my father.

"Camp." Flannery's tone changed as he brought up the case of a mutual friend who had been accused of embezzling funds from his employer. "His wife left him. He hasn't got a friend in the world at this point. He's lost everything and he's looking at a prison sentence."

"I'll give him a call when I get home," Camp said as the two men shook hands.

Even as a kid I knew I was in the presence of someone special.

As we neared Wellfleet on the way back to the house, we noticed a large crowd gathered in a field just off the side of the road. Camp slowed the car, squinting in the direction of the assembled people—men, women, teenagers, even a handful of children—before pulling over.

"Wait here," he said. "I'll be back in a minute."

I sat for a while listening to the radio and then opened the door and climbed onto the hood of the car, where I roosted and watched what was going on. My father was talking to a man with black hair. Nearer to me, but set apart from the rest, was a young man on a horse. There were other riders that day, but I concentrated my attention on him. True to form, I looked at his horse first, a beautiful bay thoroughbred. The rider slid his helmet back off his head and held it in his hands. He appeared to be waiting for something to happen. He had russet hair, a woodsy color, distinctive. His hair had the dark and light and brown and red tones of sawdust and cedar chips.

I jumped, startled, as the driver's side door opened. My hand to my heart, I slid down off the hood and into the passenger seat next to Camp, who put the key into the ignition and started the car. Hemmed in temporarily, we idled as we waited for someone to move.

"What's going on?" I asked him.

"Search party. The police are working with a hired outfit to conduct a private search for Charlie Devlin."

My interest piqued, I sat up straighter and took a long second look at what was going on around me. "Who was that you were you talking to?" I asked. "I couldn't see his face."

"That was the great and powerful Michael Devlin."

"Oh." I waited for more, but no more was forthcoming.

"I wonder who that is, over there," I said, pointing to the young man with the russet hair on the bay thoroughbred. "I love his horse. Wow."

"It's got to be the older boy, Harry Devlin," Camp said.

"How do you know?"

"Elementary, my dear Riddle. One: that is no ordinary horse, as you've already gleaned. Two: his hair color. His mother had the same unusual color. He obviously inherited it from her." He laughed. "Polly had this great pelt of hair. She used to come to school looking like she had a wild rabbit perched on top of her head."

I wondered if I looked as pale as I felt. The sun was shining down on Harry Devlin, his hair glimmering, all those autumn colors glowing under the shimmering light of early summer. My heart plummeted several stories, plunging out of control, as if someone had cut the elevator cord.

I had seen that hair color before.

Our way clear, Camp put the car into reverse and we headed for home.

"Why did we stop?" I asked.

"I offered to help search for the boy but Mr. Devlin wasn't interested in my help," Camp said as he swung out onto the highway. "To hell with him."

Chapter **Ten**

——

THE NEXT MORNING, AFTER A SLEEPLESS AND FITFUL NIGHT, I
left the house early on the pretext of going for a morning ride.
It was only seven o'clock and already sweat trickled down my face,
from the moist border of my hairline to the damp point of my
chin. After tying my horse, Eugene, under the long branch of a
huge shade tree just out of sight of where the yellow barn once
stood, I ventured tentatively toward the cold remains, still smoldering in my imagination.

I needed to go back, though it was the last place on earth I
wanted to revisit. Standing amidst the blackened and scorched ruins
of the yellow stable, I went looking for reassurance, for proof that
the mares and their foals were the only ones to have perished in the
fire that terrible night. Though the site had been investigated cur-
sorily by insurance adjusters, all its unsalvageable debris disposed of
and the few standing remnants of the barn demolished, I picked up
a sharp stick and started to poke around the leftovers.

Using the tips of my boots I cleared a path through the cre-
mated corpse of the stable, the blackened ground a barren soil.
Brilliant sunshine illuminated my path, though even the summer
sun wasn't powerful enough to polish this slag pit.

I found a barbecued bridle, the caramelized residue of a saddle, a partially melted stirrup. I continued searching through the ashes. Down on my hands and knees, I was covered in charcoal and soot when I caught a glint of something else; something tiny and silver sparkled in the area where the tack room once stood. Taking a closer look, I saw a tarnished chain coiled under the corner of a cinder block. I stood back up with the necklace in my hand. It was covered in grime but otherwise intact. There was a medal on the chain, a religious medallion, familiar to anyone who attended Catholic school in that era, the miraculous medal, the nuns and priests dispensing them like candy. I had worn one myself briefly—my family was typical of so many Catholics, about whom Camp said that being lapsed was so common it should be made a tenet of faith. I wiped it off, rubbing the familiar oval between my thumb and index finger, the dingy image of the Virgin Mary slowly appearing. Clutching it, I squeezed tightly, pressing it against my heart.

All around me was quiet. I felt the dry pressure of a hand on my shoulder. Something familiar, the reptilian dispassion maybe, told me that it wasn't a Marian apparition. Gula was standing behind me, right next to me, touching me, his head bowed, his face inches from my own, his breath a familiar, fetid, signature cologne.

My heart slowed. I hadn't even heard him coming. My arm dropped to my side. I tucked the chain into my pocket.

"What are you doing here?"

Too weak to speak, I was leaking air, a hole in my composure that matched precisely the size of Gula's hand on my shoulder.

"You were curious, is that it?"

I nodded.

"Not much to see is there? Devastation. Terrible." He extended his arm over the stable's foundation. "Well," he paused surveying the ruins, "feel free to look around to your heart's content. I must be on my way. The truck's parked over there behind the trees. Much ground for me to cover today. I have many duties, you know. So, I shall leave you to your task." He smiled. "Oh, but look how dirty you are getting." He took my hand and held it in his, turning it over, examining it. I recoiled and pulled away. If my response was instinctive, then his reaction to it was primitive and swift. Lashing out, he grabbed my wrist and, yanking me into him, held me in place with the sheer power of his will, his strength of purpose expressed in that unbreakable grip.

Unable even to struggle, I felt as if I had been molded to him, as if we two were fused in an inglorious undertaking. Taking a handkerchief from his pocket with his free hand, he held open a corner of cloth and spit into it. He wiped my palm with the moistened handkerchief, rubbing until a small round patch of clean skin appeared.

"It seems you are still there underneath the soot and the grime," he said affectionately, as if he were a parent talking to a child.

Letting go my hand, he watched as I let it fall limply to my side. Swaying in the breeze like the tall grasses outside the perimeter of the burnt ground, I was a captive of a fear so overwhelming it had stripped me of all but the most basic functions. Gula smiled, he laughed, he was enjoying my terror. His eyes shining with a kind of sadistic accomplishment, he looked me over with ruthless precision, as if I was a building project and he had just applied a final coat of paint.

"I'm off," he said pleasantly. "I have work to do around the property. Mending fences. Checking the livestock. Got to protect against predators. Always circling. Always looking for an opportunity."

He had barely turned his back before I spun around and took terrified flight. I ran to where I had tied Eugene, but he was gone. Panic-stricken and calling out his name, I looked everywhere for him. Finally, I found him just inside the woods, reins dragging, nibbling on a clump of grass at the foot of a tree. I threw my arms around his neck and clambered into the saddle. I didn't need to ask how he had come free. I already knew the answer.

EUGENE WAS FEELING THE effects of the heat, after an initial wild getaway gallop. We had slowed down and were walking along the trail in the woods heading for home when I caught unexpected sight of Gula again, through a gap in the trees. "Shhh," I whispered, reining in Eugene, not wanting to risk detection, lowering my head as I viewed Gula from between my horse's ears.

He was climbing the side of a small hill, emerging from the pasture where Gin kept a small flock of sheep. Walking slowly, he was pulling something. As he drew closer I saw blood on his hands, on the front of his shirt, on the knees of his pants.

Dragging a dead lamb by its leg, he stepped up onto the pathway where I could see everything. The lamb flopped helplessly, lifeless, its throat ripped open, its white wool soaked in red, black eyes fixed and staring.

I don't remember using my heels on Eugene. I have no memory of pressing him into a gallop. It seems to me he did it on his own, as if even he was responding to what we saw that day amidst the tall grass and the wild poppies. I held on for dear life as we raced past the forest and across the open field, and even after we arrived back at the little stable next to my house I was still shaking. Without the broad shoulders of my horse to support me, I would have fallen to the ground.

Sneaking into the house up the back staircase, I managed to avoid detection. I wasn't in any mood to explain to my mother my resemblance to a chimney sweep or my disheveled emotional state. Running up to my bedroom, purposefulness fueled by panic, my mother's copies of *Vogue* in one hand and *Harper's Bazaar* in the other, I sat on the edge of my bed frantically and irrationally hunting for photos of people—models, actors, anyone—with hair the same color as Polly Devlin's, the unusual forest-creature color she had transferred to her son.

There was a Belgian sheepdog in an ad that came close. I closed the magazine for a second to consider. Gula did say he was working on a secret project. Hadn't Gin said he was from Belgium? Maybe he and Gin were planning to raise Belgian sheepdogs. It could have been a dog—maybe Vera and the dog were playing, which accounted for all that running and scrambling. So many maybes.

I started to wonder about what it was exactly that I had heard, what I had seen. Was it as bad as I thought it was? My imagination undermined my sense of reason at the best of times. Maybe I didn't hear or see anything. Maybe Gula didn't realize how hard he had grabbed me earlier, how tightly he had held me close to him, how he had twisted my wrist.

I retrieved the miraculous medal from my pocket. Gin had taught countless students to ride over the years; it could have belonged to any one of them. I brightened. For that matter, it could have been mine. Whatever had happened to mine anyway? Who knows how long it had gone undetected in the stable? I opened the top drawer of my dresser and hid it in the back corner.

So many thoughts running through my head, none of them having to do with what had just happened to me at the scorched site where the yellow barn once stood. I rubbed my wrist without thinking about why. It was much later that I noticed the bruising and felt the ache from the barbarian band, black and blue and red that wound round my wrist like a savage variant on a tennis bracelet.

• • •

My mother caught up with me a few hours later in the laundry room, freshly showered, my riding clothes churning away in the washing machine.

"So?" She eyed me with suspicion. "What brings you in here?"

"I could ask you the same question," I said.

"What happened to your wrist?"

"Got caught up in the reins. I was walking along the road, cooling down Eugene when he got spooked and bolted."

She disappeared behind her sunglasses. "I'm heading down to the beach."

I surprised both of us by asking if I could come with her.

"Please use suntan lotion. I'm starting to see spots," my mother said, peering at me over the top of her open book as right before her eyes all those red freckles started multiplying under direct assault by the sun, covering my exposed face and my body like paint spatter.

Giving her the silent treatment, I lay down on the sand, warm turquoise beach towel at my back, and closed my eyes, covering them with the flattened palms of my hands, shutting out my mother's penetrating glare, the hard edges of the sun's unyielding rays slowly burning me to a crisp, baking me so thoroughly that at one point I thought I could smell smoke.

That night, I stayed up late watching TV, my parents already in bed and asleep as I tiptoed past their bedroom door and down the long corridor, its red walls glowing, golden light from intermittently placed antique sconces illuminating paintings stacked in sophisticated profusion, the way my mother liked. I opened the door at the end of the hall and crept up the stairs to my bedroom.

My room was steeped in a disorienting blackness, the outline of my antique four-poster bed barely visible. I stepped off the cool hardwood, my bare toes skimming the worn surface of an ancient Anatolian kilim rug, an exotic fading remnant of my mother's childhood room.

Sitting at my desk, by the warm gleam of a dim light, I pulled out the picture of the Belgian sheepdog from inside the drawer. Already I had made it into some sort of talisman, obsessively consulting it, begging it to tell me what I so desperately wanted to hear—that mysterious, missing Charlie Devlin had never been inside a yellow stable, that he had never worn a soft leather topsider, that he had never met a soft-spoken European man with a way with horses and a handshake so warm and woozy it was like dipping your fingers into a kiddie pool.

I pulled back my quilt and climbed into bed, chilled by the night air and the memory of my afternoon run-in with Gula. I closed my eyes and tried to sleep. Emotional overload tended to render me comatose.

Whoomph!

Oh, my God, what was that? Rocked by instant terror, my body stiffened as I lay rigid, pinned against the mattress, chest heaving. Whomp! Another dull thud. My brain was running wild in the street. I eyed my bedroom door and prayed that my legs would move fast enough.

When I realized what was inspiring all that terror, I felt like a fool.

"Jesus! Dorothy?"

Relief and annoyance washed over me. It was the big muffled smack of a dog paw, wide as a baseball mitt, battering against the door, scratching and clawing from within the closet. Her tail was banging away against my clothes—the basset-hound equivalent of nervous laughter. This was perhaps the millionth time she had managed to lodge herself in one of the house's many inhospitable tight spots.

Briefly considering the idea of leaving her locked up, I abandoned my impossible dream of sleeping dog-free and threw back the covers. Indulging in a round of inspired profanity, I pushed open the door. The closet's dim light clicked on automatically.

Dorothy rushed out at me, the musky smell of her captivity filling the room. Shocked and unprepared, I squealed and fell onto my backside. "Dorothy!" From my spot on the floor I looked up. Amidst the chaos of my closet, random strewn shoes, rumpled sweaters, crumpled jeans tossed on the floor, shirts turned inside out and carelessly dangling from bent hangers, was something I'd never seen before. Something that didn't fit. Something that didn't belong.

There was a small rag doll propped up against the top shelf. A doll with no face.

The doll was faded and diminished. Her hair was made of black wool, and her little dress was torn. She was old and she was dirty. Lifting her warily from the shelf, I carried her to the bed and stared into the featureless fabric, the place where her face should have been, and I wondered where she had come from. A humble no-face doll, its poignant anonymity conferring a message that spoke to me in a secret language I couldn't understand.

When I was little, I used to put my dolls in the closet at night so I wouldn't wake up to find them staring at me in the dark, so fearful was I of seeing the slow methodical blink of an eye, the hint of a mysterious smile, any furtive sign of animation, the world awash in possibilities, not all of them golden.

All of my dolls had faces. I knew each one intimately. This wasn't my doll, so whose doll was it? The base of my head began to pound. It was hard to breathe.

I don't know how long it took me to realize that the sporadic tapping on my window glass wasn't the wind. Doll in hand, I walked over to the window, drew the curtain aside and opened it up wide. Gula was standing in the grass far below, light from the back deck illuminating him in the darkness, a fistful of stones in his hand.

"Do you like her?" he called up to me.

Leaning forward, I let the doll fall from my hands. Lightweight and insubstantial, it soared upward on the robust wind, drifting this way and that, wavering slightly, struggling to stay aloft before beginning its gentle hypnotic descent to where Gula stood waiting with his arms outstretched to catch it.

I looked down at the doll, hanging limp and affectless in Gula's hands, and in the darkness I could see her face forming, see her staring back up at me.

Blinking.

Chapter Eleven

———

THE SUMMER CONTINUED TO PUT ONE FOOT IN FRONT OF THE other, dragging me resistant and rebellious along with it. I awoke each morning, riding boots at my bedside, committed to hours of rigorous cross-country work with Eugene and weighted down with the knowledge that Charlie Devlin was still missing.

Private protests aside, my mother, semi-dutiful but with a kind of violent resentment, reluctantly fulfilled my father's campaign obligations during his weeklong absence in Southeast Asia. Never one to suffer in solitude, she blackmailed me into accompanying her glowering to a sailboat race in Hyannisport designed to raise money for multiple sclerosis research. The event, held in the second week of July, was organized by a New England industrialist whose wife had been diagnosed with the disease.

"Just once I would like one of these people to work on behalf of an illness they don't have," Greer groused after threatening to cancel my dressage lessons with Gin.

"Don't you ever put me through anything like that again as long as you live," she said to my father, confronting him mere moments after he walked through the door after making the long journey from Vietnam, his forehead creased with fatigue. "You know how much I loathe good works."

The fact-finding mission was national news, and within hours of his return Camp was on the phone and in front of the camera, making the rounds of politically focused network talk shows and radio programs, until his voice was reduced to the sore sound of tires across gravel.

Camp was the kind of man who just naturally attracted attention. He couldn't help it. If you could write a prescription for charisma, it would resemble my parents' alchemical mix: a composer, an academic, a writer, a war hero, a tough union-minded guy with a blue-blood pedigree, acres of debt and a full head of hair, married to a chilly beauty, shiny, remote and unknowable, ruthless as a mirror, a movie star! Reporters covering the election campaign loved him because every time he opened his mouth, he said something worth recording.

My mother, an incredible asset or a devastating liability depending on how high the moon hung in the night sky—speaking to a journalist, she once referred to Cape Cod as a "straitjacket with topography"—was sparingly applied, her provocative layers of cachet apportioned out meagerly: subliminal flash of perfect smile, artful hint of perfect profile. Camp possessed an intuitive grasp of the aesthetics of persuasion as an apparatus of power. His campaign team was terrified of Greer, what she might say, what she might do, but Camp was smarter than that.

"Bush-league concerns," he labeled them. "You leave Greer to me," he continued to instruct immoderately timid staffers whom he privately disparaged as "conventional thinkers, unenlightened planners, ditherers. Carefully handled, your mother is not a problem. In fact, she may even deliver me a particularly resistant elitist constituency."

As for me, kids weren't taken very seriously in that era. Nobody was recruiting my thoughts or opinions, which is probably just as well. Sometimes reporters glommed on to the fact that I was named after Jimmy Hoffa; otherwise, I was generally relegated to the final paragraph of the story, along with the basset hounds.

Predictably, I hated anything to do with campaigning—at that stage of my life, my likes were so few they could have comfortably fit through the eye of a needle—and all things to do with getting Camp elected to office had begun to boil over. My father's trip to Vietnam and the resulting furor had inspired ferocious comments from those who supported his conclusions and those who opposed them. The harder they came at him, the harder he roared back, declaring to the world that he'd take on all comers with one hand tied behind his back.

UNTIL THE SUMMER OF seventy-two, my main goal was leaving childhood officially behind me and becoming a bona fide adolescent. I realized the dream on the last day of July, when I officially turned thirteen. Camp surprised me the day before with an Irish draught horse, a fantastic eventer he named Mary Harris, in memory of the labor activist otherwise known as Mother Jones.

"There goes the Pollock," my mother commented at the unveiling.

It was decided that Mary's stall mate should be a Shetland pony that Greer defiantly insisted on calling Henry Clay, after the notorious antiunionist Henry Clay Frick.

"Have you people never heard of Blaze?" Gin complained when he heard about the ensuing domestic uproar.

When I blew out the candles on my cake, I surprised myself by wishing that I could go back in time. I wanted nothing more than to be the twelve-year-old girl in the hammock that Sunday afternoon in June in what I had come to view as my last carefree moment.

There were so many things happening that I couldn't explain to myself, let alone my parents. The day after my birthday, I walked into a drugstore in Provincetown, killing time waiting for Greer and Camp who were giving an interview to a lifestyle reporter over lunch. A group of people were standing in line waiting to pay for their purchases when a man in a Hawaiian shirt picked up a newspaper from the nearby rack, an article about Charlie Devlin on the front page.

"Boy, I don't know what the big mystery is there. That kid is long dead and gone," his companion said, pointing to the large shot of Charlie that dominated the front page. "Just another kid who got drunk and got into some kind of jam he couldn't get out of. Mark my words, he's going to wash up on shore one of these days. Or parts of him anyway," he added with a chuckle.

"Anybody consider that maybe his family knows something? If it were any kid other than a Devlin that disappeared, the cops would be all over the family," his friend announced, to murmurs of agreement from other customers.

I was outside the store when I heard a man call out to me. I turned around. It was the store manager. "Excuse me," he said. "Did you forget to pay for those Life Savers?"

Reaching into my pocket, I retrieved three packages of cherry Life Savers that I had stolen. "Sorry," I said. "I didn't mean to take them. I have the money to pay for them."

"Okay," he said, leading me back into the store.

"Isn't that the Camperdown kid? Nice values her parents teach her," someone whispered as I paid for the Life Savers and ran from the store out onto the congested summer streets.

If I was crying for help, no one was listening. If I was crying at all, I had only myself to blame. In reality, the universe was telling me to put a sock in it. I could have committed hara-kiri on the front lawn of the White House without attracting any attention.

Everyone was so taken up with the election and the campaign. Charlie Devlin's disappearance was still big news—God knows my mother and Gin had plenty to say on the subject, and the newspapers kept up a regular reportage though there was no new information to sustain the front-page coverage he continued to get. Most people, including the police, seemed to feel that he had suffered some sort of accident—drowning was the most frequently mentioned possibility. Even Camp seemed less inclined to believe that he was on a rich boy's reckless escapade. As for the fire, well, nobody talked about the fire anymore. All that was left of the old yellow stable was hidden away in the far corner of my underwear drawer.

I kept to myself the secret of the miraculous medal, tiny silver sliver of light, and contemplated its mystery, the sole survivor of a conflagration. Holding it in my hands late at night, my head on my pillow, I pressed it to my cheek, untidy reminder of all that I concealed, faithless emblem of my secret nature.

TWO DAYS HAD PASSED since my birthday. I came downstairs for breakfast, ready to spend the day with my new horse. I found my father at the dining room table in animated conversation with Gula, who stood up to greet me as I entered the room.

"Jimmy!" Camp was smiling. "Look who's here! We have another campaign volunteer and I couldn't be more delighted to welcome him aboard." He put his hand on Gula's shoulder. "It seems Gula and I share a common experience of sorts. We've been discussing the war. Turns out he was a boy in Belgium during the battle of the Ardennes. He lived through the nightmare of Bastogne in forty-four. Jesus, that's one Christmas we'll both never forget, isn't it?" He posed the question to Gula, who had somehow perfected a method of nodding and shaking his head simultaneously.

"Unfortunately, I have limited time to give because of my obligations to Gin, but if you have a need, I will endeavor to fill it," Gula said.

"Look, we're having a huge fundraising evening tonight in Provincetown. It should be fun. Gin's going to be there. Please come as my guest. I can introduce you to the head of our volunteer committee and he can get you started if you'd like."

"Thank you. I will do as you suggest." Gula hesitated. "Though, if I may be frank, I had hoped for a more informal relationship. Considering the circumstances of our living arrangements, I thought it might suit us both better if you could simply ask me to help out whenever you feel the need personally. I'm a great driver," he said, laughing.

"You know," Camp said. "That's not a bad idea. I might just take you up on that."

I slunk off into the kitchen and started mindlessly banging cupboard doors and opening and shutting the refrigerator. On his way out, Gula popped his head in through the open doorway. "Looking forward to seeing you tonight, Riddle. I hope you'll save the first dance for me."

"I'm not going," I said, eyes lowered, head averted, my voice barely audible.

"Yes, you are," my father said, sounding surprised.

The two men exchanged knowing glances as my father, socially amused but privately annoyed—I recognized the familiar tones—wrapped things up by saying that Gula could expect to see every member of the Camperdown family in Provincetown that night.

"Not me," I said, flouncing up to my bedroom where I prepared to do battle. It appeared, however, that my father meant business. He sent in Greer. An hour after I had made my declaration, my dispirited floundering collided with my mother's epic prickliness.

"Riddle," she said, briskly violating the privacy of my bedroom, thumping on the door and throwing back the bedcovers. "Get up. You're going with us tonight. Enough."

"I'm not going and you can't make me," I said.

"You have a couple of hours to exercise your new horse, get washed and get dressed, and then start preparing for the inevitable. I mean it. Or no more riding."

She had my interest. "You can't stop me from riding. No one can stop me from riding."

"Watch me."

"I hate you," I snarled at the back of her head. Frightened and aggressive at the same time, striking out, I had become a monosyllabic fear-biter.

"What in God's name has happened to you? Where have you gone? I can almost see you shedding IQ points with every passing day this summer. You sound like a fugitive from *I Was a Teenage Werewolf*. I knew that adolescence could be difficult, I didn't know that it was a form of lobotomy."

"Shut up!" I shouted, rewarding her allegations with proof of what I had already come to suspect. Charlie Devlin wasn't the only person to disappear that summer. A big part of me had gone missing and I had no idea how to put myself back together again.

TEN MINUTES LATER, I bumped down the stairs, white blouse an accordion of wrinkles, riding pants retrieved from beneath the bed in a ball of dog hair.

"You should have something to eat—though a part of me hesitates to feed the beast," my mother said as Lou, looking on in bemusement, offered to make me a sandwich. Refusing, I huffed and puffed my way out of the house. After waiting outside the stable for all of three minutes, my brain working overtime, I made my decision. I took off running for the beach.

"Riddle!" my mother shrieked from the kitchen window when she spotted me hotfooting it along the trail among the tall trees at the back of the house. She ran onto the back deck, tripped down the steps and tore across the yard after me as I shot across the grass, heading for the dunes and from there the beachfront. Before I could descend the ladder dug into the sandy bluff, she caught me.

Seizing me by the shoulder, she spun me around. "You're going to this goddamn fundraiser tonight if I have to drag you all the way there by your hair."

"I'm not going. You can't make me!" Wrenching myself free, I ran to the nearest tree and started to climb. Not to be outdone, she grabbed me by my riding boots and yanked me back down and onto the ground.

"No!" I went officially nuts, hitting, spinning and swinging. To my amazement, my mother started to swing back, the two of us wildly flailing away at each other as the waves roared below. It might have ended in murder if my mother hadn't abruptly stopped, a look of shock and dismay on her face.

"What am I doing? Beating up my kid over a Democratic fundraiser? Has it really come to this?"

Bent over at the waist, hands on her knees, she took several deep breaths, stood back up and gave her head a shake. "You listen to me, Riddle James Camperdown. I'm through. Finished. Go. Don't go. It's your choice. You can live with the consequences. This is between you and your father. I'm out. Do you hear me?"

She tucked in her white shirt and then she turned around and walked across the dunes and back up the stairs and into the house. My crazy red hair blowing wildly and covered from head to foot in my mother's fingerprints, I was left alone to wonder why this felt less like a victory and more like something dangerous let loose to run urgent and unchecked, zigzagging unseen and primitive through the tall ocean grasses.

"All right," I screamed. "I'll go."

Chapter Twelve

———

A FEW HOURS LATER AND MY MOTHER AND I WERE IN THE CAR waiting for Camp. He was inevitably late and we were always early. "It's been a while since I've seen you in a dress," she said.

"Don't get used to it. I don't see a St. James bow in my future."

"Too bad," my mother said. "I think we could all benefit from you having a curtsy in your repertoire."

"Are you going to vote for yourself on Election Day?" I asked Camp as he slid behind the steering wheel of the car, his dark hair still wet from the shower.

"That's an odd question," he commented.

"It seems strange, that's all. Voting for yourself. Arrogant. Selfish in a way. I think it would be a noble gesture if you were to vote for the other guy."

"I wouldn't vote for that son of a bitch Joe Becker if my life were at stake," my father said, referring to his Republican rival, an optometrist with several clinics in and around Boston.

"Oh, I don't know," my mother said, glancing at her reflection in the visor mirror. "He's a war hero, after all."

"Self-proclaimed. Another one of these self-mythologizing rear-liners. He drove a supply truck, for Christ's sake. The worst danger he faced was from boredom as he waited for the all-clear sign. I consider it my moral duty to skin him alive at the polls."

"I'd vote for you, Camp," I said.

"Thanks, Jimmy," my father said as I leaned forward and put my hands on his shoulders. He grinned over at my mother. "What about you? Can I count on your support in November, or do you think it would be more noble to vote for the other guy?"

"Don't be absurd. What kind of question is that?"

My father laughed. "You never know," he said, turning the key in the ignition, the engine sputtering once and then reluctantly kicking into gear.

My mother, shining diadem in a royal blue dress, parted the Red Sea with her entrance at the fundraiser. She made her way through the gawkers and the fawners assembled pop-eyed and gurgling, in the old-fashioned lobby of the inn. She loved the spotlight, reveled in the social power it bequeathed, but her spectacular misanthropy curdled any real delight she might have allowed herself to feel.

"How I hate the common man. They need to install a filter on the door," she muttered, her bright smile like a veil concealing the filigree of frost that she wore underneath.

I never did get used to her daily professions of superiority. "We live in a democracy, remember? Everyone created equal and all that."

"Yes, I see your point," she said, indicating with a lift of her eyebrow a woman across from us who appeared to have swallowed a hippopotamus.

"The only thing that can improve that creature's bid for equality is a tub of vanishing cream," my mother said. I rebuked her with silent indignation while secretly sharing her revulsion. I consoled myself with the thought that at least I had the grace to feel ashamed of my prejudices. Glancing behind, I allowed myself to be conveniently distracted by the sound of my father's big laugh filling the room.

"Come with me, Riddle," my mother said, pulling me by the hand, gesturing for me to join her in shaking hands and greeting people. "The election has been a marvelous opportunity to educate our daughter in civic duty—and familial obligation," she explained, upper-register inflections on display, as the people around her nodded and smiled. "Idiots," she said under her breath. "Someone please explain to me why people have such an endless appetite for pap."

"You should be grateful. If they didn't, you wouldn't have a career," I said.

"Cheap shots represent the lowest form of insight."

"Yeah, yeah," I said, having reached the outer limits of my wit.

INSIDE THE PRIVACY OF a washroom designated for the family's personal use, Greer stopped to arrange her dress and comb her hair. "How do I look?" she asked, checking her crimson lipstick with a hand mirror. She wore a strapless dress with a fitted bodice and full skirt that skimmed her knees—the kind of dress that only a certain kind of woman could pull off. I glanced down admiringly at her coral heels.

"Fine," I said. "You look nice."

"Damned with faint praise," she said, clicking shut her compact, as she reached over and ran her fingers through my permanently disheveled mop.

"Hopeless," she said with a sigh.

I pushed her hand away. "Leave it, please."

"Do you know what your grandfather said on the day you were born? He said, 'That hair color spells trouble.' Imagine any evolved person saying such a thing." Annoyed at the memory, she impatiently walked toward the door. "That is how hopelessly unenlightened your father's parents were. Your grandmother extolled the scientific virtues of phrenology!"

"Why are you so angry?" I asked her.

"I'm not angry," she answered, looking me up and down as if she was measuring me for a pine box.

"You're so negative about everything."

"The default allegation of the true bore, and from my own daughter no less."

Forcing a smile as we rejoined the growing numbers of Camperdown supporters waiting to enter the ballroom, she watched offside as members of the press surrounded my father, who was graciously fielding both genuine and perfunctory well wishes. My mother caught his eye. He grinned over at us. She waved back, so did I, and I don't know what exactly but there was something about her expression that put me in mind of what my father had said in the car when he joked about counting on her support in November. There was just something about how she looked and something about what he said, and in my mind's eye I could see my mother entering the voting booth under the watchful eye of the election clerk and inserting her ballot—the ballot starting and stopping, bunching up, jamming slightly, she giving it an impatient poke until it recovered its slippery slide, but not before it opened and then folded, a revealing split-second bulge, time enough for me to see a jaunty little X penciled next to the name of the self-mythologizing Joe Becker.

She gave me a knowing look, as if she could read my thoughts. For a moment I wondered if she was imagining the worst of me, as I was in the habit of imagining the worst of her.

"Good god," my mother said from across a banquet table piled high with a gelatinous array of finger foods, processed meats and jellied salads, surveying the bounty with all the enthusiasm of someone being asked to choke down a pureed mulch of church lady and Old Spice. "Are those marshmallows?"

They were hanging from the rafters, the hotel ballroom was packed with campaign workers, the party faithful, the press, the rank and file, Teamsters and academics, all gathered in the ballroom of this elegant Provincetown inn to support Camp's high-profile bid for the House.

With mixed feelings, I watched him get swept away on a wave of exuberant roiling humanity, leaving me orphaned at the buffet table, munching on a gherkin pickle, feeling out of place, fielding and fending off endless inquiries from people who visibly inspected me for flaws, who spoke to me too loudly, who overwhelmed me with the vivid primary colors of their curiosity, posing questions in singsong voices that bobbed like mobiles hung over a crib.

"Are you enjoying all the excitement? You might try smiling, in any case," suggested an oversize woman in organza, her fleshy fingers swollen and laden with dinner rings of flashing sapphire and emerald. She introduced herself as Mirabel Whiffet, Gin's mother, returned to the States after living for several years abroad. I had never met this woman, though I had heard enough about her, but she immediately began rubbing against my legs like a pampered cat, as comfortable as if we had enjoyed a lifetime of intimacy.

"Such melancholia from such a lovely looking girl. Oh, well, I suppose it's the fashion these days among young people to mope." She leaned into me, her mouth mere inches from my face, her perfume a crude assailant, as I cringed and looked for escape.

"You don't look at all like your mother." She slowly enunciated each word as if she were expelling a series of hen's eggs from the rouged oval of her mouth. "I've known Greer since she was just a little bit older than you."

"You don't look like Gin, either," I pointed out politely. There was an understatement; it was as if the side of a mountain had given birth to a river rock.

I smiled, something I hadn't done in weeks—or more accurately, I grimaced in grotesque replica of a smile, as if I were working out a charley horse. My curiosity was piqued. It never occurred to me that my mother had ever been my age.

"She was the most beautiful girl in all of New England. Everyone said so. That complexion. Like a vanilla milk shake. Elegant carriage even as a child. She looked like a fairy-tale princess, but . . ." My eyes widened in anticipation. Now, this was information that I could get behind. My imagination soared like a runaway balloon.

"But she was more like Rumpelstiltskin in disguise," I said, finishing the thought.

Mrs. Whiffet laughed, relishing my enthusiasm. What Gin and his mother didn't share as far as appearance, they made up for in the pleasure they derived from things that glowed in the dark.

"Well, you said it, my dear, not me. Temperamental or not, she had suitors lined up for miles. Mind you, she was strictly look-don't-touch. Of course, she only had eyes for Michael."

"Michael?"

"Michael Devlin. Who else?"

My head gave a violent start as if I had been slapped—the kind of symbolic thump upside the head that hurtles you into a whole new way of being. Mrs. Whiffet kept right on talking, unmindful of the psychic whiplash engendered by her remarks.

"Your mother was crazy about him. Ghastly, what happened between the two of them. It was supposed to be the wedding of the decade. I'll never forget it. Everyone was there. Governors. Senators. Movie stars. Cary Grant was there! The vice president was there! The church was packed. Your mother was waiting in her white gown at the back of the church—well, you couldn't take your eyes off her, that's how gorgeous she looked, a devastating beauty, that's just what she was." She lowered her voice so I had to lean in to hear her. "Oh, but where was the groom? We waited and waited. It was a nightmare, the minutes ticking by like weeks. Michael was in a hotel in Prague. Imagine! He left her at the altar. Took off to Europe the night before."

What? Why hadn't I heard anything about this before? My mother was engaged to Michael Devlin? When? How did Camp fit into all this?

Staring blindly down at the floral centerpiece, I was trying to sort out exactly how I felt about what I was hearing. I had always viewed my parents' personal lives as being the province of archeology. The idea that my mother had the potential to be interesting was not just new, it was revolutionary. Needing something to do, a place to put my head and my hands and all those feelings, I reached for a slice of blue cheese and a cracker, something to put in my mouth.

"Oh, my goodness," Mrs. Whiffet said, expressing, too fast, a regret she didn't feel. "You didn't know? I just assumed everyone knew. It never occurred to me that your parents would be so secretive. I'm so sorry, dear."

"It's okay." The cracker snapped between my fingers, crumbs falling to the floor. I bent down to scoop them up.

"Anyway, ancient history, and it all worked out, didn't it? Your mother married Godfrey a couple of years later. People said she only did it to make Michael jealous but I never believed that to be the case. I so despise cynicism. I always wondered about the three of them, honestly. Seemed to me that there was always a queer little triangle at work. It was obvious to everyone that both boys were in love with your mother. Gin thought so, too," she said as if she were conferring the imprimatur of ultimate authority, which, when it came to gossip and superficial subject matter,

I supposed that she was. "However did they contain their feelings? Well, in the end, I suppose they didn't, did they? You know, your father and Michael were the best of friends, did everything together, even served together overseas in the same unit, but something happened and the friendship died, just withered on the vine. Terribly sad. Do you know what happened, dear?"

"No," I said, looking around desperately for something more to eat. I settled for a ginger ale.

"What's your father's opinion of Michael? Does he talk much about him? What about your mother?" Subtlety was not one of Mirabel's gifts.

"I don't know. They mention him occasionally. But they talk about so many people." I hesitated, debating with myself. Even then, I was aware of the unwritten law that exists between people; you need to give information to get information. "Sometimes they argue about him. My father doesn't respect him very much—at least, I don't think he does." Gulping down my soda, I struggled for an exit strategy. I wasn't exactly a smooth operator.

"Really?" Mrs. Whiffet's eyes popped and clicked, as if a whole series of camera flashes were exploding. Her Technicolor enthusiasm was enough to convince me that I was treading uncomfortably close to betrayal.

"I don't really know anything about it," I backtracked. "He isn't a big topic around our house."

"Oh, just one of those things, probably, the tricky business with your mother, that's what I always thought anyway. As it turns out, just as well, look at the tragedies that have dogged Michael. Polly MacLeish, the heiress to the Salinger fortune, the girl he eventually married, died prematurely: a brain aneurysm. Went just like that! Died on the kitchen floor going over a dinner party menu with the cook. Shocking. The Lord works in mysterious ways, doesn't He? Thankfully she never lived to see this terrible business with the younger boy. Something to be grateful for." She paused, searching her conversational treasure trove for more bric-a-brac. "If you think about it, had your mother married Michael it could have been you that disappeared!"

"What?" It was as if she had flipped a switch and I had no control over the automatic response it generated.

"Oh, I've upset you . . ."

"Still scaring livestock and children, Mirabel?" My mother, noticing my distress from across the room, came up from behind Mrs. Whiffet and took up a spot directly in front of me.

"Oh, Greer, I feel terrible. It seems I've upset Riddle talking about the Devlin boy, the one who has simply vanished. It wasn't my intention at all."

"Riddle's at a stage of life when feeling affronted is a biological imperative." She stared skyward, appealing to the heavens for patience before turning around to face me. I found myself in between the two women. "Pull yourself together, Riddle. It's not as if you knew him. Don't worry, it's not an epidemic. Even if he was abducted, fortunately for you, your father's bank balance would discourage all but the most bush-league kidnapper."

"Oh, my, you don't change, Greer," Mrs. Whiffet interrupted, face flushing.

"Something you and I share, Mirabel."

"How long has it been, my dear?"

"Too long, darling."

"You're more beautiful than ever, I see."

"How kind of you to say. And you are looking . . . well . . . So, tell me, what else were you two talking about?"

"Nothing," I said, fighting for composure, as Mrs. Whiffet heaved a loud telltale sigh. My mother's brows creased, her ears twitching like antennae. "Nothing worth mentioning anyway, I suspect," she said.

"Not to flog a dead horse—cover your ears, Riddle—but isn't it simply awful about Charlie Devlin, Greer? I was just saying to Gin this morning, that child is long dead and buried, you can be quite sure."

"How can you be sure?" I couldn't stand one more moment of this. "How do you know what happened to him? Nobody knows for sure. Maybe he's fine. He could be fine. Just because you're missing doesn't mean you're dead. Why do people always think they know everything?" I was panting by the end of my little speech.

"What in God's name is wrong with you?" my mother demanded. "If I didn't know better, I'd think Charlie Devlin was in our freezer in the basement."

"Now who's crazy?" I sputtered. "Can't I have an opinion?"

"No, you can't. It's illegal, like drinking under age," my mother said.

"It's not the opinion that's the problem, dear. It's the intensity of the emotion. As I always say, emotion is the great enemy of conversation. Did you have some sort of crush on this boy?" Mrs. Whiffet said.

"No! How many times do I have to say it? I never met him!"

"You never need to say it again. You need to stop talking entirely. I keep telling her father, this is why boarding schools were invented." My mother offered up her best falsely conciliatory gaze—imagine a spitting cobra composing a thank-you note written in venom.

"You never listen. You never pay attention to anything I say or think. You're too busy showing off." My desperation was bouncing off the walls. I was audibly pinging.

My mother searched the room with her eyes. "My kingdom for a kidnapper! Please carry on, Mirabel."

"Oh, it's all right. Hormones are bedeviling, or so I seem to recall."

"Oh, my God," I groaned, reaching for the edge of the buffet table to steady myself. I pulled a daisy from the centerpiece and begin to pluck nervously at the petals.

"Now. Where was I?" Mrs. Whiffet questioned herself. "Oh, yes. Recklessness no doubt played a role in what's happened to Michael's boy. And entitlement. Sometimes money and prominence can be a curse."

"Spoken like someone who has never worked for a living. That aside, it's a tragedy. He was a nice-looking boy," my mother said. "Michael must be devastated." From the incidental way she tacked on that last remark it was obvious she was conducting her own little intelligence mission.

"I'm sure he is, but you know Michael, stiff upper lip and all that. He never lets on. Oh, but they're all like that, aren't they? The ones that went to war, I mean. I think it did something to their emotional barometer, what they saw over there."

I struggled to listen, hoping to distract myself from all that made my teeth chatter and my body shake. "What's he like?" I asked, more blunt than considered. "Michael Devlin, what's he like?"

"Why do you care?" my mother said, exasperation in her voice. Mrs. Whiffet snapped to attention, drawing herself up in grand fashion, flaunting her equatorial circumference, bust the disconcerting size of a ship's prow. The coiled tendrils of her hair bounced up and down, skirting the fleshy part of her ears. Forgetting herself, she stepped out of her heels, scratching her right ankle with her left foot. She was as excited as if someone had just announced the discovery of a new planet where the inhabitants dealt exclusively in the currency of small talk and gossip.

"Would you like to hear about him? I'll tell you."

My mother jabbed me in the ribs with her elbow, but I ignored her and nodded. Hear about my mother's lost love? You bet I would.

Mrs. Whiffet laughed and licked her lips—she was about to dip her fingers into her favorite gooey dessert. "Greer, dear, would you mind passing me a pastry? I never could resist an authentic Sicilian cannoli." She took a bite, flecks of confectioners' sugar dotting her lips.

"Ricotta impasata! I'm in heaven! Now, where shall I begin?"

Chapter **Thirteen**

"**M**ICHAEL DEVLIN WAS ONLY TWO YEARS OLD WHEN HIS PARents got divorced. It was 1928. I remember clearly because that was the same year that Mr. Whiffet and I bought the property they owned next to the Cormorant Clock Farm. Or was it 1927? The Devlins owned several prestigious properties in the area. In those days, it was the fashion to buy up surrounding lands, the idea being that you make your own best neighbor. After the divorce, they sold some of their holdings. It was Mr. Whiffet's idea to call the place Settlement House. Very wicked, I know. Eventually, of course, we bought the horse farm for Gin. He always had such issues with his teeth—not to mention his nervous system—he could never undertake the demands of a profession."

Mrs. Whiffet was clearly relishing her turn onstage and didn't appear to notice or care that my mother had begun to turn blue.

"Please do not resuscitate," she said, leaning back and whispering in my ear. "Get to the point, Mirabel," she urged unpleasantly.

"Never you mind, Greer. This is my story and I will tell it the way I want to tell it."

This was a tale she had told more than once; Mirabel Whiffet was obviously invigorated by repetition. "Michael was a very rich boy, monogrammed by fate, as it were, famous by accident, yet most people still insisted on referring to him by the hated nickname, the Devlin baby."

"It drove him crazy, being called the Devlin baby. Makes him sound more like a movie title than a person," my mother said, unable to resist making her own contribution to a story they both knew by heart.

"They fought over him like jackals over a piece of meat," Mrs. Whiffet said, poised like a vulture to pick over whatever remained. "People of that era chatted about him the way people talk about Leopold and Loeb or the Scopes trial or the Fatty Arbuckle scandal. I can still see him, his picture in all the papers, this dear little boy with the curly black hair and the fat cheeks. Of course, most people don't know him in any meaningful way, which suits him just fine. He keeps to himself, doesn't he, Greer?"

My mother shrugged her shoulders. "I suppose. I don't pay that much attention to anything concerning Michael Devlin."

We all knew that was a lie, but my mother's little deceit only fueled Mrs. Whiffet's zeal to continue. "His peers inhabited the world's elite registries." Mrs. Whiffet paused to look around the room, as if she were waiting for some sort of public acknowledgment of her own place among the socially anointed. "But you would need a divining stick to find him most of the time. Such an insular man, Michael. But deep. Very deep."

She made it seem as if getting to know Michael Devlin was a form of lonely, perilous descent, like abseiling into Low's Gully.

"He's a tricky one to navigate, Michael, all those sharp angles. The Devlin baby isn't exactly the Gerber baby." Mrs. Whiffet was really enjoying herself.

"More like Rosemary's baby," my mother quipped.

"Of course there was his military service. He has quite a distinguished record, and with his money he could easily have avoided active duty. Give credit where credit is due." Mrs. Whiffet was proud of her generous spirit and rewarded herself by reaching for a glass of champagne from a passing waiter. She took a noisy sip and returned to her captivated audience—me. "He and your father signed up right away. I always say, give them full marks. I mean, I liked both of them, Michael and Camp, though God knows, they were both difficult boys, but then people with money are expected to be temperamental, though I myself like an easier-going person when it comes to companionship."

"Farmers are easygoing, Mirabel," my mother said. "Conviviality is highly overrated."

"How would you know?" I couldn't resist.

"I beg your pardon?" my mother said.

"It can't be easy, after all, to be a cultural phenomenon," said Mrs. Whiffet, ignoring our skirmishing. Her conversation traveled an uneven road, sputtering one way, lurching another.

Michael Devlin, it was beginning to seem to me, wasn't a man at all. He was an event, a circus performer, a figure of speech twirling in the lexicon like a poodle in a tutu.

"Well, but what did he expect?" my mother said in obvious agitation, waving her cigarette in the air, smoky fingers curling around her neck like a ghostly vise. "Mirabel, you know as well as I do, the rich and the famous can do many things. The one thing they can't do is whine. Apparently someone decided that God should give Michael Devlin something to complain about."

"Oh, dear, really, Greer, you go too far. The things you say. You have no heart." Mrs. Whiffet fanned herself with her plump hand, batting back my mother's words as if she were attempting to make her way through a sticky canopy of flying insects.

I was attempting with some difficulty to digest my mother's pagan logic—her mordant philosophies, almost sadistically rancorous, tended to leave a bitter aftertaste—when a loud burlesque whooping went up from the other side of the ballroom, the sudden burst of exuberance pushing aside the topic of Michael Devlin.

Three cheers for Godfrey Camperdown! Hip hip hooray! Huzzahs all round followed by great spurts of laughter. My father was addressing the crowd, bottles uncorking and squeals of excitement as women in their little black dresses ducked to avoid all that was overflowing.

My mother looked pained. "Why your father is willing to work so hard for hoi polloi is beyond me."

"Oh, Greer, you don't mean it," Mrs. Whiffet said, digging in to a slice of Black Forest cake that was roughly the size of the Black Forest. "Everyone loves him so."

My mother was astonished. "You're really not so silly as to believe that, are you?"

Then it went quiet except for an aroused ripple of expectation accompanied by soft amused murmurings and a smattering of applause as Camp began to sing "The Daring Young Man on the Flying Trapeze" in that familiar confident tenor of his, the joy he took in performing for others so irresistible that it caused a spontaneous moment of reprieve, as if both sides in a battle had decided to lay down their arms.

Such sweetness, such a genial moment, golden candles flickering, swaying to the music, warm tones of my mother's hair shining like the sun, the ballroom walls intimate as a honeycomb, dripping with pleasure, sticky with happiness. I listened to my father sing, delight like honey oozing from everywhere, from everyone, happiness, smiles, grace, everywhere glistening. My mother, in an unprecedented show of sentiment, reached for my hand and held it in her own, though she never once took her eyes off my father as he sang. Following her lead, I did the same, focused on Camp even though it was Greer who gave me cause to wonder.

Even when he'd finished singing—resisting, but just barely,

everyone's calls for an encore—the overall feeling of affability persisted. My mother gently withdrew her hand and struck up a lighthearted conversation with a couple of women who came up behind her. Camp, meanwhile, looking surprised, was extending his arm to someone who had emerged from the crowd, but the man seemed uninterested in the formalities, ignoring my father's outstretched hand in favor of immediate engagement. Gesturing, he was talking animatedly, Camp leaning in and listening intently, brow line creasing. Glancing away for a second, I turned to see what was making my mother laugh.

Somewhere in the near background, vague and unformed, I heard the sounds of excited voices, hollering, shouting, giving orders, excitement rapidly turning into alarm as the velveteen party chatter gave way to chipped sounds of skirmish, pandemonium.

"Jesus Christ!" a male voice hollered.

"Oh, my God," my mother said amidst a backdrop of shrieks and screams, covering her mouth.

"What's happening?" Mrs. Whiffet cried, clutching my forearm as I stood on my tiptoes and watched my father disappear into a sudden sinkhole, an intense pocket of energy exploding in the center of the room, the crowd receding and then flowing back into place, chairs and tables overturning, crash of glass and cutlery, dishes shattering.

I walked and then ran, ignoring my mother's orders to come back, come back here right now, and pushed my way through all those people, someone's elbow ricocheting off someone's shoulder and into my jaw as I squirmed and wiggled my way to the center of it all where my father stood over Michael Devlin who half sat, half lay on the floor, one hand partly covering his right eye, which had already begun to redden and swell. He was staring up and sideways at my father, watching him, shaking his head slowly back and forth, not talking, as arms from everywhere appeared like tentacles, pulling him up to his feet and away, arms on his shoulders, his neck, around his waist as he fought to free himself.

"Take your hands off me," he said in the manner of someone unaccustomed to restraint, blinking profusely, involuntary tears pouring down his cheek, his hand to his wounded eye.

"They were talking privately. Quite an intense conversation, it seemed, when Camp hauled off and socked him right in the face," the woman beside me said to her friend. "Imagine!"

The man on the receiving end of my father's memorable left hook gradually took form in front of me, in vivid drifts of active color: tall, slim, black hair, ivory skin, navy blue eyes, dark blue bespoke suit.

I knew who he was right away. I recognized Michael Devlin from newspaper photos, from the recent cover of *Look* magazine, from the spread in *Life* magazine, from the distant view I had of him that afternoon in Wellfleet. He was one of those men who could change the weather in the room just by showing up.

A young man, college age, eighteen or nineteen, pushing and pulling, winding in and out, made his way to the front of the crowd.

"Dad!" Stunned, he confronted his father. "Holy shit, what's going on?"

"Michael!" my mother said, gasping, finally reaching my father, standing at his side. "Camp, what's the matter with you? How could you? Have you gone mad?"

"Dad, what the hell?" Michael's son gestured helplessly as I moved in closer to get a better look. His face obscured, I noticed with a start his russet hair and lean athletic build. The boy I had seen on horseback.

"Ask him. Ask the candidate. He's in a better position to answer you than I am."

Everyone regarded my father expectantly. Camp scanned the

room, took its temperature and opted against any sort of public explanation. He ignored the rest of us and spoke directly to Michael Devlin, talked to him in low tones as if there was no one else in the room, as if they were all alone on a boat in the middle of the ocean. The water was ominously calm.

"There's a butler's pantry off the kitchen," he said. "Why don't we take this to someplace private?"

Ignoring his son's protests, hand cupped over his eye like a patch, Michael Devlin headed toward the kitchen area, followed by Camp.

"Stay here, Harry," Michael instructed his son. "Don't worry. It will be fine."

"Jesus, Dad . . ."

Michael walked past my mother, his arm brushing against her arm. She stiffened; her cheeks temporarily lost their color as the crowd parted to let both men pass.

"Hello, Greer," he said. "It's been a long time." Swerving slightly, he leaned into her. "You've still got it, I see."

"How dare you?" she said as I looked on, fascinated.

"Oh, my! Whatever happened to decorum?" Mrs. Whiffet was stuck in a loop. Like a farm collie with an ungovernable compulsion to goose stray sheep, she was restricted by breeding to a specific narrow range of reactions that caused her to alternate between feeling overwrought and feeling overwhelmed.

"Told you there was a story," a reporter mumbled aloud to the photographer standing next to him, camera in its holster. "I think I'll leave it to the Hedda Hopper crowd. Trite is their bailiwick, not mine."

My father studied both Michael and my mother from across the room as everyone else watched him, trying to chart his response. His expression gave away nothing. It struck me, despite his volatility, just what a cool customer Camp could be. He stood off by himself, waiting for an aide to find the key that would unlock the door to the butler's pantry.

Harry Devlin looked on in disbelief, shifting his gaze back and forth between his father and my mother, squinting, forehead furrowed in his quest for interpretation, shielding his eyes with his hand as if he were staring directly into the sun. His father looked mildly embarrassed and a little bit amused. Next to his son's athletic intensity, there was something vaguely dissolute and of the country club about Michael Devlin, smoky scent of the indifferent American expat.

I wanted to look away but it was riveting. I was conscious of staring at Michael but I couldn't help myself. Pulverized by events, all I could do was gawk. Unable to contain my curiosity, embarrassed but thrilled—my parents had never been so interesting to me as they were in that moment, to say nothing of the Devlins. As I moved in for a closer look at his father, Harry glanced up at me. Boom! I recoiled from the impact. I had seen that face before in newspapers, in magazines, on TV. Charlie Devlin was wearing it.

"This has been the most extraordinary evening!" Mrs. Whiffet exclaimed, overheated and perspiring, licking caramel sauce from her pudgy fingers, a dusting of pastry on her upper lip.

"There's Gin," she said, spotting her son at the fringe of the crowd near the entrance door. "Oh, Gin! Over here, Ginger darling! You won't believe what you've missed." She waved her hand over her head.

"Oh, no," my mother said, moaning theatrically, jaw set as if it had been nailed in place.

I looked for Gin, or pretended to anyway, in between sneaking protracted glances at the Devlins, as the melodramatic tango of the crowd degraded to an insistent vibrant hum. I got caught doing an inspection.

"Do we know each other?" Harry asked me.

Panicked, I had no idea how to talk to this boy whose father was the enemy of my father. I looked around the ballroom, contemplating my escape, trying to formulate an answer. That's when I saw Gin, arm extended over his head, waving, yoo-hooing. He plunged into the crowd and seesawed through, making his way toward us.

Directly behind Gin, Gula lingered in the gloaming that he wore like a cape, looming and murky, louche and intriguing, inhabiting his own dense pocket of darkness—night seeming to follow him like a feral odor. I took a step back. My mother noticed and tracked my gaze. Harry intuitively turned to look. My father, briefly pausing at the entranceway to the kitchen, did the same. Michael Devlin glanced around to see what or who we were all looking at.

Gula, smiling, sought me out with his eyes.

"Are you all right?" Harry came up alongside me. "You don't look that great."

"I'm fine," I stammered, conscious that Gula was watching me.

"I'm Harry Devlin, by the way."

"I know who you are," I said. "I'm Riddle Camperdown. Godfrey Camperdown is my father."

"I figured. Sorry about this thing with my dad. I knew he wanted to talk to your father about something but I had no idea it would turn into a fight. Jesus."

"Your father must have said something pretty bad to make my father want to hit him."

"Well, he hasn't been acting like himself lately." He paused and swallowed with difficulty, as if he was trying to digest something bitter. "I'll tell you one thing, I never expected the evening to end with my dad in a dustup with your dad. Crazy."

I was trying not to look at him except indirectly. His resemblance to his missing brother was disconcerting but compelling. Finally, I could resist no longer and turned to face him. He was massaging the back of his neck with his hand, displacing his shirt collar, his fingers fiddling with the silver chain that he wore. Tugging at the chain, playing with it, he pulled it up around his chin, tiny silver medallion reflecting the overhead light of the chandelier.

"Where did you get that?" I said.

Harry popped the necklace back inside his shirt. He looked at me, quizzical expression on his face, but answered, "A baptism gift from my mother. She gave one to my brother, too. It's supposed to keep you safe from harm. That's what my mother believed anyway. I'm not so convinced."

I felt as if I was going to throw up. My mouth was dry. My eyes fluttered. That's when it happened. No delicate perfumed swoon for me, no pretty feminine buckle onto a velvet chaise. No, I teetered like an old drunk, eyes wobbling, stomach churning, and keeled over as if someone had yanked my feet out from under me, hit the ground with a backward thud, blacked out and came to just in time to find Harry discreetly trying to adjust my skirt to its original position around my thighs rather than leave it in its current inelegant location somewhere around my collarbone.

On the plus side, I didn't vomit.

"Are you okay, kid?" Harry asked, a crowd gathering.

"I'm not a kid."

"So, do you do this often?" Harry asked me. "Faint, I mean."

"Never. I never do this . . . Shit," I said, propping myself up on my elbows, waving away his extended hand, sinking into a plush tub chair.

"Tough guy, eh?" Harry said.

If only he knew.

"What's that supposed to mean?" I asked him.

"What?" He looked perplexed. Obviously Harry had never before met a teenage girl hell-bent on persuading the world that she moonlighted as a Screaming Eagle. Taking a deep breath, I worked to stave off lumbering waves of personal mortification. It was like trying to swallow bleach. Then something darker than mere embarrassment settled inside me. I remembered what it was that had caused me to pass out.

"Good Lord, Riddle, what have you done now?" Hands on her hips, her hair smooth as satin—my hair, meanwhile, looked like it was being held up at gunpoint—high points of her cheeks flushed, my mother expended little effort to contain her contempt for the crowd's expectations. She made it clear to all within earshot that maternal solicitude was not on the menu. "Honestly, you're making a spectacle of yourself. Are you ill?"

"I tend to have this effect on women," Harry said, trying to make light of my embarrassment.

"Like father, like son," my mother said, batting her verbal eyelashes, unable to resist any invitation to banter.

"Forget power. Forget money. Forget reputation. You can bring no greater currency to any party than sophisticated banter," my father had once proclaimed to guests over an after-dinner drink.

"Well, then again, there is beauty. Beauty will fly you to the moon," my mother had demurred, ever the contrarian, indirectly proving my father's point.

"So sorry, dear, about your brother," Mrs. Whiffet said, springing forward, talent to dismay shining like her nose. "Any news about what's happened to him?"

"Thank you. No. Nothing." All levity gone from his face, Harry straightened up, reflexive formality taking hold as if he had suddenly been enfolded head to toe in a white glove.

"What a shame." Mrs. Whiffet tsk-tsked, blowing up like a flotation device. "Well, you must be strong. Try to focus on all the good things in your life. You have so many blessings, haven't you? I was just saying to Greer, if I were a few years younger . . ." The color drained from Harry's face. "I think Riddle agrees with me, don't you my dear? I mean, I've had my share of crushes too, but I never swooned over one of them, did I?" She laughed lightly and then covered her mouth in a conspiratorial whisper.

Too horrified to respond, I briefly wondered whether it was DNA-mandated or hormonally fated that every woman of a certain age decides lasciviousness is a kind of wit.

"Gin once fainted when Emma Meldrum kissed him at his tenth birthday party," his mother carried on, oblivious to her effect. "Adorable!"

"Riddle, where do you think you're going?" my mother demanded, her hand folded like a handkerchief at her brow, a flimsy gesture of pseudo-distress, watching me intently as I ungracefully pole-vaulted to my feet, retreat uppermost on my mind. I needed to get away, to escape the hollow pop and fizz of all that party chatter and counterfeit exchange. I needed a moment to recover, to find a private place where I could process all that had just happened.

"I'm going to get a glass of water," I said, stumbling toward the back of the room, resisting all offers of help along the way.

Alone in the kitchen, I closed my eyes and leaned against the sink, head sagging, my arms outstretched, hands gripping the sides of the stainless steel cabinet for support. I heard the grandfather clock toll, familiar Westminster chimes echoing from inside the inn's front entranceway. "Dum dum da dum dum dum dum dum," small bells reverberating, polishing the air until it shone like the memory of the leather topsider that I had found in the yellow stable. I knew. I knew. I can never say that I didn't know. It wasn't a rabbit or a puppy or a pony. It wasn't a Belgian sheepdog. It wasn't my overactive imagination. It was Charlie Devlin in the barn that day.

The bells rang out. One. Two. Three. Four times. I stopped counting.

Taking a deep breath, I opened the cupboard and reached

inside for a glass. My hand on the faucet, I was about to turn on the water—and the waterworks—when I heard my father's voice coming from behind the wall in the adjacent butler's pantry. The civility of his tone surprised me.

"Do the police have any idea?"

"No. Well, just what you might expect. Runaway kid." Michael's tone was bitter.

"What do you think?"

"Oh, I think Charlie is dead. What happened to him? I don't know. I know this much. He didn't run away from home. I don't give my boys reason to jump ship. All I know is that he's gone and he's not coming back. As for why, well, I stopped asking myself those kinds of questions a long time ago."

Charlie's father, convinced he was dead? His hopelessness felt airborne, as if futility were a contagion and I was being overwhelmed by its toxic effects.

"I don't understand you. Giving up on the kid that way. If it were Riddle I would search the world before I'd surrender hope."

Eyes tightly shut, I fought to block the flow of tears. I have never felt so unworthy as I did in that moment.

"It's easy enough to imagine what you would do or how you would feel when it's not happening to you."

"True enough, if you are a blowhard or a fabulist, and I am neither." Camp hesitated. I could almost feel my father pumping the brakes, steering into the spin, trying to maintain control. "He looked like a nice boy. I'm sorry, Michael. What is there to say? Life is cruel."

"You're wrong. Life is random, life couldn't give a shit. People are cruel. Which brings me to my point. What in the hell makes you think that you're fit to hold office?"

Screech of tires, smell of smoke and rubber, I braced for the crash.

"Go to hell, Michael. You want me to crawl into a hole and pull a rock over my head, because you can't face the truth about what kind of man you are."

"Oh, I know exactly what I am."

"No. I'll tell you what kind of guy you are. The kind of guy who can talk about his missing son with all the emotion most people reserve for the discussion of a disappointing golf score. You see, I know you better than anyone. Is that what you can't forgive?"

Michael Devlin laughed, though he wasn't amused. "Hard to believe. At one time I would have walked through fire for you. Camp, you're making this very easy for me."

"Don't threaten me, Michael. I don't respond well to threats, especially under the circumstances."

"Well, that's where I have the advantage over you. You can't threaten me. The worst has already happened to me."

I hardly dared to breathe. The door opened, then closed—high-pitched chatter from the ballroom briefly funneled into the butler's pantry, making its muffled incursion into the kitchen.

"Your son is missing and this is what you think about? I thought we resolved all this years ago. You never could stand to see me pull out ahead of you."

"Desperation doesn't become you, Camp." Devlin cleared his throat. "Listen. I'll do this much for old times' sake. For Greer. Step down. Plead personal problems. Resign from the campaign and I'll keep my mouth shut."

"Are you kidding me? Forget it. I won't go down without a fight. You know that better than anyone, Michael! I'm not the only one with something to lose here. It's my word against yours." He was shouting. Then just as quickly he wasn't, his voice gradually becoming a low rumble. "Why are you doing this? What's to be gained for either of us? Think of your sons. Think of Riddle. What's behind all of this? Is it malice or madness? Jealousy?"

"Jealousy? Ha! You really want to go there?"

"Tell me. Why? You owe me that much. After all I did for you. Worst mistake of my life." Camp sounded tired, and there was something else in his voice but I didn't understand its meaning.

Leaning forward, I struggled to hear the answer that never came. The door clicked shut as Michael Devlin made his exit. In the ensuing quiet my father began quietly to whistle as I had heard him whistle so many times before.

He was whistling a show tune under his breath. I covered my ears. I had heard enough.

Chapter **Fourteen**

—

I BROKE OFF FOUR SMALL PIECES OF MY BAGEL AND TOSSED
them one after the other to the dogs who sat lined up expectantly in a neat row at the dining room table, their begging a ritu-
alized staple of our family life.

"Interesting," my mother said, referring to something she was
reading in the paper.

My father looked up from his coffee. "Uh-oh," she said a few
minutes later. "Take a deep breath. Just remember, Camp, bad
publicity is better than no publicity at all. Isn't that what they say?"

"What are you talking about?"

"Listen to this," she prefaced before reciting one of the paper's
blind items:

"Who has a checkbook the size of New England, movie-star
good looks, a tragic personal history and a black eye? Ask the
Democratic congressional hopeful with the stunning left hook
and the gorgeous, brainy, icy-blonde wife. (We'd say more but it
would blow her cover.) Rumor has it that when these three old
friends talk 'triangle,' the subject is biology not math."

"Good to see the fourth estate is on top of things," my father
said. "Jumped to a melodramatic conclusion, too. That's what we

like to see in our opinion makers, predictability and dearth of imagination. Trust the press to get it all wrong."

"Well, now, I wouldn't say that," my mother said wryly. "They got some important details right."

"Yes, you're right, I do have a great left hook," Camp teased.

Squirming in my chair, I couldn't figure out why they were so nonchalant about what had happened. Finally, I worked up the courage to ask, "Why did you punch Michael Devlin, Camp?"

"I lost my temper. It happens."

"Your father's sympathy for the plight of others only extends so far," my mother said.

"Look," Camp said, growing angry, "no one disputes what an awful thing this kid's disappearance is, but . . ."

"But?" My mother interrupted. "There's a but?"

"Oh, for God's sake, Greer, the kid was a Devlin. Too bad what's happened to him, of course, it's terrible, but think for a moment about all the kids that have suffered as a result of his family's history of lousy labor practices."

"I don't understand, Camp," I said. "You're upset over people that you don't know, people you consider to be innocent bystanders, and that's fine, but you think what's happened to Charlie Devlin is okay? Why do you think it's okay to hurt some people but not others?" I bit my lower lip, trying to keep my emotions from becoming apparent.

"I'm not suggesting that what happened to the Devlin boy is right or good. I'm merely yielding to the power of greater forces. Sometimes these incidents are tied to a history of events, and within the context of that history they are, if not morally defensible, an inevitable if bitter form of correction or atonement."

"Careful, you might miss a stitch, Madame Defarge," my mother muttered, patting her lips with a napkin.

"What if someone talked about me that way?" I said, aware I

was sounding a little desperate. "What if what happened to Charlie Devlin happened to me? What if he was better than his family? You don't know."

My father looked at me for a moment before answering. "Nothing like that is going to happen to you because I won't allow it. And you're right. I don't know anything about Charlie Devlin. I'm sure he was a good kid and I'm sorry for him." He sighed. "Surely we can think of more pleasant things to discuss on such a beautiful day?"

My mother laughed in disbelief. "I can't think of a single thing. Your insensitivity is a showstopper . . . Riddle, where are you going?" she said as I pushed my chair back from the table, scraping the hardwood.

"My room," I said glumly, making my glowering exit. Did anyone ever tell the truth about anything? The adults around me loomed like tall trees that resisted climbing, pendulous, dark and mysterious. I was lost in their forest. I was lost to myself.

Kneeling on the floor, my head in my hands, elbows on the windowsill, I looked out over the blue waters of the Atlantic. The beach was empty except for the hundreds of seagulls congregated on the sand. The view from my room was as it had always been. I was the one that was different. The fundraiser the other night had changed everything. There was no more pretending to myself anymore. Charlie Devlin had been in the yellow barn that Sunday in June. I knew that now and that's not all I knew. This was no longer just about me not wanting to tell. It was about me not wanting to be found out.

"YOU HAVEN'T BEEN SENTENCED to your room, you know, Riddle," my mother said, referring to my increasingly strange love affair with solitary confinement. My life as I knew it had stopped. My training regimen fell apart. I was riding only sporadically. Mostly I had begun to hang around the house in a stupor, a self-imposed state of disgrace, which my mother viewed as a grave indicator of the state of my character.

In this and all other matters, big and small, she wasn't inclined to keep her thoughts to herself. "Slouching churlishly toward depression by way of dodgy personal hygiene and potato chip crumbs in the sheets doesn't exactly bode well for your future prospects," she called out after me as I followed the familiar flight pattern to the third floor.

For an exuberant elitist such as Greer, whose tongue seemed to lead an independent, terrifying life of its own, scorching the earth daily, my abrupt refusal to leave my bedroom, my unwashed hair, generalized dreariness, the dramatic shuttering of my social life, alarmed her more than if I had started coughing up blood.

Grabbing the morning newspapers on the few occasions that I ventured forth from my top-floor sanctuary, I spent the first part of every day the same way, scouring in vain for references to Charlie Devlin.

"Is she mentally ill? Is that the problem?" From where I sat reading in the living room, I overhead my mother talking to my father in the kitchen.

"Remember Harriet Townsend's boy? He locked himself in his bedroom for months and when he finally emerged he announced to everyone that he was a werewolf. Though with that underbite, I dare say he was one."

"Greer, she's just turned thirteen years old. She's a little moody. It comes with the territory. Anyway, she's a different type than you. She's contemplative. She's more intellectual, introverted. People like Riddle need a lot of downtime."

"Perhaps I delude myself, but I like to think that my intellect, inadequate though it may be, isn't adversely affected by my attention to personal appearance or my aversion to grunting as a form of communication. I have it on good authority that you don't need to be melancholy to be considered an intellectual—though undoubtedly it helps."

"Don't be so hard on her. Give her some space. You're going to have to face the fact that you and Riddle are two very different people. You're only going to drive her away if you don't learn how to respect your differences."

My heart warmed to hear my father take up my cause.

"Riddle and I are more alike than you know, though right at the moment it pains me to concede the resemblance."

"Back at you," I said, walking into the kitchen, raw and conspicuous, bruising the air around me. "I'm nothing at all like you."

"Oh, good, I see that you've finally decided to rise from the dead," my mother said, unfazed by my eavesdropping or my black-and-blue attitude. She was leaning against the counter, watching my father as he sat at the kitchen table looking over some documents. "Just in time, too. You can walk over to Gin's with me." She smiled slyly.

I popped open the refrigerator door and, leaning forward, pretended to search for something to eat. "No. I don't want to go to Gin's. I hate spending time with you and your wicked stepsister."

My father looked up and laughed. "Nothing wrong with her powers of observation," he said, directing his comments to my mother, who ignored him in favor of continuing to harass me.

"Well, unfortunately for you, you're not living in a democracy so you don't get to decide. You're coming with me whether you like it or not. Don't worry. It won't interfere with your predilections. That's the one nice thing about pouting, you can do it anywhere."

I pulled out a quart of milk and thumped shut the refrigerator door.

"Why do I have to go? Why can't you just go alone? Gin's your friend, not mine. Anyway, it's not like you enjoy my company."

"It's not as if I enjoy your company," she corrected. "Misery loves company, or hadn't you heard? If I have to go, then you have to go. Now put on your best scowl and let's get this over with. I don't want to hear any more about it."

"Why do you have to go? What's the big deal? Since when do you do anything you don't want to do?" I said, attempting to annoy her by drinking directly from the carton.

"I don't understand you. You've gone from spending all your free time over there to never setting foot on the place. Did something happen? Good God, Riddle, if you tell me that Gin asked about your bra size . . ."

"No! Jesus! Mother!" I banged the milk carton down on the table. "How many times do I have to tell you? Nothing happened." I was squeezing the carton in my hand so hard that milk squirted out of the open spout. I gripped it tighter, wishing it were a grenade, milk running down my fingers. "Why does everything around here have to turn into the Spanish Inquisition?" Winding up, I pitched the carton against the wall, its contents spurting across the room and streaming onto the floor, the dogs rushing in as a single unit, delighted to fulfill the role of cleanup crew.

"That reminds me, Camp," my mother said, "I'd like a Judas chair for Christmas this year." She paused to consider the noisy slurping of the basset hounds as they lapped up the deepening puddle of milk in the middle of the room, then turned her attention back to me.

"Is this something Midol can handle?" I gasped in horror and reflexively looked over at my father, who thoughtfully feigned deafness. "Or shall I put in a call to the Vatican for an exorcist?"

"Jimmy, you don't need to go if you don't want to go," my father said.

"I thought you were an advocate of solidarity," my mother said.

"I am," Camp said, looking over at me, grinning.

"Why don't you come, Camp?" I asked him. "I'll go if you go."

"No," he said, his voice pleasant but firm.

"Why?"

"I am not going to the old Devlin farm today, or tomorrow, or ever. Is that clear?" His voice was no longer pleasant, and the firmness had reconfigured into something resembling hostility.

I nodded, protest levels rising within. "Why are you getting mad at me?"

"I'm not angry with you." He took a more moderate tone. "I've got some people coming over this afternoon to go over a few things." He looked at my mother. "This Watergate break-in is picking up a little steam, especially after the *Washington Post* piece the other day. You wait and see, there'll be evidence of Kissinger in a balaclava with a skeleton key in his pocket before this thing is finished."

I was committed to making my case and stubbornly refused to yield the floor. "I don't see why you can decide you don't want to go to Gin's but I still have to. I don't want to go to Gin's either."

"I'm not forcing you to do anything you don't want to do. You're welcome to stay at home with me," he said. "I'll crack open the Ovaltine and we'll get drunk."

"Are you quite finished?" My mother snapped shut her cigarette case, anger clicking tightly into place. "May we get back to the matter at hand? Look, you two, Gin has some tedious secret he's mad to reveal. I promised under duress that I would come. He absolutely insisted." Her white skin was getting pinker by the moment.

Warning. Warning. I braced for the inevitable transition to code red. She threw her hands in the air. "So selfish. I can't abide self-centered people." Her eyes swept the counter, searching for something to decapitate, her ferocious gaze finally focusing on me. I've rarely been more grateful that human heads are not a screw-top design. "Dammit! This is the problem with having friends." She had begun to pace back and forth, puffing away on her cigarette. "It really is too much to be borne. The truth is I need you to come with me, Riddle, so that I can use your inevitable bad behavior as an excuse to leave early, otherwise I will be stuck over there forever."

Camp and I looked at each other and laughed.

She stopped and stared at us. "You should be grateful the rifle is under lock and key upstairs, because if there were guns anywhere within easy reach I would murder both of you."

"Like to see you try it," I said, bolstered by my father's proximity and his expert way with a choke hold.

"Ha! That's my girl," Camp said, reinforcing my uneasy sense that evisceration was the true shortcut to his heart.

Chapter **Fifteen**

———

"**O**H, MY GOD, SO THAT'S WHAT THIS IS ALL ABOUT," MY
mother said, stopping in her tracks as we rounded the stable
corner. Audibly catching her breath, she instinctively reached out
and placed the palm of her hand against my shoulder, stopping me
in mid-stride.

"Wow," she said.

"Wow." For once my mother and I were in perfect agreement.

Directly in front of us in a large grassy paddock was a horse
unlike any horse I had ever seen. Lush and sensuous, half black,
half white, his piebald coat shone in the soft afternoon light. He
was a midsize stallion, showing massive chest, short back and
neatly cleaved apple butt, and had thick legs with long feather-
ing. His head was refined-looking, slightly aquiline in shape, with
short ears. He had a kind, intelligent expression and startling eyes,
one blue eye and one brown. A double mane hung in long wavy
tendrils that reached past his knees. Kicking up his heels, he cantered from one end of the enclosure to the other, his wide, thick
tail so long it dragged on the ground.

"Good Lord, he looks like some sort of pre-Raphaelite paint-
er's version of Ophelia on testosterone," my mother muttered.

"Or Ann-Margret," I said, the prose to my mother's poetry.

"So where is the Son of God? This must be the Second Coming," my mother shouted out to Gin, crisp and shiny and compulsively cheerful, counterfeit as a grapefruit masquerading as an apple. I cringed with embarrassment. It was excruciating to watch my mother pretend happiness for others. Gin, meanwhile, appeared to be levitating as he approached, near deranged levels of enthusiasm lifting him several inches off the ground. He made me think of one of those flying monkeys in *The Wizard of Oz*.

"It is! It is! Isn't he wonderful? I haven't the words. I can't believe it. Isn't he the most beautiful thing you have ever set eyes on?"

Gin opened the paddock door and stepped inside as his dream horse trotted over to greet him. Closing his eyes, he locked his arms around the horse's neck, burying his face in its long mane, peering at us through the thick curling tendrils, his ecstatic face framed on every side by that waterfall of hair. "Whatever happened to Baby Jane?" my mother asked as we stood watching Gin stroke the horse's legs and back, in ways both intimate and sensuous, in what I can only describe as being three of the most uncomfortable moments I've ever spent.

"Any more of this display, Gin, and I'll be reporting you to the relevant authorities," Greer said before commenting, "Yes, he is nice," her arm extended, calling out to Gin's prize. It was the closest she had come in a long time to anything resembling a ringing endorsement.

"Nice? Is that the best you can do? Don't you want to know all about him? Aren't you dying, Greer? Oh, I can see it in your face. You are so jealous! I can't stand it!" Gin was so giddy he was about to make the existential leap from human being to Silly Putty.

"So I take it this is the great secret? Another horse?" my mother asked.

"Not just another horse, Greer. A Gypsy horse. The only one in all of North America."

"Where did he come from?" I asked.

"Ireland. That's where I first saw them. In a farmer's field. These marvelous horses, piebalds and skewbalds and chocolate palominos. I thought for a moment that I had stumbled into a fairy tale. The farmer was an Irish traveler. In the warm months he lived with his family in a horse-drawn caravan. He used to winter on a deserted farm by the ocean near the Cliffs of Moher. Honestly, Jimmy, these horses, they call them Irish tinkers, Gypsy cobs or Gypsy horses. They looked as if they'd descended to earth on a cloud.

"The Gypsies have been breeding them and trading them among themselves for years. They're a very secretive bunch and they distrust Gorgios—that's you and me, by the way. That's what they call anyone who isn't a Gypsy . . ."

"I suspect Riddle is a Gypsy at heart," my mother interrupted, lighting up a cigarette.

"Gula and I went to Appleby this year—that's the real reason I went to the UK. Gula offered to help me finally make this dream of acquiring a breeding pair come true. I intend to establish the breed in North America."

"Appleby is the great Gypsy horse fair in England," my mother explained.

"That horse is pure pornography."

My mother and I both looked up at the sound of an unfamiliar voice, startled to see someone else emerge from within the stable.

"You scared me!" I gasped, hand at my heart.

"My, you're jumpy these days, Jimmy," Gin said.

"Harry Devlin, what would a good Catholic boy like you know about pornography?" my mother said, deftly concealing any surprise she might have felt seeing him there.

Harry laughed. "Let's just say that I know it when I see it."

"What are you doing here?" I asked as I climbed onto the top rung of the fence, my legs dangling over the side.

"Riddle, you shouldn't be so direct," Gin said. "It's, well, I don't know. What is it, Greer?"

"An expression of true feeling," she said. "You always did have a morbid fear of authenticity."

"What's wrong with being direct?" Harry asked, hopping up on the fence and sitting next to me. "I don't mind." He grinned over at me as I reluctantly returned his smile.

Having him in such proximity, I suddenly felt in dire need of a blood transfusion. Harry was a living reminder of all that tormented me. The war between our fathers only magnified my discomfort.

"I wasn't aware that you and Gin even knew each other," my mother said, glaring over at Gin, who deliberately looked elsewhere.

"I guess you don't know everything," Gin said, staring down at the ground. "Gula and I were at the horse show in Rhode Island in the spring and I was so taken with Harry. He was riding Hal. Love that horse!" He looked up and clapped his hands over his mouth, immediately aware of the nuclear scope of his faux pas. "Oh!" Choking, Gin looked stricken as my mother's lips curled in antipathy, revealing the vulpine flash of grinding teeth. I could have sworn that I heard the low rumble of a growl deep in her throat.

She was violently offended by any mention of a horse-and-rider combination that didn't reference her. Gin coughed and backtracked, trying to choke down the radiation emanating from his atomic blunder. "Anyway, I was so impressed," he sputtered weakly. "Harry is such a . . . such a . . . competent rider." He was beginning to sound apologetic, drooping pathetically, like a daisy under direct assault by the sun. "I've known Michael for ages so I decided to approach his boy. Isn't it marvelous to see Harry back on the estate where his father grew up? Seems so right somehow."

He beamed at his young protégé. "Can't you just see Michael when you look at him, Greer? Doesn't it remind you of when we were all so young and beautiful and glamorous and brilliant? The dances. The parties. The world at our feet. No thought of what was to come."

"Good God, Gin, beautiful? Brilliant? You weighed all of sixty pounds and had alopecia for years. Glamorous? Your second name is Mary, for Christ's sake!"

"Greer, you know perfectly well it's a family name," Gin protested.

She turned away from Gin and directed her remarks to Harry and me. "He was so terrified of being drafted that his hair fell out and he stopped eating! I volunteered to shoot him in the foot but he was afraid I'd accidentally put a bullet between his eyes instead." She swiveled back around to confront Gin as Harry laughed out loud.

"Sorry," he said to Gin, who flapped his hand dismissively.

"Never mind. Lord knows I'm used to Greer by now. And just so you know, everyone used to say that I was the image of Roddy McDowall when I was young."

" 'Everyone' meaning your mother," Greer chirped.

"Who's Roddy McDowall?" I asked.

"Cornelius," my mother said. "Dr. Zaius! Dr. Zaius!"

"Ohhhh!" Gin, deflating like a punctured tire, emitted a long and loud exhalation of breath before resuming. "Where was I? Ah, yes, Harry makes the decades disappear, watching him walking up the driveway, the very image of Michael, well, I could feel the years peeling away."

Obviously tired of being spoken about in the third person,

Harry interjected. "Gin told me he was importing this fantastic horse. He asked me if I would work with him."

"It was Gula's idea, Harry has so much experience with show jumping," Gin said, looking around trying to recruit cheerleaders, unmindful that his seemingly innocent declaration had tripped all of my internal warning devices. I was going off like a police siren.

"Oh, really, has he? Why didn't you ask me? Or Riddle for that matter?" Greer demanded.

I wished I could disappear. Blunt as an anvil, as usual. Had this woman never heard of passive aggression?

Harry spoke up. "I don't want to cause any trouble here. I'll step aside, no problem."

"No!" I blurted out with more force than I intended. "No. You mustn't. Please."

I had no desire to work with Gin's new horse. Harry could have his new assignment and the association with Gula that would surely come along with it.

My desperation was disproportionate enough to cause three sets of eyebrows to simultaneously shoot skyward. Harry attempted to speak and then stopped himself. A look of fleeting terror crossed his face as he scanned the immediate area. He was obviously stricken and contemplating a means of escape, fearful that I was about to wrap myself around his leg and beg him to marry me.

"It would seem that Riddle skipped the chapter on playing hard to get," my mother said, at which point, already in the active stages of dying, I entered a long narrow tunnel, blinding white light beckoning to me from the beyond. Clutching at my throat, grip tightening, unable to speak, emitting a range of herky-jerky snorts and croaks that sounded something like a dog in a fit of reverse sneezing, I briefly wondered if it was possible to strangle yourself.

"I don't appreciate being overlooked, Gin," my mother said,

getting back to the matter that most concerned her, my imminent demise being at the end of a long line of other priorities. Staring dumbly at the ground, I felt the light, comforting touch of Harry's hand on my back. Looking up, I was relieved to see him smiling as if we were both in on the joke.

I smiled back at him and, looking into his face, felt a pang, my heart prolonging a beat, making its resonant point, like a sustained poignant note on a piano. He and Charlie looked so much alike that I was having trouble making the distinction between them. For a moment, I allowed myself to believe that he was Charlie, that I had somehow wished Charlie back to life with the power of my regret.

"What's going on?" Harry said, conscious of my intense scrutiny. "My mascara running?"

"Oh, Greer, you know how much you loathe time commitments." Gin was attempting to dig himself out. "I wouldn't dream of imposing on your freedom. It's taken me days just to get you over here for the unveiling."

"Well, he can't jump," my mother said, drawing circles within circles on the ground with her riding crop, redirecting the conversation. "That is painfully obvious from looking at him."

"Not so fast, Greer," Gin said. "These Gypsy horses can do it all."

"Gin, I know a jumper when I see one. That horse is not a jumper."

"Well, what does it matter? If he can't, he can't. We'll see. That's what Harry is here for. Jumping isn't the world, Greer." Gin was growing impatient. Trying to chart the highs and lows of Gin's vast range of emotions over the course of a few seconds would have stumped Magellan. "A fruit fly among men," Camp called him.

My mother, in thrall always to the dissonant moment, reached into her jacket pocket and withdrew her cigarette case as Gin's eyes watered and widened. He was visibly overheating. She lit up, her cigarette elegantly emblematic of her subversion, and, taking a deep drag, she blew smoke into the air, each ghostly puff dangling at eye level, daring Gin to object.

He had been doing a slow burn, but now he had reached the point of explosion. Pop! I could see the kernels exploding all around me. Pop! Pop!

"Greer, for heaven's sake!"

"Don't even think about it," my mother warned, giving him a vicious sideways glance.

Fortunately, Gin's brain continued to flit about from tree to tree, rarely settling anywhere for more than a few seconds. "Oh, look, here he is," he said, pointing. "The man of the hour. Gula! Hurry! The show's about to start." Gin was frantically waving in Gula's direction, urging him to join us.

"Lock up the silverware," my mother stage-whispered to Harry, who seemed to be enjoying her irreverence. With a deep sigh, she turned around to greet the new arrival. Harry, following her lead, did the same. I was the last to follow suit—my neck, my head, my eyes, all actively ignoring my brain's instructions to engage. It was as if, on hearing Gula's name spoken, all that's automatic about being alive—moving, breathing, seeing, hearing—had shuddered to a halt.

Ignoring Gin's admonition to be quick, Gula was walking slowly and methodically toward us, morphing into something that crawled toward me on all fours in an undulatory prowl, zig-zagging, yellow tongue darting, drooling with expectation, dripping poison, my world and the people in it growing smaller and narrower as with every step forward he gained in intensity and momentum and power until finally he was all I could see.

His attention was on me, the fierce unblinking intensity of his gaze holding me in place like an unspoken threat.

"Gula, you remember Harry, Michael Devlin's son," Gin

said. "You met him the night of the fundraiser. We watched him ride at . . ."

"Yes," he said, extending his hand, cutting off Gin. "I remember you. A wonderful way with a horse."

"I understand we have you to thank for this guy," Harry said, jumping from the top of the fence down to the ground, indicating with a nod the Gypsy stallion, as their hands briefly locked. "Well done."

I drew solace from the familiar formal melody of his private-school boy's lilting patois even as I suppressed the urge to make fun.

"Yes, well . . ." Gula said, averting his gaze, his eyes shooting about and finally settling on my mother and me. He nodded and withdrew his hand from Harry's friendly clasp. Was I the only one to notice that he wiped a flattened palm on his pants?

"Hello, Gula," my mother said, avoiding any sort of direct contact.

"Yes, yes." He just kept nodding. "Then there's you," he said, pointing to me. "Hello, little partner."

"Hi," I said, choking out a greeting. Partner? The tension between us was so palpable it provoked comment from my mother.

"What's all this about?" she asked, looking as puzzled as her nature would permit.

Gula's mouth contorted into a grotesque impersonation of delight. "Should I tell her?" he said.

I could hardly hear him over the din and clatter of all my internal organs in screaming collision with one another. Staring back at him, practically blithering, I scrambled to regain my equilibrium. My voice box went into spasm as I felt my throat close up.

"Tell her what?" my mother demanded.

"Nothing. It was nothing. Young people. I found her in the stable with a boy. It was the day of the fire. I told her I would keep her little secret."

What was he doing? I looked down at my feet and watched

as an invisible snake wrapped itself around my legs, my waist, my torso, squeezing the life out of me.

"I think it would be fun to let it out. No harm now. Well, she has probably told you herself. Girls this age cannot keep secrets."

"Riddle? What boy? What is he talking about?" My mother started firing off questions in brisk, purposeful succession as if she was skeet shooting and I was a plate that needed shattering.

"I . . ." I looked at all those pairs of eyes focused on my face and I could not speak.

"Didn't you say he was a boy you went to school with? You showed him the foals. He wanted to see the babies and so you showed him. Then he left. Wasn't that the story?" Gula asked me.

I looked into his eyes and I nodded.

"Oh, my God! What's this? You never mentioned anything about some boy. Now we have some strange boy on the premises doing heaven knows what?" Gin said.

Was it my imagination or was Harry looking at me funny?

"Hair like his," Gula said, pointing to a stray pile of desiccated leaves trapped at the bottom of a rotting fence post. "Same color. A bit like Harry's. Like autumn or like smoldering fire."

"Like fire? Jesus, there's a Freudian twist if ever I've heard one!" Gin proclaimed.

"Poor choice of words," Gula said. "Anyway, this is the girl with the fire-colored hair," he said, pointing to me. "This hair could cause a conflagration." He laughed. I examined the faces around me. Was I the only one drowning in all that slyness?

"What's his name, Riddle? I demand to know," my mother said.

"I forget his name," I said, speaking so softly that everyone leaned in to hear me. "He was just some boy."

"Just some boy," Gula echoed. "Not important. That's right. That's how it seemed to me. A boy who didn't matter at all."

"Everyone matters," Gin corrected, master of the meaningless.

"Thank you, Pope Paul," my mother said.

"Yes, of course," Gula said, simultaneously solemn and ridiculous. "I meant only that he was harmless. A nice boy. The situation was benign." Gula laughed.

"So you were alone in a stable with a boy you either can't—or refuse to—identify, a boy you met in secret, a boy who appeared and disappeared on the same day as the fire," my mother said, looking me over as if she was meeting me for the first time. She paused to consider for a moment, the three men watching her intently as she smoked and thought. "All right, then," she said, abruptly dismissing the whole matter, her expression visibly lightening. Even to the least astute observer—that would be Gin—it was obvious that she'd never been more proud.

"Like mother, like daughter," Gin said, striking out in lame fashion. It was a ludicrous thought, or so I assumed. My mother had led me to believe that our toaster had a more interesting sexual history than she did.

"Sexual preoccupation is endemic to adolescence. Among adults, it's symptomatic of mental retardation," she used to say. As for me, the closest I had ever come to a romantic entanglement occurred when one of the basset hounds pinned me down on the sofa and licked ice cream from my face.

"Funny, I used the identical expression just the other day to describe you and Mirabel," she shot back at Gin as Harry unsuccessfully tried to conceal a laugh.

"All right, Greer. It was just a joke. You know how to laugh, don't you? Anyway, I don't know how happy I am about this news concerning some mysterious boy," Gin said, continuing to pout.

"Now we know," my mother said, briskly uncaring. "As for me, I can think of nothing less interesting than the activities of children, secret or otherwise." She prodded Gin in another direction: "So what's this Gypsy horse's name?"

"Zindelo," Gin said. "A traditional Romany name. Don't you just love it?"

"No, I dislike it intensely. Too blatantly ethnic. It makes him sound positively Polish. If you're going for a Gypsy theme, there are other more apt choices. What about Pickpocket? Grifter?"

"Jesus," Harry said, looking at Gula and trying to discern his reaction.

"Greer, you are incorrigible," Gin said.

"I haven't a clue what you're talking about," she said. "Gula's not a child. He's an adult. Adults have no business being offended."

"It's bad luck to change a horse's name," Gula said, ignoring my mother's obvious insults.

"I'd risk it," she said. "Zindelo creates the impression that he just cleared inspection at Ellis Island."

Gin looked worried. "Oh dear, Greer may have a point."

Gula's eyes darkened. He smiled. "Why not let young Mr. Devlin name him? Maybe that will remove the curse of ethnicity."

"See? Not offended in the least. I applaud your sophistication, Gula." My mother's condescension was her art. She applied it in thick oily dabs, everyone she met a potential canvas.

"Oh, I like that idea. What say you, Harry?" Gin was mere decibels from squealing.

Harry, simple snaffle bridle in hand, bemused and polite, looking as if he had inadvertently stumbled down the rabbit hole, shook his head slightly and shot me a glance, both amused and empathetic, before answering.

"Thanks, but I think Greer should do the honors. It was her idea." He bent over to adjust his boot and whispered to me on the way down, ". . . and I don't give a flying fuck."

"Yes, fine. Greer, what do you suggest?" Gin's voice sounded strained. He yawned and licked his lips. I knew what was coming next. "I'm exhausted," he said.

"You were born exhausted," my mother said, making us wait as she lit a cigarette and considered her options. "Boomslang," she said. "What about Boomslang?"

"I love it . . . I think . . ." Gin said, stealing a glance at my mother, using all of his limited powers of deduction to determine her true intent. The simultaneous shift of her shoulder and eyebrow was enough to persuade him that she wasn't testing him just so she could subsequently ridicule him.

"It's fun to say," Harry said. "I like it. What does it mean? Where did you come up with that?"

"The boomslang is a venomous snake," my mother said. "Deadly. Secretive. Hard to detect. Patient. Lies in wait. Mercifully unsentimental."

"Oh, my," Gin said. "I'm not sure I like that."

"I do," my mother said, as if her approval was all that counted. "You want him to be taken seriously, don't you? He's beautiful, Gin, but there is such a thing as being too beautiful, you know. You don't want him to be self-parodying."

"Boomslang it is, then," Gin proclaimed, trying to make it sound as if it was his decision.

"Good," Harry said. "Now maybe I can do what I came here to do and ride this fantastic horse of yours."

"Where's your saddle?" I asked him.

He waved me off, dismissing the idea. "Saddles are for girls," he said as I bristled. We all watched him pop over the fence and introduce himself to Boomslang with a carrot he pulled from his jeans pocket. He took his time fitting the bridle, all the while talking to the horse as its ears flicked responsively. With reins in one hand, the other hand gripping that Veronica Lake–style mane, Harry hoisted himself onto the stallion's short, thick back and spent several minutes hacking around the paddock's outside perimeter, circling several jumps that were set up in the middle of the large ring.

Horses are not natural jumpers; left to their own devices they prefer a flight pattern free of obstacles. Horses run on the straight-away; they leap over objects that get in their way only because they have no choice. I was still sitting on the top rung of the pad-dock, Gin standing next to me, the two of us riveted by Harry and Boomslang as they smoothly looped in and around the ring. Gula and my mother were talking together, an incongruous coupling— Satan and Morgan le Fay in terrifying conference—the two of them watching from beneath the big oak tree a few yards away.

A rider like Harry makes other riders jealous. He sure as hell made my mother jealous. It was so obvious she might as well have hired a plane and written her invidious feelings across the sky in green smoke. She was smiling too much, for one thing, and hum-ming, for another. My mother always hummed when she was most annoyed.

"Snakes rattle, dogs growl, your mother hums," Camp said of her propensity for offering up a musical prelude before launching a full-scale attack.

Boomslang was approaching a small jump in a controlled but brisk canter. Just as he hit the conventional takeoff point, he hesi-tated and appeared to stop; at the same time, Gula, watching from the sidelines, suddenly, forcibly called out Harry's name. Unpre-pared for the horse's peculiar stalling tactic, Harry, who looked up spontaneously at the call of his name, went sailing straight into the jump, made crashing contact and landed with a loud thud on his hip, then tumbled onto his knees.

"Oh, sorry," Gula said, walking quickly toward me, my mother following. "I just wanted to warn him about the horse."

"I'm okay," Harry said, dusting himself off as he reached for my hand and I helped pull him to his feet.

"Ouch," he said, trying to put his full weight on both feet. "That hurts."

He unself-consciously unzipped his jeans and, letting them fall to his knees, turned his neck and inclined his head to check out the damage. The side of his leg, his knee and his left hip were badly scraped and had already begun to change color. For that matter, so had I.

"Harry, pull up your pants," my mother said. "For heaven's sake, consider Riddle."

"You're lucky that you don't have more than the sight of my ass to complain about," Harry said, surprising everyone with his authority.

My mother checked herself. "I'm sorry, Harry. Gula was just telling me that Boomslang has an eccentric approach . . ."

"Yes, this is my fault. I didn't know you were going to attempt a jump. I should have mentioned his, what do you call it, tic?" Gula's apology was spectacularly unconvincing.

"I think I could've figured that out on my own, thanks. Jesus, what were you thinking?" Harry wasn't fooling around. Where was the mannerly, manageable private-school boy?

"Forgive me, Harry. I assure you that I had your best interests at heart. I was trying to warn you. It was a stupid thing to do. Right reason, wrong deed," Gula offered up with a shrug, turning the familiar maxim on its head.

"Yeah, it was stupid, all right," Harry said. He reached down and hitched his pants back up. He seemed to relent a little. "Forget it. I'm okay."

"I want you to see the doctor. Gula, get Fiona Roberts on the phone," Gin said. "Your father will have my head over this."

"I don't need a doctor," Harry said. "It's only a bruise. No big deal. What do you think I'm going to do, run home and tell my old man I fell on the playground? You're not my babysitter."

"Anyone who rides can expect to fall occasionally," my mother said. "It's what we sign on for, after all." She wrapped her arm around Harry's waist. "Here, let me help you into the house. It's the least I can do."

"Thanks, but I don't need any help," Harry said, taking a step forward.

But he did need help and Gula stepped up to offer his shoulder for Harry to lean on.

"Are you coming, Riddle?" My mother, who had been following the men, stopped and looked back at me as I watched them from beneath the oak tree.

"In a minute," I said.

"Suit yourself."

THE SOLES OF MY boots chipped away at the ground, a pattern of scrapes leaving their mark in the clay. Boomslang cantered alongside the paddock fence, mane and tail blowing, the only sound the thud of his hooves beating out a rhythm on the hard clay track.

The screen door opened and banged shut. I looked up. Gula was standing on the porch watching me, not speaking. We stared at each other, both of us silent and expressionless, sepulchral stillness filling the air like incense, conjoining us, seeping into my brain, this taciturn partnership of ours a kind of ceremonial dirge.

A groundhog popped out of his hole. He was shouting, a series of discordant cries shattering the silence, taut and strained, his ordinary vocalizations breaking down, degenerating into a long litany of fearful calling. He was sending out a warning to the other animals: predator. I looked around and saw the gray outline of a coyote on the edge of the forest. Boomslang snorted and whinnied. The birds overhead shrieked.

When I was little, I thought that evil was something that made noise when it approached, that rumbled the way thunder does in the humid seconds before the universe lights up. I imagined that every bad thing had its own deafening sound track, drums and brass section rudely memorializing the thump of each wicked heartbeat. So where were the cymbals? Where were the trumpets? Where was the driving bass line to sound the alarm?

Looking back at the house, I couldn't see Gula at all anymore. By my silence I had made him invisible.

Chapter **Sixteen**

"**I**'M NOT GOING TO SAY IT AGAIN. I DON'T WANT RIDDLE ANY-where near the Devlin boy. Is that clear?"

My parents' bedroom was on the floor beneath mine. It was late at night when a turbid rumbling from below rattled my bed frame and shook me from sleep. I crept down onto the second-floor landing. The old herringbone floors were cool against my bare feet as I stood, poised to dash, listening in my nightgown outside their door. A recording of *The Threepenny Opera*—my father's great favorite—played faintly in the background, needle bouncing and skipping over the album's furrowed surface.

"For God's sake, Camp, you're being ridiculous," my mother said, her tone detached, deliberately sounding the cool counterpoint to my father's overcooked fury. It was part of the pattern—an annoying technique, one of many in her vast emotional repertoire—and specifically designed to drive my father to the outer limits of his anger, at which point he would smash something and my mother would feel justified in bursting into flames.

"Don't be so goddamn insulting. I'm not Gin, all right? I'm not your lap dog."

"You can't be serious. Who cares about Gin? What does he have to do with anything?"

"Well, finally we agree about something. We're making progress. So. For the last time, I won't have my daughter spending time with Michael Devlin's son. Do you hear me?"

"I'm sure they can hear you in Russia. What is your problem? Harry is nineteen years old. Riddle is thirteen. He doesn't know she's alive. They don't even move in the same circles. For that matter, Riddle doesn't have a circle."

"And thank God she doesn't."

"Oh, here we are, as usual, the point in the argument where you deride me as some sort of shallow socialite obsessed with Max Factor and cabana boys."

"Don't be absurd."

I shut my eyes, dreading what was to come. My mother was operating at full throttle.

"I'm sorry that I didn't drive a tank through the Ardennes, Camp. Or hurtle myself screaming and firing onto the beaches of Normandy, if for no other reason than you might take me seriously as a human being. News flash: the war is over. You're threatening to become like one of those Japanese soldiers still dug in in the Pacific, refusing to bow to the inevitable. I'd raise my white flag and surrender but I'm sure you'd shoot me on the spot."

"Shut up. Do you hear me? I'm so sick of listening to you. You don't know what the hell you're talking about. Shut up!"

"Shut up? Is that your father speaking? I've been waiting for him to make an appearance. Seems I never have to wait very long."

There was a short silence as my father considered his next step. He didn't enjoy being compared to his father, a man who once bragged to me that he chased down a deer until its heart exploded. I braced myself for one of only two alternatives, pitched battle or appeasement. My parents never did seek out middle ground.

"All right, all right. That was uncalled for." My father struggled for control; the accompanying strain penetrated the walls. "I'm sorry. This is getting us nowhere. Let's keep our eye on the ball and not get derailed into making petty attacks on each other." He cleared his throat and took a deep breath. "I don't want my daughter around Michael's son for many reasons. I assumed you'd feel the same way. Listen, I don't want to fight with you. We are on a joint mission. We're soldiers in a just cause—the cause being us, our family. You. Me. Riddle. Everyone else is extraneous. It's important to keep that in mind if we are to succeed."

"Camp, please. This isn't some sort of debriefing."

"Greer, for Christ's sake, why are we going to war about some kid that neither one of us gives a damn about?"

"It's not Harry Devlin that I'm concerned with. It's the circumstance. It's the awkward situation in which you put me. Gin and I are friends."

"That's news to everyone, including him, I'm sure," my father interrupted.

"I've known him forever. We share a number of common interests, horses being chief among them. Riddle shares the same interest, in case you hadn't noticed. What am I supposed to do? Gin's recruited Harry to ride for him. The boy has been a gentleman. Speaking of circumstances, have you forgotten his? He just lost his brother, or so it would appear. What do I do, pull out a shotgun and order him the hell off Gin's property? Demand that he stay away from our daughter, someone he barely knows?"

"That could change. You said yourself that she has a crush on the kid."

Were they idiots? Part of me wanted to kick the door in and confront both of them. For the last time, I do not have a crush on Harry Devlin.

"Remind me never to confide in you again. I thought you would be amused. How wrong could I be, by the way? You're obviously determined, for some primal reason, to play the part of the Neanderthal father. Well, don't worry, I assure you, your little princess is quite safe from the big bad bachelor boy. Since we're on the topic, would it really be such a disaster for Riddle to marry well someday? Are you so opposed to our daughter aligning herself with money and influence and power? How can such a combination hurt the Camperdown cause? Whatever the hell that may be."

"It's whatever I decide it is, wherever my ambition takes me," my father said unpleasantly. I wrapped my arms around myself. I was shivering. "A few years in the House of Representatives, then a Senate bid, then who knows? The less we have to do with the Devlins in any shape or form, the better it is for everyone. Michael is no friend of mine. He'd like nothing better than to cut me off at the knees. The less he's reminded of that, the better. Don't forget that goddamn book of his isn't going away any time soon."

"I know Michael Devlin very well. Revenge isn't his style. It would mean that he would have to take time away from the pursuit of his favorite pastime, himself. You exaggerate your importance to him, Camp."

"You're right, but you're wrong, too. His beef with me is tied up with how he views himself. Devlin's on a moral crusade, or so he thinks." His tone changed as he broadened his attack. "Boy, that guy has got some nerve. Every cent he has, everything he owns, came to him by way of the blood, sweat and tears of the workers his family exploited over generations."

My mother wasn't buying it.

"Time to change your tune, Camp. That's not what's bothering you and you know it. I think I liked you better when you were a struggling composer with no prospects."

My father's laughter struck a sour note. "Bullshit, you did."

"Oh, for heaven's sake, this is such a stupid conversation. I can't believe we're having it." My mother had decided to put a swift end to things. Her strategy, typically, was to demean the topic at hand, by branding it the province of nitwits. "Harry is footloose and fancy free and the most eligible young man in the country. The Seven Sisters are working round the clock to grind out an assembly line of girls whose parents would love nothing better than for them to fall prey to Harry Devlin's worst intentions. In other words, Camp, his cookie jar spilleth over. Whatever would make you think he's slavering after Riddle?"

Her other preferred tactic was to debase me, though I had long since ceased to take it personally. Gin used to joke that the two of us should be reconfigured as punching bags.

"Oh, that's a charming touch. That'll win you Mother of the Year. Denigrating your own daughter while elevating Michael's brat. He'd be lucky to get her."

"Well, of course, he would, I only mean . . ."

"I don't give a damn what you mean. I don't like Michael. I detest the Devlins and all they stand for. I couldn't care less about this boy and his circumstances. You're scraping the bottom of the barrel with that family. Jesus, you know that better than anyone."

"I don't want to talk about it anymore. You're being impossible."

"That figures. Too painful to discuss—or so you would have everyone believe. Michael humiliates you in front of the whole world, leaves you standing at the altar, flowers drooping, both figuratively and literally . . ."

My mother gasped. "How dare you?"

I could hardly believe what I had heard.

"I'm supposed to sit with my thumb in my mouth all these years, satisfied to play the role of second choice and second best."

"Not this self-pitying nonsense again."

"Let me stop the performance right now. I know it by heart.

I think it's time to introduce some new material into a tired old scene. You and I both know that if Michael were to show the slightest interest in you you'd set a new land speed record in your scramble to leave me for him."

"Oh, please, if only that were true. This has nothing to do with me and Michael. This has everything to do with you and Michael. Stop pretending otherwise."

"The Ballad of Mack the Knife" played along in soft, menacing accompaniment to their argument.

"You don't know what you're talking about."

"The hell I don't. Oh!" She raised her voice in exasperation, leveling a familiar charge. "Will the bloody war never end? Let him do his worst. It's your word against his."

"And you think that is an uncomplicated scenario?"

"What could be more straightforward than an impasse?"

"All right," my father said, challenge implicit in his tone. "You think it's so simple. Let me ask you something. Who do you believe?"

"Oh, my God. This is such a waste of time."

"Answer me. It's not complicated. That's what you said. So who do you believe? Me or Michael?"

Who do you believe about what? What were my parents talking about?

It was so quiet I could hear the needle scratching roughly against the vinyl.

Chapter Seventeen

———

"**G**ODDAMN IT," MY MOTHER SAID, SLAMMING DOWN THE phone just as I walked into the kitchen. "It never ends."

"What's going on?" I asked her, pausing in the doorway, already regretting the day's first encounter, the murky steam of cigarette smoke and coffee curdling the air.

"Oh, I could just scream. That was Gin. It seems that Harry Devlin has some knee strain or bruised hip or something from his fall from Boomslang the other day." She reached for her purse from the kitchen table and pulled out her cigarette lighter, agitatedly flipping it open, then shut, her annoyance clicking away rhythmically.

"That's too bad," I said, taking a couple of tiny steps backward, trying to execute a subtle withdrawal, tripping over a raised edge of floorboard.

"Much ado about nothing. He just needs to stay off it for a day or so. He's a healthy lad, he'll get over it. You'd think from the fuss that his spinal cord had been severed. I broke my arm on a trail ride and never batted an eye. Kept right on to the end."

"Okay," I said, wondering where all this was leading. My mother was opening and closing drawers, the drawers getting stuck because of her reckless handling. She rattled and banged, trying to push them back into place.

"Calm down," I said. I couldn't believe she was getting so angry over something so insignificant.

"Gin thinks we should take him something, cookies or some damn thing. For God's sake, where am I supposed to get cookies? Where is Lou when I need her? Wouldn't you know it would be her day off? Just one day, one carefree day, that's all I ask." Wringing her hands, she looked to the skies. "Why me, O Lord? Wait—where do you think you're going?" Motion detectors fully operational despite her radiating self-immersion, she caught wind of my exit strategy.

"Down to the stable," I stammered unconvincingly, one foot out of the kitchen. "Mary needs grooming."

"Oh no, you're not escaping that easily. The horses are fine. I took care of them myself earlier this morning. If I have to make a pilgrimage to Truro then you're coming with me. You can't expect me to face the Devlins alone."

"You mean we're going to the Devlin house?" I said, immediately intrigued, a combination of panic and curiosity subverting my typical default posture of recalcitrance.

"Gin is swinging by in an hour to pick us up. Go get ready and for God's sake do something with that hair. It looks as if you stuck your finger in an electrical outlet. And put on a dab of lipstick, Riddle. You're reaching an age where a little help is in order."

She squinted over at me, taking a closer look. "Is it my imagination, or are you even paler than usual?"

I started down the hallway and toward the stairs, stopped, turned around, and then walked back to where she stood in the kitchen. "Does Camp know where we're going?"

"Your father left for Boston earlier this morning. Some meeting among giants." My mother, avoiding my gaze, casually sifted through the mail. She had obviously decided to defy my father's edict concerning Harry Devlin. Putting down the letters and ignoring their careless drift onto the floor, she started opening individual cupboards, launching a scant investigation of their contents, banging shut their doors, then reopening them again. "What the hell can I take this kid?" she groused, rooting around until she spied something.

"Pudding mix," she said, inspecting the box in her hand.

"Mom! You can't be serious."

She was busy reading the label, squinting. "Banana flavoring. Good Lord. Who comes up with this stuff? Oh, well. It's fine. Boys like pudding, don't they?" She shrugged and popped the box into her purse and walked away. "I'm going to get dressed."

I looked at her in disbelief. "You're not even going to make it?"

She confronted me head-on, hands on her hips, mouth open, clearly aghast.

"Make it? Are you insane?"

GIN INSISTED ON DRIVING despite my mother's objections, the two of them arguing over his intention to cut down a tract of century-old trees next to his house.

"It's a safety issue, Greer," he moaned.

"You've never been in more danger than you are right now sitting next to me," she said as we arrived at the front door of Alcestis, the Devlin house. I thought of my father. "Living creatures have names," Camp used to say. "Houses have street numbers."

Poised romantically on high ground in a clearing offset by sand dunes, the slate-roofed and gabled residence, a house both long and tall, had a spectacular ocean view. Carefully graded steps carved into the rugged cliff side led to a private sandy beach. Essentially classical in design, Alcestis, built in the early 1800s, was a rare and much prized shell house—made from stone and pebbles and shells collected from along the shoreline. More art piece than standard dwelling, its battered exterior had become more beautiful with age. Its outer walls were the etiolated shade of yellowing newsprint.

I stepped out of the car and along with the sound of crashing surf and the soft noise of the wind blowing in the trees overhead I could hear the tumultuous minor roar of bubbling acid springs— there were several hot springs located near and around the house. My mother was walking ahead of me, pausing to wait while Gin checked his reflection in the visor mirror. She was halfway up the steps when she stopped to look out over the ocean and the beach. The lean lines of Alcestis and the sheer vertical immensity of the tawny cliff framed her as if it were a rugged natural portrait, and for a moment I found it hard to separate my idea of my mother from my idea of the great house that formed the devastating back- drop to a picture I still carry around in my head.

"Well, if it isn't the notorious Irish hooligan Greer Foley, in all her terrible beauty." Michael Devlin, summoned by the sound of our arrival, appeared in the entranceway of his house, wide grin emerging like a counterfeit halo from behind the head of his housekeeper. He stopped and put his hands on her shoulders. "Call the demolition squad, Mrs. Maguire. We have a bomb on- site that needs disarming."

"It's way too late for that," my mother said. "The countdown has already begun."

"In that case," Michael said with a shrug and a smirk, "what a way to go."

"Michael, really, you sound like a used-car salesman," my mother said, to his apparent delight and my ongoing embar- rassment. Having Greer for a mother was like having diabetes, a chronic condition for which there is neither cure nor any painless form of containment. I glanced around, taking in the view, so like an art gallery, white walls and glossy herringbone floors in cherrywood—oh, those herringbone floors, the paintings. Is that what she and Michael shared, a similar aesthetic? There were massive installations of contemporary and traditional paintings on the walls, sunlight streaming into the glazed atrium where an indoor sculpture garden flanked a reflecting pool.

"This must be Riddle!" Michael turned on the high beams, flooding me with the contrived brilliance of his full attention. "Killer intelligence in those eyes," he said. "I hardly dared to wonder what the combination of Greer and Camp would produce. Must say, with all my imaginings I never expected . . ."

"Huckleberry Finn?" my mother supplied.

"Good girl. You know enough to ignore your mother—a rare talent but in your case a useful one. Anyway, you're not what I expected at all."

"What did you expect?" I asked him.

"Horns," he said, looking bemused.

I would say that he was casually dressed, but men such as Michael Devlin never dress casually. In defiance of the aphorism, he really didn't put on his pants one leg at a time the same as the rest of us. We may all be born with three basic layers of skin, but Michael, along with my mother, possessed multiple additional varnish enhancers. Gin and I were a couple of decidedly matte finishes, tragically unadorned when considered against their combined brilliant sheen. It was as if Gable and Lombard had accidentally stumbled into a meeting of Quakers.

Classically handsome, slim but powerfully built, Michael Devlin suggested a panther with his glossy black hair and cobalt blue eyes, his sleek and graceful physicality, dangerous disposition and aggressive intellect. He was restless, always circling, pacing back and forth, rarely sleeping, tail flicking, surveying his kingdom and its tenants from the top of the highest branch of the tallest tree. Harry may have shared some physical similarities with his father—high, broad cheekbones, for one—but the resemblance ended there. Harry was about as feline as a Norwegian elkhound.

"Hello, Michael. Did you forget about me?" Gin said, a slight trace of annoyed resignation in his voice, his face partially obscured by a massive bouquet of white and pink lilies.

"Gin! Hello. Hello! How could I forget you? Wonderful to see you. How are you, my dear friend?" Michael extended both hands, warmly clasping Gin's forearm.

Gin's minor bout of prickliness quickly evaporated, much to my mother's amusement.

"Michael!" He proclaimed our host's name with such gushing subservience that even the housekeeper looked embarrassed.

"Don't forget to curtsy, Gin," my mother said, making Michael laugh out loud.

It was hard to imagine that this amiable man with the big laugh was the same glowering gladiator my father had knocked to the ground mere days before. I searched his face for any sign of sorrow, but Michael Devlin was adept at concealing his private griefs. Schooled in the primacy of sociability, he had absorbed well the lessons of his caste, for whom emotional exhibitionism was the ultimate breach of etiquette.

"And they say having a Labrador retriever makes you feel like a king," my mother said as Gin launched into a rhapsodic review of the house and all its contents. "For heaven's sake, toss the poor creature a bone."

"Does your husband know where you are?' Michael teased, turning all his attention back to my mother. I felt instantly defensive at the mention of Camp.

"I understand women are permitted all kinds of freedoms

these days," she responded. "Now if men could only learn to walk upright."

Gin, acting oblivious, thrust the trembling bouquet of flowers into Michael's chest. "We are just so sorry about Harry and the incident the other day. I've been beside myself over it. How is he?"

"Don't worry about it. These things happen. My biggest problem is keeping him in bed and off his feet. He's had a few health issues over the years and it's hell to get him to do as he should."

"Harry has health problems?" I said.

"Oh, that's right," Gin said, snapping his fingers in recollection. "I do remember! Didn't Harry have polio when he was a little boy?"

Michael nodded. "We were traveling. He was five. At first we thought it was the flu. He'd been immunized, but he was among the small percentage for whom it didn't take. We almost lost him. Fortunately he made a full recovery. Polio is a strange thing, though. It has residual effects. Sufferers feel pain more acutely, for one thing. Greater fatigue, too. When something like this happens, it can set him back a little. He has to be careful. Try telling that to him, by the way."

"He seems so healthy," I said.

"Oh, he is," Michael reassured me. "He just needs to be mindful, that's all."

"Riddle's in love," my mother said.

"Mom!"

"Don't worry, Riddle, I never pay attention to anything your mother says, least of all when it concerns affairs of the heart," Michael said.

The fragrance from the lilies was distractingly powerful. Michael inhaled deeply, then handed them off to the housekeeper. "Take care of these fabulous flowers for me, won't you, please, Mrs. Maguire?" As she was leaving, he stopped her, and, plucking a single white lily from the bunch, he presented it to me.

"I hear that that you're a marvelous rider, like your mother," he said.

"I think Harry is a wonderful rider, too," I said, self-consciously twirling the lily stem between my fingers, like some sort of refugee from a Shirley Temple movie. Did I really think I was that adorable?

"Harry and Riddle are the finest young riders I think I've ever seen and I've seen plenty," Gin piped up in a rare spontaneous act of bravery, as my mother snorted in disbelief.

"You don't agree, Greer?" Michael said with a knowing glance in my direction.

"I haven't given it much thought. For God's sake, they're teenagers." My mother had a habit of using one word, "teenagers," to imply another word, "cretins."

Her imperiousness was astounding. I couldn't help both admiring and being appalled by her arrogance, the way she wore it! Like an apparatus of fashion, matching ocelots trotted out for snarling effect.

Michael surveyed me kindly. "You're not like your mother," he said.

"No, she's not. Not one little bit," Gin said with a little too much vehemence to suit my mother. He shrank under the ferocity of her unfiltered glare.

"Or your father, either, for that matter," Michael continued, unperturbed by my mother's reflexive hissing and scratching. "So, where did you come from?"

"Camp insists she's heaven-sent, but offhand I would guess some place less celestial. Buffalo, maybe," my mother said, as a strong wind off the ocean blew in through an open window. "Come block the breeze for me, Michael," she said as she pulled another cigarette from her silver case and made several frustrated attempts to light it in the wind.

"Still at it, I see. How many of those bloody things do you consume in a day?" Michael asked her.

"I have no idea," she half purred, half growled. "It doesn't interest me to keep track. Maybe that could be your project," she said. "So what do you think of our little monster?" she asked as he put himself between her and the wind.

"You mean me?" I asked, pointing to myself.

"Wasn't it John Steinbeck who observed that the distinguishing characteristic of monsters is that they think everyone else is a monster, too?" Michael posed the question, as we made our way into the living room, whose massive walls of glass showcased the Atlantic Ocean and miles of private beachfront.

"Spectacular!" Gin proclaimed, and even my mother observed a moment of silence as we all paused to take in the view. Michael had had the original house both refurbished and revolutionized, so that it felt old and new, a contemporary palace with warm underpinnings. It possessed a location not unlike ours, the difference being that the Devlin view was open and friendly and instantly available. The view from our house was a trick of the eye. It wasn't until you stood at the edge of the dune that you could feel its terrifying effects, the desolation of its beauty, as if you were being shown a fleeting glimpse of infinity.

My mother's attention was instantly captured by a portrait of a woman with strikingly colored hair that hung over the fireplace.

"Polly," she said.

"Yes," Michael said.

"Polly always was a lovely girl," Gin said gallantly.

"Hmm," my mother said, seeming deep in thought. "If only a lazy eye could be so successfully dealt with in life as in art."

Horrified, I was too stunned to speak. I waited for the inevitable, justifiable angry response from Michael. To my everlasting astonishment, he laughed. Laughed! A big, loud, appreciative guffaw. If that had been my father, I would have been reaching for bulletproof armor. Gin started to speak but quickly thought better of it, clearing his throat instead, swallowing whatever mild rebuke he had in mind.

"By God, I've missed you," Michael proclaimed. "What's it been? Ten years?"

"Eight. We ran into each other at Cannes. Obviously you've forgotten."

"No, I haven't forgotten anything."

I wasn't enjoying the suggestive subtext, though I knew not to take it too seriously. My mother could inflame the reading of a grocery list if that was her intention.

She swept across the room. "Marvelous portrait of Harry," she said. "Such a handsome boy. Like his father." Michael acknowledged the compliment with a half bow. She looked around. "But what of the other boy? Where are the paintings and pictures of Charlie?"

I could hardly believe what I had heard. Charlie Devlin and his disappearance was the elephant in every room in this house.

"Greer!" Gin began to noisily swallow and gag, as if he had a pencil lodged in his throat.

"Mother!" I was barely able to say the word. She didn't care.

"Why are there no portraits or photos of Charlie?"

Once she embarked on a course of action, there was no stopping her.

Michael, mildly taken aback, took a moment to compose himself before answering. "I had them taken down," he said finally. "I can't stand to look at them."

"Well, you should put them back up. You can't pretend he doesn't exist. You can't just obliterate him. It's not fair to him. Put that boy back where he belongs. For your sake, too. You'll feel better to have him where you can see him."

Michael just kept shaking his head as she spoke.

"Michael!" she said softly, interrupting herself, startling all of us. "I never took you for a coward."

"Oh, my God, I need to sit down," Gin said, clutching his heart and toppling into the nearest armchair.

"Perfect illustration of my point," my mother said, nodding in Gin's direction as I looked on appalled, convinced I could feel my hair turning prematurely white, strand by stricken strand.

"Greer, have pity. Charlie is gone. All indicators are he's not coming back. He was fifteen years old. I'm not staging a performance. Let me mourn in my own way."

"Maybe not. Maybe he's not dead. Maybe he's still alive," I said, hands thrust forward, gesturing wildly, unable to contain myself. "You don't know for sure. There's always hope."

Michael looked surprised at my outburst.

"Riddle," my mother said, with surprising equanimity, "I have a vast closet. Trust me. I know when black is the appropriate color."

"Nobody knows. You can't say that. You don't know," I just kept repeating myself, my eyes glistening.

"Naïveté is a poor substitute for hope," my mother said.

"Oh, when will this nightmare end?" Gin moaned. "This was supposed to be a pleasant call. I do so apologize, Michael . . ."

"Gin, for Christ's sake, after everything, do you really think I can't handle Greer?" Michael said. Gin looked as unconvinced as I felt.

Michael turned his attention to me. He took my hand in his.

"You're absolutely right," he said. "We must never give in to despair. There is always hope. Thank you, Riddle, for helping me to remember what it means to be young."

"Good God, Michael, who's writing your material these days?" my mother interrupted. "Hallmark?"

My face burned with shame. "I'm sorry," I said, head bowed. He couldn't imagine the true scope of my contrition.

Michael smiled at me, offering reassurance. "I had forgotten how amusing your mother can be. Don't worry, Riddle, Greer always was good for what ails me. Her bark is worse than her bite."

"Double, double, toil and trouble," Gin muttered under his breath.

"What was he like? Charlie?" my mother asked. "Was he like Harry at all?"

For the first time, Michael seemed truly distressed, as if being asked to talk about his younger son was too much to bear. He turned his back on us and walked over to the window and looked out over the ocean. He stood that way for a long time, and even Greer respected the silence in the room. Closing his eyes, he seemed to go inside himself. When he emerged, he smiled and still he took his time before speaking.

"He was high-spirited like Harry, but where Harry is more direct and to the point, Charlie was sensitive. I remember one time," Michael sat down, perched on the edge of an Eames chair, one of two in the living room, "he was just a little guy, maybe six or seven. I had an art book tucked away in the closet, photographs of nude women, never thought a thing of it."

"An art book?" My mother raised an eyebrow suggestively. "So that's what they're calling it these days."

"In the eye of the beholder, Greer," Michael said. "Anyway, he had some little friends over that day and when they went home he came and asked if he could speak to me." He cleared his throat before continuing. "Before I could reply he ran up to me and grabbed me around the waist with both arms and started to cry. It seems he had shown the boys the book and he was horrified by what he had done and wanted to come clean." He laughed. "Charlie wouldn't have made much of a criminal. He couldn't keep a secret if his life depended on it."

I often think about that story, and every time I think about it

I feel as bad as I did the first time I heard it. No one spoke until finally my mother walked over to where Michael sat, unable any longer to conceal his pain, and she put her hand on his shoulder.

"I'm so sorry, Michael. Perhaps Riddle is right after all," she said. "We don't know what's happened to Charlie. No one can predict the future. I want so badly for him to come home to you." Embarrassed by her genuine expression of feeling, she blinked rapidly and said, "I generally get what I want, too."

Michael looked up at her gratefully as Gin buried his face in his hand.

"Let's show you some horses, shall we? I know you're dying to see them," Michael said, rising to his feet, his voice artificially brightening, clasping her hand between his two. "Riddle, why don't you go find Harry? I'm sure he'd love to see you. I think he's bored."

STANDING AT THE BOTTOM of the long winding staircase, my hand on the balustrade, I took a deep breath before making my ascent, taking each curve slowly, nervous about what I might find around the bend. Standing at the top of the second-story landing, I paused to gaze down the vast corridor with its hand-painted walls. Running my fingers along the beautiful deep green surface, I traced the outlines of bluebirds and seagulls, dahlias and hydrangea, recurring vines abloom with violet-colored wisteria. Long and meandering, the hall had several mysterious tributaries that flowed into separate private areas, with bedrooms making up distinct suites.

I tapped nervously on the first closed door to my right. There was no answer. Turning the knob, I walked into an empty bedroom, slipping inside, not wanting to be found out, and closed the door behind me. Hesitating at the threshold, feeling as if I had entered a church, I almost genuflected. It was so quiet in there and motionless, a still life—the timelessness of the decor contributing a sense of ceremony. Bronze-colored silk fabric covered the walls. There was a traditional set of antique bed and dresser, made of mahogany, along with a matching desk with leather inlay.

It was a classically masculine room. The bed was made. White cotton sheets. A summer bouquet made up of white and blue and pink flowers looked pretty in a pale yellow ceramic vase on a windowsill.

It wasn't until I slid open the desk drawers that I discovered fragments of the boy concealed from public view by all that good taste. A deck of cards, a desiccated sea horse, a pair of sunglasses, leather riding gloves, baseball cards, a pack of gum, an orphan sock, a schoolbook, a volume of poetry. I opened it: "Charlie Devlin," written in black ink, the handwriting big and sloppy and capacious.

Seeing his bed, touching the pillow where his head had once rested, surrounded by all his things, I was overwhelmed by a sense of his loss, the boy who never kept a thought to himself.

Standing up, looking around, I made no effort to control my curiosity; I felt the same way I did the day I went back to the burnt-out stable. In the front corner of the drawer I spotted a small stone, dark gray with orange and black flecks. It was smooth to the touch and shiny, as if it had been lovingly polished to a high sheen—the kind of stone that a kid might pick up and hang on to, knowing in his heart that it was worthless but making a secret treasure of it just because he liked the way it looked and how it glowed. Holding it in my hand, I closed my fingers around it and put it into my jeans pocket. I shut the drawer, took one last look around and left, the door clicking quietly into place behind me.

Continuing to walk, I heard the repetitive sound of a bouncing ball as it collided repeatedly with a wall. The noise led me to Harry's room at the opposite end of the house.

"Hey, Hoffa, get in here," Harry said, catching sight of me through the open crack of his door.

I stepped inside and looked around his room. Books stacked in a tall pile on the floor. Some pieces of abstract art on the walls. A football. A basketball. Riding boots. A cactus. A guitar. Simple, but expensively furnished, unadorned, not like Charlie's room at all. Charlie obviously left the decorating up to his father. Harry was different. Harry could be felt in every corner of this room. Clothes on the floor. Stuff under the bed. It was 1972, nobody under the age of thirty cared about decorating then, not the way they do now, especially boys. A bedroom was a place you slept.

Harry was slumped against the brass headboard of his bed, pillows rolled up at his back, punched into submission. A little red dog came bounding forward to greet me. I was thrilled for the diversion. I knelt down on the floor, pretending to focus all my attention on his shih tzu.

"What's his name?"

"Spartacus. Forget the dog, I've got a use for you," he said pulling himself up into a sitting position, wincing a little from the pain. He pitched a tennis ball into the corner with so much force that it ricocheted off the walls, narrowly missed beaning me and landed in the bookcase, knocking over a porcelain bowl that shattered into pieces on the wooden floor.

Spartacus was thrilled by all the excitement. He skittered across the floor and bounded up onto the bed and into Harry's arms, putting both front paws on his chest and licking his face. Harry laughed and licked him back.

"Don't lick the dog's face," I exclaimed, aghast.

"Why not? I like him."

The muffled sound of voices rose from outside. They were coming from the rear of the house, conversation and laughter drifting upward to Harry's room on the second floor. "They must be taking the official tour," he said, grinning. "Kill me now."

He leaned forward. "Okay, here's what you do. I want you to go to the cellar—the stairs are just off the kitchen—and bring me a bottle of Irish whisky. You can't miss it. There's a healthy inventory, believe me. Bring it back up to my room, please. Oh, and get me a glass while you're at it."

"I'm not your servant," I said, staring at him in disbelief.

"Come on. Don't waste time. You're going to wind up doing it in the end; so let's get the bullshit protesting out of the way."

"What makes you so sure?"

He cut me off. "Please. You're putty in my hands. Admit it."

I stared at him. "No," I said. "Get it yourself."

"Thanks, hoffa. want some?" Harry asked, proffering a glass. I couldn't decide whether he was serious or not. He was stretched out on top of the bedcovers wearing gray sweats and a matching long-sleeved top. Only his legs were covered—by an electric blanket, its frayed circuitry exposed.

"Your dad said you had polio."

He rolled his eyes. "Oh, Jesus. I was a kid. My dad talks too much. Who cares?"

"I have to go," I said, feeling queasier with each passing moment.

"Don't go. Keep me company."

"But . . ." I shifted uncomfortably from one foot to the other. Harry was the best-looking boy I had ever seen and I was alone with him in his bedroom. My stomach did a weird flip-flop.

"Stick around, won't you? I can't sleep. I don't want to read. I'm going nuts. I'd like someone to talk to. Seems like you're all I've got." He gestured toward the armchair next to his bed.

"Here," he said, pouring me a drink and extending his hand.

"No." I shrank back in my chair, sitting on my hands, palms melting, sticking like wax to the seat, sweat gathering like mist at the nape of my neck. I felt as if I was being lowered naked into a hot tub of toga-clad men at the Playboy Mansion. How can I begin to describe the great divide that existed between Harry Devlin and me?

He was about as relaxed as a person can be who isn't asleep, while I was expecting to turn into a pillar of salt.

"Come on. You could use a drink, believe me."

"All right," I said as I looked around to see who it was who had agreed that I would accept his offer of a drink.

"Hoffa!" Harry exclaimed as I took a sip.

"It tastes horrible."

"You'll get used to it."

"Why would anybody want to get used to it? He's so cute," I croaked, pointing to Spartacus. "Is he yours?"

"He is now."

"What do you mean?"

"He was my brother's dog."

"Oh," I said. Any mention of Charlie was inevitably followed by a moment's silence.

Embarrassed, I took another sip and called to Spartacus, who leapt from the bed into my lap. "Harry, do you know why your father hates my father?"

"No, not really. It seems to me it's mutual, not one-sided. I'm pretty sure it has something to do with the war. What else, right?"

"My parents think that your father is going to do something to hurt my father's political career."

Harry considered me for a moment before answering. "I don't know. Maybe. He seems to think your father doesn't deserve to be a congressman. My dad is a traditionalist. He thinks public service is a privilege—only the great need apply."

"That's not true," I said, angry and suspicious and ready to shoot flares out the top of my skull. "What does he know about my dad? My father is the bravest and best man I know."

"Come on," Harry said, mildly. "Take it up with my old man."

"You seem like you know more than you're saying." I took another drink.

I had suddenly become interesting to Harry. "Are you sure you haven't done this before?"

"No! Stop trying to change the subject."

"Look, I don't have any interest in this stuff. Anyway, I think maybe the time has passed. He was going to do something but then my brother . . . and now, well, I think he goes back and forth about it."

"His book . . ."

"If your dad is the man you say he is, then you have nothing to worry about, right?"

"What could it be?" I couldn't conceal my worry.

"Forget it. It's probably no big deal. It will blow over. These old guys and that goddamn war of theirs," Harry said. "Everything is the war. The war. It's like they came home from Europe and made us all prisoners of war stories."

"I like to hear my father's stories about the war. He's not a wind-bag, talking about hokey stuff. Everything he says is so impor-tant—inspiring," I said, feeling curiously warm as Harry looked at me with something approaching pity.

"Wow. You're quite the little campaign manager," he said. "You've really bought into this crap."

I was trying to fend off Spartacus, who kept scratching and sniffing at my pocket. I lifted him down onto the floor, but he jumped right back up and began rooting around even more aggres-sively. Using his two front legs, he started to dig vigorously at my pocket.

"What is it?" Harry said.

"Nothing," I answered, a little frazzled.

Spartacus stopped his excavation and barked. "No, no. Good boy," I said, but he wouldn't stop barking.

"What's he want?" Harry said.

"I have to go," I said, standing up, feeling dizzy, the little dog slipping off my lap and onto the floor. He jumped up on his hind legs and continued to sniff at my pant leg.

"What have you got there? The family jewelry?" Harry joked as he climbed out of bed and stood up alongside me. "Come on, let's see. Give it up," he said, holding out his hand.

I was too terrified to respond. I knew I was done for.

"Jesus," he said, finally, reaching for me. I fought back a little, not much, but he pinned my arm and reached into my pocket.

"Where the hell did you get this?" he said, his mood shifting dramatically from playful to serious. "You got this from Charlie's room, didn't you? What are you doing with this?"

I looked at the stone in the palm of his outstretched hand. My mouth was open but nothing came out. Fight-or-flight kicked in—minus the fight part. Dropping my drink, the glass shattering on the wooden floor, I dashed from the room and down the stairs, running as if my life depended on it.

Chapter Eighteen

——

I ALMOST COLLIDED WITH GIN AT THE BOTTOM OF THE STAIR-
case, his mouth firmly set as he looked out toward the house's
ocean side, so preoccupied with his own thoughts that he didn't
notice me at all until I was right next to him.

"Where are the others?" I asked him, breathless, touching him
lightly on the shoulder. "I want to go home."

He jumped, startled. "Oh, Jimmy, you scared the heck out
of me! How's Harry doing?" He took a closer look. "Are you all
right?" He sniffed the air. "Heavens, have you been drinking? You
smell like a distillery."

"No! I'm fine. Harry's fine. Can we go now?" I glanced up the
stairs, but there was no sign of Harry.

"That's good. Thank God he's okay. It could have been so much
worse. We can leave when your mother gets back." He seemed as
shaky as I did. For a moment I thought his knees would buckle, or
maybe that was just projection. "Your mother and Michael are still
down at the stable. I was feeling a little off so I thought I would
come up to the house and make some tea."

He continued staring in the direction of the stable.

"Would you like me to make it for you?" I asked as I eased my way past him and into the hallway. I kept expecting Harry to come bounding down the stairs after me.

"Oh no, thank you. Aren't you a doll to offer? The housekeeper is taking care of it. Anyway, Jimmy, I really do wish your mother would finish up her visit. I need to get going. I didn't anticipate an all-day affair."

He began to fiddle with the open neck of his shirt collar. I noticed that his hand had a slight tremor. Not wanting to stare, I watched out of the corner of my eye as his emotional state continued to degrade.

"Oh no. No," he said. "Oh dear. Oh my." Hand at his forehead, he walked briskly toward the living room and took up a spot at the window, where he stood and stared out at the water. Following slowly behind him, wary and wondering, I stopped inside the door.

Spinning suddenly around, his eyes darted furtively from corner to corner. "I can't stand one more moment in this house."

"I don't understand . . ." I said, taking up a spot next to the fireplace, rubbing my hands together though there was no fire burning.

"That poor child. I can practically hear the beating of his heart. Don't you feel it? It's terrible. He's everywhere."

Now I was really confused. Why was Gin thinking about Charlie? Gin never thought about anyone but Gin. Appearing simultaneously distracted and single-minded, he scanned the room, spotted his keys on an occasional table and, moving quickly, grabbed them and stalked toward the door.

"Tell your mother I had to go."

"I'll come with you," I said, eager to make my escape, but he ignored me.

"Apologize for me, please, Jimmy. Michael will simply have to drive you home or have his driver do it. I'm sorry. I really am."

Through the glass door I watched him jog from the portico, accelerating into a run along the flagstone pathway. Sliding behind the wheel of the car, pausing neither to wave nor to take a final look around, he threw the car into gear and shot out onto the narrow winding roadway, quickly vanishing from view.

Holy cow. Even for him, this was kooky behavior. For that moment, I felt weirdly grateful to Gin for making me seem steady as a rock by comparison. And for giving me someone besides myself to think about.

NOT WANTING TO STAY in the house with Harry, I wandered woozily down to the stable where Michael kept a few of the thoroughbreds for which the Devlins were renowned. Black clouds blocked the horizon. There was a wicked wind and it was unseasonably cold. I watched my hat blow over the side of a cliff and disappear into the crashing waves below. There was a loud crack of thunder and a sudden downpour.

Inside the barn, I could hear my mother and Michael talking and laughing in the distance. Taking my time, pausing to admire the horses in their impeccably maintained box stalls, I meandered along, their voices growing louder as I approached. I rounded a corner and saw them together inside the stall of a showy thoroughbred.

For reasons I can't entirely explain, I ducked into an empty stall where I could both hear and see them without being seen or heard myself. Speaking softly, Michael reached into his back pocket and offered the horse a cube of sugar on his outstretched palm. "Wico is a great guy," he was explaining to my mother, "but horribly spoiled. You can't go into his stall without having your pockets full of sugar and apples and carrots." My mother was shaking her head.

Wico, sensing an easy mark, nudged Michael forcibly on the shoulder. Michael obligingly produced more sugar.

"So tell me more about hand rubbing," Michael said. "I've been thinking about instituting it around here."

"Oh, it's fabulous," my mother said, launching into an explanation of the process that she had adopted after seeing its benefits on a trip to Europe.

Our horses were hand rubbed every day as part of their grooming ritual. After you've combed and brushed the horse you strap him with a soft brush, lightly at first, then progressively harder. Horses enjoy a good strategic thumping. Then you begin hand rubbing for about fifteen minutes. You use both your hands and your forearm to rub, and to polish, moving your hands in a circular motion along each side of the horse from the head to the tail.

"How hard? How much pressure?" Michael asked. He was squatting down beside my mother while she showed him how to massage up and down the front and back of the cannon bone and up over the fetlocks.

"Michael, you've been around horses all your life—you know you can reasonably apply a fair amount of pressure. You should feel tired after fifteen minutes of hand rubbing."

He took her hand and drew her up on her feet. They were standing side by side. He turned around so that his back was facing her and, reaching behind, he put her hands on his shoulders.

"Show me," he said. "Demonstrate."

She hesitated and then complied. I didn't want to watch, but I couldn't help myself.

"I see. You mean like this," he said when she had finished, and he began to rub her shoulders. His hands massaged her back gently but firmly. He started at her shoulders and began to gradually work down along her spine to her lower back. "So, let me get this straight. You rub along the top of the head, behind the ears, along the belly, up and down the legs, inside the thighs . . ."

"I think you've got it," she said, stepping—with some small reluctance, it seemed to me—just out of his reach.

"I could give you the full fifteen-minute treatment." He smiled.

"I don't mind, I've got the time and I think Wico would appreciate it if I practiced first."

"That's all right. I think you know what you're doing. You don't need any more help from me."

He grinned and shrugged his shoulders. "Thanks for teaching me. It's all enough to make you wish you had four hooves instead of feet, isn't it?"

I watched her reach out and rest her palm against the hollow of his back. He leaned in closer, his head barely touching hers. Her long blonde hair obscured his profile; its silken tassels hung down the square of his shoulder.

It was a painfully intimate gesture.

Beyond them, I could see the gray-blue sky darkening, smoke from somewhere, someone burning something, floating over the dunes and over the ocean. There was this cessation of movement between them; it rose up like cinders from a bonfire, sailing outward in indigo ribbons of smoke and searing the air around me.

I recognized the idleness that develops between two people who are very used to each other. Seeing it that way, framed in the half-light by the bowed arch of an open stable door, there could be no mistake.

My throat ached. I closed my eyes. So that's how it was.

I WAS ON THE ROAD walking, fury and upset propelling me along the gravel shoulder, when Harry pulled up next to me in a car.

"Get in," he ordered as I briefly hesitated, slowing my pace.

"Get in the car, please," he said, trying a softer approach. "Let me drive you home."

"What's with you?" he said as I slid into the seat next to him, staring straight ahead as he pulled out onto the empty road.

"Harry, I'm sorry I took the stone," I said. "I didn't mean to steal it. I only wanted something of Charlie's."

"Why? You didn't even know him."

"I just wanted something to make me feel as if I did know him."

"It's okay," Harry said, reaching into his pocket and retrieving the stone. "Here." He nudged my knee with his clenched hand. "Take it."

"Thanks." I held it for a moment and then put it in my pocket for safekeeping.

We drove along in silence. "Look, Hoffa, I'm sorry, too, about giving you the drink. I shouldn't have done it."

"It was my choice. Nobody forced me. Anyway, I'm paying for it. I feel horrible."

"It was a bad thing to do. I can't believe I did it." Harry shook his head and glanced into the rearview mirror as if he was trying to identify the person behind the wheel.

Jesus. He was nice, he was cute, he was a wonderful rider, he was interesting. It never occurred to me that he might be good.

"What was Charlie like? Was he like you?"

"No. He's smarter than me—you have no idea how much it pains me to admit that, by the way," he said, laughing. "On the plus side, I'm better looking. More conventional. Charlie has a gift for getting himself in trouble. He's more temperamental than me. He likes to tackle things head-on, is always in an uproar about something, kind of like the old man. I prefer to glide."

Listening, I watched the countryside pass by. Sometimes I imagined that I had become one of those Russian nesting dolls, a doll within dolls, each doll growing smaller and smaller until there was only a tiny voiceless replica left of the girl that I was once. It seemed an insurmountable task to go through all those incarnations of me before unearthing the authentic version. What would

I find if I looked? I felt reduced to nonexistence by the enormity of the secret I was keeping.

"So how come you took off that way? Back at the stable, I mean?" Harry asked.

Ignoring his question, I countered with one of my own.

"Did you know that your father left my mother at the altar?"

"Can you blame him?"

"Why does everyone know about this but me?"

"Don't get all worked up. The only reason I know about it is because we were watching some old movie starring your mother, and my dad, after half a bottle of wine, told me the whole story."

"Did Charlie know?"

"Yeah. What do you care what Charlie knows?"

I shrugged.

"Charlie and my dad are joined at the hip. They talk about everything."

Surprised by what his tone implied, I looked at him inquiringly. "What about you and your dad?"

He shook his head and laughed knowingly. "Uh, no."

Sensing a dead end, I pursued the original topic. "I wonder why he did it? Why didn't he show up at the wedding?"

"Have you met your mother?"

"Well, he must have liked something about her."

"Have you met your mother?" Harry's eyes gleamed with deliberately exaggerated lasciviousness. " 'The woman men hated to love,' that's how my dad described her." He seemed amused as he charted my woebegone response. "What the hell's the matter with you?"

"He could have called it off."

"He did," Harry said, shifting his gaze momentarily away from the road.

"What do you mean?"

"He told me they got into a big fight the night before the wedding. Something stupid. She told him the wedding was off. He was shocked, started backtracking. He apologized but she wouldn't listen, said she wanted nothing more to do with him. Told him to go to hell. The whole thing knocked him on his ass. He told her if it was over then she'd have to be the one to tell everyone and then he stormed out and took the first plane to Europe. My old man's got a bit of a temper and he's used to getting his own way. The next couple of days the press was full of stories about how he had dumped her at the altar. He couldn't believe it."

It took me a few seconds to digest Harry's version of events.

"You're saying that my mother pretended to be jilted?"

"Yup."

"Why would she do that?" What was wrong with her?

"You know her better than I do. Why does anybody do anything? What the hell? She's an actress, right? Greer strikes me as someone who likes to turn in performances, the more dramatic the circumstances the better. Being dumped at the altar is more exciting than calling off a wedding."

"Why didn't your father come forward and just tell the truth?"

"My dad has a serious case of manners. He's a gentleman and old school about privacy—and he has this weakness. He likes to be entertained. I think what she did amused him. I think she still does—entertain him, that is."

I rolled my eyes. Harry noticed and eyed me with suspicion. "What exactly did you see in that stable anyway?"

"Nothing," I said too hastily. "I didn't see anything in any stable."

"Okay. I don't know you, but even I can see that you take things way too seriously," he opined before adding, "Makes a great story, no? The aborted wedding."

"Maybe my mother held out the hope that he would show up after all."

Harry made his skepticism all too apparent. "Whatever helps you get through the school day."

"Quit making fun of me."

"Come on, Hoffa, you need to develop a sense of humor."

Laughter wasn't exactly a big staple of my repertoire, especially of late. "Is anyone what they seem to be?" I lamented.

"Oh, I don't know. I think for the most part, people are exactly what they seem to be. You just need to pay better attention, that's all."

Harry slowed the car as we turned down the lane leading to my house. As we were passing the Cormorant Clock Farm, we spotted Gula out in the field with Boomslang.

"That guy, for example," Harry said, squinting in Gula's direction. "His soft voice and that phony deferential manner, his false gentleness. He's not fooling me for a second."

"What do you mean?" I could feel my heart rate accelerating, my hand reflexively covering my chest.

Harry shook his head. "Just something about him. You should stay away from him."

"What do I have to do with Gula? Stay away from him? You don't know what you're talking about. When am I ever around him?" I struggled to find the door handle.

"Jesus," Harry said as I lurched from the car. "Calm down, Hoffa."

"Don't tell me what to do," I said, banging shut the car door to draw attention away from my lame riposte, striding melodramatically up the lane leading to the house. A few feet into my petulant march I got the strangest feeling that I was being watched. I looked around.

There was only the sight of Harry's rear bumper disappearing down the road. Gula, his back turned to me in a gesture of vast indifference, vanished behind the trees, Boomslang's tail dragging on the ground behind him.

Gula had been ignoring me for the most part, just as I had

been avoiding him—as if what happened to Charlie Devlin on that June day was a sort of minor social embarrassment best handled by polite throat-clearing and an undeclared mutual understanding that criminality is a matter of etiquette.

The leaves, pale green and glistening, murmured as the tall grasses rustled across the dunes. My hair blew back off my face. The wind was getting stronger, white seagulls spinning against the conflicting air currents, the sky growing darker, the day erratic and unpredictable.

"Jimmy!"

I turned and looked down the lane in response to the familiar voice. Camp waved goodbye to his driver and started walking. I ran back down the driveway to meet him. He was wearing a suit and tie; no half measures for my father. The suit's gray fabric intensified his green eyes and the ruddiness of his complexion.

"How come you're home so early?" I asked him.

"I got out of there fast. They were the biggest collection of bores and windbags, each one with plans to deliver the same self-aggrandizing speech over and over. I thought I would go mad listening to them. There are many things worse than death, Riddle, beginning with committee meetings convened by people with good intentions."

He loosened his tie. "So, anything of interest to report?"

"Nope."

"Were you talking to anyone? Did you go anywhere?"

While other fathers I knew craved nothing more than to be left alone with a beer and a recliner, Camp loved to hear the latest. He never could resist a story about the crazy thing that someone we knew had said or done. Even as a kid, I felt more pressured than Walter Winchell to come up with the daily scoop.

"Oh, I know! One thing—Gin wants to cut down all those old trees behind the house."

"What? Those trees are hundreds of years old."

"He's afraid they may fall on the house during a hurricane and land on his bedroom while he's sleeping."

"We can only hope." Camp was both delighted and disgusted—his favorite combination of feelings. "You've got to be kidding me."

Camp's highest accolade! My inner high beams switched on, flooding me with light.

"That imbecile would obliterate all of nature if it meant keeping himself alive an extra day. The guy is absolutely terrified of his own mortality. Why else do you think he's so obsessed with taxidermy?"

"He says it's because he's not afraid of death."

"Ha!" With Camp savoring the opportunity to renew his boundless contempt for Gin, I searched my inventory for more material. While the visit to the forbidden zone of the Devlin house had given me an infinite supply of talking points, I decided on a less volatile but always reliable topic.

"Camp, did you ever think you were going to die in the war?"

Not looking at me—he always avoided eye contact when the subject was the least bit personal—he began to talk. They'd been marching for days, crisscrossing the Ardennes, he said. "We knew there was a river crossing ahead," he told me. "I couldn't shake the feeling that I wouldn't make it to the other side of that river."

His platoon started across the water and that's when the Germans attacked. He was halfway across when he was hit. Shortly after that he was sent back home to the US on a stretcher. I asked him how he knew he wouldn't make it across the river.

"I don't know how I knew," he said in a matter-of-fact tone. "I just knew."

We were almost at the house. I hesitated before blundering in. "Camp, if you knew that someone had done something wrong and you knew that by telling someone about what you knew you were going to get into big trouble, would you tell?"

His demeanor changed. He gave me a hard look. "You're god-damn right I would. Do you know something?"

"No."

"Don't lie to me. Tell me what has you so upset."

"Well . . ." My brickwork crumbling, I had barely begun to speak when we were interrupted by the architect in charge of my demolition. Gula called out to us from the road. He was on board Boomslang, taking a shortcut to the beach.

"Hello!" He waved and cupped his hand at his mouth, shouting, "Magnificent day for a ride!"

"Fantastic animal!" Camp hollered back. "I'm referring to the horse, by the way."

Gula laughed, though there was no mirth in his eyes. Pulling up alongside us, Boomslang acting up a bit, sidestepping and refusing to settle, Gula, unfazed, looked at me with such ferocious precision that I felt as if I were undergoing a full-body X-ray.

"I'm sorry. I seem to have interrupted something. My little friend here seems to be upset. I hope nothing bad has happened."

"No. We're fine, just enjoying a little father-daughter time," Camp said as I stared down at the ground.

"Riddle, why don't you saddle up and join me?" Gula said. Shocked by the invitation, I stared up at him, speechless. He grinned, the force of his gaze pressed against my chest. I was finding it hard to breathe. "I'll even pass on some of my trade secrets. Nothing like a great ride on a spectacular day to make us forget whatever it is that is bothering us."

My father spared me the agony of an answer.

"Next time, Gula. Riddle and I have plans."

"Of course. Next time," Gula said as he tipped his hand to his forehead and eased Boomslang into a collected canter.

I bolted ahead of Camp toward the house.

"Hey," Camp said, catching up and taking me by the arm. "Not so fast. You're not going anywhere until you tell me what you're hiding." He paused and added, "Look, I'm not going to get mad at you."

He wasn't going to let this go. Camp wasn't averse to using torture to extract information. Desperate to get out from under his inquisition, I knew I had to tell him something.

The last few weeks of my life flashed before my eyes. The barn. The fire. Gula. Charlie. I stared into my father's eyes. I could have told him the truth, but I took another path. My words spilled out in a tumbling rush of tears. He had no way of knowing that I was confessing my cowardice.

"We went to the Devlins today to see Harry because he hurt his knee and he asked me to go to the basement and get him some whisky and I did it."

"Jesus Christ. I thought I smelled something. Where is your mother?"

"She's still there."

"That little twerp was trying to ply you with liquor?"

"No! It wasn't like that. I was in his bedroom and . . ."

"In his bedroom? What is your mother thinking? What is your mother doing? Supplying underage girls to the idle rich? You're thirteen years old, for Christ's sake!"

This was getting out of hand.

"Harry's not like that. I'm not like that! I just took a couple of sips. Camp, you promised you wouldn't get mad." I swear he was leaking rocket fuel.

"Yeah, well, I lied. By the time I'm finished with that Devlin kid he'll be drinking his dinner through a straw for the rest of his life."

Ignoring my entreaties, Camp tore off his suit jacket and took off running. He hopped into the driver's seat of the car, slammed it into reverse and disappeared down the lane in a swirl of dust and gravel. The wheels screeched as the car turned onto the highway and sped toward Truro. I watched the car until it disappeared.

Seabirds cried out overhead and, glancing skyward, beneath the acrobatic swoop of their disrupted flight patterns, I watched and listened, wary and attentive, full of regret and self-recrimination, waiting for what I knew was to come.

I looked down the road and Gula was there, stopped at the edge of the dunes, watching me, Boomslang fussing and prancing, rearing up, Gula fixed and unmoving in the saddle. A lesser rider would have been in a panic; a lesser rider would have been in big trouble. Gula might as well have been on a rocking horse, staring at me as I walked quietly toward the house, struggling all the way to keep myself from breaking into a run.

Chapter **Nineteen**

———

"**S**O ARE YOU MAD AT ME?" I FINALLY GOT THE COURAGE TO approach my mother later that day as she sat outside on the deck, sipping tea and staring out over the ocean.

"Why would I be angry with you?"

"Because I told Camp we went to the Devlin house."

"So what? We did. I have no intention of concealing what I do from your father. If I had wanted a warden, Riddle, I would have opted for a life of crime. Obviously, I'm not happy about you drinking."

"I wasn't drinking. Taking a few sips isn't drinking. What happened?"

She shrugged. "The usual. Camp made a great scene. Michael threatened to call the police and your father invited him to call in the Marines and the FBI. You get the picture." She shut her eyes as if she was trying to stave off the painful effects of a migraine.

"Oh no." I slid down on to the nearest chair. "Did he say anything to Harry?"

"Oh yes. Must say I was impressed with him. Harry, not your father. He took it like a man, faced down the werewolf, graciously apologized and offered up his throat."

"I'm going to kill myself." Pulling my feet onto the chair seat, I hugged my legs and buried my head in my knees.

"It might not be a bad idea considering the day's not done. It will be a few more hours at least until your father assumes human form again. God knows what awaits."

"Where is he?"

She tossed her hands in the air. "Combing the dunes, looking for cobwebs to fuel his wrath. I haven't a clue. Oh, wait. Sounds like him now."

The door opened and closed. We heard him as he walked up the stairs heading for the bedroom. My mother and I waited in silence for his inevitable appearance. Twenty minutes later, the garden doors opened and Camp, suitcase in hand, stuck his head outside.

"Riddle, your mother and I are separating."

I looked over at Greer, who took a brief puff of a cigarette before answering my unspoken question: "I forgot to mention the divorce. It slipped my mind."

Ignoring her, Camp continued. "Your mother will be keeping the house and all our possessions. You are free to join me. The decision as to where you wish to live is up to you. I'm checking in to the Blue Hydrangea and then I'll look for a more permanent place to live. Think about it and let me know your decision."

My mother kept shaking her head even after he had gone. "Even if he would just switch up hotels," she said, wringing her hands in frustration.

Camp retreated to the Blue Hydrangea in Chatham every time he and Greer had a serious fight or disagreement. Each time he left, he invited me to make my own custody arrangement pending the divorce. Three days later, without explanation or fanfare, he would simply return home and act as if nothing had happened until the next blowout.

Greer leapt to her feet, leaned over and snuffed out her cigarette. "On the bright side, given the separation, I'm available to see other men for the next seventy-two hours. What do you think? Shall we make reparations and invite Harry and Michael over for a late dinner?"

"SORRY, HARRY, FOR HOW my dad acted." We were sitting on the beach watching the seals play on the sandbar, the sun setting in the background. My mother and Michael were on a walk; we could see them in the distance. I had no desire to look too closely. Greer carried her shoes in her hand and stopped occasionally to let the waves wash over her bare feet.

"You don't need to apologize for your father. I don't blame him for being mad. Just for the record, though, I wasn't trying to get you drunk."

"I know. I told him."

"Why did you tell him anything? I don't get it. You had to know he was going to erupt."

"I'm sorry. I didn't mean to tattle, but he just kept at me until I finally broke down and told him about it to get him off my back."

Harry ran his fingers through the sand, considering. "You know, Hoffa, you've really got to stop letting people push you around. You didn't want to get the booze for me today but you did it anyway. You let your dad bully you into being a tattletale. You're going to wind up being a professional victim if you don't develop some balls." He leaned in next to me. "One more thing. If my old man came after me about where I got the booze, I would never have given you up."

I started to sputter reflexively just as the sun dipped beneath the horizon, the evening sky the same deep crimson color as my face. Distracted by the intensified chattering of the birds, I looked up to see Gin and Gula approaching.

"Hello, you two," Gin called out. "I saw Michael's car in the driveway and Lou told us you were down here. Honestly, Harry, I can't believe that Greer invited you and your dad over for dinner and didn't include me in the fun."

"It was last minute," I said, squinting over at them, my heart bumping, pinging arrhythmically in my chest as it did whenever Gula was near.

"Where's Camp?" Gin asked, eyebrows arched in perfect synchronicity, two cats hissing.

"The Blue Hydrangea," I said.

"Oh, dear. Fear not, Jimmy, on the third day he will rise again. Is that Michael and Greer down the beach?" Gin asked, cupping his hand over his brow. "What the devil? Think you two can shun me and get away with it?" He appeared to be talking to himself. "I'll show them." He set off at a run, careening shamelessly along the sand, like a wobbly torpedo programmed to hit its unsuspecting target.

"Why go where you're not wanted?" Harry said as hundreds of seagulls, strewn across the beach like driftwood, dispersed squawking into the air to avoid Gin.

"Intrusion is the best that some people can hope for," Gula answered as he strolled toward the edge of the water. He dipped his toe into the breaking waves. "On that note," he looked at us, smiling, "I will leave you two young people to yourselves as I go for a swim. Forgive the interruption."

"Not at all," Harry said agreeably as Gula slowly stripped off his pants and shirt, folding both neatly in a tidy pile on the sand. As he bent over, the last remnants of sunlight caught the glint of a tarnished silver chain hanging from around his neck.

"Hey, you've got one, too," Harry said as he instinctively reached beneath his shirt collar to retrieve his medal.

"So it seems we are both good Catholic boys." Gula smiled.

"I don't know about that," Harry said. "Mine was a gift from my mother. I wear it to remember her."

"Ah, yes," Gula said. "Mine came to me from my grandmother. A lovely woman. She adored me. I told you about her, Riddle. Do you recall?" I nodded and looked away even as I marveled at his ability to deceive. Ironically, it never occurred to me that my own growing skills in that department warranted some of the same concern. He had never told me anything about any grandmother. Did she even exist? Gula seemed to have sprung fully formed from Vlad the Impaler's forehead.

"I'm so grateful to Riddle for recovering it for me," Gula said, running his hands through his hair, scanning the beachfront. Harry looked puzzled. I smiled and tried not to look stricken.

Gula took his time. He was enjoying himself. "She found it in the ruins of the yellow stable after the fire," he explained. "I must have lost it in there when I was working. All I knew was that it was gone—I thought, forever. I can't tell you what it means to me to have it back. My grandmother gave it to me during the war. All she wanted was for me to be safe in an unsafe time."

"Is any time safe?" Harry said a bit desperately.

"You're thinking of your brother—Charlie, isn't it?" Gula said after a brief interlude of silence. "So sad. Terrible. No wonder you have lost your place. I have been through a few things in my lifetime, too. Don't worry. After a time you will feel safe again." He paused. "Though whether any of us should ever feel safe is the real question, isn't it? Who, after all, truly knows the thoughts of another?"

I shifted uncomfortably, trying to suppress the urge to be sick, a surge of adrenaline poking me like the sharp fragment of a seashell. The medal had been hidden in the far corner of my underwear drawer. The unwholesome thought of Gula handling my intimate apparel, sniffing the air around him to avoid detection, was an image so quiet in its violence that I almost felt the pornographic thrust of his palm against my chest, the sheer psychic force of it temporarily paralyzing me, a low thrum of blood rushing through my veins.

These elegantly planned time-release revelations of his, malignant playful challenges in which he took almost sensual pleasure, were like perverse inverted seductions.

Harry and I watched Gula jog into the water and plunge into the noisy surf, vanishing beneath the indigo waves.

"Look out for sharks!" Harry hollered with fingers visibly crossed. Enjoying his wickedness, I perked up considerably at the thought of a great white shark biting Gula neatly in half.

"I always feel so much better after talking to Gula," Harry said. I lay back down on my stomach and laughed into the top of my clenched hands, fists filled with leaking sand.

"Jesus Christ, the guy is like a haunted house," Harry added, as I giggled away.

I don't know what I was laughing about. Anyway, I wasn't laughing for long.

Chapter Twenty

——

IHAVE A CLEAR MEMORY OF THE WAY THE NEXT DAY STARTED: blue sky, white clouds, green leaves, yellow light, and an even more vivid memory of the way it ended. It was 3:30 in the afternoon, a hot day, the beginning of the second week in August, and I was riding home from the library in Wellfleet, the wheels of my old bike churning along the narrow, winding Cape roads. I was reading *The Collector*—and, enamored of a certain kind of repetition, renewed it to read again; in those days, my masochism outranked my sense of irony.

When I turned onto my road I saw them. All those police cars, blunt and startling, like a poke in the eye. They were parked along the lane, four or five black-and-whites flanked on all sides by the dunes, tall brown grasses waving in the breeze; behind them, the indigo ocean, sunlight sparkling on its rolling surface.

My mother met me at the door. "Riddle, you're home," she said, her voice showy and decorative, sounding positively sprightly, as if she were a sales rep greeting a potential customer. Immediately, I recognized the symptoms. Acting. There were men and women in uniform and men in plainclothes. All of them looked up simultaneously as I stepped inside the door. The women smiled sadly.

"Camp!" I said, surprised into exclaiming. My father was standing among the police officers, deep in conversation, convivial, nodding and laughing, gesturing expansively. He looked up when I called his name, smiled and waved his index finger at me, then refocused his attention on the police, who laughed appreciatively at something he said.

"Your father came home when he heard," my mother said.

"Why? What's going on?" I asked, unable to hear the sound of my voice over the loud beating of my heart. Were they here to arrest me?

My mother pulled me into the kitchen, where Lou was making coffee and looking worried. "Some man walking his dog along the beach found Charlie Devlin's jacket in the dunes."

"I don't understand," I said.

"No one does, Riddle," she said frowning with impatience. "Who knows how long it's been there? Or where it came from? It could have drifted in on the water. It may have been there all along, buried by the sand. Who knows?"

"How do they know it was Charlie's?" My mouth was so dry I was having trouble formulating speech.

"His initials were sewn into the lining of the collar, apparently. His wallet was in his pocket."

"What does it mean?"

Bang! Bang! I jumped at the sound of rapid pounding on the door accompanied by shouting. There was an eruption of loud voices in the entranceway.

"Whoa! Whoa!" I heard someone shout.

"What in the hell is my boy's jacket doing on your property?" A recognizable voice rang out, ragged and tinged with fury.

"Oh my God," my mother said, running from me and into the

living room as I walked slowly behind her, soaring anxiety levels like braces on my legs.

"Calm down, Michael," my father was saying. "You're upset."

"You're goddamn right I'm upset. Of all the places in the world, Charlie's jacket shows up here? Yards from your house? Camp, for Christ's sake! Mother of God. What have you done? You hate me this much?"

"You need to get ahold of yourself," my father said. "I don't know any more about this than you do. I came home the moment I got the news."

"You son of a bitch," Michael said. "You goddamn lousy son of a bitch. I knew you were capable of . . . But this?"

"Jesus," my father said, going on the offensive. "Control yourself, man! What do you think, that I'm in the habit of murdering children and then littering my property with the evidence? Are you insane?"

One of the detectives jerked his head with enough force to give himself whiplash. The others were obviously astonished by what they were hearing.

"Michael, Michael, you need to listen," my mother said, rushing over to him, linking her arm through his. "You're overwrought. You don't know what you're saying."

"I know what your husband has inside him. Nothing! A great vacancy. There's is nothing there, do you understand?"

I was stunned. What was he talking about?

Camp looked at him, incredulous. "Have you gone completely mad?"

"Oh God," Michael said, overwhelmed, as if he was being toppled by the weight of the world. "Where is he? What's happened to Charlie?"

For a moment I thought he was going to collapse. He leaned into my mother for support. The policewoman had her arm around his shoulders. The detectives looked grave. Someone offered him a glass of water. He shook his head.

My mother whispered something into his ear, withdrew her arm from his, vanished and just as quickly reappeared. She had a glass of something stronger in her hand.

"Here. Drink this," she said extending him the glass. He slid down into the nearest chair, took a sip and closed his eyes. I had rarely seen her be so solicitous.

"Are you all right?" she asked him.

"He's fine," my father said drily as Michael nodded and thanked her.

Outside I could see a group of men dotted in clusters around the dunes, a dozen officers or more. Some were down on their hands and knees, raking their fingers through the grass and sand, using sight, using touch, using everything at their disposal in an attempt to dig up some tiny piece of Charlie.

My father never let anyone walk on the dunes. He was obsessed by the need to protect their integrity. Over the years, I'd seen him come close to blows with people—tourists mostly— who ignored his admonitions. Now he was watching all these cops swarm over their sandy inclines, his jaw clenching and unclenching.

The doorbell rang. I looked over at my mother. She was kneeling in front of Michael, their foreheads practically touching. They spoke quietly together. Her head popped up at the sound of the door.

"Harry!" She rose to her feet as Harry, ignoring all of us, limping slightly, entered the room trailed by a couple of the detectives.

"Dad," he said, spotting his father, who refused to look up at him. "Did you tell them?"

"Harry, please," Michael said. "You need to go back home."

My father, in solemn discussion with two of the detectives, stopped in mid-conversation.

"Dad, it's gone too far. I mean it. If you don't tell them, I will."

I grew rigid with fear, wondering what he had to say, terrified of the possibilities.

"Harry, you shut up. Shut up right now! Do you hear me?" Michael said, blunt as lead and almost threatening, invoking the parental power of veto over his older son.

His mind made up, Harry turned to the nearest police officer and began to speak in a firm, steady voice. "My brother came home the night he disappeared. He banged on the door and my father wouldn't let him in. He walked down the road toward town and found a pay phone and he called . . ."

Michael let out a long, slow sigh and buried his head in his hands. "Jesus," he said. "Harry, stop, please. That's enough."

The detectives exchanged a brief glance, multiple sets of eyebrows raised as if they were synchronized swimmers in a competition. My mother and father looked at each other, my father releasing a long, low whistle as he shook his head, a knowing smile briefly crossing his face.

"How long have you known about this?" one of the policemen asked.

"I just found out today," Harry said. "My dad told me when he heard about Charlie's jacket."

"Go on," one of the detectives said in that affectless way the police possess.

Harry looked over at his father imploringly. "Dad, tell them. They need to know. How else are we ever going to find Charlie?"

Michael sat for a moment. We all stared at him expectantly. Dorothy wandered over to him as we waited for him to break the silence. She put her big head into his lap. He rubbed her ears, took another sip of his drink and then began to speak. I was so on edge that I jumped, startled at the sound of his voice.

"I'd been having a few problems with Charlie. Nothing serious—in hindsight, nothing serious at all. He was just a boy, typical of his age. Experimenting. Challenging the rules. He was getting in trouble at school. I had gotten quite a few complaints from the priests about him sneaking out at night, missing curfew, that sort of thing. Same thing when he was home. Right, Harry? You remember?"

"Yeah, I remember. It was no big deal."

"We had a few scenes. The usual father-son stuff. The weekend he disappeared, he sneaked out of the house after being grounded. I was so mad at him that I decided to lock him out." He looked imploringly around the room. "Try to understand. I was trying to teach him a lesson. Around two or three in the morning, I heard him banging at the door. I wanted to let him in. I really did. Jesus, Jesus, why didn't I let him in? He was home, for Christ's sake." Michael covered his face with his hands.

"Take your time," one of the detectives said before Michael resumed his story.

"A half hour passed, when the phone rang. I answered. Charlie was calling from a phone booth. He wanted me to come and get him. He wanted to come home."

"Don't say it," Harry said, exhaling long and painfully.

I stared at him, the full horror of what I was hearing beginning to take hold of me.

"I said no. I told him that it was time he started facing some of the consequences of his actions. I told him not to bother coming home because the doors would be locked. I told him that someday he would understand. I told him that someday he would thank me for teaching him what it meant to be a man. He just listened and then he said, 'Okay, Dad.' I said goodbye and he said, 'Dad, please,' but I hung up."

"Holy Christ, I can't listen to this ever again," Harry said before his father could launch a second wave. Harry turned and walked toward the French doors leading to the hallway. He walked with difficulty. His limp was more pronounced than when he had first arrived, his pace less sure. I heard the front door open and then shut.

Michael looked up, tears streaming down his cheeks. "I hung up on him. I hung up on him." He repeated himself, as if he couldn't believe what he had done. "When I got off the phone, I felt proud of myself for taking such a tough stance. Proud." He paused, shaking his head, staring sightlessly ahead, vision turned inward.

"I see," one of the detectives said, stammering a little, struggling to construct a proper response.

"Please," Michael said. "I'm begging all of you, this is not for public consumption. Please, I couldn't stand it."

When I remember that moment, the sound of the front door shutting, the sight of Harry alone and limping, the despairing picture of Michael Devlin, his sorrowful admission, the limitless scope of his shame, the sadness a kind of enveloping gray fog, I remember it as being one of the worst moments of my life.

Even my mother seemed moved. She stole another glance at my father, who was listening intently, making a meal of it, concentration etched along his brow line.

Finally, Camp cleared his throat and spoke. "You've got to be kidding if you expect me to keep any more secrets for you. You've got a hell of a nerve, Devlin."

Michael stiffened but otherwise betrayed no response, just continued staring down at the floor. As for me, I couldn't believe what I was hearing, so astounded was I at my father's seeming callousness. The police were paying rapt attention—the air in the room crackled with so much tension it was as if we were waiting for something to explode.

"Camp!" my mother rebuked him as Michael looked up at her gratefully, causing my father to laugh out loud.

"Priceless," he said as the police studiously avoided looking at one another, the intensity of their unspoken communication a soft, stingless buzz.

"Hmm." The lead detective leaned forward from his spot on the sofa and set his empty coffee cup down on the table in front of him. "Well." He finally looked back at two of his colleagues sitting alongside him. "That's quite a story. Naturally, this is information that I wish we had had from the start. It's a very serious omission. Certainly we can't overlook it in trying to piece together the puzzle of Charlie's disappearance."

"Yes, yes," my mother said, hurrying him along, "you're absolutely right. So, now we know. What's to be gained from releasing this information to the public?"

"How about finding out what happened to the kid, for a start?" Camp said.

One of the cops shrugged. "What's to be gained? Everything, potentially. We have a timeline. We can place him according to that timeline. We have his state of mind to consider. Was he drunk? Did he seem under the influence of something?"

Michael shook his head. "He sounded okay."

The detective continued: "Those aren't incidental details. Maybe he was mad enough to run away. Although," he paused, "finding his wallet and his jacket seems to point away from that conclusion."

"I'll never forgive myself if I've done anything to hinder the investigation," Michael said.

"Oh, I'm sure you'll find a way to let yourself off the hook eventually," Camp said.

My mother ignored him and spoke directly to Michael. She talked slowly, as if she were picking up rationalizations like wild-flowers along the way. "You thought you were doing the right thing. You're human. Sometimes our mistakes have . . . unintended consequences. People behave differently under pressure than they do under normal circumstances. I promise to take this story to the grave with me."

"Well, that makes one of us," my father said. "You are aware, aren't you, Michael, that you aren't the victim in all of this? Your son is the victim here. You know that, right?"

Michael said nothing. He and my father looked at each other for a long time. I held my breath. My mother seemed suddenly compelled by the state of her fingernails. There was a secret negotiation going on. I was too scared to look at the police. Surely they sensed the same undercurrents that threatened to sweep me away.

"I don't need any reminders about who the real victim is here," Michael said.

"Look," one of the cops said. "We don't need to make public the contents of your conversation with Charlie, if that's what you're worried about. We can simply say that new information leads us to conclude that Charlie was near home in the early morning hours of the day he disappeared."

"Thank you," Michael said as he stood up to shake the detective's hand and carry on with a series of extravagant apologies.

I slipped from the room, nobody noticing but the dogs who trailed behind me, going from the living room to the hallway to the kitchen and out the door onto the porch. Tripping down the stairs, four basset hounds bounding after me, I ran down the winding path that led around and past the irregular lows and highs of the dunes, waves crashing, wind gusting, summer grasses blown sideways. I ran past the police officers, who barely looked up as they searched the area for signs of Charlie.

I was out of breath by the time I reached Harry. He was standing alone at the edge of the tallest dune, a towering cliff of white-and-rawhide-colored sand. The dogs circled him, barking happily, tails wagging, as he bent down to pet them.

He stood back up and stared out over the ocean, taking in that terrifying view.

"Unbelievable," he said.

I RETURNED TO THE HOUSE alone an hour later and overheard some police officers in conversation. Walking toward their cars, idling in deflection by the rose garden, unaware of my presence, they seemed to be trying to postpone their return to the real world.

"God forbid Devlin should be publicly embarrassed," one of the detectives was saying. "Anything else that we should cover up for him while we're at it? Weeks of investigatory work undermined and we're just supposed to defer to the right of kings to do as they please. If he's lying about this, what the hell else is he lying about? For God's sake . . ."

"Please. He's probably got God on his payroll," the woman detective whispered, the two of them suppressing chuckles.

Laughing? Was it possible? They were laughing?

"How did I sound? Was I okay? Jesus, Greer Foley looks just like she does on the big screen. Camperdown's an intimidating guy—a little daunting, you know? To say nothing of Devlin, the playboy of the Western world." A younger cop spoke to an older cop as they filed out of the house behind the two detectives.

"You were fine. Anyway, between you, me and the lamppost, when all is said and done, I figure this kid got pissed out of his mind, decided to go for a swim and either drowned or got eaten. It's a bad year for sharks. He got taken for a seal. End of story."

He was just getting wound up, using Charlie's disappearance as an excuse to pontificate. "These kids today, I'm telling you, they haven't got a clue. You know, I was reading this article the other day and it claimed that in a survey of high school kids, ninety-five percent of them couldn't identify a photo of Spiro Agnew but they had no trouble recognizing the Cowsills, for Christ's sake. Ask some of these little bastards what happened at Galilee and they look at you as if you just shit on their sneakers, meanwhile, they can all tell you where they were when Brian Jones died."

I had just come back from a riding lesson when I got the news that Brian Jones had drowned.

"Devlin really went after the candidate, huh?" the younger cop said. "Pretty outlandish."

"Something's going on between those two, that's for sure. You can practically taste it. Wonder how the wife fits into all this? She and Devlin seemed close, if you get my drift."

"What about the kid? The girl? The one with the weird name. Waddle? She's cute, kind of serious, seems out of place among that crew. Sort of like a mascot."

I crept back into the house, tentative and disoriented. Lou was busy cleaning up. Michael Devlin was gone. Two policemen drove with him to his house, fearing for his state of mind. My father stood in the entranceway in animated discussion with the lead detective. "Surviving a bombing is not a measure of character or courage," he was explaining. "Believe me, it's just a matter of dumb luck and geography."

The detective was nodding and listening intently, obviously fascinated.

"Mr. Camperdown, given what's happened, we'll leave a couple of black-and-whites here round the clock for the next few days for the protection of you and your family."

Camp shook his head vigorously. He detested personal security, viewed it with utter contempt, as if it were a scathing review of the state of his manhood; he treated security protocols as if he were a ten-year-old squirming under the constraint of tie and Sunday-best outfit.

"No, thanks. I appreciate your concern, but we'll be just fine." He patted the detective on the shoulder. "Bring your father around for a drink. I'd enjoy meeting him. Sounds like we've got a lot in common."

The detective nodded, smiling broadly as he shook Camp's hand and promised to come back soon with his father for a visit.

The door had hardly closed behind them when my mother spun around and confronted my father. "My God, Camp, I thought he'd never leave."

"Ah, but he left happy and that's the important thing," my father said, eyes twinkling. "Your father knows how to work it all right, Jimmy," Camp said, as my mother groaned impatiently.

"No big secret," she said. "First rule of thumb: avoid meaningful conversation at all costs."

"Listen to your mother," Camp said, grinning, walking toward the living room. "She knows whereof she speaks."

"I thought the detective was kind of nice," I said, though I suspected I was talking to myself.

"Well, that was interesting," my mother said, cheeks flushing, eyes flashing in excitement as she trotted next to Camp. With a glance in my direction, my father lightly furrowed his brow, then allowed himself the tiniest smile. The two of them shook their heads, sighing loudly, taut shoulders giving way in relief.

"Look, it's awful about the boy," my mother said, tucking her legs beneath her on the sofa, beginning with the obligatory solemn preface.

"Yes," my father said, sitting across from her, getting the preliminary niceties out of the way.

"But . . ." she said, her tone picking up.

"But," my father interrupted, "I'm starting to think Devlin's totally lost it. I can't figure out whether he's insane or it's an issue of character, or both."

"What are you talking about?" I asked.

"Well, as you know, Michael is publishing a book about his war experiences," my mother explained. "He keeps intimating that he intends to embarrass your father with certain information that could, if it became public knowledge, threaten his political career."

"I know all that. What information?" I asked.

"Crazy stuff," my father said, his voice thick with resentment. "The guy has gone right off his rocker. I know the truth about what happened overseas and he resents the hell out of it. This thing has been brewing for years. I should have handled it differently from the start, but I never expected him to go completely nuts."

"It's a complicated story, Riddle," my mother said.

"No, it's simple as hell. He's lying and I'm telling the truth."

My mother's unusual silence said more than words ever could.

"You like Michael, it's so obvious," I said in mildly accusatory fashion.

"I like him. So what? I feel sorry for him . . . and I've been known to enjoy his company. Despite what your father says, he has some attractive characteristics."

"Greer, I don't need to listen to your bullshit about Devlin right now," Camp said. "For Christ's sake, he practically accused me of murdering his son! He's threatening to destroy me with his lies and I'm sick of feeling as if I need to defend myself to you. You still act as if this is some sort of he-said-he-said situation, my word against his. We're not back in high school competing for your attention. For the last time, Devlin is lying. I foolishly agreed to protect him years ago and the decision has come back to haunt me. Even my own wife suspects me. How do I stand a chance with anyone else?"

"I believe you, Camp," I said.

"Thanks, Jimmy, I can always count on you," Camp said. "It's never good to be the guy on the defensive."

Despite his aggressive stance, and willingness to trade punches with an opponent at a minute's notice, Camp seemed oddly agitated, which had me a bit confused.

"One thing for sure, his moral hypocrisy is alive and well and in excellent working order. Can you believe what he did to that kid of his?" Camp said, directing his remarks to my mother.

"Have a little compassion," my mother said. "He's paying a terrible price."

"Who are you and what have you done with my wife?" Camp said. He looked over at me. "Always remember, you can call me any time, day or night, and I will never ever turn you away."

"I know," I said before adding, "I can't help it, Camp. I feel a little bad for him, too. He did something wrong but he's so sorry for it. Doesn't that count for anything?"

"No, it doesn't," my father said. "Save the contrition for the confessional. Regret isn't worth a damn to anyone."

"Is he accusing you of doing something bad?" I persisted, trying to get to the heart of the matter. I was frustrated by all that was going unsaid.

"Listen, Riddle, I don't want to get into it for many reasons. Let's just say, the only one who did anything wrong is Michael Devlin."

"Come on, tell me," I said, exasperated.

"Hey. You. Know your place," Camp commanded. "You're thirteen years old. You're not entitled to know anything more than I choose to tell you."

Greer, who had made a quick trip to the bar, was delivering a mixed drink to Camp. She held up her own drink and, bowing slightly in my direction, toasted the air.

"To young Harry Devlin," she said. "Beacon of truth and fine young manhood. Surely you have no problem toasting all that you purport to admire even when it comes wrapped in Devlin packaging?"

My father held up his glass in grudging concession. "The devil his due. Harry Devlin," he said.

He took a drink and ran his finger around the circular edge of the glass.

"About Harry," he said to me.

"What about him?" I asked defensively.

"You're much younger than him, Jimmy. I realize that intellectually you're light-years ahead of most of your peers, but . . ."

"But it's not your intellect that your father is concerned about," my mother interrupted.

"Harry's not like that," I said. It was true, Harry wasn't like that; from his nineteen-year-old vantage point, I was not an exploitable resource. Regrettably.

My expression betrayed my thoughts, to my mother at least, whose radar was permanently attuned to unstated wicked intentions.

"It's not Harry that I'm worried about," she said. "Amor tussisque non celatur."

"For crying out loud, Greer." Camp smiled over at me in conciliation. "Don't worry. Gandhi himself couldn't stand up under your mother's withering judgments." Responding to her derisive laughter, he sat back in his chair, shoulders square, and pointed at her with his forefinger. "By the way, Foley, don't be so goddamn pretentious. You're in deep trouble when you start recruiting the support of foreign languages to make a point."

"Big heavyweight fight tonight, Camp," I said, looking for ways to sustain the room's shifting momentum.

"Oh, Jesus, I almost forgot. You and me at ringside, right?"

I nodded eagerly. For that moment I allowed myself to believe that everything was fine. Sitting back in my chair, I wrapped myself up in the comfort of the moment and watched my father as he scratched little Vera's ears. Dorothy shook her head, her collar clinking in concert with the ice cubes in my father's drink, a dissonant metallic note.

Camp was keeping this damnable secret, just as I was holding fast to mine—buried in a grave so shallow I could unearth its partially decomposed remains with my fingernails. That night as I went up to my room, I heard "Prisoner of Love" playing softly from behind their closed bedroom door. I knew the lyrics intimately from hearing them so often.

Greer loved that song. She listened to it all the time. My father used to kid her about having an unrequited love. She was uncompromising in her preference for the Perry Como version. But that night it was Billy Eckstine I heard, the rendition my father favored.

My mother laughed as the music played on, looping continuously; did she never grow tired of that song? My parents were deep in animated discussion, their voices low and intense. I leaned my forehead against the door and willed them to let me in. My hand was poised to knock, but I didn't rap on their door that night.

It was late. Whatever we had to say to one another could wait. Anyway, I really didn't want to know. I already knew far too much. Let them keep their little secrets as I kept mine, for the moment anyway.

My mother said it. Amor tussisque non celatur.

Love and a cough are not concealed.

Chapter **Twenty-One**

———

THE NEXT DAY, MY MOTHER AND I WENT FOR A RIDE TOGETHER. Pure duty call—the horses needed exercising. We rode along in silence for most of the way, me aboard Mary, my mother riding her favorite mount, Joe Hill. Our horses walked in tandem along the path leading through the woods and down toward a small stream located in the middle of Gin's property. Dismounting by the water's edge, we sat across from each other on the stony incline, the fast-moving amber water flowing alongside.

"You're awfully quiet today, Riddle," my mother said, pulling off her riding gloves and folding them, one neatly on top of the other. She rested them on her thigh, continuing to stroke their worn leather surface.

"I don't have anything to say," I said, staring moodily off into the horizon. My mother cleared her throat and tried again.

"Don't be so difficult. As if I haven't had enough to contend with in the last little while. You think you've had a bad week? Are you kidding me? You're a child. What the devil do you have to worry about? How would you like to be me? Finding Charlie Devlin's jacket and on our beachfront, of all places. Hearing Michael's dreadful confession about the night he disappeared."

She paused, considering. "I don't think that boy was taken. Why wouldn't there be a ransom demand if that were the case? I'm more inclined to suspect misadventure, given the circumstances. I got the impression the police think so, too."

"Well, what do they know? What does anyone know? The police thought they had all the facts from Michael and that wasn't true at all. Who knows what's true about anything?"

"Welcome to the world, Riddle," my mother said, coolly appraising my pulsing contrariness relative to her notoriously unreliable tolerance. "At least your father's polling well," she said, trying a fresh approach as I nodded with a simmering blend of listlessness and hostility.

"I guess." I was picking at a loose strip of bark.

"What do you mean, you guess? Even to someone as disagreeable as you, it must be obvious that your father is taking everyone by storm."

" 'Taking everyone by storm?' Since when are you the queen of clichés? You've been hanging around Gin too long."

Her head snapped back. I'd hit pay dirt with that one.

"Anyway, that's such an exaggeration," I said, churlish stew of emotions erupting into a boil. "I hate it when you do that—make things sound like more than what they are. You don't care about ordinary things. All you care about is money. Power. Fame."

"That's a charming way to speak to your mother. I'd think you'd be happy that I'm so supportive and proud of your father's accomplishments." She reached up to stroke Joe's muzzle.

"Please, spare me. You are such a phony." I rolled my eyes.

"I'm not interested in your insults, Riddle. Maybe you should keep a diary, then you could rant and rave about me to your heart's content. You'd be guaranteed one avid reader."

I could feel my entire body clench. "I really can't stand you, you know that? You never listen to me. Do you ever listen to anyone? I think you like intimidating people, making them feel like second-class citizens."

Seconds away from crying, I struggled to regain my composure. How I hated being a girl! How did my mother manage to keep her cool the way she did?

"I was embarrassed for you, for our whole family, the way you treated the police." I wiped my nose with my hand. I was cracking. "What makes you think you're so perfect anyway? I've got news for you, Greer, you think you're the only one with opinions—well, other people have opinions, too. They're just too polite to speak up. Those detectives were disgusted."

I choked back a sob.

"Oh, well, then, stop the world I want to get off." Her dispassion was infuriating.

"That's what I mean." The dam broke. "There you go. Charlie Devlin has disappeared from the face of the earth and all you care about is how our lives are affected."

Greer rolled her eyes.

"Don't do that! Don't roll your eyes at me! You act as if it's a good thing that's happened."

"Pardon me if I'm grateful for the opportunity to be able to live and breathe another day. It's terrible what's happened to Michael and his family. I wish it were otherwise, but I'm not so foolish as to wish away the fact that it means he has bigger fish to fry than the Camperdown family. I'm not going to apologize for that."

"We aren't the only people that matter," I yelled at her.

"Of course we are," she said, looking at me as I wept.

"What's wrong with you? You just don't get it."

"Get what? All of this?" She made a sweeping gesture with her hand. "The shared properties, the ocean view, the horses, oh and let's not forget about Harry. You don't meet a boy like Harry at the local Laundromat, you know. Where do you think all of this comes from? You think it falls from the sky like manna from heaven?"

"Stop making fun of me!" She was making me crazy. "How many times do I have to tell you that I don't have a crush on Harry?" I picked up a rock and threw it into the stream, where it made a big splash and sank to the marshy bottom.

Greer laughed out loud.

"Where is all this coming from? Take this stuff up with your father, not me. He's the one with the axe to grind. You've hardly said a word to me since our visit to Truro, and now this."

"You want to know? You really want to know? I saw you! I saw you with him. I saw you with Michael Devlin," I said, rising to my feet, startling the horses with my vehemence.

"Saw us? What's that supposed to mean?"

"In the stable. I saw you. Don't lie. Don't deny it. I'm so sick of all the lies."

She flushed in rosy discomfiture, a pinkish hue dotting the surface of her white skin, but quickly reinstated her characteristic cool. In the face of nearly any challenge, my mother turned into a tranquil monument to self-possession. Meanwhile, I was doing my best impersonation of the sun's core, all those volatile combinations of particles slamming together.

"I don't know what you think you saw. And aren't you the little sneak, by the way."

"Don't even . . . don't you dare turn this around on me. You've got the nerve to talk to me about Harry. When we're just friends." I wiped my eyes. I felt as if I'd been crying for weeks on end, which I had.

"Not if you have anything to say about it," she said, as I huffed and puffed with indignation. "Don't worry, darling, your not-so-secret is safe with me. Believe it or not, I understand." She scuffed the ground with her boot and ran her fingers through her hair.

She looked out across the fields. "Life is so strange. When you're young and your blood is racing you crave these romantic connections with all your heart—you think you will die of love for him—and the whole disapproving world stands in your way, tsk-tsking and deploring your every thought and desire. When you're older and you no longer give a damn about love or sex, the world is your oyster. What does it matter then?"

"I don't want to talk about this with you."

I smoldered away as she took the time to retrieve a cigarette from her cigarette case, tap it, light it, inhale and exhale before responding. Her reflective moment had passed.

"We were flirting. So what?" She blew a perfectly formed circle of smoke into my face.

"So you admit it?"

"Admit what? All right, I confess to being married, not dead. I admit engaging in a few moments of lightly infused banter with a man I've known my entire life. Perhaps you would prefer that I don a gingham housedress and talk to chickens about the price of eggs."

"I hate you."

"Grow up, Riddle. This Pippi Longstocking routine of yours is getting old."

"Poor Camp."

"Poor Camp? Ha!" She started to laugh. "Now that really is funny."

She stood up and, brushing off her riding breeches, reached for Joe's reins and gathered them up in her gloved fist. Hooking her foot in the stirrup, she hoisted herself aboard.

I reached for the bridle and looped my fingers tightly around the leather strap.

"What's that supposed to mean?"

"You're so clever, little girl, you figure it out. You've got all the answers."

"Are you trying to make me believe that Camp knows about whatever it is that's going on between you and Michael Devlin?"

"Knows about it?" She tapped my fingers with her riding crop. "Darling, it was all his idea."

I released my grip, my fingers lightly stinging, and she pressed Joe into a canter, setting out alone across the open field, hair blowing in long, silky, yellow streamers—no riding helmet for Greer Foley. I watched her disappear down the winding path surrounded on all sides by dense forest, the trees seeming to part to let her pass, the birds taking to the sky, crying out, their calls reverberating in warning echo along the way.

I URGED MARY ALONG, THROUGH long stretches of pasture and daunting tracts of woodland with endless secret coverts and thick pockets of scrub and swamp. Cross-country riding at the Cormorant Clock Farm demanded an experienced rider. Even so, there were elements of risk. Horses are naturally skittish and there was a lot to startle one on the way. Riding to where the land was most hilly and ruggedly endowed with dense tree growth, I cantered over the rise, jumping over any obstacles in our path.

As the day got lighter and grew warmer with the progress of the afternoon sun, Mary and I meandered along the overgrown trails, me leaning forward in the saddle, my chest against her neck, my face against her mane, dodging the low-hanging branches that burdened the narrow path. I looked out over an unbroken line of trees and longed for my world to give up its secrets. So many disturbing questions, answers as elusive as something lost in the woods, a hidden presence wanting to be found. Sitting on my horse, still and silent, watching as each revelatory breath rose up over the trees like a trail of smoke fixing location, listening as each beat of the unseen heart gave itself away.

Sliding down onto the wet ground, I led Mary along the convoluted trail to the center of the forested area. I had been there many times before, to where the trees finally open up into a windy marsh and beyond it a large kettle pond, a wilderness sanctuary for ducks and birds.

I walked toward the water and let Mary enjoy a quick taste. Her ears flicked forward and, stamping her foot, she raised her head, stretching her neck in the direction of the deep pond concealed just beyond, behind overgrown vegetation and chest-high grasses. She whinnied in alert recognition. The reins jerked in my hand. I read her message immediately—another horse.

Lashing the reins to a tree branch, I ran past the swampy area and, rounding the corner, was surprised to see Boomslang grazing in the tiny clearing. Something in the water caught my eye. Squinting, I could see the outline of Gin's old wooden canoe and someone stretched out on its floor, head and shoulders propped up against the seat, eyes closed, the sun shining its spotlight on him.

"Harry," I called his name.

He lifted his head, hand at his brow. "Hoffa!" he shouted. "What the hell are you doing here?"

"What the hell are you doing here?" I countered unimaginatively. I pulled off my helmet and reflexively combed my hair with my fingers, confident my wit wasn't the only thing that was sagging.

The pond wasn't big, but it was deep. He wasn't going anywhere in the boat. There was nowhere to go. He was just aimlessly floating.

"Hey! Wait there. I'll paddle over and ride back to the house with you."

He pulled himself up onto the seat and began to row toward me. I met him at the water's edge. "Are you following me? This obsession of yours is getting out of hand."

"Very funny. I was just doing a little cross-country stuff with Mary."

We decided to ride back together. Aboard our horses, we walked along in silence, side by side along the wide forest path. Harry was the first to breach the void.

"Okay. What's on your mind? Whatever it is, just say it," Harry said.

"I was thinking about what happened the other day at my house."

"Oh, yeah."

"Aren't you curious about what made our fathers go from being best friends to bitter enemies?"

"That's what's on your mind?" He reined in Boomslang and stared at me.

"Harry?"

"You gotta be kidding me. It's ancient history, whatever it is. Who cares? Frankly, I'm not too impressed with either one of them right at the moment. They stand around trading insults and meanwhile, what about Charlie? Charlie vanishes into thin air and all they can think about is one-upping each other. I couldn't care less about their goddamn war."

"How can you say that?"

"You know what concerns me about the other day? Where the hell is my brother?"

A few moments passed before we spoke again.

"Harry, you're right. I'm sorry."

"Charlie and I used to sometimes ride our bikes to the back of Gin's property and sneak out here when we were younger. My dad told us about the pond and how he used to go fishing when he was a kid. Did you know the canoe belonged to my grandfather?"

Faltering, I just shrugged my shoulders and shook my head.

"Cut it out," Harry said. "Quit feeling sorry for yourself. Forget about all this stuff between your dad and mine. You want to feel sorry for somebody, feel sorry for Charlie." His voice caught in his throat and he squeezed his eyes shut, grimacing in pain. "Chances are he's missed his chance to become a middle-aged pain in the ass."

Chapter Twenty-Two

―

THE RIDE BACK TO THE HOUSE TOOK AN HOUR. IT WAS AN uncomfortable journey and Harry's leg was acting up again.

"I'm fine. Would you forget about it already?" he said, as the horses walked the long trail leading to the stable and the house, passing the caretaker's cottage where Gula lived.

"Shit," Harry said, mouth grimly set.

"What is it?" I asked him, turning around in my saddle to see what had caught his attention.

"I hate the way he treats that dog," he said, nodding in the direction of Gula's tortured pet, huddled on the ground, tethered by a heavy short chain to an empty wooden box.

"I know, me too," I said, averting my gaze.

"Don't look away," Harry admonished. "What do you think that accomplishes? Why does Gin allow it? There's something about Gula . . ."

If you only knew. "He scares me a little bit," I said, a rare admission.

"Well, he doesn't scare me."

"Maybe he should."

"What's that supposed to mean?"

"He just gives me a creepy feeling, that's all."

"Nobody ever died from a creepy feeling. Man up, Hoffa," Harry said.

"Screw you," I said.

"That's more like it."

Once back at Gin's house, Harry was having a rough time. Sighing deeply, wincing in pain, he leaned over, shifting his weight, first onto one leg and then the other as he tried to make himself comfortably upright. I walked alongside him into the open yard. He was moving slowly and paused to lean against the paddock fence, which was painted a brilliant white, like the stable.

"Are you all right?" I asked.

"Yeah."

I helped him over to a wooden bench near the stable door. "I'll find someone."

He closed his eyes and leaned his head back against the wooden slats of the stable wall. Just then Gin, Gula and my mother appeared from the rear of the stable, heading up to the house. I called them over.

"Oh, my, does your father know where you are?" Gin said, reaching Harry's side. "Boomslang's training can wait, you know. Are you in much pain? We need to get you home."

"I'll just sit here for a minute and then head home."

"No. Your father would never forgive me if I sent you off on your own in this condition. I'll drive you home myself. Gula can follow in my car."

"No, thanks. Jesus, it's just a sore knee. I can drive myself," Harry said as he rose to his feet and limped alongside Gin.

"Finally, some perspective," my mother said, Harry looking over at me, trying not to laugh.

"This is turning into quite a day." She shot me an unpleasant accusatory glance. "Gin and I were exercising Clancy and Naiad. Clancy stumbled and went down and his knee looks to be quite a mess. We had to walk back."

"What does the vet say?"

"I'll be back in a moment," my mother said, not answering my question, sprinting up the walkway and disappearing through the front door of the house.

"I've got to get going," Harry said. "Holy shit!" He was looking past me and toward the house. I followed his line of vision.

"Oh no," I said as my mother approached, rifle in hand, her intent apparent.

"Don't start," she said, raising the palm of her hand in a stop signal. "It needs to be done. Gin and Gula both agree."

"Just call the vet, please, Mom. I can't believe you're going to shoot him." I was desperate.

Harry spoke up. "Let's just have the vet take a quick look at him and see what can be done. Where's the harm?"

"This is not a committee meeting. The decision is made. Clancy is finished for hunting. I don't need a vet to confirm what I know. That's the end of it. He won't suffer. It'll be quick and merciful. I'll make sure of it. He's lame. There's nothing to be done with a lame horse."

"Greer's right," Gula said. "The horse must die."

My mother looked at him with something approaching respect. I was terrified.

"Gin," I said, trying a last court of appeal. "Don't let them do it!" Gin just covered his face with his hands and shook his head. "Gula knows what he is doing," he said.

"Greer, for Christ's sake, this isn't the sad chapter from *Black Beauty*. Don't shoot the horse," Harry said.

"I'm sorry, but I don't intend to indulge your sentimentality at Clancy's expense. All you're doing is postponing the inevitable. He's suffering. Why prolong it when you know the outcome? The vet will euthanize him. Should someone else do our dirty work for us? By the way, you two, no one's asking you to do it. Toughen up."

"Maybe you better shoot me too, while you're at it," Harry said, pointing to his knee.

"Don't tempt me," she said.

"Greer, you're just making matters worse," Gin wailed.

I stood next to Harry, as my mother, accompanied by Gin and Gula, walked away, her stride purposeful and brisk, rounding the corner to the back of the stable.

"Mom, please!" I shouted out to her. Gin ducked back from around the corner, hands covering his ears. Seconds later we heard a single rifle shot, and that was the end of poor Clancy. I started to cry. Harry looked over at me in disbelief.

Greer reappeared and walked toward us.

"Mom," I cried out. "Did you really do it?"

But she wouldn't answer me. She looked at me with contempt and walked on. I kept asking her, calling after her, hoping for a different answer.

Harry stared at me, not speaking, deep in thought, his arms at his sides, palms resting on his jeans, his fingers tapping out a message that I couldn't decipher.

LATE THAT NIGHT, LYING in bed, I was reading by the dim light of an old lamp when I heard someone calling for me in a kind of loud stage whisper. "Hoffa!"

"Harry?" I stuck my head out of the open window. "What is it?"

"Get dressed and get down here."

That was all I needed to hear.

"Over here," Harry whispered, stepping out from behind a cluster of willow trees. The night was a chalky blue-gray color, the moon casting its surreal silver glow. I felt as if I had stumbled into a painting, a kind of nocturne.

"What are you doing here?"

"Never mind. Just follow me. I'm parked down at the road."

"How's your leg?" We were half running, half walking down the lane.

"It's fine. That's why God invented drugs and alcohol."

"So what are we doing?" I was trying to keep my voice steady, not wanting to betray my excitement at this midnight rendezvous even as I suspected that his answer was not going to live up to my expectations. At that point in my life, anything short of a glass slipper and a golden carriage would have come up lacking—though I might have settled for an impassioned declaration of love and a marriage proposal.

"Come on. Follow me," he said, touching my elbow, which I made immediate plans to have laminated.

"Where are we going?"

"You'll see," he said as he drove a half mile down the road and turned down the concealed back entrance to Gin's property. I went along as if it was the most natural thing in the world—certainly the most thrilling—to sneak out of the house in the middle of the night and accompany Harry Devlin deep into the woods.

"What are we doing here?" I asked him, apprehensions growing as we ducked down behind a wide overgrowth of wild shrub roses overlooking Gula's cottage.

"We're going to steal Gula's dog," Harry said, oblivious to my sudden onset of respiratory distress.

"We can't do that." I moved away, shaking my head. "Let's go home. I want to go home."

"You go home if you want. I'm getting that dog."

"No! You can't. We can't. Please, Harry, don't." I was shaking.

"Jesus. What's wrong with you?"

"You can't just steal someone's dog. Anyway, Gula's crazy. Who knows what he'll do if he catches us?"

"I don't have any problem taking that poor dog away from that bastard. Let him catch us. I couldn't care less what he does. Somebody's got to help that dog. Why not me?"

"I can't do it."

"Yes, you can."

"Harry, please."

"Fine, run along home. Do what you want. I'll do it myself."

He started to walk away. I was riveted in place, afraid to stay and afraid to go. An owl hooted in the tree overhead, making the decision for me. I dashed after Harry. He wasn't impressed.

"Either you're in or you're out," he said. "No whining and no independent thinking. Okay?"

I nodded and struggled to keep my voice steady. "What do we do with the dog when we get him?"

"I've got it covered. A friend of mine is going to take him. He's going to live on a farm in Maine."

"What do you want me to do?"

"Nothing for now. You wait here. I'll get him. I want you to take care of him once we get to the car. I don't know how he'll react. He knows you."

"Where are we going? Are we driving to Maine?" Crossing state lines was something that outlaws did, so why was I so captivated by the idea?

"No. My friend is going to meet me back at my house. So, will you help me?"

"Yeah, I will," I said, my internal organs marinating in adrenaline.

"Listen to me. This guy Gula's got some kind of weird radar. If I get caught, you run like hell. Okay? Don't look back. Just run. Get away."

"What about you?"

"I can take care of myself."

I wasn't so sure about that. Harry picked up on my reservations.

"Hey, if it makes you feel any better, if you get caught, I promise I'll take off running without a thought for your safety, okay? Is it a deal?"

"Harry." I grabbed him by the wrist as he got up from his crouching position behind the wall of roses. "Don't get caught."

"What's the dog's name?"

"Hanzi."

Gula's cottage was a board-and-batten construction with traditional Cape cedar shakes. It was small but had a wide verandah out front and a screened-in porch at the rear. There were lights on in the living room, though the blinds on all the windows were drawn. They were always closed, even on the sunniest days.

His dog was tied to an overturned wooden crate positioned a few yards from the front door. Alerted by our presence, Hanzi emerged from his crate, ears pricked, watching without barking as Harry darted across the front yard, dropping down behind an old car up on blocks in the dirt driveway.

I held my breath, watching as Harry popped up and prepared to dash toward Hanzi, who looked on timidly but with interest. Harry stepped out from behind the front of the car just as the main door to the cottage opened, screen door squeaking and banging against an outer wall. Clapping my hand over my mouth, I repressed an instinct to shout out an alarm as Harry dropped behind the car again.

Hanzi looked up and shrank back down to the ground at

the sound of loud voices; the voices weren't angry, but they were intense.

"Whatever I can do to make it happen. Whatever it costs. I don't care. Just get me that mare."

Even now, if I close my eyes and concentrate, I can smell the wild roses, hear the shaky sound of Gin's voice vibrating in the early morning night air.

"Yes, yes," Gula said wearily. "Be patient. You'll have your mare." He walked from the front door to the edge of the verandah, looking over at Gin, who was standing a few feet away from him at the top of the steps.

"So you say, but where is she?" said Gin with childlike impatience. "You've been promising me now for months."

"What are you suggesting? That I don't keep my word?" Gula's tone was stark and inhospitable.

"All I know is that I want what I want when I want it and I want my breeding pair yesterday. I need a brood mare. I've made promises. I'll look like a fool if I don't deliver on them. This is very important to me." Gin was behaving like some sort of thwarted infant god in the throes of a tantrum.

There were loud footsteps as Gula surged across the porch in a singular violent lunge, knocking into Gin's chest with his own. Gin reeled backward, crying out in surprise and fear. He briefly struggled with his balance and then fell down the stairs, tumbling to the ground. Hanzi fearfully scrambled back into his crate and peered out at Gin, who lay in a distorted heap.

"You want? What you want? You talk to me this way? Me?" Gula shouted, looming over him as Gin cringed, curling up as if he had been kicked.

"I'm sorry. I'm sorry, Gula." Gin held his hands up in a posture of submission. "I know you're doing the best you can. Sometimes I'm too single-minded for my own good." Tentatively, he straightened up into a half-sitting, half-lying position. "Are we friends? I hope so. We're still on? Are we?"

Gula stared down at him as Gin kept up a steady stream of conciliatory chatter. "Oh, I'm so relieved. We've come so far. Once I get my mare I can work to develop the Gypsy horse here in North America. It will all be worth it. I know I'm terrible. I do know that. I'm spoiled. I am. My mother spoiled me. She really did and, you know, I went along with it. Well, why not? I never could stand to be disappointed. It's just the way I am. Come hell or high water. My father used to say to me, 'Gin, are you really so eager to reap the whirlwind?' Of course, I didn't have a clue what he was taking about. Still don't for that matter. I just know what I want and I know how to get it. Is that so terrible? Some people might even consider it a talent."

Gula snorted noisily, throwing out his arm in a derisive gesture that Gin, eagerly extending his own arm upward toward Gula, misinterpreted as a helping hand.

"Oh, thank you," he gushed, delighted and grateful at first but then, as it dawned on him that Gula had no intention of assisting him to his feet, seamlessly changing course, a man used to making social accommodations. "Never mind. It's all right. I'm fine. Don't trouble yourself," he said. Gula wasn't listening. He turned around and walked back into the house, door thumping shut behind him.

Little Hanzi crept from his crate and crawled along the ground toward Gin. He put his front paws on Gin's lap and licked his cheek. Gin sat silent for a moment, then pulled Hanzi close and hugged him. "Aren't you a dear little fellow for caring," he said. He sat up and remained in place, petting Hanzi all the while, and then, recruiting the support of the porch railing, he pulled himself onto his feet, took time to brush himself off and bent down to offer Hanzi a final grateful pat.

"Thank you, Hanzi," he said, withdrawing his keys from his jacket pocket, the keys jingling as he walked to his car, the car slowly reversing, low beams glowing, turning toward the dirt road leading back to the main house.

The cottage door opened again. Gula appeared, moonlight flooding the tiny clearing in the woods, illuminating him and the retreating car even as Harry and I remained concealed among the silver shadows.

Gula spat on the ground as he watched Gin drive away. Then something seemed to catch his eye. I froze as, with Hanzi's eyes on him the whole time, he sighed and walked toward the dog, who wagged the tip of his tail in greeting. I held my breath and watched mesmerized as Gula sat down on the steps of the verandah and, making a quiet little chirruping sound, summoned Hanzi to his side.

Hanzi maneuvered himself into Gula's lap, his ears flattened, and remained still and devoted as Gula rubbed his head and stroked the length of his thin body, speaking to him soothingly in a language I didn't understand. He reached into his pocket and pulled out a biscuit. Hanzi accepted it gratefully. Withdrawing from Gula's lap, tail wagging, he bit the biscuit in half, crumbs falling to the ground.

Gula watched him until he finished eating the biscuit, then with one last glance around he went back inside. I heard the latch of the cottage door as he locked it. The living room light snapped off. Neither Harry nor I moved, nor did we make a sound for what seemed like hours.

Harry was the first to get up. He snaked across the open space of the yard and, reaching Hanzi's side, quickly unlatched the chain from his collar, snapped on a leash and, with the compliant dog pressed to his side, ran back to where I remained hidden, the faint trace of a limp inhibiting his sprint.

"Let's get the hell out of here," he hissed. I rose shakily to my feet, feeling as if I might faint. Harry and I started toward the woods and the clearing near the road where he had parked his car.

"Come on, Hanzi," Harry urged softly as the dog hesitated, stopped and turned around. He looked back at the little cottage as if he knew that he would never see it or Gula again. Harry let the leash go slack as Hanzi said his silent goodbye.

POOR LITTLE HANZI CURLED up next to me in the backseat of the car, his head in my lap, black eyes gazing up at me. I was stroking him from his head to his tail, over and over, trying to reassure him.

"Jesus, what the hell's going on with Gin and Gula?" Harry asked from the driver's seat, glancing up into the rearview mirror.

"I don't know," I said.

"I thought Gula worked for Gin, not the other way around. Did you see Gula bump him across the verandah and knock him down?" He whistled. "Wouldn't you know Gin would fall on his ass. For a minute I thought I might have to intervene. Then that son of a bitch wouldn't help him up. Jesus. Poor Gin. Gula did everything but piss on him. What was with the spitting and the whirlwind stuff?"

"I don't know, Harry," I repeated.

"A little intense. I'm starting to wonder if 'Gypsy horse' isn't code for world domination. That generation is obsessed with reaping whirlwinds in one form or another. They won't be happy until the whole world is sucked up into a massive spinning vortex."

I leaned down and kissed Hanzi between his eyes. Holding him close to me, I stared out the window, trying to empty my brain.

"Look, I wouldn't worry about it. Don't let your imagination run away with you. These old guys are wired so tight. We're thinking they were plotting an assassination or a military coup, meanwhile they were talking about something they had for dinner. Besides, what in hell could Gin be involved in? Obviously, Gula smells Gin's desperation and is exploiting the hell out of it."

I nodded. "That's the first time I've ever seen Gula be good to Hanzi."

"Yeah, well, Hitler loved his German shepherd. Just because they're monsters doesn't mean they aren't just as inconsistent as the rest of us."

"I know, you're right."

"So then." He reached for something in the passenger's seat. "Snap out of it, Hoffa," he said, tossing a fistful of Cheez-Its at my head. Hanzi flinched but then wagged his tail, thin and taut as a whip. It bumped weakly against the leather upholstery as I picked Cheez-Its from my hair and fed them to him one by one. He licked the tips of my orange fingers in gratitude.

I lay back, cheek against the leather upholstery, my legs curled beneath me, night breeze blowing through the open window and ruffling the stillness inside the car. My whole body ached.

I was sick with love for Harry Devlin, an illness for which there continues to be no cure.

It was almost lunchtime the next day when I awoke to the sound of banging on the front door so loud and violent that the glass rattled in the windows, as if someone had decided to pummel the door to death.

"Hey, there, what the hell is going on?" my father shouted as he approached the entranceway, my mother exclaiming as she followed behind him. I jumped from my bed and hastily scanned the floor for something to wear. Grabbing a pair of shorts and a

T-shirt, my hair tangled with Cheez-Its dust, I dashed down to the second floor where I hid on the landing, arriving just in time to see Gula, accompanied by Gin, as they were entering the house.

"Where is my dog? Where is Hanzi?" Gula's voice was raspy and full of emotion.

"Good Lord," my mother said. "Who do you think you are? How dare you burst in here like some sort of lunatic? What are you talking about?"

"Someone took my dog! What do you know? Was it Harry Devlin? He is the only one who would take my dog," Gula hollered, pointing his finger, advancing dangerously close to my mother.

My father stepped in between them. "Watch yourself, my friend," he growled.

"I can take care of myself," my mother said, stepping out from behind my father and confronting Gula. She took one step forward and using both hands, flattening her palms on each of his shoulders, she pushed him as hard as she could, sending him spinning. He struggled to maintain his balance, falling backward into Gin, who caught him before he fell.

In a matter of seconds, the situation had transformed so dramatically that now my father had to step in to restrain my mother, who seemed hell-bent on murdering Gula. For his part, Gula was so stunned at the unexpected turn of events that it had the weird effect of calming him down.

"What do we have to do with Harry Devlin?" my mother demanded.

"I tried to stop him from coming over like this. I did, Greer. You must believe me. Oh, my! Gula, please!" Gin said, looking like a damp spot on a bed. Even at the best of times, Gin was something that needed fanning.

"For heaven's sake, Gin, pull yourself together," she said.

"Think about it. Hanzi has probably fallen victim to a predator. The woods are full of such things. Look what the coyotes have done to your sheep."

Composing himself with great effort, Gula seemed to think better of his conduct and began to apologize, frantically rubbing his hands together, generating so much friction I thought he would burst into flames.

"This was not the work of a coyote. I feel it inside." He was pounding on his chest. "No. He's gone. Taken. Stolen from me." He stopped, as if he was reconfiguring something in his head. "Try to understand," he beseeched. "He is all that I have in the world." For a moment I almost felt sorry for him. Hanzi's disappearance seemed to unhinge him.

"Well, I, for one, am delighted," my mother said, never able to leave well enough alone. "It's monstrous the way you treated that dog. I hope you never get him back."

"I'm sorry you feel this way," Gula said slowly and deliberately, his eyes never leaving my mother's face, his gaze sharp as a knife to the throat.

My father had had enough. "This is preposterous, Gula. You can't come over here behaving in such a threatening way."

"It was the Devlin boy. Of course, it was. Who else?" He clenched his fist and held it to his forehead. "Understand me. All of you. I have had everything taken from me in my life. I won't stand for this. It's too much for a man to bear," Gula said.

"Did you report the missing dog to the police?" my father asked, directing his question as much to Gin as to Gula.

"Maybe I should call in the FBI, what do you think?" Gula said sarcastically. "Let me tell you something, all of you. I handle my problems myself."

"Well, that makes two of us," my mother said as she and Gula squared off.

"Stand down, Greer," Camp said wearily.

Gin put his hand on Gula's shoulder. "Let's go back home. He might show up yet. We'll find him. Don't worry." He looked up at my parents. "I'm so sorry. Please try to understand. He's just so distraught. Hanzi is everything to him."

Gula, head bent, moved in sync with Gin toward the door.

"I take care of things in my own way and in my own time," he said, one foot on the porch, the other still inside the house. "Harry Devlin will come to regret meeting me as much as I regret ever having met him."

Chapter **Twenty-Three**

———

THE NEXT DAY AND FOR DAYS AFTER I SPENT EVERY FREE moment I had, on foot, on horseback, via astral projection, surreptitiously checking out Gin's place to see if Harry was there. There was no sign of him, nor anyone else for that matter. Only the Gypsy horse, Boomslang, who ran free in the pasture, cantering alongside Mary on the opposite side of the fence when I rode her early in the morning or at dusk.

He made his own wind, that horse, galloping across the field, mane soaring and tail streaming, rippling like an unmoored kite. I half expected him at any moment to leave the ground and take flight, vanishing into the blue sky and the clouds.

"Run into anyone interesting?" my mother said, glancing up slyly from where she sat in her tan leather club chair, feet elevated, smoking and drinking Coca-Cola, her singular concession to populism. The four basset hounds, arranged lifelessly on the floor around her like chalk outlines, barely lifted their heads, batted their tails and fell back to sleep, as she continued reading, poring over a story about Charlie Devlin and the various theories floating around about what happened to him.

"No," I said, draping my jacket over the back of an occasional chair and flopping onto the sofa.

"Not for lack of trying, I'll bet," she said, making a point not to look up from her reading.

"Why don't you just leave me alone?" I whined, my familiar unchanging refrain, chiming on the hour, never more conscious of futility than in my dealings with my mother.

"No problem," she said, her concentration deepening.

The grandfather clock ticked loudly in the background. "Where's Camp?" I said, conscious suddenly of the house's unaccountable breadth of silence.

"Boston," she said. "You knew that. You've just forgotten."

"Oh yeah. I guess." Index finger at my mouth, I began to shred my nails.

"Don't bite your nails," my mother ordered.

"Don't tell me what to do," I countered reflexively, chewing on my fist.

My mother put down the newspaper. "Look, there's nothing to worry about. We're perfectly fine here, the two of us."

"What about Gula? What if he comes back over here and causes trouble when Camp is away?"

"Believe me, I wish he would. I'd love another crack at that cretin. I'd take out Gin, too, while I was at it."

"You're always looking to start a war."

"You can't appease a predator, little Miss Chamberlain. You must cut off its head."

"Why can't you be like every other mother and play tennis and get your hair done and go for lunch?"

"Ha! You've just described the deadliest faction of all."

I stood up and headed for the stairs. "Why am I arguing with you? I don't even care," I said.

"Riddle," my mother called out to me as she left her chair. I felt an attack of maternal empathy coming on.

"I know you're upset about Harry, but at this time in his life, the age difference between you creates a gap as big as the Grand

Canyon. You're only thirteen; he's got a year under his belt at Yale. You must be realistic."

I started up the stairs, intending to ignore her.

"I do know what it feels like, Riddle."

Stopping midway on the staircase, I heaved a great sigh.

"I was once your age. I remember what it feels like to labor under the romantic delusion that life is full of possibilities, all of them exhilarating and hopeful, a world in which it's always Christmas, never winter. But it's not like that. The events of your life creep along on all fours, they don't dance, they don't twirl. You're thirteen, you think everything is going to happen to you. Meanwhile, nothing ever does, nothing you'd dreamt would happen anyway."

She extended an arm over her head as if stretching, reaching for the ceiling, and then she raised her other arm, her fingers linking over her head. She lowered her hands onto the top of her head, resting them there, elbows extended like wings.

"Is this something you've been saving up for a special occasion?" I asked her, automatically suspecting and rejecting any attempt at intimacy on her part. "Just because you want to persuade me to become as miserable and cynical and hopeless as you are. Anyway, what right have you to complain? You grew up rich. You were a movie star."

"Are a movie star. There's no expiration date," she corrected.

"Fine. Whatever you say. You married Camp and now he's going to be a congressman. Everyone thinks you're so beautiful and mysterious and interesting. What more do you want?"

"I'm not miserable. I'm not hopeless. I am not a cynic," she said. "Quite the contrary."

"Oh, that's convincing. Please. I know your little secret, even if no one else does. You are an unhappy person and you want to make everyone around you unhappy too."

"I know what it feels like to be your age and to think you know it all, when the truth is that you know nothing at all. It doesn't get much better either. You want to know what I know? Nothing. Neither does anyone else."

My fingers gripped the balustrade. Finally, something we both could agree on.

"Mom, can't you just say you're sorry? 'I'm sorry, Riddle, that you're upset. Wish there was something I could do to help make you feel better. Hey, Riddle, how about we share a bowl of ice cream?' Ever hear of ice cream, Greer?"

It was no use. She was looking at me through the wooden rails of the staircase, listening the way you might listen to snow fall.

That evening i was lying on top of the bedcovers fully dressed and staring at the ceiling—in those days I had an intimate relationship with the acanthus-leaf medallion overhead—when I heard a brisk rap on the front door.

Jumping from my bed, I ran to the top of the stairs. "Don't answer!" I called down to my mother. Too late.

"Michael!" My mother's voice floated skyward, lyrical and welcoming like the notes on my father's piano. "What brings you to our humble home? If I'd known I would have arranged for an Air Force flyby."

"Hello, Riddle." Michael spotted me on the landing. I smiled back and sneaked a peek at the empty space behind him, praying to see Harry, my hopes dashed when my mother pushed shut the door, took Michael's jacket and directed him into the living room.

I ventured down the stairs, inexorably drawn to the mystery of Michael Devlin. Given his feelings about Camp, he should have been my enemy, but he intrigued me. That world-weary elegance, combined with such pleasantness and something else—there was a certain feeling of tragic inevitability about Michael that made him seem as romantic as a lit candle. I liked him, though I didn't want to like him. More than that, I wanted him to know I liked him, wanted him to like me.

He was so different from Camp. Michael made me see that there could be power in containment. Standing at the edge of the living room, I looked on from the doorway as he sat down in the living room in my father's favorite chair, my mother offering to make him a drink.

Wreathed in smoke, the indolent haze of my mother's habitual cigarette curling round him, he was burning away like incense, sending off aromatic smoke signals into the atmosphere. He wore a soft white shirt, open at the collar; one long sleeve was casually rolled to just below the elbow, the other sleeve hung loose to below his wrist. His shirttail was partly tucked and hung over a pair of seamless khakis. He had on a pair of sandals, the left one looking as if it were missing some crucial buckle. Skin politely tanned, he gave the impression of being long and lithe—although he wasn't exceptionally tall, standing just less than six feet.

Something about him was different, as if I was looking at him through soft focus, or maybe it was the way he chose to present himself that particular evening. Every time I saw him I saw a subtle variation on the theme of Michael Devlin, as if he selected separate aspects of his character to highlight, depending on his mood or the way he wished to be seen by others. Most of us are integrated parts of a whole. In Michael's case, all those fragments resisted the governance of adhesion. It made him interesting, as if he had wings to fly while the rest of us wore cement shoes. Then there was the sadness, a sorrow about Charlie that he bore lightly, giving him an appealing air of vulnerability, which elicited something in my mother that I had never before seen—or that she'd taken measures to conceal: caring, solicitude.

"Harry's been a little under the weather. I can't get through to him about taking it easy for a few days," Michael was saying in response to my mother's inquiry.

"Is he okay?" I interrupted.

"He'll be fine." The two of them seemed amused by my concern. He paused as she handed him his drink—she knew what he liked—and sat down across from him. "Actually, that's what brings me here tonight. I wanted to talk to you, Greer. You, too, Riddle, if you have a moment." He waved me into the room. "What do you know about this incident with the dog?"

My mother scrunched up her brow as if she were trying too hard to recall something unmemorable, a phone number or the name of a cereal. She reached for a copy of *Life* magazine sitting on the coffee table in front of her and casually flipped through the pages, as Michael waited patiently for her answer.

"Well," she said taking her time, "I know that Harry was upset at the way Gin's stable manager was treating his dog. The suspicion exists in certain quarters that he took the dog. Is that what you've heard?" She looked at him through the corner of her eye.

"I first found out about it when I got this phone call from Gin earlier today. He was upset, begging me to speak to Harry, imploring me to have Harry return this dog that he's supposed to have taken. Well, of course, I told Gin that the whole idea of Harry stealing this man's dog was ludicrous. He just kept insisting that it must have been Harry and that he understood why he did it. Please just return the dog, he said, and all will be forgiven."

My mother snapped through the pages of the magazine, her cheeks flushing, disgust her natural blush.

"Gin is such a gutless wonder. Honestly, I'd like to take a stick to him sometimes."

"Naturally, I told him that Harry didn't have any part in the dognapping. Gin was ready for the butterfly net by the time we'd finished talking, just kept saying that it was going to cost him his Gypsy mare, that this fellow that works for him was going to quit and go back to Europe before bringing him the horse."

"Please God," my mother said prayerfully. "Gin has gone stark raving mad over these Irish tinker horses. I swear he would sell his mother to ensure that he gets a breeding pair. On second thought, I could be persuaded to sacrifice Mirabel for a whole lot less inducement than a horse. Her life for a Mars bar seems like an equitable trade to me."

"Greer, just between you and me, Harry did take the dog. Admitted it right away. Unbelievable."

"I thought as much, but I'd be hard pressed to criticize him for it. It's an abomination the way that repulsive man treated that poor creature."

"Should I be concerned about this man? What's his name?"

"Gula Nightjar."

"Good Christ. Seriously? Sounds like a fugitive from *The Twilight Zone.*"

"His provenance is far less distinguished than episodic TV, believe me," my mother said. "The man is a praying mantis. He's an insect. No brain to speak of, just a fusion of dangling ganglia. Oh, wait, I'm confusing him with Gin."

Michael looked over at me and laughed out loud, totally enamored of my mother's subversion.

"Harry tells me he does volunteer work for the campaign. What does Camp think of him?"

It was strange to hear Michael recruit Camp's opinion, even indirectly.

"He thinks that Gula is a bit of a force to be reckoned with, as those quiet types inevitably are. Harry should avoid Gin's for a while. Let things settle down."

"He won't listen to me or anyone else when he's made up his mind, as you may have noticed. He's really taken with this Gypsy horse and it gives him an interest, something to take his mind off . . ." Michael's voice trailed off.

"Understandable," my mother said, observing a respectful moment of silence before exploding. "I'm so sick of hearing about that goddamn horse." She shut the magazine and thumped it onto the table.

"There, there, Greer, don't fret. I understand that he has thick ankles and a big ass," Michael said, reaching out to pat her hand. "What if I offer this Gulag fellow some money? That usually does the trick."

"No!" I felt panic rising. Michael and my mother were caught off guard by the intensity of my response.

"Why the devil not?" My mother stood up and tried to stare me down, hands on her hips.

"You'll make him angry. He's not for sale. He's not like everybody else." I was flushed and aware that I was sounding like the script of a soap opera, but I couldn't help myself.

"What the hell is going on here?" Greer asked me, brows furrowed.

I ignored her. "Mr. Devlin, please make sure that Harry doesn't go to Gin's place again. Gula hates Harry."

"What's wrong with this man? Why does he have it in for Harry?"

"I don't know," I said, backtracking a little, "it just seems that way to me. Well, he knows that Harry took the dog."

My mother interjected. "For God's sake, Michael, you should know by now, everyone hates the Devlins a little in their heart of hearts. Even the people that love you, hate you. People are jealous! Is this really such a surprise? I, of course, have good reason for disliking you. As for you, Riddle, what strange power does this Gula creature have over you? After all, he's just some grubby immigrant. What can he do? Hurtle profanities at us in another language? No need for the world to stop rotating. Michael, you know as well as I do that you cannot give in to these types, otherwise they will own you, lock, stock and barrel."

"I don't know, Greer," Michael said. "Maybe his feelings run deeper than jealousy, maybe he has a grudge against the family based on some old grievance with the company. God knows my grandfather and my father made enough enemies to keep me on my toes until the end of time." He looked reflective.

"Anyway," he brightened up a little. "It's one thing to take defensive measures, it's another to poke the snake with a stick." He looked over at me gratefully. "Thanks, Riddle. I appreciate the warning. I'll do everything in my power to keep Harry away from Gin's—even if it means I have to tie him up and confine him to the cellar."

"Good for you, Riddle. Looks as if you've earned yet another merit badge. Isn't it past your bedtime, darling?" my mother said through gritted teeth. "In other words, time for you to take a powder."

"Are you sure you don't need a chaperone?" I asked her as Michael glanced downward, interested all of a sudden in inspecting the floorboards.

"You go too far, Riddle," my mother said, unamused.

"Good night," I said, heading up to my room, a queasy feeling overtaking me as I contemplated the dismaying notion that even this rich and powerful and famous man was no match for the wingless insect next door.

I THOUGHT I WAS DREAMING. "Hey, Hoffa," Harry was whispering and nudging me, hand on my shoulder. "Wake up."

I sat forward, gasping for air, jolted awake by an enormity of dread so ominous I thought I was being sealed in a narrow coffin and buried alive. Unreasonably panicking, I quickly looked around, grasping hold of Dorothy, trying to make sure I was still among the living.

"Jesus!" I lurched from under the bedcovers, almost tumbling onto the floor.

Harry laughed lightly. "Sorry," he said, not meaning a word of it, relishing my shock. "The front door was open. There's nobody downstairs. Christ, that was quite a response. Do you have a guilty conscience or what?"

"What are you doing here? Your dad said you weren't feeling well." I knew better than to suppose he was coming to see me, and I was right.

"I'm fine," he said, exasperated. "I had to get out of that house. I couldn't stand it anymore. It's like a mausoleum. I was out with some friends and on my way home I'm driving past your place and I see my father's car in the driveway. What's going on?"

"The door was unlocked?" I said, instinctively reaching for a sweater and pulling it over my head. I was at an acutely self-conscious stage of life, especially around Harry, and felt overexposed in anything less than a beekeeper's uniform. "What time is it?"

"Two o'clock," he said, sitting down on the edge of the bed, Dorothy licking him all over his face. I suddenly became conscious of the jostling currents of synovial fluid in my knees and for a moment fantasized about the joys of being a basset hound.

"She's quite a watchdog," Harry joked.

"Where are they? My mom and your dad, I mean? They were talking in the living room when I went to bed around eleven."

Harry grabbed my hand and yanked me out of bed. "Pull on a pair of pants and let's go have a look around. I'm sure the answer to that question isn't nearly as interesting as what you're imagining."

. . .

WE WERE APPROACHING THE utility shed on the ocean side of the property when we heard muffled voices and laughter. Shifting uncomfortably in reaction to the intimacy of the sound, I walked uncertainly toward the voices. Wordlessly we made the intuitive decision to conceal ourselves—Harry and I were at risk of becoming professional sneaks, with the amount of spying we had done of late—using the black of the night and the thick, razor-edged summer foliage that lined the winding path leading down to the beach. The voices grew louder—so loud I can hear them still. My mother. Michael. She poured him a glass of wine. He sipped it slowly. They were laughing and talking, watching each other intently, smoke rising above their heads.

"Jesus," Harry whispered. "I've never seen my old man smoke."

Michael got up and walked toward the edge of the water. He was staring out over the dark expanse of ocean. His arm fell to his side as my mother sidled up next to him and took the cigarette from between his fingers. She stood apart from him and finished his cigarette before tossing it into the waves, a tiny flare in the night sky destined to go almost unnoticed.

I looked at Harry. He looked back at me. "Seems harmless enough," he said unconvincingly. I stared at him. "Okay," he conceded, "so nobody here is being anointed with rose water. What are you gonna do?"

"Easy for you to say. What about my dad?"

Harry took me by the elbow. "Come on," he said, leading me along the darkened, graduated path over several levels of dune that led to the house. "Listen, Hoffa," he said as we walked along side by side, "things aren't always what they seem to be. Don't jump to any conclusions. I think they're just messing around with each other. You know, flirting with the possibilities. Entertaining themselves. Nothing more. Your mother isn't the type. In her own weird way she has scruples." He paused, amused, considering. "I think."

I stopped walking. "Really? Honestly, do you mean it?"

"Yeah, I do. You need to forget about it. Anyway, you know her better than I do. Why am I doing your job and sticking up for your mother?"

We were standing at the edge of one of the lower-level dunes, next to an old wooden bench and a couple of weather-beaten Adirondack chairs positioned to overlook the ocean. There was a large, black, wrought-iron lantern standing next to the bench like a sentinel. It cast a warm glow out over the water. I could hear the waves lapping against the sand on the beach below us.

Harry's eyes, reflected in the silver light of the moon and the golden light of the lantern, stared back at me in the darkness.

"What the hell, Hoffa? Even if they're up to something, it's only sex." He laughed, an easy, reassuring, boyish laugh. He was completely at ease—Harry was always relaxed—leaning gracefully against the wooden back of the bench, casually loitering.

Slightly taken aback, I pretended a sophistication I didn't feel. "I wish I could be more like you."

"You might as well enjoy yourself while you're young and you have the chance. Before you wind up making a good match with somebody's son that your parents manipulate you into marrying."

"Who are you to talk about somebody's son? You're the ulti-mate somebody's son."

"Oh, interesting," he said. "We have a reverse snob in our midst. I knew it."

"You have a way of making me say things I don't mean."

"That's a hot one. You mean exactly what you say."

"No one cares anything about what I think," I said, generously larding my comments with self-pity, my favorite condiment.

"Don't tell me you sit up nights worrying about Greer's indifference or Gin's. Quit being so grave."

"I'm not."

"Yeah, you are." He surveyed me playfully. He poked me in the shoulder.

"So, do you have a boyfriend? Someone at school you like?"

"No. Why are you asking me such a stupid question?"

"Come on. There's someone, isn't there?" Harry was a born teaser.

"No."

"Yes there is."

I shook my head.

"Is he rich? Is he from a famous family? Is he everything you actively despise?"

I didn't dare look at him. I caught my breath.

"Oh, Jesus Christ." He laughed. "It's me."

I was trying to restart my heart when Harry, who hardly had a moment to enjoy the sweetness of his victory, grabbed me by the forearm, gripping it tightly.

"Quiet," he said, finger to his lips. "What the hell is that?"

"What?" I said, gradually regaining the feeling in my body. "I don't hear anything." At that point I was so grateful for the interruption I would have welcomed the Zodiac Killer with air kisses.

He took me by the hand. "Come here," he said, pulling me along behind him. "Listen."

Closing my eyes, I was trying to hear what he heard.

"There it is," he said. "Someone's walking along the path. It's coming from behind us."

"Let's go inside."

"Come on," Harry said as we reversed direction and, moving quickly, backtracked toward the beach. We came to a clearing just above the spot where my mother and Michael continued to talk and laugh and drink their wine.

I gasped as I realized that someone was about to emerge from the opposite side of the path, overhanging branches snapping, tall grasses rustling.

"Camp!" I said as my father came into clear view.

"What in God's name?" my father said at first sight of Harry and me.

"Hoo boy," Harry muttered.

The sound of my mother's laughter drifted upward, curdling round us like the smoke from her cigarette. My father turned around to see them sitting together on the beach below us.

"Greer! Michael!" He shouted their names. "What is this? I go away for a day or two and come home to find a bacchanal in my own backyard?"

"Camp?" My mother got up and hands on her hips looked up at us. "Harry? Riddle? What's going on?"

"That's what I'd like to know," Camp hollered down at her as she and Michael abandoned their wine glasses and, shoes in hand, walked barefoot up to meet us.

"You better have a goddamn good explanation for what's going on here," Camp said as they approached. If his plan was to put my mother on the defensive he should have known better, both as her husband and as a seasoned combat soldier familiar with sussing out enemy strategy.

"What do you mean, explanation? How dare you? I don't need to explain myself to you, or to anyone else for that matter. Michael and I were sharing a quiet conversation on the beach talking about old times. What is wrong with you?"

"Greer . . ." My father was digesting his mistake, reformulating his thoughts. I knew the routine—this could either get better or it could get a whole lot worse.

"I'm not finished. What I do, when I do it and with whom is none of your business, do you understand me? You owe Michael an apology. You owe me an apology. You owe the whole bloody world an apology!"

"Forget it," Michael said. "It's a misunderstanding, that's all."

"No, it's aggressive stupidity and I'm sick of it," my mother said as I died a little. Please, Mom.

"Okay," my father said, edge vaulting back into his voice, as he fought to maintain some control. "I may have overreacted, but it's the middle of the damn night."

"Come on, Harry, time to go," Michael said, unaffected but resigned, as if he was in all-too-familiar territory. He stopped, something occurring to him. "What are you doing here?"

While Harry explained, I watched my father's face for some indication of his intentions. He had grown progressively quiet and calm, and it was unnerving.

"Look, Camp, I'm sorry," Michael said, suddenly turning to face my father as he and Harry made a movement to leave. "Given our differences, I probably didn't show the best judgment coming here tonight. Don't be angry with Greer. She didn't know I was coming. I was trying to get to the bottom of this thing with Harry and the dog and I wanted to get her take on things. I can see why you might jump to the wrong conclusion."

My father listened impassively, nodding his head. "You fascinate me, Michael."

Michael stiffened. "What's that supposed to mean?"

"It's amazing. Your ability to frame everything in a way that either flatters you or exonerates you or makes you an object of pity, which ironically has the same effect of casting you in the best possible light. Deflection, revision, manipulation. I've got to hand it to you, Michael, you have truly found a way to make style seem like substance."

"I can see that I'm wasting my time."

"Camp, hasn't Michael been through enough?" My mother chastised him as Harry groaned and shook his head.

"I don't know. Ask him. He was so concerned with appearances that he didn't even tell the truth to the police about his own son's disappearance." He began directing his remarks to Michael. "Then you use the natural sympathy of others—including my wife, or should I say our wife?—as a shield to protect your image of yourself as a man beyond reproach."

Harry inhaled sharply. Michael stepped forward. He and Camp were facing each other. "You think I don't know what I did? You think I wouldn't change it if I could? I would do anything to bring Charlie home. Anything. How dare you question my love for my son?"

Michael's voice quavered. Harry was struggling to keep his composure.

"I'm sorry, Harry," Camp said. "You deserve better. So did your brother. As for you, Michael, congratulations, I didn't think it was possible but you're giving your old man a run for his money in the son-of-a-bitch department."

"Now you attack my dead father, too? Come on, Harry. Good luck, Greer. You'll need it." Michael started up along the trail toward the house.

"Oh, please," Camp scoffed. "You and I both know that the only thing that stood between your father and a stint in a federal penitentiary was a plastic bag."

My mother gasped. "Camp!"

Michael stopped and stared at her. "You told him, Greer. How could you? You swore . . ."

"What are you talking about?" Harry asked his father, who seemed unable to find the words to respond.

"Let me enlighten you, Harry," Camp said. "Your grandfather was about to be indicted for a long list of labor violations, long enough to ensure a substantial prison sentence, but he took the cowardly way out and killed himself instead. Your father and Greer found him in the living room on the sofa with a plastic bag over his head. How old were you, early twenties? Not much older than Harry is now?"

"I thought he died of a heart attack," Harry said, as Michael looked on helpless and angry.

"That's the story your father concocted to conceal the truth about what happened. He recruited Greer's silence and support by playing the sympathy card. His usual modus operandi. Just another day in the lie of Michael Devlin."

"My God," my mother said, struggling to light her cigarette in the wake of the aroused offshore wind.

Chapter Twenty-Four

———

WHACK!

"Greer, for Christ's sake." Camp held his hand up to his cheek. We were in the living room. Michael and Harry had barely pulled out of the driveway before my mother launched her attack. Unheeding, she wound up and slapped him again.

Her palm must have been burning. I could practically feel the imprint of her hand on my cheek. Tears streamed down her face, but she wasn't weeping in any traditional sense. She was crying bloody murder. Camp's arms dropped to his sides in standoff. They stood still and their eyes circled one another.

"If only that spirit could be harnessed for good instead of evil," he said finally.

"How could you?" my mother shouted at him, echoing Michael's words to her.

My father looked over at me where I stood frozen in place across from them.

"Go to bed, Riddle," he said. "This is between your mother and me. It has nothing to do with you." Paralyzed, I couldn't seem to make anything work. Walking seemed to be out of the question.

"Do you think she's an idiot? Do you think you can bundle

her off to her room the way you did when she was a toddler and she'll forget all about what happened here tonight? That she'll carry on blissfully assuming her father is the heroic figure he pretends to be?"

"Go to your room, Riddle," my father said. I would have liked nothing better than to disappear but I was immobilized.

"Yes, go to your room, Riddle, and put your fingers in your ears. Cover your eyes and hold your nose, too. Put a goddamn bag over your head, while you're at it."

"Stop it," my father said.

"How dare you humiliate me that way! How dare you violate my confidence! And for what? Because you're jealous? For years I've had to tolerate you whining and mewling and fuming with jealousy over Michael Devlin. You had no right to attack him that way. His son is missing. His father killed himself. You weren't there that day. I was. He was devastated. It was horrible. So what if he pretended his father died of natural causes? People have been lying about that sort of thing since the beginning of time. Have you no feelings? Have you no heart? You should be ashamed of yourself. Pretending to care about Harry! Say what you will about Michael, he isn't afraid to be wealthy. He isn't afraid to let me in. You know what else? He actually likes me just the way I am."

My father, resigned to my presence, decided to my horror to include me in the conversation.

"You see, Riddle, your mother never loved me at all. Her heart, such as it is, always belonged to Michael Devlin, but he wasn't in it for the long haul. He was smart. He got out while the getting was good. As for me, well, I didn't have enough power or money to hold her attention for longer than it took for the signatures on the marriage license to dry. All your mother has ever cared about is the almighty dollar."

"Please," I said, wanting to be anywhere in the world but where I was.

My mother laughed and reached out to touch the lapel of his jacket, pure cashmere and imported from Italy. "Oh, I see. That's right. It's all me." Now it was her turn to recruit my support. "Your father pretends to have dirt under his fingernails while living like a second-rate pasha and taking my name in vain."

She started furiously pacing the room, Dorothy worriedly trotting alongside her. The other two dogs and little Vera were curled up hiding under the sofa. I looked longingly in their direction. She stopped abruptly, spun around and resumed her attack.

"Am I laboring under a delusion or is the cost of the clothes you're wearing equal to the gross national product of a third world country? Who paid for them, Camp? I did. Who asked me to? You did. So what? News flash, Camp: you're not perfect. Human beings weren't meant for perfection. Why do you insist on trying to change the unchangeable? Why don't you forget the greater world and devote a little time to working on yourself instead?"

"Don't." My father held up his hand as if he was holding back traffic.

"Don't tell you the truth? You don't have a monopoly on point of view here, Camp. I have a few thoughts of my own. I know the idea of being a hypocrite terrifies you. You think by punishing yourself with labor history and public service, by committing death by boredom, maybe you'll even stop wanting to go to parties. Is that what you think?

"What would you have me do, Camp? Quit washing my hair, wear flats, and wrap myself in a cardigan with holes in the sleeves? Will that make me good? Will that make you better by association? You know something? I'm not that bad and you're not that good."

It was as if a lifetime of grievances, expressed in daily trickles of archly expressed resentments, had swollen into a tsunami of plain unvarnished fury.

"You're hysterical. Calm down."

"You think because you're quiet for the moment you're not frantic? I've got news for you. You're berserk. You're so busy pretending to be a humanitarian you've forgotten what it's like to be human. And you and I both know that you are all too human, don't we, Camp? All the secrecy and the denials and the lies can't make it otherwise."

Camp gradually slid downward under her barrage until he was sitting sideways on the cushioned seat of an armchair, his long legs stretched out in front of him. Slightly shaking his head from side to side, he ran his hands through his hair and loosened his tie. He sighed loudly and lay back on the seat.

"Hand me that pillow, will you?" he asked, pointing to the sofa. I was standing next to the fireplace. Moving automatically, I walked over, picked up the small yellow pillow and gave it to him. He reached behind the back of his head and set the pillow in place. He relaxed into it and stared up at me. "Thanks, Jimmy."

I knelt down on the floor beside him and stared into the open hearth.

My mother, seeming depleted, sank down into the sofa across from us. "What a mess everything is. Why did you do it, Camp? Confront him that way? Nothing will stop that book from coming out now." She paused, reviewing matters silently. "I think you need to act preemptively if you're to survive."

"It's too late, Greer. The time for candor has long since passed," my father said quietly. "I was a fool. I made the wrong decision all those years ago and I'm going to pay for it."

"What did you do, Camp?" I said.

"It's what I didn't do, Jimmy," he said.

"But he says you're the one who did something bad."

"He's lying. It's been eating him alive, knowing that I know the truth about him." He seemed contemplative. "Well, I suppose I did do something bad, too."

"It was war, Camp," Greer said, mildly exasperated. "You all did what you thought you had to do to survive. What the hell difference does it make who did what?"

"It makes a difference. I didn't come home just so I could answer to people who don't know what the hell they're talking about."

"I'm telling you that I understand. I don't hold you accountable," my mother said. "You can't see that. You don't get it. You never will." She reached into the silver cigarette case and, withdrawing a cigarette, she got up and walked over to the fireplace. She reached into the fire, lighting the tip of her cigarette in the flames.

"For Christ's sake, Greer," Camp said, a mix of despair and horrified recognition on his face. "You think it was me. You believe him, don't you? You believe him and you don't believe me."

Even now, all these years later, I can't stand to think of the pain I saw in my father's face that night.

Standing up straight, my mother briefly lost her bearing. She leaned against the end of the mantelpiece.

"Mary, Mother of God," she said, staring over at my father, the smoke from her cigarette seeming to freeze the air around her, crackling and bursting into tiny pops of ice. "What do you want me to say?"

Chapter **Twenty-Five**

———

Camp was gone by the time I got up the next morning. I came downstairs and went into the kitchen where my mother was sitting at the table reading the newspaper. She looked up briefly, said hello and resumed her reading. I went to the pantry, opened the cupboard door and tried to decide what I wanted for breakfast. Lou was visiting her family in Chicago.

"I'll make pancakes, if you'd like," my mother said, an offer so unexpectedly maternal I was temporarily speechless.

"Well?" she prompted. "It's a yes or no question, Riddle. No need to prepare formal remarks."

"Yes," I said. "Please."

She put down the paper and slid back in the chair, stood up and went over to the refrigerator where she retrieved a quart of milk and a carton of eggs.

"Please bring me the pancake mix," she asked, searching for a mixing bowl.

"It's in the bottom cupboard," I said finally, after listening to her systematically open and bang shut the same cupboard doors over and over again.

"Where's Camp?" I finally worked up the nerve to ask, half afraid that he might be in pieces in the bathtub.

"Washington," she said. "No need to panic. It was a planned trip. He decided at the last minute to drive himself to the airport in Boston. He'll be home in a few days."

"Are you two speaking?"

"We're speaking. Whether we're enjoying it or not is a whole other conversation." She inexpertly cracked an egg on the edge of the mixing bowl, small shards of the shell spraying the pancake mix. "Dammit. How does anyone do this?" she said, helpless and annoyed, scraping the contents of the bowl into the garbage bin and preparing to start over.

"Here, let me," I said, sensing a lifetime of culinary failure ahead, taking the new recruit from her hand and tapping it on the side of the rim, the shell splitting neatly down the middle, the egg landing in a perfectly formed oval in the center of the mixture.

Having stumbled her way through the rest of the preparation, she turned off the heat under the skillet and wiped her hands on a dish towel, sighing with relief.

"Thank God that nightmare is over," she said, pancakes made at last. She looked wrung out—knots of hair poking out from behind her ears in disarrayed tufts and twirls. If her hair had been a sweater, it would have been missing a few buttons. My mother could have led the siege of Iwo Jima while balancing a book on her head, but don't ask her to boil pasta unless you're prepared to spend the evening talking her down from a ledge.

I sat down at the table and sprinkled brown sugar over my plate of buttermilk pancakes, four of them, one on top of the other, all varying sizes and irregular shapes, slightly burnt on the outside, the inside lumpy, wet and runny.

"They're good," I said. "Thanks."

"You're welcome," she said, looking at me as if she couldn't imagine what I was talking about, pouring herself half a glass of grapefruit juice. She took a sip and then another and dumped the rest down the sink. Breakfast. Eating gave her no pleasure. For the most part, she appeared to view it as a form of weakness, a vaguely vulgar display of human frailty.

"So, I need to drive into Provincetown and run a few errands," she said, letting the water run in the sink. "Would you like to come?"

"Sure," I said, reaching for a glass of milk, finishing off my pancakes as she took a few moments to restore order to the kitchen before going to her room to change, the four dogs thumping up the stairs behind her, the water still running in the sink.

She came back down wearing a calf-length, licorice-colored cigarette skirt with a kick pleat in the rear and a form-fitting gray sweater with an envelope neck. She had on black high heels. Her blonde hair was pulled back in a sleek ponytail. Her lips were tulip red and her skin was white.

"You look nice," I said in solemn understatement. I wasn't being stingy. I was enjoying the novelty of a domestic encounter conducted in lowercase for a change.

"Thank you, Riddle," she said. "You're just full of compliments today. What's the occasion? Are you and Harry planning to elope?"

"You always have to spoil things," I said.

Dorothy came toward me, wagging her tail, holding up her right hind leg, lifting it off the ground as she walked. Panting, she stopped and smiled up at me before limping off to her bed in the corner of the kitchen.

"I spoke to the vet the other day about Dorothy," my mother said. Chattiness, however awkward, constituted her best attempt at an apology. "You know all the problems she's been having . . ."

I nodded. Dorothy's health had been on a steady decline over the last few years.

"He doesn't know what's wrong. She has so many different symptoms, but they don't point to a single obvious conclusion. He prefers not to attempt a diagnosis since even educated guesses are invariably wrong and an incorrect treatment can be worse than no treatment at all."

"I hope it's nothing really bad," I said, kneeling down beside Dorothy and stroking her head.

"Me, too." She was rooting around in her bag looking for her sunglasses.

"What do we do in the meantime?"

"The vet said we'll just have to watch and wait and see, nothing else to do in these complicated cases. Her condition will manifest itself eventually. Whatever is wrong will become clear in time. It always does."

THE CAR WAS CLIPPING ALONG, windows open, sun and wind streaming in as we drove up and down the narrow curving roads. My mother drove too fast, piloting the car as if it were a sailboat heading into the wind. With Greer at the wheel, I always felt as if we were hurtling toward something. We drove in silence, both of us thinking about what had happened the night before but declining to discuss it directly.

"Why did you marry Camp?" I asked her, breaking the impasse, my oblique way of addressing what was on my mind.

She shifted her gaze away from the road and toward me. She was wearing sunglasses but I didn't need to see her eyes to read her expression; the slightly bitter curve of her mouth told its own tale of resignation and disappointment.

"Because he showed up," she said, looking away, eyes focused straight ahead as she navigated the sharp turns of the road.

"I don't want to be like you when I get older," I said.

"Oh, come now," she said. "There are worse fates."

"Like what?" I said.

"How would you like to be a chocolate eclair alone in a room with Mirabel Whiffet?"

I stared out the window for the next five miles.

"For God's sake, Riddle, I loved him. I couldn't live without him. All right? Are you happy now?"

"Did you love Michael Devlin more?"

"That's for me to know," she said.

WE SPLIT UP ONCE we reached Provincetown—it was safer that way. I wasn't interested in clothes and was especially resistant to my mother's persistent desire to remake me in her likeness. Around noon I walked into Crunchies, a gentrified hamburger joint on the main drag, where we had agreed to meet for lunch before heading back home. The restaurant was nearly full. Loud and exuberant, it crackled and popped like an accidental collision of hot oil and water in a skillet.

"Hey, Hoffa, over here!" I heard Harry shouting at me, his voice rising up over the collective din of tourists and hungry regulars.

Harry was here? At first, I couldn't believe my bad luck, then I couldn't believe my good luck. His hand over his head, he was waving at me from a crowded booth at the rear of the restaurant. Still mortified from the events of the night before, I looked around for an escape route. It was a reflex destined to pass quickly. My desire to spend time around Harry overrode any impulse I had to flee.

I walked toward him, feeling intimidated when I realized that he was with a bunch of friends. Six or seven of them, maybe more, sat jammed into the booth. Windburned and steamy, they were an industrial-strength wrecking crew, with a talent for making a bright Saturday afternoon seem like a dingy 4 a.m. downtown prowl.

"Sit down," Harry said, standing up in greeting, seeming remarkably unaltered after last night. "What are you doing wandering around unattended?"

"I'm meeting my mother for lunch," I said. "She's shopping."

"Your mother eats here? Must appeal to her wicked sense of adventure," Harry said, making a spot for me next to a girl sitting beside him. How had I missed seeing her?

"This is my girlfriend, Jemima," he said.

Girlfriend. I blinked rapidly. I didn't dare cry. There wasn't an ark big enough to protect the world from the flood of my tears. Was it just me or did the sky seem suddenly beige? Swept free of color and no breeze to lift the terrible stillness that covered everything like crepe, all blessings mislaid or turned to stone.

Harry had a girlfriend.

"Have something to eat," Harry invited, unaware of my devastation, gesturing toward a plate of French fries and onion rings in the middle of the table.

"No, thanks," I said.

"I like a girl with no appetite," Harry said, grinning over at Jemima.

"Harry," she said, pretending to sound annoyed. She smiled up at me and said hello. My heart sputtered and backfired. I had never seen a prettier girl. She looked like Snow White, which only succeeded in making me acutely conscious of my own status as a dwarf.

Despite her feigned shock and disapproval, she was transparently charmed by his antics, but then again so was I. I sat in silence for the next twenty minutes, checking the door constantly, looking for my mother as Harry and his friends engaged in the conversational equivalent of arm wrestling.

"Harry tells me that you're quite an equestrian," Jemima said, as she made a point of not eating what was in front of her.

"Not as good as he is," I said, truthfully.

"Is he really as good a rider as people say?" Jemima asked.

"Oh, yes," I said. "Don't you ride?" I already knew the answer to that one. An experienced rider who had seen Harry on horseback would never have asked.

"No," she said. "I'm terrified of horses."

I was just young enough and ruthless enough in my judgments to hold such an admission in contempt. For the first time I understood what Patton felt like when he slapped that soldier suffering from battle fatigue. "He should have pulled out his revolver and shot him on the spot," my father said, as he held me to the same standards of attitude and performance.

She had her hand on Harry's knee and was running one long, slender finger casually along the inside of his thigh. He was laughing at something someone said, not even paying attention to her. She leaned over and kissed him on the ear. She looped her leg over his. How could she be so blasé about being so brazen? Did boys really like that sort of thing? I finished off my chocolate milk shake feeling like the table mascot—feeling, for all the world, like a pygmy among giants.

"Jesus, it's almost 1:30, my old man is going to kill me. I was supposed to meet him an hour ago," Harry said, grinning over at Jemima before he dove for the last onion ring. "We're driving into Boston. We're supposed to fly to Palm Springs tomorrow morning."

"How long are you going to be gone? To Palm Springs, I mean," I asked.

"Couple of weeks," Harry said.

"I'll miss you," Jemima said. "I wish you weren't going."

"I guess you won't be coming to Gin's hunt tomorrow then?" I said. Harry shook his head.

"Nah. I don't like hunting. Killing animals for sport is not my idea of a fun way to spend the day."

"Most of the time the fox gets away," I mumbled, staring at the table.

"You don't admire it, but you're going to do it anyway? What's that all about, Hoffa?" Harry wouldn't let me off the hook.

"I just love riding to hounds so much," I whined. It was a pitiable response and I knew it. Every year Gin held two major events at the farm—a hunt in August and a horse auction in early September, the highlights of the summer as far as I was concerned. Hunting was illegal in the off season, but Gin didn't let that worry him. He considered himself above the law. "If there's any trouble, I'll just pay the fine and be done with it," he used to say.

Harry was just getting wound up when a server approached, his latent contempt preceding him to the table like a charmless cologne. "Devlin?" He sniffed, surveying the table.

"You're looking for me?" Harry asked.

"There's a phone call for you," the waiter said, lip curling in the direction of the front desk.

"Shit. Gotta be my dad. Tell him I left, okay? Will you do that please?" Harry jumped to his feet and reached for his jacket.

"Well, no, I won't do that. You can do that yourself. Follow me."

Harry amiably took his direction and loped along after him. He was amused by the waiter's intransigent snobbery. It would never have occurred to him to raise hell about anything. Jemima followed him with her eyes and then she turned around, took a sip of her drink and leaned into me. "I'm surprised your mother lets you wander around Provincetown all by yourself," she said. "At your age."

"I don't know what you mean," I said, though I knew exactly what she meant.

"Oh, no offense," she said with exaggerated contrition. "I almost forgot what it was like to be a kid."

"Does Harry know what a bitch you are?" I asked, marveling at my own brashness.

"What did you say to me?"

"Oh, no offense," I said.

The truth is that's what I wanted to say, if only I had been brave enough to say it. What I actually said was nothing at all. I never said a word, just stared down at the table and felt my legs grow shorter with each passing moment in her company.

"HARRY DOESN'T BELIEVE IN hunting," I said to my mother as we drove along the winding ocean-view road toward home, brilliant sun illuminating a familiar journey. "He thinks it's cruel."

"Well, it is when you get right down to it. I would be hard pressed to make an argument otherwise."

"Don't look so amazed," she said, briefly averting her eyes from the road to confront my astonished expression. "Must you wear every emotion you feel on your face? No one likes a gaper, Riddle."

"If you think hunting is wrong, then why do you hunt?"

Greer let out a deep sigh. "Oh, God," she said full of exasperation. "There is only so much is-it-right or is-it-wrong that I can pack into a day. Think of the suffering that went into your riding boots. Are you going to stop riding? For that matter, look at the way horses are abused in the name of competition. Do you intend to stop competing? Think about how your father tortures himself—and others, too, by the way—by constantly invoking his principles."

I wasn't impressed.

"Why do I bother? You're just like your father with his constant moral hectoring."

"Do you ever wonder why Camp is the way he is?"

"What do you mean?"

"Do you think he killed anyone in the war?"

"I have no idea. You would have to ask him that question."

"Yes, but what do you think? Do you think he killed someone?"

She considered for a moment before answering, as if she were mediating an internal debate.

"Yes, I would imagine that he did."

"It must be awful."

"Oh, come now. I think everyone deserves to be killed at some point."

Greer looked into the rearview mirror and adjusted her makeup. She always seemed poised to hear a director yell "Cut!"

"He talks a lot about the war, but he never talks about that."

"Riddle, here's a little grown-up tip for you. When it comes to telling stories, it's not what you tell that matters, it's what you leave out that's important."

No kidding. I couldn't argue with her about that.

I stared out the window, as was my habit. Greer wasn't exactly offering me much in the way of moral counsel. She was generally annoyed by any discussion that involved ethics.

She leaned forward, grinding her cigarette into the ashtray. I waited as she lit up another one.

We drove along in silence, my mother releasing her ponytail, blonde hair flowing freely to her shoulders, hair shining, hair always shining.

"Riddle," she said finally, glancing in my direction. "Semel insanivimus omnes."

"Speak English, please. Is that a line of dialogue from one of your films?"

We've all been mad at least once.

My mother and i were sitting down to supper when we heard the jiggle of a key in the front door, the dogs' tails thumping in unison against the floor giving away the intruder's identity.

"Camp! What are you doing home?" I asked, jumping to my feet, my mother looking on quizzically from her spot at the dining room table.

"My flight got delayed. Then there was some confusion around scheduling in Washington. I decided someone was trying to tell me something, so I came home. To hell with it. I'll go tomorrow."

"How did you get home?" Greer asked. "Did you hire a car?"

"Gula drove me, believe it or not. I ran into him at the airport picking up guests arriving for Gin's annual massacre of the innocents."

The August hunt tended to attract riders from neighboring states who were serious about fox hunting. The auction, still a couple of weeks away, drew a more international crowd interested in buying and selling top-of-the-line competition horses. Gin also held a deer hunt that weekend attended by friends of his and Greer's, social acquaintances, prominent people in the arts, politics and society, some of whom hunted, some of whom were interested in buying horses, all of whom wanted to be seen as important enough to warrant an invitation.

"We know how you feel about hunting, Camp," my mother said. "Have you ever considered keeping your thoughts to yourself, or must you be heard on every topic?"

"You might be surprised at the things I keep to myself," Camp said, a trace of bitterness creeping into his voice.

"You seem a little weary," my mother said. "Are you not feeling well?"

"I am tired," Camp said, a rare concession for him. "Think I'll have a shower and relax."

I don't think I had ever heard my father use the word "relax" in a sentence before that moment. My mother was equally taken aback. "Should I arrange to have you buried, or would you prefer cremation?"

"Just throw me out with the garbage," Camp said, undoing the top button of his shirt and loosening the knot of his tie as he headed out of the dining room and up the stairs.

Chapter Twenty-Six

———

I F YOU'VE NEVER HUNTED ON HORSEBACK, YOU PROBABLY HAVE a mistakenly refined notion of what it means. Imagine it as a piece of music where the bottom notes repeat in jarring, thunderous sequence until all you can hear is a throbbing bass line. There are no real high notes in hunting. There's the odd soaring relief when it's lift-up and over a hurdle you sail, but most of the time it's pounding, relentless, digging up the earth as you go, and all the while there's that meditative tremor of hoof to ground like fist to drum.

A hunt starts in silence. Hounds are sent in to rout the fox. The field is quiet and well back. When the pack finds they immediately give tongue and then there's a period of intense listening, of holding still, to hear the direction of the chase, to decide the course, to evaluate the freshness of the line. Dry ground and dry air do not hold scent well, wind and temperature have their own roles to play.

If hounds run with heads held high, the scent is off the ground, so strong it owns the air. Sometimes the scent lies still and flat against the earth; other times it moves like an invisible cord. When the pack hits it they take possession of it; occasionally they get beyond it or behind it or run riot when they encounter the distracting scent of deer or rabbit or coyote.

You want hounds with head to ground, otherwise they may lose interest. When you hunt on horseback, you're in pursuit of the invisible. You're being guided by instinct, following the lead of a quarry seldom seen. There's no greater thrill than when you catch sudden sight of a flash of red, simultaneously appearing and disappearing, existing only in the moment, coming into view in a way so ephemeral that it makes you question whether you're in pursuit of anything at all.

Some hunters determine to kill what they chase, stop the fox in its tracks, have it all end where it ends. Others, like me, enjoy nothing better than being led around in circles, as the object of all that desire gets far away, until a vibrant slash of color, a startling crease of memory is all that remains.

The fox broke cover that day. He led us over many miles—running, evading, circling, appearing and disappearing, reversing himself and taking us back almost to where it all began near the big kettle pond on Gin's property. That's where we lost him. Struggling to find his scent, the dogs cast about until all but one of them gave up. Bruce, the lead hound, never would say die but kept his head to the ground until he recovered the line or had to be leashed and dragged back to the kennel, his defeat imposed by others.

The other riders decided to head back to the stable—all but me. I watched Bruce and looked around, examining the countryside for a clue, for something to guide my way. Cantering off after him, the two of us were trying to recover the scent. He led me deeper into the woods to an old stone fence.

The fox had broken the line of scent by jumping up and running along the length of the fence and into the dense coppice wood beyond. Bruce ran alongside Mary as we followed the fence to its end, to where it crumbled and fell away and we were able to enter into the thickets of hazel, so dense at points I could barely make my way. Bruce was ahead of me when I heard him. I followed the sound of his cry and was about to call him back when a pair of deer ran from the bush, startling Mary, who shied so dramatically she almost unseated me.

Pressing Mary onward, my heart banged in my chest. There was no trail left to follow, and in the near distance I caught a brief last sight of the fox as he went to earth.

I called for Bruce to come away and as we struggled through the dense undergrowth, the old dock and canoe visible ahead in the clearing, the canoe latched to the dock, my eyes settled on something jarring, its effects disturbing.

Alarmed, I hesitated, then urged Mary forward. What was I looking at? A decaying animal. Is that what it was? My eyes focused on a hank of hair caught at the base of a sycamore tree, visible among a crucible of coppice stools. Squinting, I drew nearer and with each closing step I realized with a sense of mounting horror that along with the school bag and the topsiders and the artfully arranged miraculous medal and the tarnished silver chain, I had found Charlie Devlin.

THE POLICE GUESSED THAT Charlie had died the same weekend that he disappeared. The timeline seemed right. Determining the cause of death was a problem, they said, because there was so little of him left—his skull and bones, stripped bare, were scattered erratically across the forest floor by purposeful scavengers and by the random forces of nature. Adding to their initial confusion, his bones were charred. Easily enough explained when Gin told them that he had done some controlled burning in that area to protect against the incursion of nonnative plants.

Privately, they speculated that Charlie had gotten drunk or high or both and had decided to go to the pond at Gin's where he and Harry had gone so many times before. That would explain why his jacket was found on our property. He had obviously dropped it or discarded it along the way.

Charlie Devlin lost his life as a result of misadventure, just another one of those sad but inevitable casualties of youth.

Determining the cause of death may have been a problem for the police, but it wasn't a problem for me. I sat down far from his remains, sun shining through the leaves of the overhanging trees, Mary peacefully grazing on lush clumps of tall grass, wind whistling through, and I thought about all of it, the running, the scuffling, the violent banging, the shattering glass and the plaintive cry. Why?

THE REALITY OF THOSE BONES, stark and stripped bare, quiet and unremarkable—they could have been the remains of a lamb or a fox or a rabbit—possessed, for all their plainness and their simplicity, the power to elicit from me a brutal admission about the cost of my silence. Gula had killed Charlie Devlin in the yellow barn that Sunday in June, and I hadn't lifted a finger to help him.

"She never shed a tear," one of the hunters that found me marveled when discussing me with the police. "Most girls her age would have been hysterical, but she was so calm and composed. She said she was afraid to go for help. She thought she might not be able to find her way back to where he was. Most girls wouldn't have cared. They would have just gotten the hell out of there and as far away from the body as they could."

I had spent the summer crying for Charlie Devlin—at least, I thought it was for Charlie. Finding him strewn among the grass and the leaves, wan and dispersed and rendered anonymous, I felt such shame, such guilt, even as I was ashamed to feel shame, disgusted by my feelings of guilt.

My failure to act disentitled me. Feeling nothing is the worst feeling of all. Since finding his remains that day in the woods, I've never shed another tear for him. How could I? By what right? However would I dare?

Chapter **Twenty-Seven**

———

"'POLICE' AND 'THINK' ARE TWO WORDS THAT ARE NEVER TO be used in the same sentence," my mother said, no occasion too somber to warrant a moratorium on the expression of her opinions. "Gin told me they used divers to search the pond this morning but found nothing illuminating. Apparently, Charlie and Harry used to occasionally visit the pond unbeknownst to anyone, so it was familiar to him."

"Sad state of affairs all around," Camp said. "Quite a blow for Harry, though I suppose at least now he knows what happened. No more agonizing about whether his brother's dead or alive."

"A terrible thing for Michael, losing a son," my mother reminded him.

"Yes, that too." Camp cleared his throat and ran his finger around the rim of his glass. "How is Gin reacting to the tragic discovery?"

"Oh," Greer said. "That's the other thing. I think he's terrified that the police suspect him of being involved in the disappearance. So bizarre. Honestly, it's enough to make me wonder."

"Gin's total ineffectiveness as a human being is his best asset in this case," Camp said. "Unfortunately, it sounds as if Charlie Devlin got himself into a jam. Lots of kids do these things. Inevitably, some of them pay the ultimate price. It's a good lesson for you." He pointed at me, as I stared back at him without speaking. "Though I'm sorry you had to learn it in such a difficult way."

My mother sought to inject a little vitality into the numbness I was emanating from my corner in the room.

"What about you?" she said, pressing him for information about his trip to Washington. He'd cut it short when he heard the news about Charlie.

"Went well, despite the standard nonsense. Very well. Stupendously, in fact. I think I can safely report that the party is amenable to my ambitions."

I marveled at my parents' ability to carry on as if nothing had happened.

"Really?" my mother said, eyebrows raised. "Will I be expected to refer to you as Your Grace?"

"Only on Saturday nights," Camp said, as they laughed and I looked on.

KISSING MY MOTHER ON the cheek—the discovery of Charlie Devlin's remains seemed to have had a restorative effect on their relationship—Camp announced he was going to get changed. Greer walked on ahead of him. Pausing at the doorway, Camp called my name.

"So you're fine." It was less a question than a pronouncement. No inquiries from Camp as to my emotional response to finding Charlie Devlin's remains.

"Shipshape," I said.

"You cooperated fully with the police? Told them everything." I nodded.

"Good. I'm proud of you."

Oh God. Proud of me?

Camp seemed relieved. It was the most relaxed I had seen him in ages. His relief was evident in the way he walked, the animated spontaneous way he talked.

"You don't seem tense anymore, Camp," I said.

"You might be a little tense, too, if you were being accused of murdering a fifteen-year-old boy," he said. "Now we can finally put this thing behind us."

Charlie had been found, the tragedy satisfactorily defined. Any connection to our family had ceased to be of interest or concern to anyone. Anyone but me, that is.

Sometimes it seemed to me that my parents never met a catastrophe they didn't like. The day-to-day stuff—cooking, laundry, simple parenting—undid them, but give them a war or a murder, set the whole world on fire, and they were like a vaudeville team that you couldn't extract from the stage without a grappling hook. Camp, especially, rose to the occasion. Lou once told me that she had talked to some of the men he served with and they all said that even in the worst situations, Camp used to tell jokes and make funny remarks. "He was always able to make us laugh," they said.

No question about it, Camp was the sun; the rest of us were orbiting lesser planets. He was exciting to be around. Incapable of a lukewarm response, he made things happen. A creator of worlds, he possessed a deep need to monitor and control the people he loved. A few minor personal adjustments, the occasional pruning of free will, a chop to point of view here, a trim to independent thought there—it seemed a reasonable trade-off to me. Besides, he was a merciful god and he dispensed favors in a dizzying flurry. The air was dense with his blessings; like a cloud of cherry blossoms propelled on a gentle wind, they soared then settled. I was forever knee-deep in petals and perfume. If ever he administered

discipline, it was swift and straightforward and readily compre-
hended.

I WALKED SLOWLY TOWARD THE car, my father and mother
uncharacteristically silent, preoccupied with their own thoughts,
following a few feet behind me. I climbed into the backseat and
looked down at my hands folded in my lap. Camp slid behind the
wheel and stared straight ahead. My mother looked out the passenger window and never once spoke the whole way to the church.

Charlie Devlin's funeral mass was held at Our Lady of Lourdes
in Wellfleet, the church he had attended as a boy. It was simple
and private, unadorned, no eulogy—his father's decision, and one
that earned grudging respect from Camp, who considered speech
making to be an unacceptably Protestant manifestation of grief.

I remember some things from that day, forget other things.
My father's businesslike demeanor. He shook hands with Michael
and their brief exchange was brusquely formal, sterile as a military
salute. Despite their differences, my father wouldn't have considered for a moment not attending Charlie's funeral. I remember
how handsome Harry looked in his dark suit.

I remember searching for my mother. Going from room to room
and not finding her. Seeing her finally, outside, with Michael, the
two of them alone in the rear of the churchyard, standing under
a large tree. I came on them from behind, Michael's face buried
in his hands, his shoulders shaking, silently sobbing, my mother's
arm around his shoulder, her hair a yellow shroud.

They never knew I was there. I never knew you could be too
sad to cry.

Wandering down into the basement, I sat by myself in the
kitchen for a while. Then I went upstairs and into the church where
Harry stood next to the parish priest, the bishop and a church car-

dinal, their presence a tribute to Michael Devlin's stature, Harry smiling and shaking hands, thanking each person for coming.

He greeted my father politely. Later, I stood in the vestibule watching as Harry and Camp helped Gin to his car. His grief seemed vulgar and out of place, self-indulgent and insincere, as if someone had shown up to the funeral drunk and disorderly and demanding a beer.

"Why did this terrible thing happen? At the farm of all places!" he cried as he leaned into Harry while they walked down the church steps. Gula, playing the role of chauffeur, stepped out from behind the wheel of the driver's seat as they approached. He opened up the passenger door, spoke to my father and then extended his hand to Harry and told him how sorry he was. As Harry and my father turned their backs to him and walked back toward the church, Gula smiled up at me and waved.

Something in a hood. Something in a cape. I looked at him and all I could see was soot and grime and charred bone, a piece of skull, russet hair with crimson tips. I saw him as if for the first time and he was awful to behold. What did he do? Why did he do it? What had I made possible?

I felt a hand on my shoulder. I jumped. It was Harry.

Shaking my head, I managed to eke out a stilted expression of sympathy.

"How did you find him when I couldn't?" Harry said, his face white and stricken. I looked down at the ground. I knew what I had to do.

"Harry . . ." Just as I found my voice, his attention was diverted when Jemima emerged from the crowd and took his hand and whispered in his ear and led him away.

Would I have told him if she hadn't interrupted? I don't know. I'd like to think so.

Standing at the open doorway of the church, I glanced down

at the book of condolences, multiple expressions of sympathy on every page. Camp had written something. I picked up the pen and thought about what I wanted to say. Gula came up behind me, waiting his turn. I fled without signing.

You get the epitaph you deserve. That day at the funeral I earned mine.

She fled without signing.

CAMP DROVE US HOME from the funeral, my mother in the passenger seat, me behind her in the back, the only sounds the tires rolling along the road and the wind whistling in through the open crack of my window. It was a beautiful summer day, a pretty day to be alive. The birds sang and the sun shone. The ocean glittered in alternating shades of blue: sapphire, cobalt, indigo.

"Camp," I said, breaking the silence, "what did you mean when you wrote to Michael in the book of condolences, 'I will see you in the morning?' "

"Never mind, Riddle," Camp said.

More secrets. I started to protest when he cut me off.

"It's private. Do you understand? It's none of your business. It's between Michael and me."

Once inside the house, my mother removed her hat, a gesture that felt somehow ceremonial, and set it on the table in the entryway and left it there, a solemn memorial of where we had been. She pulled off her gloves, tucked them into her bag and ran her fingers through her hair, glancing at herself in the hallway mirror, then went into the kitchen to make coffee.

My father sidled up to the piano and casually tapped out a tune. Walking over to the tall windows overlooking the dunes and the beach, the ocean, he paused to look, take it all in, then he reached for the crank at the bottom of the sill and opened wide the windows on either side, sunlight and breeze pouring in, flooding the house with brilliant light and a rush of fresh air.

"Greer, I've been thinking, we should have a party," he said, turning to face her as she stood in the doorway of the living room, a sudden gust of wind blowing her hair back off her shoulders.

Chapter **Twenty-Eight**

———

DESPITE MY MOTHER'S AVERSION TO THE HUMAN RACE, SHE was an accomplished and generous hostess and beautiful to see, like a string of white lights stretched across an evening sky. "Why do you look so glum?" she asked me as I lay across my parents' antique bed watching her dress for the party. "How would you like to be me? You're lucky. You can hide up in your room. I'm the one who's stuck front and center all evening with these professional windbags and their vacant wives. I'll tell you something, Riddle, this is my enforced stint in the army and I only intend to do one short tour of duty. I feel like a preacher's wife."

"You don't look like one," I said, turning over onto my abdomen, elbows on the chenille bedspread, chin in hand. "You sure as hell don't act like one."

She stood up, wearing a strapless cobalt blue dress with ruffles on a boned bodice and more ruffles on the front of a full skirt that had its own red tulle crinoline. She was the world's most sophisticated cupcake.

"Come, zip me up," she said.

"It just seems weird, that's all," I said.

"What seems weird?" she asked, leaning forward, staring into the mirror, curling her long black eyelashes.

"Having a party after what's happened. I mean, to the Devlins. It doesn't feel right."

"As Mr. Kipling once noted, grave digging is not cheerful, Riddle," she said, powdering her cheeks, reaching for her lipstick, the same red shade as her crinoline.

"It's only been ten days."

"Life goes on."

"I don't understand why Camp wants to have a party. It's like he's celebrating."

"Well, that's the conventional interpretation, anyway," my mother said. "A more enlightened thinker might conclude that he's seen too much death in his time on this earth and this is his way of having the last word."

"Or not caring. Or gloating."

"Would you prefer crocodile tears? Would that satisfy your sense of propriety?"

"Do you think that Camp is happy that Michael is suffering?" I asked.

She sighed and hesitated, her hand faltering briefly before she resumed applying her lipstick.

"No," she said finally. "I do not."

I COULD HEAR THE DULL thrum of honeyed party chatter from my perch on the landing, the main floor slippery and sliding in the dross of panegyric, doggerel and indiscreet divulgence. As far as I was concerned, my parents' get-togethers were the social equivalent of a doily.

This little get-together was further distinguished by the noisy presence of campaign workers and handpicked supporters and a number of big-ticket donors being rewarded for the size of their contributions to Camp's campaign. Camp enjoyed a significant lead in the polls against the hapless Joe Becker, and he seemed determined to enjoy the moment. If he was worried about Michael's threats, he kept those concerns to himself.

"Gorgeous, as usual, sheer poetry, that's what you are, Greer," Gin said, taking both of my mother's milky white hands in his, surveying her as if she were someone's idealized artistic vision, an impeccable piece of writing or a painting, as he searched in vain for a clumsy phrase, a single visible brushstroke, anything that might break the spell.

"Why, thank you, Gin, you look as cute as a button yourself," my mother said, kissing him on the cheek, her arm wrapped lightly around his shoulders, skimming his aura rather than his person— my mother had perfected a style of hugging that was essentially devoid of human contact—a lit cigarette poised between her fingers, like a glamorous extension of her signature French manicure, inducing in her guests a sweet asphyxia.

"What a wonderful idea to have a party," Gin said. "There's been too much sadness. Let's celebrate life. What better way to defy death? Oh, and here's Mother," he said, as Mirabel appeared behind him on the threshold of the open door.

"Greer, darling!" Mirabel exclaimed, walking right past her only child and into my mother's arms. "Beautiful! Sensational! You are breathtaking, my dear," Mirabel gushed, as my mother strained manfully to return the compliment.

"My, what an unusual dress, Mirabel," she said. "Are those peacock feathers?"

"Oh, my goodness, no, dear, it's llama. Isn't it marvelous?" Mirabel said.

"I don't care if it's desiccated bull penis, you look fabulous," my father said, lifting her off the ground with his bear hug. "If I were twenty years older . . ."

"My, you're terrible, Camp," Mirabel said. "Oh, and there's dear little Quiz," she gushed, spotting me in my pink and orange dress—my mother's choice.

"Nobody else in the world has hair this vivid, might as well exploit the hell out of it," she had said.

"Her name is Riddle, Mirabel," my mother said.

"I knew it had something to do with being perplexing," she said.

As THE HOUSE FILLED, as guests grew more familiar and well oiled, the conversation ricocheted back and forth as predictably as a tennis ball, from politics—the election, Vietnam and the Watergate break-in—to people, to pop culture, to the state of things.

"We simply must find a way to convince the blue-collar chap that the opera has something to offer him." Harold Bristol, a New York philanthropist with an interest in the arts, was holding court, expressing, to nods all around, his frustration with the common man's preference for low culture.

"Oh, you're so right, Harold," Mirabel quickly agreed. "I always say to Gin, if I do nothing else in my life, let me impart my deep love of *Don Giovanni* to the man in the street."

Sitting alone on a little embroidered stool, burying my face in a sofa pillow, I tried to suppress a giggle.

"Please," my father said. "Who are you trying to kid? The day you find yourselves sitting next to a welder during a performance of *Carmen* is the day you'll find another interest to inflict yourselves on."

I reappeared from behind my protective pillow, exhilarated by Camp's recklessness.

Generally speaking, among my parents' set, where mortal sins were visual infractions measured in pounds and polyester,

Camp's social activism was about as welcome as a teetotaler at a wine tasting.

"Well, if it isn't the poor man's Che Guevara. I must say, you're looking suitably lean and hungry. What's new in the revolution business, Godfrey?" Gordon Crenshaw, a family friend, Scotch and soda in hand, narrow legs supporting a thick girth, hollered across the room.

"You've got it all wrong, Gordon. I'm just a humble, hardworking candidate from Massachusetts, an anonymous drone. I've got more in common with a carpenter ant than with an insurgent, let alone a name-brand revolutionary." Camp, who had already downed a few fortifying drinks in preparation for the evening's familiar challenges, was trying his best to be agreeable to this disagreeable man, even making a good-hearted attempt to change the subject.

"You've lost some frontage this year to erosion," he said brightly enough as Gordon made his way across the room, but his efforts failed to distract.

"What the hell are you thinking, giving ammunition to the enemy with this Trang Bang business? Fact-finding mission? What unmitigated nonsense. We need to stay the course in Vietnam, unless of course you want to see all of Southeast Asia fall into the hands of the Communists? Next thing you know they'll be marching into Washington Square. You fought a war, Camp. You know what it's all about—or you should, anyway. If we pull out now, all we'll be doing is dishonoring the sacrifice of the thousands of men that have died over there. Assuming you give a damn, of course."

"Where's Harriet?" my mother hastily inquired. She was being courteous but somewhat supercilious in her manner. She despised Gordon's thuggish CEO demagoguery.

"She's gone with her friends to some hen party at the Hendersons in Boston. Thank Christ. I'd heard enough of their prattle.

They're planning to spend the night. They're very disappointed not seeing you tonight, my dear. Harriet loves to show off her friendship with you."

"I can't imagine why," my mother said coyly, fully conscious of her high-wattage appeal.

"Come, come, Greer, you are every inch the movie star and you know it," Mirabel chided, fanning her face with her fingers. "I never get tired of your performance as Maude in *The Fragrant Letter*. Oh, my, what have I said now?" She was reacting to my father and me laughing out loud, in unison. My mother hated that picture and despised the character of Maude. Inevitably, it was the role she was most identified with.

Despite Greer's best efforts, Gordon refused to be dissuaded from his mission.

"By the way, Camp, I've been wanting to talk to you. Rumor is you might be sitting on the wrong side of this inheritance tax business. That's crap. Why in hell should my family's hard-earned wealth wind up in the hands of the government? I'll tell you why. So they can hand out my dough to some street criminal on welfare who'll use it to buy drugs, Kentucky Fried Chicken and a gun so he can mug me and continue to rob me blind. Is this what you're supporting?"

"I understand your frustrations, Gordon, but I like to think it's a more complex issue than that," Camp said.

"Yeah, well, I'd like to think that everyone's interested in working for a living, too, but I know goddamn well they're not. Why not sit on your ass and let someone like me pay your way? Nice work if you can get it."

"Time to turn down the sheets at Bellevue," my mother whispered in my ear as Gordon, heartened by the supportive rattling of jewelry, reached for another drink. Despite my best efforts otherwise, I was beginning to enjoy myself.

"You listen to me, Chairman Mao, my grandfather and my

father worked hard. I work hard. I've earned every bit of money and success that has come my way. I deserve it."

"You work hard?" Uh-oh, it was official, Camp was coming undone. The tables in the room began to shake. I could hear the tinkling of glass in the china cabinet. The gardenias in the glass vase on the coffee table trembled and disseminated in invisible odorous waves. "Doing what? Struggling through three-hour liquid lunches and terrorizing your employees? I don't care if you work from dawn to dusk—you're amply rewarded. You think those kids from poor countries imprisoned on rock piles and tethered to sewing machines for eighteen hours a day don't work hard? What do they deserve? Your contempt, apparently."

"Do you talk to all your supporters this way? You might recall, Camp, I crossed party lines for you. Out of loyalty to your mother and respect for your wife's family, I've been a big contributor to your campaign, but if I thought for one moment that you were serious about this socialist garbage . . . You need to get this hippie claptrap under better control, my friend. After all, you have ambitions beyond the House, so I hear. Unless you'd prefer to go back to writing songs that nobody's ever heard of."

"Why don't we all just take a deep breath and calm down?" Greer urged. "Camp tends to be idealistic and impassioned. He's a true romantic. They're a scarce commodity. All the more reason to cherish him."

"Jesus Christ, Greer, I'm not Howdy Doody," Camp protested.

"I think it runs a little deeper than idealistic intemperance or exuberance, Greer. Have you read this man's books? Sheer claptrap." Gordon was talking about Camp as if he were invisible, or at least beyond the reach of rational discourse.

"Oh, Gordon, come now, we're so fortunate to have Camp at the intellectual helm. He makes the hard decisions so we don't need to. It's very restful," my mother said.

Crenshaw laughed, a deep appreciative guffaw, as empty in its own way as the champagne glasses spread out on the bar next to him in trim opportunistic hedgerows. "You know, you're absolutely right. I always say that in his own way Camp is a brilliant guy. It's only that I look around and everywhere I see a lack of ambition, people content to sit back in their little wartime houses with their ugly wives and their drab surroundings and their dumb kids and let debt and life happen to them. What has become of ambition? When did it become a dirty word?"

"Edmund Burke made a rather interesting observation about ambition," Camp said. "Ambition can creep as well as soar."

"Whatever the hell that's supposed to mean," Gordon said.

"So now that's settled," Gin piped up, "I hear the Devlins have left the country for a while. Terrible, what's happened."

"Wouldn't surprise me if Michael decides to live abroad," a lady in a green dress said.

"Yes, after all, what is there for him here?" a woman in a red cocktail dress spoke up. "It may even be dangerous for him. Who knows? Very mysterious what's happened to that family."

"My, but the son is a good-looking boy," another woman said. "But then Michael was always so handsome, wasn't he? People speak well of Harry, too, from what I understand."

"Harry's wonderful," I said dreamily from my spot in the dining room next to the table. I realized in horror that what I was thinking about in such earnest I had spoken aloud. All eyes were upon me as I clapped my hand over my mouth.

"Well, I won't be shedding any tears for the Devlins. The world's their oyster," Gordon said, coming to my rescue, an unlikely savior. "As for the younger boy, what do you expect when you drink and take drugs? Sure, they've taken a tumble, but hell, don't we all? They have a nice, big, fat, fluffy cushion to land on."

"They're not the only ones," my mother whispered to the people around her, raising her eyebrows in the direction of Crenshaw's amply padded rear.

"Well, that may be a little harsh, Gordon. Poor Michael. It's a good thing we don't know what the fates have planned for us." The woman in green glanced over at my mother, who listened dispassionately, her face a mask. "Is there any news? Do the police still think the death was accidental? Do they suspect foul play?"

"I'm sure the police would gladly exhume Bruno Hauptmann and charge him with a kidnapping if they thought they could make it stick," my mother said. "I think the consensus is that the boy died as a result of misadventure."

"What about enemies? Does anyone come to mind? What possible motive would anyone have to hurt Michael's son?" The lady in the red cocktail dress was determined to build a case.

"I think there is some ancient holy man in the mountains of Tibet who isn't jealous of his money and celebrity, but that's only a rumor," my mother opined.

"Oh, it must be terrible for you, Camp," Mirabel said. "You went through so much together overseas. Michael survived a war only to have his heart broken with the death of his wife and now his son. There is a lesson there—though I would have to think about what it would be."

"I had heard that you served with Michael, Camp," Harold Bristol said.

"Yes," my father said. "We were in the infantry together. Joined up at the same time."

"The Ardennes, right?" Bristol asked as Camp nodded.

"Were you with him at Bastogne?"

"I was."

"That was a hell of a situation."

"It was."

"Michael and I talked about his experiences over there. He was very troubled by things he had seen. He told me he was writing a book. Expiate a few demons. Right a few wrongs. Whatever happened to the book, I wonder?"

"I think it has taken a backseat to events." Gin said. "Just as well, I suspect. Why rehash all these things? It just makes everyone unhappy."

"I'll bet he was a good soldier," Bristol said, pushing my father for an answer.

"Michael was a good soldier," Camp said.

"I was absolutely amazed to find out that he was a sniper. Of course, you knew that."

"Who told you that?" my father asked.

"Why, he did. He'd had a few drinks. It was late, you know the drill. I had no idea. I don't think anyone did. Not the sort of thing one talks about. You'd need to be a certain type, I suspect," Harold continued, as my father listened without comment.

"Oh, this is far too depressing, all this talk of war and death," Gin said. "How about a little change of pace? I have the most wonderful news. I'm getting another Gypsy horse, a mare. She's coming from England very soon, within the next week or so. I'm so excited to have a breeding pair."

"What in hell is a Gypsy horse?" Gordon demanded. "Some nag that can read your fortune? Steal your fortune, more like it," he added, laughing at his own cleverness.

"Looks like you and Gordon have more in common than you think," I whispered to my mother as I came back into the living room. She wasn't impressed.

"Just the most beautiful horse you can imagine," Gin said. "I'll have the first breeding pair in North America."

"Honestly, Gin, if you say, 'breeding pair' one more time," my mother interrupted.

"I intend to establish the breed over here," Gin said. "The Gypsies have kept them a great, glorious secret for generations. It will be my legacy."

"What in hell would some Gypsy have that I might want? For my money, you can't beat a good old-fashioned quarter horse. To hell with this foreign nonsense," Gordon said.

"By the way, Gin, I'm really excited about next week. I always look forward to your garden party weekend. Nothing like the illicit pursuit of deer to get the blood pumping," Harold said.

"Oh, yes, I've decided that everything is going to go ahead right on schedule, despite the unfortunate events of the hunt, so awful what happened, finding the Devlin boy. I do think it's important to try to keep things happy and upbeat and normal in sad times. So things shall carry on as always. Labor Day weekend, big auction of yearlings and foals on Saturday, deer stalking on both days as usual."

"Can we expect to see you there, Greer darling?" Mirabel asked my mother.

"Yes, I'll be there. Wouldn't miss it," my mother said, as Gin looked at her approvingly.

"What about you, Camp?" Harold said.

"Oh, no, not me," Camp said. "I don't derive any pleasure from killing animals."

"Jesus Christ, did you go to Bleeding Heart University?" Gordon said as he approached the bar. "Fill 'er up," he said to the young man hired to serve drinks for the occasion.

I could see my father's mouth twist into a telltale grimace. He ran his hands through his hair and sighed deeply as he turned to confront Gordon. "Listen, you . . ."

"Camp," my mother said, rushing over to his side, taking his elbow. "Would you mind giving me a hand in the kitchen? Riddle, you too, please."

. . .

SAFELY ENSCONCED IN THE kitchen where Lou was supervising the menu, my mother grabbed a tray and began to pile it high with hors d'oeuvres. "You stay here with me, until you cool off," she ordered my father, pausing to light up a cigarette. Within moments, there were lit cigarettes all over the kitchen, little plots of smoke curling skyward like charmless snakes. In her agitation, she just kept lighting cigarette after cigarette, puffing on each one, then abandoning it to light another.

"Camp, who are these people? That woman with the big hair, Harold Bristol's mistress. I can't believe he brought her here along with his wife. She looks as if she represents Arkansas in a frog jump-off. The only woman more unattractive than her is his wife. Such a royal pain in the ass. Silly manners and affected demeanor. Meanwhile, I can see the dirt under her fingernails. As for that wretched couple from your campaign office, they have all the appeal of a mime struggling against an imaginary wind. That repulsive Gordon Crenshaw—the man is a primitive reminder of what life would be like without vitamin C."

"What about your pal Gin?" Camp said. "Just one time I would like to enjoy a party in my own house without that nitwit dominating the landscape. I swear to you, Greer, the minute that jackass pulls out his guitar, I'm going to start shooting," Camp warned. "I refuse to sit through one more of his renditions of "The Age of Aquarius." It's not funny, Riddle," he said, as my mother glared at me from across the table.

"You obviously need a job," she said, handing me the tray of goodies.

I struggled to balance my tray and open the swing door to the kitchen at the same time. Camp came to my rescue. "Thanks," I said, smiling up at him. He smiled back. "Good work, soldier," he said. Then he looked out through the slanted door opening. Gordon was loudly burdening a handful of visibly pained party-goers with more of his unsolicited worldviews.

Camp extended his foot into the corner of the door frame, using the tip of his shoe to hold open the door. His hands free, he used them to fashion an imaginary rifle and, squinting, he held steady aim and then he blew the back of Gordon Crenshaw's head off.

"Oh look out, Riddle!" my mother cried out as the tray slipped from my hands and clattered to the floor, food tumbling every-where, the four basset hounds joyously pouncing.

A few minutes later, the tray replenished, I held the door open for Camp who stepped out ahead of me with a new platter of finger foods. My father's shoulders stiffened. Gin was strum-ming a guitar and singing "The Age of Aquarius."

"Come on, camp, you know you want to," Gin said after sev-eral migraine-inducing encores. "Play a little something for us." He pulled out the piano bench and gestured for Camp to take up position.

"I suppose I could be talked into playing something," Camp said.

There was a smattering of applause and then the room fell silent as he began to play "Soon It's Gonna Rain."

I curled up in a corner of the sofa away from the rest of the guests, who gathered round the piano, my father's voice an authentic soaring counterpoint to the room's wholesale romantic delusion, all those clean jawlines grimly set, everyone's determi-nation not to feel bad as decorous as their choices in clothing, their declamatory festive spirits as shallow as a fading Palm Beach tan.

When he finished singing, someone spoke up and proposed a toast to Michael Devlin. I slipped away into the kitchen as glasses were raised and voices joined in sentimental tribute. Through the glass door I saw Camp standing near the window next to a fifty-year-old Boston fern in a hand-painted urn. As the others sipped their champagne and reminisced, he quietly emptied the contents of his glass into the plant, champagne bubbling down into the soil and soaking the roots.

I looked around for my mother, but she had vanished. I found her a few minutes later at the front of the house. She was alone and looking out over the oily black ocean, the whitecaps of the waves illuminated in the moonlight.

"Needed a moment away," she said as I came up alongside her. We stood together in silence, listening to the roar of the waves. "I suppose I should ride back into battle," she said, reluctantly deciding to head into the house. She put her hand on my arm. "Shhh," she whispered as Mirabel, in the company of the woman in red and the woman in green, stepped out onto the deck. "I can't face those three without a drink in my hand."

Concealed by the trees and the darkness we listened to them talk, their voices amplified in the night air.

"Well, you can hardly blame him. She is gorgeous, even if she's a nightmare," the woman in red was saying. I could feel my mother's sudden tension.

"Oh, yes, Michael has always been drawn to Greer, no question—for her beauty, understandably, and he does enjoy her wit. She's a saucy one and he likes that," Mirabel was saying.

"Everyone knows they're carrying on. It's a disgrace," the woman in green said, sounding angry. "With Camp running for office too. You would think she would be more discreet for his sake. To say nothing of their daughter! And under the circumstances . . ."

"Hell's bells, he jilted her!" the other woman interjected. "In the most embarrassing public way. Then he married Polly. He comes back and she abandons her husband and falls into his arms—is she a fool? What's in it for her, except more humiliation?"

My mother grabbed my hand and squeezed it. She looked at me and shook her head.

"Well, my dears, think about it," Mirabel said, preparing to set everyone straight. "If you knew Greer as I do, the answer is simple. Michael appeals to her vanity. He is the epitome of the romantic leading man. They're playing out scenes together, don't you see? Camp is just her husband, a supporting role. How can he possibly compete against the romantic fiction of Michael?"

Greer gasped and dropped my hand. She walked away, disappearing into the darkness, appearing in the living room moments later smiling and laughing and tending to her guests. "Mirabel," she said taking her glass. "Please. Let me refresh that for you."

"Mom! What are you doing?" I asked as I followed her into the kitchen and found her mixing a drink for Mirabel using soupy water from the dog bowl. She looked up. "Oh, I know," she said. "It's much too good for her. I tried to get Madge to piss in the glass, but she wouldn't cooperate."

It was 2:30 in the morning. The last guest had gone. The moon disappeared behind gray clouds and the wind off the ocean picked up in a spirited surge and the sound of the waves rocked the house to sleep as a devout quiet descended. My father was in bed, soft strains of recorded music wafting into the hallway.

My mother sat on the sofa in the living room, dog next to her, lights dimmed, stroking Dorothy's head with one hand and smoking cigarette after cigarette with the other, the smoke dissipating into the shadows.

Not wanting her to see me, I tiptoed outside and onto the deck where it had grown stormy. A wilder wind picked up a newspaper left outside and blew it onto the dunes and the grass. I chased after it as it dispersed, all those billowing sheets of newsprint.

My hands full, I headed back toward the deck when Gula stepped out of the shadows and stood in front of me, between me and the house. Too terrified to scream, I dropped the pages from the newspaper and watched as the wind reclaimed them, blowing them up into the sky and carrying them out over the ocean.

"A bit late for a young girl to be out wandering around in the dark alone," he said. I couldn't see his face. There was no light where we stood. It was as if the night itself had found its voice.

"You should be careful. You never know who or what is lurking," he said. "There are bad men about. A girl alone. You never know what may happen."

The sound of the wind and the tumult of the waves receded into the background. All I could hear was that voice. "Have you recovered from the funeral? So sad. Heartbreaking, really. Whatever happened to that boy? I can't imagine. Can you?"

Gula was used to my nonresponsiveness by now. There was nothing he liked better than not hearing my voice.

"Poor Charlie Devlin. I'm sure the police are right. It was a terrible accident. Alcohol poisoning, maybe. A drug overdose. What do you think?"

I wasn't thinking at all. Was he mad? Could it be that I had imagined everything? All I really knew was that there was safety in silence.

The door opened. "Riddle, is that you?"

I had never been so happy to hear Greer's voice as I was at that moment. I struggled to answer her, and in that second Gula was gone; like a black dog, he appeared and disappeared into the night, undetected.

I wanted to call out to her, I wanted to tell her that I was there but I couldn't speak.

"Riddle!" she called to me again. Getting no response, she closed the door.

My hand wrapped around the collar of my dress as I squeezed my throat, attempting to quell the telltale throbbing of my pulse, a relentless, lurid pounding, so noisy I was certain it would drown out the urgent thundering of the waves and the insistent beating of the wind against the tall grasses along the shoreline. So deafening, I thought for sure she must hear it.

If only she'd been listening.

Chapter Twenty-Nine

———

"So, almost time to go back to school. What are your plans for the fall?" my mother asked me. "Please don't say, 'nothing.' I don't think I can stand it if you do."

"I'm going to keep on working with Mary. I want to start competing in the spring." I was sitting on the floor in the bathroom, Dorothy's head in my lap, steam rising from my mother's lavender-infused nightly bath.

"Well, I don't know how you expect to make gains when you keep canceling your training sessions with Gin." She extended her long neck and, resting her head just above the waterline, she lay back in the old claw-foot porcelain tub, the damp ends of her hair curling in the heat.

I rolled my eyes. "Mother, please. I'm going to go back. I've been concentrating on . . ."

"Harry Devlin," she supplied.

"No. Cross-country. I'll work on my dressage in the fall and winter."

"Whatever you say, darling." She closed her eyes and swished through the water with the tips of her fingers. "Are you looking forward to tomorrow?"

"I guess. It'll be good to see the yearlings."

"Uh-huh," she agreed. "The horses never disappoint. The guest list, unfortunately, is another matter. Hand me the towel, will you, Riddle?"

I gently lifted Dorothy's muzzle from my leg and stood up. I paused to consider the loose dog hair clinging to my pajamas before reaching for the large white towel hanging from a hook on the back of the door.

"Thanks," she said, standing up in the tub, tall and slim and softly curving, skin flushed pink from the heat of the water and the room. I caught myself wishing that she and I had more in common than a surname. She stepped out of the tub and onto the mat, wrapping herself in the towel. Leaning over the sink, I looked into the mirror, but there was no reflection staring back at me. Using my forefinger, I reached out and wrote my name in the steamy fog clouding the glass.

"Let's hope the weather cooperates," she said. "There's supposed to be a big storm brewing."

"One of those scary ones?"

"Sounds like it. The winds pick up tonight. Tomorrow is going to be a little dicey. They're calling for gale force winds by Sunday night."

"Why did you have to tell me that?"

"The weather wasn't designed with only your preferences in mind, Riddle."

"Why do you and Camp have to turn everything into a sermon?"

"Just one more quality that I share with Jesus," she said, patting her face dry with a hand towel. "Oh, by the way, Gin tells me that Harry is coming to the auction tomorrow," she said with practiced nonchalance, as if she was wondering about the whereabouts of her slippers, instead of delivering news so momentous that at any moment I expected David Brinkley to make an unscheduled appearance in my parents' en suite.

Silence prevailed as I contemplated the sheer wondrousness of her unexpected announcement. Harry was home? He and his father had gone to Ireland to visit family shortly after the funeral. I continued to stare into the mirror, as each letter of my name drooled down the glass, leaving a watery trail. My mother was staring at me, a knowing expression on her face. By saying nothing, I had said it all.

"He's interested in one of the yearlings from the Sexsmith stable, or so Gin tells me." Dropping her towel, she pulled a white cotton nightgown over her head. "Do you have any idea how much money that boy has to play with? Unbelievable."

"I don't care. That's gross."

"Spare me your uninformed teen ideology." She stopped mid-insult. "Riddle, you know him. Do you think he gives a damn?"

"About the money?" It was so rare for my mother to recruit my opinion about anything that I was caught off guard, stumbling around in my head, trying to find my balance and respond.

She nodded, waiting for my answer.

"No," I said. "I don't think he cares about money at all."

Groaning, she slipped an arm into the sleeve of her robe. "I suspected as much. Of course, he can afford to be indifferent. There is no God. Wait. I take that back, there is a God. There must be. The universe is just too perverse—there must be an idiosyncratic mind at the helm."

"All you think about is money," I complained, not for the first time.

"Well, let me tell you something, darling: money, elite social status and the power they confer are every bit as wonderful as they're cracked up to be."

"Is Michael coming home, too?"

"That's the scuttlebutt," she said, leaning over the sink, her face inches from the mirror as she began to apply moisturizer to her forehead, her chin, her cheeks.

"That should make you happy."

"Don't bait me, Riddle. You don't know what you're talking about, for one thing." She stood up straight and picked up a hairbrush. "The truth is, I'm not that thrilled about his return, especially with the election only a couple of months away."

"Why? I don't think he's thinking about the campaign anymore, or about Camp. Not since they found Charlie."

"You're probably right."

Had I heard correctly? There was something unnerving about hearing my mother make such an agreeable remark. She began to brush her hair with more force than necessary.

"I don't know. In my experience, neither Michael nor Camp can be counted on to perform according to expectations, and they're both used to getting their way. They both have a lot to lose—they're like two countries poised to detonate nuclear weapons against each other."

"Isn't that what's supposed to keep us safe?"

"Ostensibly. In the hands of moderates, yes. When it comes right down to it, Camp and Michael would think nothing of blowing up the whole world in support of their points of view, and to hell with everyone else. I'll be glad to get this damnable election behind us, that's all."

I WALKED AMONG A SERIES of white tents erected on Gin's front lawn, passing dozens of long tables draped with white linen set amidst the silk rustle of elegant, formal, late summer gardens. Hundreds of people wandered among the tents and the tables and the gardens as individual horses were showcased to almost ecclesiastical effect, their coats gleaming under the shifting sun and cloud, their manes and tails aloft in the wind, their high spirits kicking up dust as they cantered into the paddocks, the auction in full swing.

Live music played as each horse was led by halter into the paddock by a uniformed attendant, who first posed and then released animals so otherworldly beautiful they looked as if Hans Christian Andersen had imagined them.

It was the Saturday of Labor Day weekend, the opening day of Gin's celebrated annual garden party, by coveted invitation only. Guests had flown in from around the world—some of them people Gin knew personally, others people Gin only knew about and wanted to know personally—and were congratulating him on the horses, on the beauty of the setting, extolling the excitement of the hunt to come. Everyone was preparing for a lavish lunch up at the house, exquisitely prepared to accommodate riders and buyers and socialites alike, all of whom were making note of every detail of every moment to recall on command for their curious associates, inquisitive colleagues, jealous friends.

I scanned the crowd, searching for Harry. I can still see him, as if he were a painting. He was sitting on the top rung of the paddock fence, despite Gin's orders to the contrary. He was wearing faded blue jeans and a dark T-shirt. Beat-up running shoes. Everything about his posture was casual. His looks were so pure and unadulterated, I swear I could hear a nightingale singing.

The way he looked, how he dressed, the way he talked, the way he thought, the way he carried himself—I loved all of it, his honesty, his confidence. He smiled and I wanted to reach out and polish his luster. Every time I saw him, I found something new to admire. He raised his arm over his head and waved when he saw me.

"Hoffa," he hollered. "Over here!"

"Harry!" I broke into a run and reached him just as Gula— no attendant's uniform for him—led a magnificent horse into the ring. His sudden appearance stopped me in my tracks.

"Jesus," Harry said, pointing. "Gin finally got his Gypsy mare."

The crowd was oohing and aahing over the new arrival, a piebald with blue eyes and a mane like a veil that hung to her knees, her tail dragging along the ground like a wedding train. Gin, taking up his position in the center of it all, the rich man's version of a circus ringmaster, talked about who she was, what she was, what he intended to do with her, as Gula put her through her paces.

"Got to give him credit," Harry said. "He did it. Wow. She is fantastic, isn't she?"

I nodded, though I don't think my full attention was on the mare.

"How are you, Harry?"

"I'm okay. I'm all right," he said a little evasively.

"Are you happy to be home?"

"I wouldn't go that far," he said, pausing to reconsider when he noticed the devastation on my face. "What the hell? Sure I am."

Gula was leaving the ring, leading away Gin's newest acquisition, when he noticed Harry and me. He stopped and performed his customary, brief half bow in salutation. Harry laughed and waved. "Son of a bitch," he said, loud enough so I could hear him.

"How is Hanzi?" I asked him.

"He's great," Harry said, patting my knee. "We did good, Hoffa." I stared down at his hand. The beautiful strains of the cello and the violin, the music of the birds from the branches on the trees—was it my imagination or had the whole world exploded into song?

A growing crowd of gaily chattering onlookers was gathering around the paddock in anticipation of Boomslang's imminent moment in the sun, Gin leading the troops, my mother next to him as he sidled over.

"So what do you think, Greer? Riddle? You too, Harry. Aren't they fantastic? Oh my, I could look at them forever. If God were to strike me dead right here and now, I could die happy." Gin was so ecstatic he was trilling, filling the summer air with his own perverse twittering.

"How many times must I say it?" my mother demanded impatiently. "They're beautiful. There never has been nor will there ever be two horses such as these two horses. Are you happy?"

"These two horses will make my place in the history books. They will make me immortal."

"Now, there's a terrifying thought," my mother said. "I wasn't planning to do any hunting, but you've put me in the mood to murder something."

An appreciative murmur that quickly developed into a loud round of whooping and applause heralded Boomslang's arrival in the ring, where his halter was removed and he was allowed to move freely around the fenced-in arena. "No explanations needed," Gin said theatrically, as Boomslang pawed the ground and surged dramatically forward like a directed explosion of smoke and spark.

Harry hopped down from the fence and was standing next to me when Boomslang ran toward us and stared at Harry, who reached in and rubbed his ears until he took off again at a canter. Churning and spinning, he abruptly stopped, stood up on his hind legs, dropped down again on all fours as the crowd clapped, and then he lashed out with his rear hooves, violently kicking the middle rung of the fence, smashing it into several pieces, large and small, and knocking an onlooker to the ground with a dull thud.

Harry was up and over the paddock fence trying to calm the unruly stallion as the shaken but uninjured observer dusted himself off. Boomslang, obviously agitated by the noise and the people, by the events of the day, shook his head and scraped the ground with his hoof. He swung his rear legs around and kicked the air as Harry neatly swerved out of his way.

Reaching into his jacket pocket for a lump of sugar—Harry was always carrying around treats for horses—he held his open palm out to Boomslang, who considered for a moment before accepting. Harry, talking to him all the while, took his forelock and mane in his hand and led him to Gula, who was making his way toward them with halter and lunge rein as the crowd broke into long, spontaneous applause.

Needing no excuse, I loped over to Harry, who was standing just outside the paddock next to Gin and a large group of people that included my mother. They were making a big fuss over him for his intervention. Gula asked me if I would hold on to the Gypsy mare while he took Boomslang back to the stable. Not knowing what else to do, I nodded as the others, Harry and Gin and my mother, drifted off toward the house so that Harry could get cleaned up and changed. He was covered in dust and dirt and clay and his shirt had got torn on a nail protruding from the fence. "You can borrow something of mine," Gin said as Harry politely demurred. "Anything you'd like. Please, I insist."

Harry never looked more horrified than he did that day at the prospect of wearing one of Gin's outfits.

Momentarily alone with Gula, I studiously avoided his eyes by looking down at the ground. I could feel him looking at me.

"Aren't you going to ask her name?" he said when he transferred custody of Gin's new horse to me. "Oma," he said, as she fixed her pale blue eyes on me.

He smiled, and then he reached out and stroked my cheek with his fingers. I froze. For some reason, not clear to me, I intrigued him. I know that I did. Tightening my hold on the lead rope, I got out of there as fast as I could, Oma trotting alongside me.

There's something satisfying in fascinating the devil. It's not a good feeling to indulge.

I LOOKED AROUND FOR HARRY, searching everywhere, going from one tent to another, but I couldn't find him. One of the attendants told me that he had gone for a little ride on a horse that he was interested in buying. "Stay in the designated area if you're going to look for him," he cautioned. With hunters on the prowl, it was a dangerous day to walk or ride the woods of the Cormorant Clock Farm, but I was confident of the route I had chosen. I knew exactly where Harry had gone. I saddled up one of the horses and went to look for him.

Gin maintained a large herd of Sikka deer, mainly for the purposes of the annual hunt. Shy and secretive, they made a pleasant whistling sound in the forest. Off in the distance, I could see groups of relentlessly social men and women in green and brown tweeds, with gloved hands and wearing lightweight Wellingtons, attended by rifle-toting gillies, spooky stalking in thick woodland glades or at the edge of the woods, waiting for the deer to appear to begin feeding. It was quiet but for the hollow sigh of the wind through the long grass and the melancholy whistling of the hunted Sikka mourning the loss of their own as gunshot after gunshot rang out in black volley. A grief so soft, a death so hard, side by side amidst the tall grass.

EMERGING ON HORSEBACK FROM the forest trail into the clearing, I knew I would see Harry, and there he was, his back to me, sitting at the end of the dock, feet dangling inches above the water. He glanced over his shoulder and waved, watching as I dismounted and walked toward him.

"I thought you might be here," I said.

"Yeah, I'm here," he said.

"Are you okay?"

"No," he said. "I'm not."

"Oh, Harry . . ."

He held up his hand. "That wasn't an invitation for you to start crying. I mean it, Hoffa. Don't."

"I'm just so sorry about Charlie. About everything."

"I know. I'm sorry you had to be the one to find him."

"Me, too," I said, though I knew that if anyone deserved to find Charlie, it was me.

"You know, I'm just not buying it, this stuff about Charlie dying from drugs and booze and exposure. It's bullshit. He was a fifteen-year-old kid who sneaked the occasional beer. He wasn't Jimi Hendrix, for Christ's sake."

My heart pounding, my fingers gripped the dock. "What do you think happened to him?"

"I don't know, but something bad happened. Don't you think it's strange that he was found here? My dad's boyhood home? Sure, we came here, once in a while. We were just goofing off. It didn't hold any real significance other than the obvious. The papers made it sound as if we viewed it as some sort of pilgrimage site. Anyway, you and I both know he just wanted to come home that night. So what did he do? Hang up after talking to my dad and decide to go for a drunken canoe ride miles away at two in the morning?"

I felt a rush of panic. I had hoped that Harry would eventually accept the police version of events. I mean, if I could accept their explanation for what had happened to Charlie, then why couldn't Harry?

"I don't know why. I don't know who. My brother's dead. For what? Jesus, sometimes I think I'm going crazy."

Tears streamed down his cheeks. I turned away from my obligation to relieve his misery.

"Shit," he said, wiping his eyes. "My mother's dead, too." He laughed unhappily. "Sorry, Hoffa, I'm doing a pretty good job of feeling sorry for myself."

I wanted so much to tell him. I wanted to end his suffering. I could hardly hold up my head for the weight of my conscience. The problem of not telling had grown to epic proportions. I'd gotten to know Harry. I knew what it would mean if I were to tell him the truth.

I was no longer keeping the secret. I was protecting it.

"What does your father think?"

Harry shook his head. "You don't want to know what my old man thinks."

He took my hand in his and we sat that way for a long time not saying anything.

Sometimes when I'm upset or frightened, I draw on the memory of Harry's hand in my hand and it makes me feel better. There was a day when it made me feel worse. Not so much anymore.

WE BOTH HEARD IT, a rustling sound in the area behind the dock, a thump and then the urgent sound of breaking branches. "Let's get out of here," Harry said, withdrawing his hand, looking toward the noise, the horses lifting their heads, ears pointing in the direction of the waning trample, now a whoosh through the woods as if something had been launched.

"What do you think it is?" I asked.

"Deer maybe. I don't know. Poor things. I hope these guys wind up shooting one another."

Harry rubbed his face with his hands, as if he were scrubbing up with a washcloth. "You know what?" he said, jumping to his feet. "I think I know why I'm so depressed." He pointed to what he was wearing, a preppie uniform of bran khakis and white linen shirt. "Gin's clothes. If I don't get out of this outfit soon I might be tempted to kill myself."

Reaching for my hand to pull me to my feet, he inclined his head slightly, face glowing, hair shining, eyes bluer than the sky. My mother was right! I was in love with Harry Devlin. I could have happily spent the rest of my life looking at Harry's face. He was smiling. He was bending toward me. I hardly had time to say his name when I heard the report from a rifle as it rang out, birds scattering from overhead branches.

I fell back down onto the deck, then I scrambled to stand up as Harry, blown off his feet, fell facedown in the dirt, blood pouring everywhere, and I was standing over him and in that moment I finally found my voice. My screams drew the attention of a group of hunters on horseback. I saw them as they appeared on the crest of a hill, the horses coming toward us at full gallop and I screamed and I screamed and I screamed until I had no voice left to scream with.

"JIMMY, WHY IN GOD'S name did you and Harry go into the woods when you knew there would be people out hunting?" Gin was begging me for an answer.

"We weren't anywhere near the hunting. We were at the dock," I said. "I was being careful. It seemed safe."

"But you're always near the hunting when you venture away from the house," Gin said, beseeching everyone to see his point of view, pleading for understanding. "You're not safe anywhere when there's a hunt going on. Didn't I tell everyone? Wasn't it clear?"

We were at the hospital in a private waiting room—my mother, Gin and Gula and a pair of detectives, one dark-haired, one fair-haired, who had been called in to investigate the shooting. I recognized the dark-haired one. He had been at the house when Charlie's jacket was discovered. I was sitting on a long vinyl sofa, my clothes stained with Harry's blood.

My mother stood alongside me. Gin was gesturing and bleating, ringed on either side by the two policemen as Gula looked on, casual and detached, removed from it all. He might have been an armchair for the extent of his seeming engagement, leaning against the open window, fingering the tangled cord of the aluminum blind.

We were waiting to hear about Harry. There was so much blood.

"Who among my guests would deliberately shoot Harry? I have members of the Dutch royal family in attendance, for God's sake," Gin said, addressing his final remark to the two detectives, who didn't look especially impressed.

"Gin, if you make one more reference to European aristocracy I will take you out and shoot you myself," my mother said, to the veiled amusement of the dark-haired detective.

"All right. That's enough. This isn't helping," the blond detective said, before turning to ask me, as he had asked me multiple times already, if I had seen anyone at the boathouse.

"We heard something by the boathouse in the bushes. Harry thought it was a deer, and then a few minutes later that's when it happened."

"Well, Jimmy, you were out and about in the middle of a hunt," Gin whined, looking like the injured party, staring over at me.

"Which brings me to another important matter." The blond detective turned to address Gin. "You're aware, I assume, that we have laws governing when deer can be legally hunted in Cape Cod, and you, sir, are in direct violation of those laws."

"But everyone knows about my garden party weekend!" Gin said, sputtering and waving his hands in front of him. "It's been going on for years. It's an institution. Ordinary restrictions simply do not apply! The state attorney general was there! If it doesn't bother him, then I don't see why it concerns a couple of beat cops." Gin carried on as he always did, inured to the impact of his remarks on his listening audience. "For heaven's sake, it's not as if anyone is wandering around in camouflage and hip waders holding a beer in one hand and a sawed-off shotgun in the other. It's my land and they are my deer, after all. Anytime I want I could ship the whole lot of them off to the slaughterhouse and no one would bat an eye. So what sense do your laws make? Why do I need anyone's permission to hunt my deer on my land?"

"Next time someone decides to rob a bank, I'll be sure to tell him to put on a tux," the detective replied. My mother looked at him with newfound appreciation.

"Surely you don't think I have anything to do with what happened?" Gin said suddenly. Everyone looked at him as if he was crazy. "Why, I've never had a violent thought in my life. I adore those children, Riddle and Harry. Greer and Michael and Godfrey are my dearest friends in the world. I've known them since I was a small child. We're a family! That's what we are, aren't we, Greer?"

"Oh, yes," she agreed, adding for the benefit of the detectives, "we all have plans to change our last names to Borgia to make it official."

Before anyone had the opportunity to respond, we were distracted by the sounds of a commotion in the corridor outside the waiting room. My mother's shoulders drooped, then just as quickly squared off as she and I both recognized the loudest voice among several loud voices.

"My God, Riddle, are you all right?" Camp appeared at the waiting room door surrounded by flustered nurses and an ineffective and apologetic security guard. Bypassing everyone else, he headed to where I sat. "Jesus Christ," he said at the sight of Harry's blood soaked into my mushroom-colored jodhpurs, spattered on my white riding shirt, soaking the tips of my hair.

He spun around to confront my mother. "I told you I didn't want her anywhere near that Devlin kid. Look what's happened. She could have been killed. You," he pointed at Gin, who shrank behind my mother. "See what your goddamn hunting is good for."

"I'm fine," I said, reaching for my father's hand. "It wasn't Harry's fault."

"You shouldn't have been anywhere near those lunatics and their killing spree. This was Harry's doing," Camp said as Michael Devlin suddenly appeared in the doorway.

"What did you say?" He moved toward my father, the room filling with the odor of burnt acetone. Michael stepped in closer to Camp until there was little more than a shaft of light separating them. "Where the hell were you this afternoon?"

My mother and I gasped in unison.

"It was too much for you, wasn't it? My family. My money." Michael paused before continuing. "Your wife." I looked over at my mother, who gave no sign she had even heard let alone understood the implications of what Michael had just said, unless you count the slightest elevation of a single eyebrow.

Camp laughed. "That's right, I killed Charlie, then I went after Harry. Look out because you're next, Devlin."

"Camp," I said. "Please don't."

"What was it that pushed you over the edge? Was it to punish me? Did you hope to distract me by murdering my sons?"

I burst into tears. "Harry's dead," I cried.

Michael looked dazed. "No. No. I'm sorry," he said. "Harry is going to be all right. Thank God the bullet only skimmed the flesh. It entered at an angle above the temple, sparing him from permanent damage." He glared at Camp. "No thanks to you."

"You're insane," my father said. They were so tightly bound together they cast a single shadow on the wall, as if in combination they made up a third man, dark and unknowable.

I looked over at Gula, who was no longer fiddling with the cord. Taut and motionless—was he breathing?—he stared at Michael and Camp, his expression ruthless as piano wire.

Michael was the first to break eye contact. "Detective," he

turned to address the blond policeman, "I want this man investigated. I want to know where he was this afternoon."

"This isn't the first time you've made this type of accusation against Mr. Camperdown," the dark-haired detective said.

"Michael, Jesus, are you kidding me?" Camp extended his hand, desperate and disbelieving, his bravado on the wane. I had never heard my father sound that way before. Michael knocked his hand away.

"Michael, it was an accident," Greer said, reaching out to touch his forearm. "No one wants to hurt Harry, least of all Camp."

"An accident?" Michael said, his voice rising in anger and frustration. "I've got one dead son, the other lying in an emergency room, both of them found in the same goddamn location, and you want to tell me it's a coincidence? Or worse, you want to blame them?"

Camp decided to take charge. "I'll come down to the station and you can ask me anything you want and I'll answer you."

The two detectives thanked him for his cooperation.

When he passed by me, Camp reached out and squeezed my shoulder. I can still feel the pressure of his hand, as if he made a permanent compression. I will never forget what he said next. "I just want to make one thing perfectly clear to everyone." Camp was pointing now, his hand raised to the same height as his face, gesturing with his index finger. "If I had aimed a rifle and shot at Harry Devlin—and his father knows this better than anyone—I wouldn't have missed."

"My God, Camp," my mother said.

"Let's get this over with," he said, the detectives on either side of him.

"I'll join you," my mother said, reaching for her bag, an offer that elicited a pointed glance from Michael, part inquiry, part appeal.

"No need for you to come, Greer. I'm fine," my father said as my mother's face flushed.

"Let me come with you," I said to Camp. I didn't like the way people were looking at my father.

"No. It's late and you need to go home. Lou is waiting for you." He looked around the room.

"Gula." He gestured to the window, where Gula stood. "You can drive Riddle home when you take Gin." Gula stiffened at being talked to that way, as if he were a servant.

"No," I said, a sudden rush of adrenaline causing me to jump to my feet. "I want to go with you."

"I will be happy to help in any way that I can," Gula answered, recovering, as he approached. "It would be my pleasure."

"I want to see Harry." I tried another tack, the wrong one.

"Over my dead body," Camp said. "You go with Gin and Gula."

"But . . ." I was just getting ready to make my case. Ignoring my entreaties, Camp headed for the exit in the company of the dark-haired detective.

"Enough, Riddle!" my mother said, opting for the direct approach. "Hasn't there been enough drama for one day? Do as you're told and quit arguing. Go home!"

"I'm coming with you, Camp." She followed behind him but he turned and stopped her. "No. Stay here with Michael. He needs you more than I do."

She stared at him. Her eyes widened in quiet fury.

"If that's what you want," she said.

"I do."

I reached for my mother's hand as Camp vanished into the corridor. "Don't listen," I pleaded. "Go with him."

"He doesn't want me to, Riddle. Can't you see? He prefers to handle things on his own. What would you have me do about it?"

Michael had been watching intently the freighted interaction between my parents. She turned to him. "Camp did not shoot Harry," she said, as if she were imposing conditions on whatever was passing between them. Michael shrugged and held up his hands as if he were surrendering, an obvious act of convenience rather than of conviction.

I felt Gula's fingers on the back of my neck, in barren contrast to the warmth of my father's touch, as he directed me toward the door, Gin bringing up the rear. I looked quickly behind me. Michael was sitting alone on a bench, his head in his hands. My mother stood over him, looking at him, her posture a dichotomy, surrender in the slope of her shoulders, defiance in the tilt of her chin, harsh hospital lighting tracing the outline of her silhouette, a raw beam whose crude power did nothing to diminish her solitary beauty.

It occurred to me that my mother was a better person than she seemed to be—or wanted people to think she was.

COLD AND DAMP, IT was a bad night. The ground was slippery and wet, trees leaned in the wind, fog obscured my vision, rising mist infected my imagination. Gin was passed out in the backseat after essentially crying himself to sleep over the catastrophic turn his garden party had taken. His determination to prostrate himself meant that I was forced to sit in the passenger seat next to Gula, who was blindly navigating the treacherous turns and narrow slopes of the road that led to Wellfleet and home.

It's an isolated stretch of road. He was driving too fast at a point where one turn followed another and there was a dramatic swing in the road. The front end of the car veered to the right, Gula steered left, lifting his foot from the accelerator in an attempt to avoid the car parked in darkness at the side of the road. He slammed on the brakes as the car came to a skidding, swerving halt mere feet from a woodsy incline that sloped down into the marsh. Gin moaned and rolled over, his face buried in the leather upholstery.

"I suppose I should slow down," Gula said, laughing a little, turning up the radio, the classical strains of a violin filling the car. He seemed nervous and that made me nervous. His voice was low and soft, empty as an echo.

We were miles from home and there wasn't another vehicle on the road as Gula reduced his level of speed until it seemed as if we were barely moving at all. I stared out the passenger-side window and into the black night, the lonely whistle of the wind the only sound.

One hand on the steering wheel, Gula stared straight ahead as the car, tiptoeing stealthily, so slow and so quiet that it seemed to be relying on the wind for power, crept up and down the lush roads, wavering at times, gently swerving to the right, sometimes stopping, at which point I would renew my focus on the view outside my window and say nothing until the car gradually resumed its long, slow, silent, torturous journey home, neither one of us saying a single word.

I didn't move, I didn't breathe as the air in the car filled with the deadly vapor of whatever it was that he was thinking. That night in that slowly moving car, Gula's crouching thoughts wore a hood. I don't know how I knew, but I knew that a single whispered word from either one of us would ignite the fuse and trigger the explosion.

The lights of my parents' house burned through the fog as we approached, Gin's oblivious snoring an ugly companion to the beauty of the music.

"Do you still think your father is a good man?" Gula asked me.

Lou was waiting on the verandah. She waved and I waved back as I opened the passenger door and climbed out. For a second I worried that my legs wouldn't support my weight. Gula got out of the car and, taking my elbow, walked toward the house with me, stopping some distance from the verandah.

"My grandmother was a mean old witch," he said, as I watched Lou step back inside the door. "Ugly, too. She enjoyed frightening me when I was little. She used to repeat this gruesome lullaby every night before bedtime: 'Old black sheep, where's your lamb? Way down in the bottom, the buzzards and the flies, pickin' at its eyes, and the poor little thing cries, "Maa-maa!"' I used to beg her to stop but it did no good. You know why?"

"No."

"Neither do I, though I do know this," he said, the glimmer of a distant light in his eyes. It wasn't a reassuring glow. "She had her reasons."

Chapter Thirty

———

"**W**HAT HAPPENED AT THE POLICE STATION?" I ASKED CAMP the following day. Exhausted by the day's events, I passed out before he got home early in the morning.

My mother came home three or four hours later, explaining that she had stayed with Michael at the hospital until they were assured of Harry's good condition.

I followed my parents into the dining room.

"Nothing happened," Camp said. "What could happen? They asked me a few questions. I volunteered some answers and that was the end of it."

"Do you think they believed you when you said you didn't hurt Charlie or Harry?"

"I don't think either one of them ever seriously entertained the ludicrous proposition that I did. I wouldn't be surprised if they've concluded that Devlin and I are both nuts, though. Anyway, nothing for you to worry about."

"That's right, Riddle," my mother said, reaching for a cardigan from the back of a chair. "If your father is charged with anything he can always plead insanity, a highly provable defense in his case." She searched the sweater pockets for her cigarettes and a cigarette lighter. Finding them, she sat down at the table and lit up and ignored my glare. I didn't see the humor in her remark.

"How are you? Did you get all that blood washed from your hair?" She paused as if she had finally heard herself. "Now, there's something every mother wants to say at least once to her thirteen-year-old daughter."

"Are you sure Harry's okay?"

My mother nodded as my father picked up the morning newspaper, where news of the shooting was on the front page.

"He's fine, Riddle," she said. "He has a bad headache and stitches, but he should be able to go home today, according to the doctors. A lucky boy."

"Can we forget about the Devlin family for a few moments, at least?" Camp asked.

We were just about to sit down to lunch when the phone rang.

"Shall I tell them you're busy?" Lou asked. My father shook his head and jumped up from his chair, my mother's annoyance reaching epic proportions as we listened to Camp boisterously greet some colleague from the party. Unlike Greer, I was happy for the diversion and relaxed into the vibrant, reassuring sound of his voice.

Camp had been appointed to a Democratic committee hastily devised to develop party policy concerning international terrorism, inspired by the attack on the Olympic athletes in Munich a few days earlier.

"It's a bloody disgrace," he said, referring to the disastrous rescue attempt, passions instantly inflamed, feet planted square on the floor, receiver at his ear, gesturing broadly with his free hand. "They bring in a handful of inexperienced weekend sharpshooters—alleged sharpshooters—surround them in darkness, give them second-rate firepower, minimal support and invite them to shoot one another. What the hell did they think was going to happen? Jesus, who did they put in charge of planning? The president of the local PTA? First thing you do in a situation like that is bring in snipers with legitimate combat experience and equip them properly. You want quantity and quality. You need at least two snipers on each known target. To hell with their restrictions about using the military."

He paused for a moment, listening, considering. "No. No. Hogwash. The idea of a lone sniper is a myth. TV stuff. Sniping is a two-man operation, although, ultimately, in the purest, most existential sense, given the nature of the task, the sniper is a lone operator."

My mother tapped her fingers on the tabletop impatiently and quietly gestured for me to start eating. "Have a little mayhem with your salad," she whispered. "We should be liberating the camps by dessert."

"Shhh," I said, trying to hear.

"Christ, at Bastogne, we sat on that goddamn rooftop for days. No food, no sleep, no water. The crazy part of it was there was booze everywhere. It flowed like water from the tap. We took up position on top of a building that had housed an after-hours club. We found cartons of vodka in the basement. We were literally bathing in the stuff. I shaved with vodka." He laughed. "I kid you not."

"Lou, where did you buy this produce?" my mother said. "It tastes like a farmer's field."

"What should it taste like?" Lou asked her.

"The inside of a sterile plastic bag," my mother said, as the two of us watched Camp's dinner grow cold. "I prefer my vegetables to taste as if they were grown on a supermarket shelf."

"Please, I can't hear," I said. Why were they talking about such stupid things?

"Yeah, the Springfield got the job done," Camp conceded, "but

I managed to commandeer an M28/30, Finnish rifle, a piece of art. Never missed a target."

We finished up, my mother watching as I helped Lou clean off the table.

He was listening again, a look of frustration on his face, exasperation mingled with contempt. "Well, all I can say is that you've obviously never been at the front lines, my friend. Believe me, that Christmas at Bastogne, everyone was a target."

I stacked the dishes in silence in the kitchen as Lou opened wide the faucet, the coarse rush of water running, pots and pans clanging, drowning out the sound of my father's voice.

"So, did you go to Michael Devlin's house last night and tuck him in?" I asked my mother, bitter as only a teenage girl is capable of being bitter. I was angry at my mother and wanted to punish her. Lou gasped and fled the room, the dogs trailing after her.

My mother laughed. "That's none of your business. Although I suppose I should thank you for caring enough to ask, which is more than your father bothered to do."

At that moment, Camp came into the kitchen, grabbed a piece of candy and headed back to make another series of calls. Sipping her coffee, my mother watched him walk from the room.

"Would you like to split a brownie?" I asked her.

"Why the hell not?"

I stood on my tiptoes, reaching for the plate of brownies on the high top shelf of the pantry, the tips of my fingers connecting with the porcelain tray. I never felt so small.

Chapter **Thirty-One**

THE NEXT DAY I WAS UP IN MY ROOM WHEN I SAW HARRY'S CAR drive along the road and turn into Gin's driveway. Stunned, I threw on some clothes and ran down the stairs, two at a time. I rushed to the barn and saddled up Mary.

A few moments later, I was cantering up the hill and down the long road leading to Gin's. I arrived just in time to see Harry leading Boomslang, saddled and bridled, to the training ring where Gin had set up a series of jumps.

"I didn't expect to see you here," I said as Mary and I trotted up alongside him. His hair had been shaved around his ear, where the stitches were visible. His right eye was black and blue and red and inflamed.

"Funny, 'cause I was sure I'd see you here, though maybe not quite this fast. You made it in record time, Hoffa. I've been here, what, ten, fifteen minutes?"

"I don't know what you mean," I said, acutely aware that my skin was the same sick-making shade of beige as tapioca pudding.

The tip of his boot in the stirrup, he eased himself up into the saddle.

"What are you doing here, Harry? Do you feel okay?" I watched him adjust the length of his stirrups, his face averted as he concentrated on the task at hand.

"I'm fine. I felt like a ride and I promised Gin I'd try to get a better feel for Boomslang's jumping capabilities. Today seemed as good a day as any." He sat up straight in the saddle and gathered the reins. "What's the look for?" he said. "What am I supposed to do? Turn out all the lights and sit in the dark? My brother died, not me."

He moved toward the ring and I followed behind, sliding down to the ground and holding open the gate for Boomslang and Harry as they entered. I tethered Mary to a low-lying branch of an old tree near the stable and took up a spot along the fence to watch.

It was apparent from the start that things weren't going well. Boomslang reluctantly cleared two small hurdles but balked at the bigger fences.

"Hello, Jimmy," Gin said, coming up behind me, his hand on my shoulder in a welcoming squeeze. "Surprised to see Harry here so soon after . . ."

"I know," I said.

"They don't seem to be clicking this morning," Gin said, after watching Boomslang refuse the same jump three times.

"It's Harry," I said.

"I can see that," Gin said, calling out some suggestions to Harry, who finally steered Boomslang to where we stood at the fence.

"Do you want to hand me that?' Harry asked Gin, pointing to a leather riding crop slung over a post. "Thanks."

The next time they approached the problematic fence—and they came at it fast, Harry opting for speed—he gave Boomslang a sharp tap with the riding crop. It didn't have the desired effect. Boomslang swerved at the last minute and sent Harry sailing headfirst over the jump, just as he had done only weeks before.

Harry jumped to his feet as Gin and I ran into the ring to see if he was okay. He charged at Boomslang, crop raised over his head, ready to strike out.

"Harry!" I shouted, shocked. He stopped, stood motionless for a moment and then let the crop fall to the ground. He walked past Gin and me without saying a word, disappearing into the woods behind the stable.

I was leading Boomslang back to his stall when Harry reappeared.

"I'll do that," he said, reaching for the halter. He looked pale.

I stared at him. He nodded. "I'm okay." He was stroking Boomslang's neck. "I'll take care of him."

Back in his box stall, Boomslang was relaxed and happy as Harry began currying his coat with a rubber brush, working in circular fashion from his head to his hindquarters. I sat on a bale of hay in the stall and watched.

"I'm going back to college this weekend," Harry said, the words I had been dreading.

"Are you going to be home for Thanksgiving?"

"I don't know," he said. "I doubt it. I figure I'll just live in New Haven."

"You're not going to live in the house in Truro anymore?" I hoped I didn't sound as devastated as I felt.

"No. Maybe someday. Not now."

"I'm so sorry about everything, Harry."

"I know." He paused for a moment, leaning into Boomslang, face buried in his mane. "I know it's crazy, but I worry about what would happen if Charlie were to come home and there'd be nobody there. How would he find me? How would he know where to look?"

"Harry. He's dead. I don't understand."

"Jesus," he said voice full of emotion. "I can't go and I can't stay. What the hell do I do?"

"I don't know," I admitted, as Harry resumed brushing. He seemed to have something else on his mind. I looked at him expectantly.

"Look, I don't want to upset you, but I think there's something you should know," Harry said, breaking the silence. "Only if you want to. It's your decision."

"What's it about?"

"Your dad. Your dad and my dad. I know what's behind their beef."

"You do?"

"It's not pretty." He paused. "Look, Hoffa, after what happened to me the other day, my father just kind of lost it. He got on the phone and gave an interview to the *New York Times*. I overheard him. He had something to say about your dad and it wasn't good stuff. They'll be calling your father soon to get his side of things, I guess. I figured you deserved a heads-up. You want me to tell you?"

I nodded. Harry dropped the brush and sat down next to me and began to tell me a familiar tale about Christmas in Bastogne—only this was a version of the story that I had never heard before.

"They were in Bastogne. Your father and my father were snipers. They worked as a team." He flinched. "Not exactly the way you want to imagine your dad. They were positioned on the partially demolished roof of a bombed-out building, surrounded on every side by Germans, by freezing cold, by darkness. They had no food and no place to hide. Artillery fire and bombs were falling everywhere. Small-arms fire was all around them."

I think I was listening but I can't be sure. It felt as if I was listening.

"They were shooting at anything that moved. Everyone was a threat. The locals were warned to stay inside or risk being shot. It was Christmas morning when this little girl crept into view trying to get water from a well." He hesitated.

"Say it. Just tell me," I said.

He took a deep breath.

"Your dad shot her. On purpose."

"What?"

"She's dead. He killed her."

I grabbed his arm.

"I don't believe it," I said. "That's a lie. My father wouldn't do such a thing."

Harry shook his head.

"It's true, Hoffa. He killed her and then he and my dad got into a big fight about it. Your dad said that in war even children were fair game. How did they know who sent her?"

"How did they know who sent her?" I was repeating him.

"Or what her true purpose was? Anyway. They started fighting, I mean, a physical fight, punching each other."

"It doesn't make sense."

"A couple of the other guys in the platoon who knew about what happened wanted your dad charged with murder but my dad defended him—not what he'd done, killing the little girl, but because, in the end, he couldn't bring himself to turn your father in since he had been such a heroic soldier and they were friends. So he worked on the other guys and they finally agreed to keep quiet about what happened. The soldiers that knew about it were killed in battle a few days later. So only my father and your father knew what had happened. My dad vowed to keep it a secret. Over the years it ate away at him and he started having doubts about his promise. When your dad ran for public office, he felt that he couldn't keep silent any longer. I heard him say to the reporter, 'He's going to get elected to the House. Next he'll be a senator and then, I know him, he'll be after a presidential nomination.' He said that in good conscience, he couldn't allow that to happen. He said your dad was a bad man."

"It's not true," I said, shaking my head, jumping up, pacing back and forth in the stall.

"I'm sorry. I didn't want to tell you. I know you've been going crazy wondering. You deserve to know the truth. Hey, where are you going?"

Tears blurring my vision, I vaulted from the stall and into the corridor of the stable. "I want to go home," I said. "I've heard enough. Your father is lying."

"Why would my dad lie?" Harry said, standing up, calling after me.

"My mother, for a start!"

"Come on, Hoffa, calm down. Let's talk about it." He began walking toward me.

"Why is your father trying to destroy my family? Why does he hate my father so much? What's wrong with him?"

Harry looked pained. "Look, I don't want your family to get hurt. It's crazy, what's happening. My dad thinks your dad tried to kill me, for Christ's sake! He thinks he killed Charlie."

"That's insane. He would never . . . He didn't. I know he didn't. And no matter what, Camp would never kill a little girl in cold blood."

We were standing outside the stable door. One thing I knew for certain, I had no desire to fight with Harry. "Harry, why did you tell me?"

He looked surprised. "Because I'm your friend. You can't keep this kind of thing a secret."

I stared into his eyes. Something passed between us. I know it did. It wasn't my imagination. "I have to get out of here," I said, climbing on board Mary, cantering across the yard and toward the field and into the forest, navigating the winding trails, sunlight streaming through the tops of the trees illuminating the cool, canopied path.

The journey back home was littered with obstacles; fallen trees presented themselves at every turn. I pressed Mary forward, refusing to believe my father was capable of shooting down a child in cold blood. Mary cleared the low-lying jumps with ease. Then the obstacles grew in size and frequency, three feet, four feet; up and over she sailed. We kept going. Five feet. Mary was tired. I was tired. Each hurdle loomed larger than the last one.

By the time we reached the open pastures of home I was covered in dirt and mud, and Mary's neck was speckled with spit and lather. The way was clear, but there were too many hurdles in the getting there. Reining Mary in, we stood still in the middle of the field, amidst the birdsong and the tall grass, as I tried to process fragments of overheard conversations and obscure references, mysterious behaviors and irreconcilable emotions, a jumbled collage of information, all of it running through my head like film in a projector.

"Nothing makes sense," I moaned, and then I remembered something that Camp used to tell me. "When nothing makes sense, everything makes sense."

"What does that mean?" I begged him to tell me.

"Someday, you'll understand," he said. "You need to figure it out for yourself."

"When nothing makes sense, everything makes sense." I repeated it out loud and, pulling my feet from the stirrups, I stretched out on Mary, the back of my head on her warm rump, my eyes closed tight against the penetrating rays of the late summer sun.

"You look like you had a rough ride," Camp said, surveying the damage when I walked into the kitchen, where he and my mother were locked into a huddle.

"I saw Harry today," I said.

My father roared to his feet. "I told you that you were never allowed to see that boy again!"

"Camp, did you kill that little girl?" I started to cry. It was as if I had sprung a million leaks. Crying had become my job for the summer. "Harry's dad talked to the *New York Times*. He told them that you deliberately killed a little girl in cold blood in Bastogne. He said that you were a murderer and that you don't deserve to hold office."

Camp recoiled as if he had been punched. He stared at me in disbelief. The expression on his face! I had hurt my father. I didn't think it was possible. I will never forget how he looked at me that day.

"You think I would kill a little girl?"

I tried to take it back. The question. The implied accusation. The doubt. He wasn't listening to me. I was kid stuff, and he had neither the inclination nor the time to indulge me. He was reaching for the phone. My mother looked over at me and shrugged.

"Aren't you going to say anything? Aren't you going to explain? I'm sorry. Just tell me, please," I begged.

"Can you hang on a minute please? I'll be right with you," Camp said to the person on the other end of the line. He put his hand over the receiver.

"Those goddam Devlins. Jesus, I knew he was crazy but . . . You look here. I don't need to explain myself to you, or to anybody else for that matter. Is that clear? You ever walk into this house again and start barking demands and allegations at me, you will have reason to regret it. Understand?"

I nodded. His manner was so cold, I felt as if I was adrift in frigid waters, and in a way I was. My hands were shaking, every part of me vibrated and stung. Even my internal organs felt raw and inflamed. I stopped at the bottom of the staircase and I felt unsure of taking that first step. I had climbed those long, winding stairs to my third-story bedroom a million times before and not thought a thing of it, so why did the ascent now seem insurmountable?

Chapter **Thirty-Two**

———

IMAY HAVE GONE TO BED CRYING, BUT I WOKE TO THE SOUND OF my father laughing. I got dressed and crept down the stairs. Cars jammed the driveway and I could hear the steady military drum of conversation, punctuated with jokes and challenges and the sporadic gunfire of arguments and collisions of opinion.

Camp was locked away in the library with members of his campaign. I peeked in at him, but he only glanced my way briefly before ignoring me. My mother appeared from in the kitchen.

"What's going on?" I asked her.

"Life marches on, Riddle. The campaign awaits."

I must have looked as stunned as I felt. She put her hand on her hip and cocked her head.

"You didn't expect him to take this lying down, did you?"

I think it wasn't until that precise moment that it even occurred to me that Camp could fight back. It took me another minute or so to absorb what was in front of me: Greer Foley, the movie star. She wore a low-sheen, dove-gray dress with a wide, plunging neckline, cap sleeves and an A-line skirt. Her hair was smooth and loose and fell in a gentle, creamy wave to her shoulders. The effect was both demure and decadent. Behind her, I could see campaign staffers peering through the glass doors, taking a second and third look. She was hunting for her car keys.

"Where are you going?" I asked her.

"Out." She didn't look up, just kept on rooting through the top drawer of the occasional table in the hallway. "Where are those damned keys?"

That's when it hit me. "You're going to talk to Michael, aren't you?"

"What I do doesn't concern you."

"I want to come. Let me come, I'm coming."

She paused for a moment, expressionless, fingering the diamond buckle at her waist as she considered my request.

"All right," she said, keys jangling in her fingers. "Hurry up."

WE PULLED UP TO the front door of the Devlin house after a quiet ride together in the car. Occasionally I looked over at her but she ignored me in a way that was the pointed opposite of ignoring me. It was overcast, the whole world painted in shades of gray, as if all of nature, in deference to my mother's color preference that day, conspired to art-direct her visit.

We got out of the car, and I looked beyond the house toward the ocean. I couldn't separate the gray water from the gray horizon. Had my hair turned gray?

Greer straightened her shoulders and arranged the skirt of her dress before rapping on the double doors. One, two, three insistent knocks. Mrs. Maguire answered. She looked mildly taken aback when she saw us. "Yes," she said, "may I help you?"

My mother stepped forward, which caused Mrs. Maguire to step backward. "I want to speak to Michael," my mother said.

"I'm sorry," Mrs. Maguire said, "but that's not possible."

My mother popped the car keys into her open bag, then clicked it shut. "What do you mean, that's not possible?" She walked past the housekeeper and into the living room. Mortified, I trailed behind her. By now I was sure I was gray from top to bottom.

"Mom," I pleaded. "Let's go."

"Mr. Devlin isn't here, I'm afraid," Mrs. Maguire said, her demeanor more friendly than formal.

"Then I'll wait until he comes home."

"You don't understand. He left the country last night." There was something disconcerting about the intimation of kindness in her manner.

"Left the country? Where did he go?" Greer, a bit disarmed by Mrs. Maguire's sympathetic disposition, strained for control.

"Why, he's in Ireland. He's joining Miss MacNamara and her family . . ."

"Kathleen MacNamara?" my mother demanded.

"Yes, that's right."

I had never heard the name before, but the effect on Greer was seismic. For the briefest of seconds, her self-containment wavered. Her lips parted. There was a revealing slight inhalation of breath, her back stiffened and her head snapped backward, though you had to be paying close attention to catch it.

"Patrick MacNamara's oldest daughter, the unmarried one, thin lips, wide . . ."

"Yes, that's her." Mrs. Maguire staged a merciful interruption. "Irish aristocrats, so I understand."

"Maguire. Scottish, isn't it? Well, take it from someone with the last name Foley, Mrs. Maguire. The term 'Irish aristocrats' is an oxymoron. Does Mr. Devlin intend to stay in Ireland for any length of time?"

"Yes. I believe he does."

"In that case, I've already wasted enough time waiting. Come on, Riddle, let's go."

Once in the foyer, she paused at the door. "Mrs. Maguire,

would you give Michael a message for me?" She smiled. "Would you tell him please to beware the sheerie?"

"I will let him know, Mrs. Camperdown," Mrs. Maguire said, looking puzzled, her hand on the doorknob.

I paused just outside the door, turning around before it closed behind us. My powers of resistance failed me. "Harry?"

"Harry is still here, though he's gone off somewhere this morning," the housekeeper reported. "He's leaving for Yale this weekend." She was looking over my shoulder, seeming distracted. "Oh, Mrs. Camperdown!" she called after my mother, who paused at the open car door.

Mrs. Maguire scuttled quickly down the steps and over to where my mother stood waiting. "I hate to impose, but would you mind signing this for me?" She retrieved a pen and a small black-and-white photo of my mother from her apron pocket. "You'll think I'm silly but I've been carrying this around hoping you would pay another visit. I'd just about given up but here you are! I'm a huge fan of yours. I've seen *The Fragrant Letter* a dozen times if I've seen it once. You were wonderful in the role of Maude. You were so beautiful when you were young!"

There was a long pause.

"Thank you, Mrs. Maguire," my mother said, obliging her request for a signature. "You are too kind."

Mrs. Maguire vanished into the house, clutching her autograph. We got into the car. My mother put the key in the ignition and her hands on the steering wheel. She stared straight ahead and sighed and then she looked over at me.

Something in her eyes. It might have been her heart.

It was too much. I started to cry. Unbelievably, so did she.

Camp was right. When you start crying, you never stop.

• • •

WE PARKED NEAR CAPE COD LIGHT and walked to the edge of the Truro bluffs and stared up into the early night sky, the last light of the sun appearing and disappearing behind dark thunderclouds. The whole world was black and blue and crimson. Below us the waves, stained bloodred by the encroaching sunset, rolled onto the beach.

"Why didn't you and Michael get married?" I asked.

"I caught him in bed with the maid of honor, a couple of days before the wedding."

Startled—my mother wasn't in the business of giving straight answers—I stared over at her as she gathered her blowing hair into a ponytail.

"Michael Devlin?"

"Yes, Michael Devlin. He swore it was meaningless, blamed drinking, blamed her, blamed the war. He used every excuse in the book, but I wasn't having it. I called the wedding off but he wouldn't accept it. Phoned me round the clock. Came to see me. Bought every long-stemmed rose in the state. Begged for my forgiveness."

"You wouldn't forgive him."

"Oh, no. I forgave him."

"I don't understand. Harry told me that his father said that you two had a fight over something minor. Things got out of hand and he got mad and called off the wedding. He said that you carried on as if everything was fine, that you went to the church knowing he wouldn't be there but that you wanted everyone to see you as a tragic heroine, the jilted bride."

She laughed. "Well, that's the self-serving folklore anyway. You believed that story?" She shook her head. "I can understand why strangers would eat it up, but you're my daughter. Didn't it occur to you that even I am not that shallow? When I went to that church, I assure you, I fully expected him to be there. He never showed up."

"Why would he do that? Why would he lie to Harry about it?"

"Because he's a liar!" Greer gave me a hard look. "That's what liars do. You don't think it's any more complicated than that, do you? I found him in bed with my best friend. He was horrified, not because of his moral shortcomings but because he couldn't stand that I knew the truth about what he was really like. I knew where the body was buried, Riddle, to reference one of your father's favorite expressions. I called him on it. So he punished me by humiliating me in front of the whole world."

"If all that's true, why did you continue to care for him, even after all these years?"

"He wasn't all bad. We all have shortcomings. What is it they say? Too bad for heaven, too good for hell. You liked him, didn't you?"

I nodded.

"The good in him was real. What can I say? Human behavior resists logic. I loved him. Not that I don't love your father." She opened up her hand and, looking down, traced her palm lines with her finger.

"Do you think Camp killed the little girl?"

She shifted in her seat. "Michael told me about it when he came back from overseas. So much for the infamous pact. I eventually confronted Camp and he refused to talk about it. Said it was between him and Michael. Can you imagine that I thought Michael was telling the truth? I suppose I succumbed to the obvious. Camp seemed the more likely candidate to have committed an impetuous, violent act. Of course, unlike Michael, he honored his agreement never to discuss it."

She appeared to be deep in thought.

"Before Harry took Hanzi, I saw Gula be kind to him. He was petting him and talking to him. He gave him a biscuit. I still think about it sometimes."

My mother looked reflective. "Sometimes I think we only imagine ourselves. The rest we conduct in secret. It's hard sometimes, coming face-to-face with your truer nature—the part that you conceal even from yourself." She thought for a moment and then abandoned whatever was on her mind. "Oh, well, what you lose in citizenship medals you gain in insight and self-knowledge."

She looked out across the red ocean as the fiery sunset exploded across the horizon. "Welcome to Apostasy Island, Riddle."

Chapter Thirty-Three

THE STORY BROKE THE NEXT DAY AND THE RESULTING MEDIA madness felt like trying to keep your balance in a rock slide, all these nasty strikes and hits, sharp pokes and jabs and choking dust, the cumulative effects of a million little cuts, always feeling as if we were one boulder away from obliteration. Camp just kept digging out from under and he even managed to throw a few rocks of his own, knocking down a few targets here and there, though the momentum was against him. Predictably there were calls from inside and outside the party for him to withdraw from the race, but he wouldn't hear of it. Camp didn't understand the meaning of retreat.

My mother read bits of the *Times* story aloud at the breakfast table as we listened. Camp, still maintaining a formal distance from me, provided animated commentary, lively as always, refusing to give in to despair.

"Listen to this," she said, quoting an unidentified source, "'I always knew something happened over there. I just didn't know what it was. I assumed it was the triangle, you know, the two boys vying for Greer's love. God help them!'"

She threw the paper down on the table in disgust. "Well, you don't need to be clairvoyant to figure out who that is—the trembling print gives it away. I hope the *New York Times* has its own witness protection program, because that spineless little weasel is going to need it."

A FEW HOURS LATER, MY mother confronted Gin in the middle of the pasture, where he had gone to spend time with his two Gypsy horses. I could barely keep pace with her as she hurtled across our two properties.

"How dare you? You traitorous gnat," she said, running toward him, scattering the horses. For a second I thought Gin was going to take off, but habit triumphed and he stood, head hanging, hands wringing, awaiting his terrible fate.

"Isn't it better that it was me rather than someone with an axe to grind? I was thinking of you, Greer, and what was best for you and your family. My family! You're my family! I adore you. I would never do anything to hurt any of you."

"Your family! The only family you'd be comfortable inhabiting is the Julio-Claudians," my mother shouted at him. It occurred to me that I might have to intervene if Gin was to emerge from this in one piece. I was trying to figure out how to subdue my mother without getting myself killed in the process.

Ducking behind me, Gin gripped my shoulders with both hands, as if I were a human shield.

"Oh, Greer, I don't care what happened in Europe during the war. I'm sure if Camp killed that little girl he had a good reason. Who knows? Maybe she was a spy."

"Camp did not kill that little girl," Greer said, sounding as if she meant it. My heart warmed to hear her speak up in Camp's defense.

"Try to understand, Greer," Gin pleaded, his head bobbing back and forth above mine. "I'm only human, after all. Call it the terrible accumulation of events—am I to ignore all of it?"

"What are you talking about?" my mother demanded.

"Well, the boys, Charlie and Harry. Camp knew that Michael had this terrible story he was planning to tell, which threatened Camp's election to the House, and not only that but threatened to ruin him utterly and completely. What better way to stop all that than by destroying Michael? Greer, you know as well as I do that people have been killed for a lot less."

I listened in horror. If Gin was willing to entertain the idea that Camp might be guilty of any of the allegations being leveled at him, what hope was there that he would ever be exonerated by the wider world?

"Et tu, Brute? You've known Camp since we were kids. You really think he is capable of killing children in cold blood? Are you suggesting that Camp murdered Charlie and shot Harry to avenge himself on Michael? You've gone mad," my mother said. "I can understand the press jumping on board, and the general public, but you know better. Where did this come from?"

"I'm not accusing anyone of anything, just pointing out how easily suspicions can shift based on gossip and innuendo and damaging speculation." Gin's face was flushed and he appeared to be in the throes of some sort of attack. He was practically vibrating with emotion.

"There is such a thing as guilt by association. Why, even my own dear mother asked me what I have to do with all of this. My mother! I'm forced to defend myself even though I don't have anything to hide. I didn't shoot some little girl in France or Belgium or wherever it was," he sneered. "God knows, I am completely ignorant as to what happened to Charlie Devlin, let alone Harry. Oh, wait, I know." He snapped his fingers in rapid succession. "The horses. The Gypsy horses. Gin would overlook anything to get his Gypsy horses. Is that what you think?"

"Oh, for heaven's sake, why do you always come back to this

ridiculous line of thought? Gin, no one is accusing you of anything. You're the only one accusing you of anything. No one other than Michael suspects anything untoward concerning the boys. He's using the boys to bolster his vendetta against Camp. The truth in this case is something so banal it's almost funny. Let's face it, the Devlins were undone by all that's ordinary. A teenage boy on a bender. An idiot hunter behaving carelessly with a gun. Murder would be an upgrade. As for Michael, well, you know Michael . . ."

"Please, Greer, let's banish all bad thoughts," Gin said, covering his eyes with his hands and shaking his head vigorously back and forth. "Let's be friends. Please! You know how I hate conflict. Anyway, on to more pleasant things. I was thinking that maybe you and Riddle might like to help me work with the horses now that Harry's not available. What do you think?"

"That I should tell you to go to hell," my mother said.

"Greer, you are the most awful woman. And look how you've upset Jimmy with your nonsense."

Something inside me gave way, as if I was a levee under assault from the waves and the wind and could take no more. I was shivering and crying, tears running down my face. My fingertips tingled. My mouth was dry and I had the sensation I was outside myself looking on. I couldn't catch my breath. My chest felt as if it was going to explode, as everything around me began to spin.

Panicking, I reached out for my mother, seizing her arm to steady myself. She looked at me, a mixture of disbelief and concern on her face. "Good heavens, what's wrong with you? If I didn't know better, I'd think the two of you were in this together. What were you and Gin doing the day that Charlie Devlin disappeared?"

"Stop it! Stop it!" I wailed. "It's not a joke. It's not something to make fun about. What will it take for you to stop acting?"

"Riddle," she said, grabbing me by the shoulders. "You're going to tell me what's wrong and you're going to tell me right now!"

I broke free of her, dashed across the pasture and continued running for home, Gin and my mother watching, mouths agape, as Boomslang and Oma ran alongside me. Graceful and high-spirited, manes and tails dragging on the ground like mythological creatures, they galloped in circles around me.

Running on ahead of me, they stopped at the far end of the fence, where they pawed the ground and tossed their heads and waited. I stared into their unknowable blue eyes.

Gin got what he most desired. He got his Gypsy horses. Gin wanted nothing more than to be left alone with his secrets and his dead kittens under glass, his movie star and those beautiful other-worldly horses.

I reached out to pet Boomslang. My fingers got tangled in the cottony web of his mane. Gin's dream had come true, and I wondered, not for the last time, at what cost?

DOROTHY AND THE OTHER three dogs leapt up to greet me as I entered the house, gaily trailing behind me, their nails clicking against the floorboards as I raced ahead of them and up the stairs leading to my room. The bedroom door slammed shut with so much force that the framed black-and-white family photographs on the wall fell to the floor. One, two, three bangs, and the sound of glass breaking.

IT WAS LATE AT night before I finally came back downstairs. My mother, opting for avoidance rather than confrontation, had gone to bed. I got myself a bowl of cereal and then sat down at the kitchen table and picked up the newspaper.

"Camperdown's Campaign in Shambles! Murderous Allegations and Mayhem in Massachusetts!" the headlines screamed, the articles populated with references to movie stars and American princes and heirs to fortunes, racehorses and private schools and labor disputes and left wings and right wings, betrayals and accidental shootings.

My father stared back at me from the front page. My mother. Michael Devlin. Charlie Devlin. Harry. I touched Harry's cheek with my hand. It might have been a personal photo album: "How I Spent My Summer Vacation." The only one missing was me.

I turned the page. There was a story about the Israeli athletes killed at the Olympics. A nameless man in a hood stood on the balcony of the athletes' residence.

MY DAD AND I were speaking, though not in any way that mattered. He was lying on the floor in the living room, stretched on his back surrounded by the dogs. The TV was on, the volume turned low. The lights were dim. Outside the wind was blowing. He was softly singing "I'll Be Seeing You," Dorothy licking his cheek. He was staring up at the ceiling, making a triangle with his fingers, holding it aloft over his head.

"Camp, you're singing," I said.

"You caught me," he said.

The distance between us evaporated as I turned up the sound on the set and walked over to the sofa. Camp got up from the floor and joined me, sitting in his favorite leather chair in front of the fireplace. I used the remote control to change channels as I stared at the screen.

Charlie Devlin's image abruptly flashed across the monitor. It was so familiar by now it made my teeth ache. His hair a livid imprint, his eyes an amber light. He was all the colors of the woods.

I listened to a woman with pastel lips, serious intentions and limited insights, who had never even met him, speculate about what had happened to him.

Murder or misadventure? She wanted to know, wanted to unravel the mystery, wanted answers. He was there one moment and then he was gone. Disappeared into the night. Now, she said, his grieving father, Michael Devlin, was calling for his death and disappearance to be reexamined in light of the recent revelations concerning Camp and himself.

She listed the possibilities: It was fame. It was money. It was youthful folly. It was carelessness. It was the evil that men do. It was late. I wanted to reach out and grab her by the shoulders and shake her until she knew: It was Gula. It was Gin. It was Michael. It was Camp. It was Greer. All with good reasons for doing what they did. I shut my eyes. It was me.

I looked over at Camp. He sighed and glanced downward and noticed a single strand of hair on the sleeve of his sweater, and as the woman on TV continued to speculate, her voice occupying an empty place somewhere vaguely in the background, my father held the strand of hair lightly between his fingers and up to his lips and, at the first veiled opportunity, gently blew it into the atmosphere, watching it disappear into the twilight air, lost to sight among the shadows, forever vanished, watched it evanesce in a world that hung on an amber thread.

Chapter Thirty-Four

———

THE WIND THAT NIGHT WAS SO LOUD I COULDN'T SLEEP. MY room rattled, a powerful gust swept my desk clear, glass vase shattering, fresh-picked stalks of hydrangea scattered and helpless as the water drained into the floorboards. Maybe because I grew up next to an ocean, the wind has always engendered in me a feeling of standing on the brink. That's the way I felt that night, as if I was wavering, blowing in the wind, buffeted between all that mattered and all that didn't.

My mother liked to say that it wasn't a black-and-white world, but the more I thought about it the more I thought that applies only to decorating. When it comes to right and wrong, most of the time, the choices are clear—it's the consequences that hang you up, it's the reasons that you give yourself that turn your world into an obliging shade of gray.

How had it come to this? I wanted to be good. There's always time for being better, isn't there?

I GOT UP EARLY THE next morning. My parents were still sleeping. I pulled on my riding boots and, shuttering the disappointed dogs inside, I quietly shut the front door and started walking. The front door opened again behind me, and my mother stepped out onto the verandah. She was wearing a gray cashmere robe. I was conscious that she was watching me, and yet I kept right on walking.

Funny, the incidental ways that life plays out. Had it been my father who appeared on the doorstep, I don't think I would have had the courage to ignore him. Had it been Camp, I would have turned back.

Loyalty was everything to Camp. It trumped all else. Disloyalty was the only sin he couldn't forgive. That Christmas Eve in Bastogne in 1944, my father and Michael would have been nineteen years old, the same age as Harry, not that much older than me.

I walked down the lane and imagined what it must have been like. There was no moon that night, but the sky was flooded with light from the German bombardment from above. They were laughing. Laughing until they cried, tears streaming down their cheeks. Camp told me that's how it used to be: the worse the situation, the graver the danger, the funnier it seemed. Nobody gets it right, he said, when they talk about life at the front. We were always crazy laughing, he told me.

"That doesn't make any sense," I said to him.

When nothing makes sense, everything makes sense.

I let myself into the tack room and threw a bridle over my shoulder. With both hands I carried a saddle, the scent of leather warming me to my task. Mary eyed me with some curiosity as I entered her stall. I took a few moments to brush her. Gave her a hand rubbing and a carrot. Her ears flicked temperamentally. She had a little edge, but I like a little edge in a horse. Beautiful dark eyes. Not like the soft blue eyes of the Gypsy horses. My father never liked blue eyes on a horse. He said women have blue eyes, horses have brown eyes. Camp loved horses but had no interest in riding.

I once asked him what bothered him most about the war. He thought about it for a moment, and then he said that maybe it was the sight of all those dead animals in the fields, the dead horses, the dead sheep, the dead cows.

THE WIND HAD SUBSIDED to a whisper, a light, lovely, early autumn breeze. My hair blew back from my face as I eased Mary into an effortless canter and relaxed into her rocking-horse gait, as together we loped down the long lane away from the house and past the Cormorant Clock Farm.

"HEY, HOFFA," HARRY SAID, opening the door to his house, surprised to see me. He stopped in his tracks and stared at me. "Come on in. Are you okay? How did you get here? What are you doing here?"

I followed him into the living room, the ocean spread out before us like an endless summer. White-capped waves rolled in, the early morning sun glimmering on the water's dark surface, seagulls circling. A portrait of Charlie hung over the mantelpiece—those amber eyes staring back at me.

"Before he left for Ireland," Harry said, "my dad put Charlie's portrait back up."

I took him in, Harry, memorizing his face, the way he looked back at me, knowing that he would never look at me that way again. We were standing next to each other where the glass wall opened up onto the beach and the sky and the ocean, the waves crashing against the rocks and on the sand. I reached out and took his hand in mine.

"What the hell? What's going on?" Harry smiled, bemused.

I did it for love. For Camp. For Harry.

"Call me in five years, kid," he cracked. He let my hand go.

Not every dream deserves to come true. Sometimes you forfeit the right to your dreams.

Harry's expression changed. His eyes darkened. "Hoffa?"

Chapter **Thirty-Five**

―――

OR ONE TELLING MOMENT I THOUGHT HE WAS GOING TO HIT me. He pushed me down onto the sofa and left me there while he disappeared into another part of the house. He came back in the room, grabbed me by the arm and dragged me out to the car. Harry always did know the right thing to do. Harry didn't know how not to tell. Within minutes, I was repeating my story to the police. By the end of the day, I was back at home telling it again, this time with both my parents present. At one point, Camp jumped from his seat and grabbed me by the shoulders, his feelings of shock and disappointment shaking the life out of me, the detectives rushing to pull him away.

"My God," he said. "Riddle, why didn't you tell us?"

I can still see my mother through the living room window after she sought refuge on the deck. She was trying to light a cigarette, but her hands were trembling so much that she couldn't do it. "Jesus Christ," she said, trying again, turning her back to the wind. She just kept trying to light her cigarette, one after another, flame flaring and extinguishing simultaneously.

That night, my father wrapped his arms around me and told me not to worry. He would protect me. No matter what, he loved me.

"This, too, shall pass," he said. My mother, all four dogs accompanying her, came up to the third floor where I lay in my bed unable to sleep and presented me with a cup of hot chocolate. "I made it myself," she said.

By the next day, the story had exploded, generating headlines. I had finally found my place in the story. It seemed as if every law enforcement agency was looking for Gula, who had simply vanished.

The blond detective, the dark-haired detective and a third detective I had never seen before talked to me.

"Why did he do it?" they asked, their faces an uneven blend of curiosity and skepticism, sympathy and disdain.

"I don't know. I don't even know exactly what he did. But whatever it was, I think he had his reasons."

Meanwhile, nobody knew quite what to do with me.

"Why didn't you tell someone? Your parents? Anyone?"

"At first I didn't know what was going on. I wanted to tell. I did. I was too scared. I waited too long."

"It's never too late to tell," the dark-haired detective said.

"It was too late for me."

"What did Gula do to scare you into silence?" asked the blond-haired detective.

I looked at everyone looking at me. I closed my eyes. It came to me.

"He killed the boy."

THE NEXT DAY I watched Camp on TV as he announced his resignation from the campaign. "I did not have anything to do with Gula Nightjar and what happened to Charlie Devlin. He occasionally volunteered to help out on the campaign, drove mostly, and that was the extent of my involvement. As far as what Mr. Devlin is alleging—I did not kill that child in Bastogne," he added, though he admitted concealing what happened. "About that," he said, "I will say no more."

He tried to mitigate the extent of my involvement and blame in what had happened to Charlie. "She was only twelve years old," he said. "She was being manipulated into silence by this man who terrorized her."

The only time Camp faltered was when a reporter asked him directly, exasperation in his voice, why I didn't tell anyone. Surrounded by all those microphones and whirring tape recorders, all he could do was stand before the assembled members of the press pool shaking his head in sorrow and disbelief.

"I don't know," he said. "Why do any of us do anything? Perhaps it's my fault. Why didn't I tell anyone what happened all those years ago on Christmas morning? I was an adult. A soldier. I knew the difference between right and wrong and still I chose not to tell. I have to face the possibility that I may somehow have inadvertently taught her to value silence. God knows, I've got the biggest mouth in Massachusetts, but maybe Riddle sought refuge in the unwholesome silence at the heart of all that noise."

HARRY WOULDN'T TAKE MY calls. I rode over to see him. The house was closed up and he was gone. I just stood there knocking on the door of that empty house. I knocked and knocked but nobody answered.

Chapter Thirty-Six

A FEW DAYS AFTER MY CONFESSION, I WENT FOR A SOLITARY walk with Vera. I should have been in school but, given the circumstances, the decision was made for me to study from home for the time being. Vera ran on ahead, stubby legs pushing through the sand toward the tract of woods bordering the property. She barked and then disappeared into the trees.

I called after her. "Vera!" I ventured into the dense trees and swamp. "Vera, where are you?" I wailed, never far from hysteria in those days. There was a rustle and swish of grass as she finally appeared ahead of me on the trail, tail wagging, attention diverted. I followed the direction of her gaze.

Gula was standing on the path. He smiled and nodded.

"Hello," he said.

"Hello," I said, struggling to appear calm, electricity surging through my body. I remember thinking that this is what it must feel like to be struck by lightning. "What are you doing here? Everyone is looking for you."

"That's fine. Let them look. I came to see you."

I wanted to run, but my legs wouldn't obey the command to move.

Sitting down on a tree stump a few feet from where I stood, he looked back at me in the manner of someone who had come to a decision. My throat was so dry it was as if sawdust papered the lining of my esophagus.

"You finally told," he said.

"Leave me alone."

"You must wonder and yet you don't ask," he said. "You must wonder what happened. You must be curious."

I just stood there looking at him.

"Maybe the truth is that you don't want to know."

I remained silent. I could never find the words to speak to this man. It was as if he had bound and gagged me; that's what it felt like to be in his presence.

He was taunting me, teasing me—that's just the way he was—but he was serious, too, and not quite in the moment. I felt as if he were talking to me from a different time, a different place.

"Life is shit. People are shit," he said.

"No, I don't believe that." Panting. I could hear panting. My heart was racing as if it were being chased, scurrying across my chest.

"What do I care what you believe? How do you believe, for example, a person should act when they stumble across a boy being held in a stable?"

I could hear the sound of my breathing magnified in my ears, so loud it drowned out the noise of the waves.

"We all have our reasons for what we do. I knew from the start that you wouldn't tell. Ha! I could smell it on you."

The winds off the ocean swept through the sand dunes, the sand cutting my skin like gunpowder, flattening grass, rushing through the barrier of ancient copper beeches and tall pine trees. The ocean sounded like a thousand jet planes landing all at once.

Gula stood up. I took two steps back. He held up his hand.

"You have nothing to fear from me," he said. Bending down and reaching behind the tree stump, he retrieved a plain box, crudely wrapped in Christmas paper. "A present," he said. "For you."

Slowly he walked toward me, gift extended. "Take it," he said, his eyes never leaving mine.

"I'm sorry about the boy," he said unexpectedly. "Charlie was a brave boy. Too bad it wasn't Harry. Now that I might have enjoyed. Oh, well. Too late for regret. Anyway, here is my advice to you. Have patience. You will know why soon enough. God knows, patience is my greatest virtue. I have an uncommon degree of patience. I recommend it." He laughed.

"Where will you go?"

"Away," he said. "My business here is all but done." He reached out and touched my hair. Speaking softly, he continued, "Very soon you will understand what I'm telling you about life. When I say that life is shit, that people are shit, the proof stands right here before me. You need look no further than the mirror to know that what I'm saying is true."

Did he hit me? It felt as if he did, everything around me exploding. A gust of wind swept over the dunes like a vanquishing wave. "Why are you doing this?" I cried out. I closed my eyes against the stinging invasion of sand and spray. When I opened them again he was gone. Looking down at the package he'd given me, I fell to my knees, overcome by a mixture of terror and relief and sorrow and regret.

God help me, but the pity I felt at that terrible moment was for myself.

Chapter **Thirty-Seven**

———

CAMP WAS TALKING TO MY MOTHER IN THE LIVING ROOM when I returned to the house. Sneaking up the back staircase, I tried to avoid him, but he heard me and called me down the stairs. "Just a minute," I said, shoving the present from Gula into the linen closet.

Summoning up what little courage I had, I came down the stairs. My parents looked up in unison to greet me.

"Riddle, we need to talk," my father said, not unkindly.

"I don't want to talk," I said. "There's nothing to say."

"I'm sorry, kid, but there is plenty to say," Camp said. "Come here and sit down and listen to me."

My mother nodded her agreement as I took my place on the sofa and stared up at Camp, who was standing by the fireplace. She sat down across from me in an armchair.

"First, I didn't kill that little girl, regardless of what Michael Devlin claims. Nor do I know anything about Gula or his involvement in anything. I feel quite confident in saying that Michael is as ignorant on the subject of Gula Nightjar as I am.

"It's entirely probable, given the circumstances, that Gula tried to kill Harry, as well as Charlie. Why? How the hell should I know? Harry, because of the dog. Charlie? Maybe it was a kidnapping for ransom that went deadly wrong. Some things aren't knowable, starting with why you never told us about the Devlin boy. Which brings me to another crucial point in the discussion. Frankly, Riddle, the only person who knew anything about what was going on here was you."

Shame and guilt covered me like a second skin. Desperate for a place to hide, I reached for the afghan thrown over the back of the sofa and covered my face with it as I lay back into the cushions.

I felt my mother's presence next to me. To my everlasting surprise, she took my hand in hers and held on as my father carried on talking.

"Why didn't you come to us? Why didn't you come to me?" He stopped talking, as if he was fortifying himself. "I think it's time for me to tell you what happened all those years ago. Maybe if I had done so when it first came up . . . Well, both of us will have to live with the consequences of that choice. Anyway, you deserve to know what happened overseas.

"The truth is, I was with Michael Devlin on the roof in Bastogne, but I did not shoot that child. Michael did." He paused. "There. I've said it. Finally." He took a few deep breaths before resuming. "She appeared out of nowhere, I can still see her in her white blouse. It was cold. She wore a ragged jacket with no buttons. Her coat was open. She walked over to the well with her little metal pitcher and he took aim and fired. He dropped her on the spot. I couldn't believe it. One of the worst things I've ever seen and I've seen a lot. I went nuts. I took a swing at him. We got into it right there on the roof, rolled down the incline and fell onto the ground. I fractured my collarbone. A couple of guys from the platoon broke us up. They wanted to turn Michael over to the military police. Mad and sick as I was, I argued against it. Worst mistake of my life. The irony is that he never forgave me for it."

"Why would you defend him?" I was talking to him from behind the safety of my blanket.

"I grew up with him. He was a good soldier. I'd fought alongside him all through the Ardennes. I couldn't bring myself to turn against him. I swore to keep it a secret."

"I don't understand. Why would he say that you did it? Why would he want to harm you when you were only trying to protect him?"

"You have a lot to learn about life, Riddle," my father said. "I have enough trouble trying to figure out what makes me tick, let alone try to understand what winds someone else's clock. Michael wasn't the man he purported to be. God help anyone who discovered otherwise.

"I shouldn't have kept it a secret. I should have come forward. I should have talked to you about it when Michael came back. I thought I had good reason for not talking about it."

He stopped and threw his hands up in the air.

"For Christ's sake, Jimmy, I never even talked to myself about it."

CAMP DECIDED TO TAKE a walk on the beach.

"You go ahead," my mother said. "I'll be along."

Declining an invitation to join them, I withdrew to my bedroom after retrieving my gift from Gula. I was trying to make up my mind about whether to tell my father about Gula's visit. I decided to tell him. He was right: no more secrets.

Soon. I thought there was time.

The low flat box, with its frayed and clumsy Christmas wrap, a cheerful snowman leering at me, sat in the middle of my bed, a threat and a lure at the same time.

I ripped through the paper and took off the lid. Inside was a young girl's blouse, white originally though grown yellow with the passage of time. Tiny pearl-white buttons fastened in place, collar sweetly turned down, it was an old-fashioned girl's blouse, delicately invested with the fragrance of warm recollection, like a sprig of alyssum pressed between the pages of someone's memory.

I hesitated before touching it. It seemed so old, I thought it might turn to dust. Taking it from the box, I held it up to the light of day. Only then did I notice the dried-blood spatter on the blouse's back panel, though the color, once a violent crimson, had faded so that now it was a depleted, almost graphic palette, in some spots gentle as mauve, in others blunt as stone. Whatever happened to the girl that wore this blouse had long since ceased to be a matter of red and was now a thing of gray.

Underneath the blouse were a handful of pictures and some newspaper clippings. One photo was of a little girl, long dark hair, black eyes, smiling. I looked on the back of the print.

"Oma," someone had written, "neuf ans, 1943" and then, beneath that inscription: "October 14, 1934–December 25, 1944."

There was another picture of the same little girl. This time she was sitting beside a young boy, thirteen, maybe fourteen years old. I would have recognized that face anywhere.

"Oma avec son grand frère, Gula."

"Oh, my God," I said out loud, combing through the rest of the photos and clippings—news stories about Michael Devlin, pictures of Charlie and Harry, stories about the Devlin stables, the Cormorant Clock Farm, articles about Camp, about his books, about his announcement that he was running for Congress, shots of my mother staring back at me glowing like a pinup girl.

I pulled out a full page torn from the *New York Times* six years earlier. It was a feature story about Michael and the history of the Devlin family's contribution to thoroughbred racing, and it was illustrated by a lifetime of photos tracing his eventful biography, including a shot of him as a toddler captioned "The Devlin Baby."

There was a picture of him with his dead wife, Polly, a candid shot of him with Harry and Charlie on ponies, a black-and-white photo of him with Greer Foley, "The Toast of Hollywood." There was a picture of Michael and Camp—identified as his Wellfleet neighbor and boyhood chum, "the noted biographer, labor activist, and musical composer Godfrey Camperdown."

They were in uniform, teenage boys, carefree and laughing, their arms around each other, the picture taken a few days before they left for Europe. The photo had a circle drawn around it in red—not one circle, but several red circles, violent with recognition.

Beneath all the books and the photos and the newspaper clippings there were several layers of beige tissue paper, the kind used for wrapping fragile objects. Carefully, tentatively, I drew back one layer and then another and that's when I saw her again—the doll with no face.

"WHERE'S CAMP?" I SAID, breathless, racing down the stairs into the kitchen.

"He's out on the dunes," my mother said. "What is it? What's going on?"

"I know! I know!" I shouted, running from the kitchen through the back door and out onto the deck. My father was standing at the top of the highest dune overlooking infinity.

"Camp!" I screamed as I ran to meet him. He looked up and waved, both arms over his head.

I caught up with him at the edge of the cliff. Out of breath, I bent over, gasping.

"What the hell?" he said, covering his forehead with his hand, blocking the glare of the sun from his eyes. I followed his gaze. Down below us was Boomslang, a black-and-white apparition, running free along the sand, tail and mane blowing wildly, galloping in a straight line down the deserted beachfront, ocean froth at his hooves.

The Gypsy horse was the last thing my father ever saw.

The shot from the rifle sheered off the top of his skull. In the midst of the terror and the tumult, in the seconds that it took Camp to fall from the top of the world to the ocean's floor, I had found this quiet spot inside myself and I saw him, right in front of me, there he was, all of his colors beginning silently to fade, his green eyes, that chestnut hair. He was disappearing, his luster waning, soaking into the ground like the mist from the ocean, hemorrhaging into the roots of the tall grass.

In the end he was gently subsiding in the fury of a September day, conveyed on a cold nomadic wind to places unknown.

I watched my father disappear amidst the waves, until all there was left was the ghostly outline of bubbling foam on the ocean's surface and the memory of something vivid.

Epilogue

———

"I RAN INTO HARRY DEVLIN last night."

Outside a robin sang, its familiar morning chirrup slicing through the gradually receding cover of night. White tulips bloomed. Blue wildflowers covered the front yard. A gentle ocean breeze blew in through the open living room window.

I was lying on the sofa in my nightgown, freshly bathed and snug under a hand-knit wool afghan, my basset hound, Archie, coiled up on the floor at my feet.

My mother looked up from her novel. "How was he?" she asked, eyes shifting back to the open page.

"Handsome as ever. A little older. The same. Harry doesn't change."

"Like his father."

"Not at all like his father," I corrected. For once, she didn't argue with me.

"All right. Like your father," she said. "Did he speak to you?"

I shook my head. "No. Did you think that he would?"

"I suppose not."

"What is there to say that hasn't been said, after all?" I reached down to scratch Archie's ears as he grinned up at me, tail battering against the tired herringbone floors.

"Not much," my mother said, setting aside her book and standing up to stretch, her sleek hair skimming the tips of her shoulders. "Having said that, it wouldn't kill him to forgive you."

"Mom, please, it isn't a matter of forgiveness. It runs deeper than that."

"You were a child dealing with a monster in a monstrous situation. You did the best you could. Anyway, we've all paid for our sins."

"I didn't think you were capable of sinning," I teased gently—something that had only become possible in the sorrowful aftermath of Camp's death.

"Let's just say that my sincere wish for Harry is that like me, he lives long enough to enjoy the great gift of being able to recognize his shortcomings and do something about them."

WE TOOK A WALK to the top of the bluffs, to the same spot where my father stood on the last day of his life. It was probably his favorite place in the whole wide world.

"Where the waves never cease to break," my mother said, referencing Thoreau. "I wonder if Harry will decide to revive the farm?" she said. "I suppose you're hoping . . ."

"No," I said. "No one has been near the place for eight years, not since Gin died and Harry bought it. The windows on the house are shuttered, the furniture is covered. The stables are empty. It's like a remnant of Gin's taxidermy collection, the whole place frozen in time and preserved under glass."

"Pity no one saw the value in having Gin stuffed. Wouldn't he have been thrilled?"

I laughed. "You know, I think he would have been."

"Your father would have been so happy about Gin being killed hunting. Score one for the animals. Remember how delighted he was whenever a hunter got shot or fell from a tree?"

I nodded.

My mother shrugged. "I so wish your father had outlived the bastards." She put her arm around my waist, and we stood and looked out over the water and listened to the noise of the cresting waves. "To think those goddamned Gypsy horses of his never produced a foal."

"You miss him—Gin, I mean?" I asked her.

"I know who you mean. No," she said. She sighed and laughed. "Yes."

She shook her head. "Well, I'm going for a ride," she said finally. "I think I can still handle a horse. Care to join me?"

"No, thanks. I think I'll just go back to the house and sit on the deck."

"Whatever you like," my mother said. "I guess I should think about packing. I have an early flight to New York tomorrow morning. I start rehearsals for the play next week."

After Camp died, my mother had made the decision to go back to work. "May as well get paid to pretend," she said.

"It's been nice having you," I said. "I wish you could stay longer."

"Why don't you move? Come to New York. Honestly, Riddle, I don't know how you stand living alone in this godforsaken place."

"We've been through this a million times. I'm happy here."

"I don't like to think of you here by yourself," my mother said, turning to face me.

"I'm fine. Really, I am. I can't imagine living anywhere else."

There was a brief interval of silence. "Harry could find you just as easily in New York as here in this house," she said.

"I'll come see you when the play opens."

"I should hope so," she said, reaching for her sunglasses as she made her exit. "You and everyone else. You can put it on my epitaph: 'Here lies Greer Foley, she didn't know much but she sure as hell knew how to fill a theater.'"

. . .

STEPPING OUT ONTO THE deck, Archie trundling along next to me, the wind took my breath away, scattering the potted geraniums, wicker chairs tumbling, striped cushions taking flight, my cotton nightgown billowing around my knees.

I don't think I'll ever make my peace with the wind. A few years ago, on another windy day, not far from home, while walking at night along a conservation trail, I heard a frantic commotion ahead and joined several others in investigating the noise. Someone shone a flashlight into a small clearing in the bush. A coyote had a young deer, wide jaws clamped around the poor creature's long muzzle. Both animals were locked in place, the coyote quietly asphyxiating its terrified prey. We clicked off the light, and we went back to where we were as if nothing had happened. As if, having caught sight of a ghost, the ghost on second glance dispersed as if there was never any ghost at all.

I was left again with an almost mythic sense of discomfiture, the feeling that there is something that exists just out of plain sight, something that wears a hood.

IN THE AVALANCHE OF scrutiny following Camp's death, Gula vanished from the face of the earth. His going was as secretive as his coming.

Michael Devlin never again spoke publicly about what happened in Belgium after Camp died. He was killed five years ago in Ireland, the victim of a hit and run after threatening to divorce his wife, the thin-lipped, wide-hipped Kathleen MacNamara.

Speculation was that she was behind the wheel. Speculation was that my mother was behind the wheel, though I suspect that she started that rumor herself.

. . .

EVERYONE, IT SEEMS, EVEN all these years later, has an opinion about what happened that Christmas Day in Bastogne. Some people think Michael Devlin killed the little girl. Other people are convinced it was Camp. Still others think there is enough blame to go around.

Those who believe in Michael's guilt think that Gula killed Charlie in retribution. A son for a sister. Still others argue that Gula wanted Michael to experience the pain of personal loss so he would understand the power of the secret he chose to keep.

As for Camp, well: Camp, with his professed volatility and his temperament, fit the profile better than Michael, and Camp died in the same way that Oma had died. The proof, some will argue, is in the manner of death. "Unfortunately, sometimes looking the part," as my mother would say, "is the closest guarantee you have for getting the part."

As for me, I know who killed that little girl at the well and who didn't.

Harry loved his father. He experienced him as a good and honorable man, incapable of murdering a child in cold blood, even amidst the moral haze of war. As far as Harry is concerned, my father killed that child, triggering all the horrors that followed.

Harry doesn't lie but that doesn't mean he's always right. It doesn't mean he knows the truth.

THE WIND WHISTLING, I watched as my mother, still slim and athletic—in so many ways, still the same beautiful girl she was—tripped down the stairs in her cream-colored jodhpurs and her white shirt, elegant gray hair blowing. I looked on as she strode purposefully across the dunes and toward the stable, and with each step another year slipped away, until the barriers that existed between then and now dissolved, Dorothy and Madge and Hilary barking and spinning and running on ahead, resisting her efforts to call them back, tubby little Vera bringing up the rear, the horses, Mary Harris and Joe Hill and Eugene Debs, and that disagreeable pony, Henry Clay, grazing in the grassy paddock under the spread of an ancient tract of trees.

The music of the waves soaring in concert with the notes of the piano, my father singing, that wonderful tenor voice of his carrying its distinctive message across the dunes and the open fields. Sometimes you could hear him singing as far away as the cormorant clock tree.

My mother thinks that I stay here for Harry, in the hope that one day he might come looking for me. Where else would he know to look, if not here? How could he find me if I were to go away? If she wants to believe that I'm waiting for Harry to come home, that's okay.

The truth is it isn't Harry I wait for. It's Camp.

Acknowledgments

By HER INTELLIGENCE, HER warmth and her humor, you shall know her—the elegant Molly Friedrich elevates the role of agent to the status of a calling. It's a privilege to have her in my corner. Many thanks as well to Lucy Carson for her insights and support, to Nichole LeFebvre for her thoughtful comments and to the always cheerful staff of the Friedrich agency, especially Molly Schulman.

I am so appreciative of my publisher, Liveright Publishing Corporation, with its rich history and its remarkable overseer Robert Weil, whose fantastic editorial and production staff have made this entire experience an honor and a pleasure.

Special thanks to the marvelous Katie Adams, one of the finest editors I have ever dealt with and who made immeasurable contribution to this novel. She has the rarest of editorial gifts, a talent to inspire. In no small part did she help me better understand the true nature of the story I was telling. I can think of no greater gift to bestow on any writer than the opportunity to work with Katie Adams.

Much gratitude also to the fabulous authors, editors and friends, Lauren Baratz-Logsted and Emily Heckman, the most generous of spirits. I am forever in their debt.

Acknowledgments

Thanks and much love to my sisters, Rooney and Virginia, for everything that they do and for *laughing at my jokes* (to my kids: take note) and to Andy for always being there and to my mother and all that she has meant to me. To my husband, George and my children, Caitlin, Flannery, Rory and Connor—you have my love, my respect and my faith and to you I bequeath my prolapsed uterus and my treasured dog-hair collection; may the latter cling to you as it has clung to me. Thanks for keeping my life real!

I would like to take a moment to credit the poetry of the Indonesian writer, Chairil Anwar, from whose beautiful poem, *Aku*, I borrowed the memorable phrase: I want to live another thousand years. Also, when Greer comments that grave digging isn't cheerful, she is referencing an observation from Rudyard Kipling that appears in his short story, *At the Pit's Mouth*.

Elements of this story were born in my first experience of the life-altering view from the edge of a soaring dune overlooking the Atlantic Ocean in Wellfleet, Cape Cod—a moment from which I am still in recovery. Although I have tried to remain true to the spirit of Wellfleet and the events of 1972, I have taken some liberties, such as tweaking dates and inventing locations, in keeping with the status of this story as fiction—in other words, I reserve the right to make things up.

So if the more gimlet-eyed among you stumble upon any inaccuracies when you're reading, please be assured these aren't mistakes—they are intentional. You will be doing both of us a favor.

It's worth noting that the magnificent Gypsy horse, also called the Gypsy Vanner, didn't make an official appearance in the United States until 1996, through the dedicated efforts of Dennis and Cindy Thompson, though I like to believe that Gin Whiffet tried mightily to make it happen two decades earlier.

I would be remiss to leave unmentioned my three little buddies, the canine watercooler of Paddy, Ned and Archie, who not only keep me daily company as I write but who also share my abiding passion for *The Housewives* franchise—short of a diet consisting only in cupcakes and grape crush, who could ask for anything more?

Finally, to my late father, Arthur J. Kelly, with whom I shared the most wonderful creative partnership and to my daughter, Flannery Dean, with whom I continue to enjoy the same great blessing—thank you.